THE SOUL KILLER

A DI BARTON INVESTIGATION

ROSS GREENWOOD

B

Boldwood

First published in Great Britain in 2020 by Boldwood Books Ltd.

1

Cover Design by Nick Castle Design

Cover Photography: Shutterstock

A CIP catalogue record for this book is available from the British Library.

Paperback ISBN: 978-1-80048-398-9

Ebook ISBN: 978-1-83889-546-4

Kindle ISBN: 978-1-83889-547-1

Audio CD ISBN: 978-1-83889-539-6

Digital audio download ISBN: 978-1-83889-541-9

Large Print ISBN: 978-1-83889-545-7

Boldwood Books Ltd.

23 Bowerdean Street, London, SW6 3TN

www.boldwoodbooks.com

FSC www.fsc.org MIX Paper from responsible sources FSC® C020471

To my wife, Amanda. This one's for you

Repent in this life
Rejoice in the next

1

THE SOUL KILLER

My earliest memory is from my reception year at school when I was five. That was twenty-five years ago. It was the day we broke up for Easter. Many people's first recollections are dramatic or bad. Perhaps that's why they stick in the mind. But it's not the pain that remains vivid all these years later. It's the shock and confusion. I simply didn't understand. However, I believe that was the moment I realised I might be capable of murder.

My mother picked me up from school, and we marched back together. We never held hands, but we talked. Well, she talked. The air of tension around her was already present. It matched the stark streets where we lived. She asked what I'd done that day. My eyes watered with the cold wind as I struggled to remember. When we reached home and entered the narrow kitchen, I opened my satchel and stared at the small Easter basket that I'd made. I stroked the shiny surface of the foil egg, knowing on some level I should keep it hidden.

'What's that in there?' she said.

Guile is beyond most young children, and I was no different so I closed my bag.

'Give it to me.' She grabbed the handles, removed the little cardboard box, and held it as though it might detonate.

'I made that,' I said.

'I warned the school about this sort of thing. They'll regret not listening to me.'

I didn't see her point and I was desperate to have the basket. 'Can you give it back to me, please?'

'It's confiscated.'

I remember thinking that *I* owned it. *I'd* built it using cardboard and foil with the other boys and girls in the classroom. The sense of excitement in the air as we'd queued to leave that afternoon had prickled my skin. The teacher had helped me with my coat and wished me happy Easter but although I'd heard the phrase many times in lessons, the idea of Easter being happy confused me. Easter, when mentioned at home, was said with solemn awe, and triggered fear in me. There was no talk of chocolate and Cadbury's creme eggs.

I knew not to upset my mother. She never shouted, but I would receive a look – one that warned me of impending discipline, which would stay on her face, sometimes for days, before I received my penance. My brain hunted for something to say.

'It's for a joyful Easter.'

She stopped in the doorway. I'd heard the word joy many times at church, but her reply was a growl. 'We do not celebrate it in that way. Don't let me hear you mention it again.'

'Why not? I want to be happy. I want to be like other children.'

Back then, I hadn't learned the value of silence. I also hadn't learned that I wasn't like other children. Only my father was relatively normal in our house.

She returned to stand in front of me. Her ageless brown shirt and jacket combined with severely pulled back greying hair made her seem featureless, despite the large glasses she wore. Perhaps these enabled her to see sin more clearly. Through these her piercing light blue eyes stared down and, with total certainty, she made things abundantly clear.

'God does not approve of that. It's for pagans. We are pure.'

At that moment, I decided I'd be a pagan. And I still wanted what I made. A flash of pure rage swept through me, I believe for the first time. My foot lashed out, and I kicked her in the shin. Quiet seconds followed. It's hard to remember if she smiled or grimaced. Whatever, I cowered to my knees and wrapped my hands around her thick tights. She kicked my arms away.

'Wait there,' she said.

The anticipation is worse than actual physical pain, which only really hurts for a while. I'd experienced the impact of rolled-up newspapers and cooking spoons on many occasions, and so my mind had stopped imagining the worst because I thought I'd seen and felt it all. I didn't know about the cellar.

As she seized my jumper at the back collar and dragged me past my father in the dining room, I noticed someone had moved the dinner table. A trapdoor yawned open. Wide eyed, I implored him to save me as he rose from his seat.

'You go too far, Marjory.'

After a final glance at me, he left the room and strode out of the house. He might have returned to get his things at some point, but I never saw him again. When I look back, I remember hints of happiness and positivity, but he had retreated from us, like an ever so gradual cloud drawing over the sun. The eclipse came that day.

I stared down into the abyss. There were no steps, only blackness. She shoved me hard and firm in the back, and in I dropped, landing on a thin mattress. I gasped in agony as my knees compressed the material and jarred on the floor. Inside, I could just make out the contours. The space was about two metres high and wide. I slumped onto my side and, with an outstretched grasping hand, pleaded for her to pull me up. She loomed above me, so large and powerful. Her voice boomed down.

'Repent in this life, rejoice in the next.'

Her words meant nothing. She was always boring me about one thing or another. I glanced around with blurred eyes as she dropped the trapdoor in place. The only other items I could see before complete darkness enveloped me were a pair of my father's shoes and a blanket. Had he been down here too?

I knelt in the chilled space and imagined the walls pressing in. I believe any other child, whatever their age, would have screamed, but I did not. It makes me think I've always been different. I reached for the blanket and kept silent while listening to the sounds of the table scraping back into place. Sitting in the dark, I focussed on how I could recover my basket.

I wasn't fully aware of my intentions at that moment. The only sound in my prison was the rhythmic ticking above of my mother's pendulum clock. It was a noise to go mad to. Recalling my thoughts is difficult. My whole body tensed. I stifled the scream that yearned to erupt, knowing my mother would recognise its fury, when she craved to hear fear. After a while, I unclenched my jaw and rolled my shoulders. A surprising emptiness washed over me, leaving only a cold, controlled motivation. That focus made me understand, for the first time, that I was capable of anything.

2

THE SOUL KILLER

I've no idea how long I waited down there that first time; no more than a few hours, probably. Using spaced hands in the pitch black, I checked the floor for other objects but found myself in an empty square except for my father's things. I sat and thought about my actions and accepted the truth. Mother made the rules, and I had disobeyed them. Kicking her was just plain dumb. Five year olds might be inexperienced, but they aren't necessarily stupid. I knew from then on that if I wanted special things, I'd need to keep secrets. She would have to be obeyed, or at the very least think she was.

The table scraped the floor, and the trapdoor creaked open. The light above stung my eyes. Judging eyes scrutinised me, but she remained silent.

'Sorry. I won't do that again,' I said.

She nodded. She knelt and held out her hand. I was always strong. Jumping up, I pulled myself out and found dinner set for two. Already the place appeared drabber without my father. He'd been working away much more of late, staying in hotels or leaving early. I could tell my mother missed him too because her eyes strayed to his seat, so we ate in silence, except for that clock. Eventually, I had to ask the most important question a child will ever need to know; words they should never need to speak.

'Do you love me, Mother?'

She opened her mouth and closed it without saying anything. Finally, she spoke as though reading from the good book, but she looked unconvincing.

'God's love is all you require.'

There was no television in our house, but I had jobs to keep me busy. Later, if I'd worked hard, she treated me to biscuits and milk. Then she'd follow me up the stairs and tuck me into bed. Each night we read a story about years gone by. My favourite was always the tale of David and Goliath.

Afterwards, we'd stare at each other and I'd smile as though I understood the message she was trying to impart. The Bible stories she read seemed contradictory to me. Some taught to turn the other cheek, whereas others seemed to condone slaughtering at will. Few suffered damnation for their sins. God forgave most, but He could be the cruellest of all.

Sometimes, I'd see a half smile as though she wanted to connect. I believe she loved me at that point, and I can't blame her for everything. This world sickens and corrupts, and it drove her madder. Loss can make you ruthless.

I don't think I responded to her in the way she hoped. My problem – to others – is that I'm unfeeling. I have a narrow range of emotional responses. Little bothers me, or excites me. It's why I'm good at my job. The strange antics in my house might have unsettled another child, but I just got on with it. Perhaps she wanted me begging for warmth.

As time marched on, my mother changed. She'd stare at my father's picture, occasionally running a finger down the frame. I knew to escape the room or I would be blamed for his absence. Sometimes she'd holler that I'd cost her a soul mate.

When I was ten, a solicitor came to our home but my mother refused to let him in. I was sitting on the lounge floor doing a jigsaw and heard him report that my father had died after a heart attack. His new partner had instructed him to inform us. My mother said he was dead to her the day he left and she closed the door. After he'd gone, I studied her. That was a lie. She had looked high and low for him. Many a time I'd put myself to bed and woke up to a cold breakfast in an empty house. She caught my appraising glance. I rose to leave, expecting harsh words and blame. Instead, tears streamed down her cheeks. I'd never seen so many before, not even in my own mirror.

I stood next to her, only the steam from our hot breath meeting in the cold air of our lounge. I raised my hands but didn't know where to place them. Her fingers flexed, too, but also remained at her sides.

'Don't do what I've done,' she said.

I shook my head in confusion.

'I lost everything. He was my better half and the joy in my heart. It would have been better if he'd died with me rather than have him escape.'

She blinked a couple of times at my shocked face and frozen-open mouth.

'But what about me?' I said.

'Don't make the mistakes I did. I will teach you the way of this world. God has given me a burden to carry, I must bear it.

With that, she took care not to touch me as she left the room.

* * *

Five hundred kids attended my senior school. There were naughtier ones than me, and others who had it worse. I perfected hiding from attention there and at home. I told neither place about the other. My mother's threats of home-schooling were enough to make me conform.

I'd recovered my Easter basket from the outside bin after the first basement incident. I kept it in a cardboard box hidden on the top shelf at the back of my wardrobe. Over the following years, I gently placed inside it the other things that my mother disapproved of. But I was to discover that I had chosen a poor hiding place and it would alter the course of my life.

A boy at school had been bothering me; a short lad called Jimmy. He wasn't usually violent, only quick and smart. Every opportunity he had, he belittled me, and I couldn't cope with his intelligent humour. The other kids laughed at his put-downs, not realising how much they hurt me. I learned to keep quiet and stay away from him. Jokes ranged from my voice cracking in class to the musty smell I carried. Even the teacher chuckled.

It was hard to live in such a powerless vacuum. I coped by showing no emotion, but there are those who notice such insignificance. Once, three much older boys grabbed me as I left the school library. Two held my hands out as the third pretended to punch me in the face; only stopping when his fist was an inch from my nose. Jimmy happened to wander by and they told him to thump me. He looked more scared than me. My nose bled afterwards but he could have hit me much harder.

I dawdled home, but my mother took the shirt off me and soaked it in water. She knelt to my level and her harsh breath drove home a lesson.

'He is watching. Their punishment will be just.'

Jimmy once slipped down some stairs while running at school. While others jeered, I rushed to help him up. The Bible usually taught you to forgive. We had a moment where he softened and he even gave me a smile. The others noticed the moment and stayed quiet. I beamed for the rest of the afternoon, but my reprieve lasted for just one day before the taunts continued. Life taught me different lessons.

Luckily, he moved school after the first year, but it was as though he had infected me with a virus. No one came too close. My confidence plummeted further. It made me long to be invisible, in case the others like him noticed me.

My mother and I visited many places of worship over the years. A few at the start were happy-clappy, but they became more sombre. One even made me consider that the world was doomed, and that I was partly responsible. Most expected you to attend in your smartest clothes, yet a couple had all manner of beggars inside. We attended huge churches and had candle mass in people's lounges. I sat wide eyed and scratching my head at almost every denomination people worshipped. We even dabbled in religions where the congregation prayed to humans with animal heads. Strangely, those beliefs made most sense to me.

I realised that there were two consistent things about all of them. They all believed that life carried on after we died. Some talked about being reborn as something else, while most dangled the lure of everlasting life in heaven. Ascending there to be judged as worthy by Him should be your aim.

The second thing was that my mother didn't fit in. Her views often didn't align with any of the people who attended these churches, even the nice ones. It took a while for me to conclude that her opinions wavered to suit her mood. Whatever she searched for in these places remained elusive. After my father left, she rarely sang. Instead she'd stare at the altar with grim conviction.

She used to attend confession. Afterwards, as she drove home, she would whisper to herself the same lines over and over.

'I know that I am saved. I am born again. I am a child of God.'

Confession stopped when she decided she knew better than those giving out the advice. Not everyone agreed with her views on eternal damnation. She believed that only a special few would be spared the wrath of God. The criteria to qualify were a shifting sand that I struggled to get my head around. More than once I found myself considering the kitchen table and what lay beneath. She'd shake me and explain that good people sometimes had to do bad things that would save their souls and banish others into permanent darkness.

Occasionally, she'd shoot out of her seat and bellow at the pulpit and we'd have to leave mid-service, or I'd be hauled from Sunday school. She'd tell me on the way home about the brutality of life, and how everyone had their own interests at heart. She'd stop in the street and lean down to look in my eyes.

'We don't need them in our lives. Only those who are saved are worth anything.'

'I was having a good time.'

'We don't worship to have a good time. Our goal is heaven and life everlasting.'

'Are we going there?'

'Yes.'

'With father?'

Her grip tightened and I was dragged along.

'Of course.'

I wondered what his last girlfriend would think about that. Whatever, it was serious stuff when I'd rather have been reading comics.

She always said not to worry about this life because happiness existed a final heartbeat away. When someone maddens over years, it's hard to see the exact point when they become crazy, as opposed to just different from the rest of us. Mother was lucid then, but, with my father gone, little outside influence crept within our walls. The gospel according to Marjory held sway and I was destined to be her disciple.

At age twelve, I was plunged through the trapdoor for the

final time. She'd burst into my room and found me enthusiastically exploring my puberty. My cheeks still burn when I recall that frozen second. For a long while, I thought of her whenever I became aroused. I wonder if I ever truly got over it.

At that embarrassing moment, she screamed at me. 'What do you think you're doing in my pure house?'

I assumed, correctly, that she didn't want the actual answer.

I fumbled for my clothes. Even though our heights matched by then, her determination overpowered me. She grabbed my ear and pulled me down our dangerously steep stairs. I almost tripped and plummeted down while trying to cover myself up. I stood with my hands between my legs as she dragged the table back and lifted the rug. Again, she thrust me in from behind. I didn't reach for help, nor feel the cold. I only scowled into the darkness.

3

THE SOUL KILLER

My relationship with my mother changed after that incident. She left me down there until darkness fell; at least ten hours. When the trapdoor lifted, I returned her glare until she stepped away. I climbed out to an empty room. She never mentioned what had happened: her part in it or mine. I don't recall her touching me again, in punishment or in love.

I continued my education but tried to remain unseen and was mostly successful, although Jimmy's acquaintances still bullied me. Their nicknames stuck throughout the years. Even now, if I hear the words mentioned, my body tenses. That said, some people started to include me, and I slowly made some friends. I even joined the cross-country team and excelled. It suited my nature to run ahead where no one could bother me.

My mother didn't insist I earn money to contribute to the household finances, but there were no free rides. Conversation and story time ended. Instead, washing and ironing the family's clothes became my job. It took a year until I got the hang of it and stopped burning my hands and ruining things. I never minded the pain.

I impressed the teachers with my exam results and told my mother I wanted to go to university. She left me gobsmacked by telling me God expects us to seek knowledge. Perhaps she wanted to see the back of me. I think she'd become confused as to the point of life. Cleanliness used to be next to Godliness, but mould crept into the corners of the rooms and surfaces gathered dust.

By that time, Barney Trimble – her new partner – had been with us for a while. He was a dopey sort with a beaten expression, and the type of guy who you could see every day for years but never recall any details about him.

He spent most of his time in my father's chair. The similarities in looks were so strong, even down to the side parting that showed a glistening head, that I imagined he'd been grown in a test-tube for the role but errors had crept in. He had very few opinions of his own and was not dissimilar to a quiet dog, but their relationship was different. Muffled groans of violence escaped from their room at night. I contemplated investigating, but many of the howls were his. He stayed though, so perhaps he had nowhere else to go.

Barney owned a white and black campervan: a real plus point. Of course, my mother believed it ungodly. She considered it some kind of sex wagon. But Barney and I took numerous weekend trips to a peaceful place called West Runton in Norfolk. We didn't speak much to each other the whole time, but instead we relaxed in the peace and quiet away from Mother's sermons. He worked an allotment, too, where he spent many hours. I don't know what he grew there because he rarely brought anything home.

I once pulled his leg about his name almost being Barney Rubble. A playful smile lit up his face for a second; an expression I only saw on a few occasions. He told me that his friends called him Flintstone at school. It seemed weird to think of him in that way: a person with a life and a future, when he ended up such a non-entity. But I liked that he'd told me that.

Cambridge University disorientated me at first. I could barely cope with the people and noise. The halls of residence sometimes reminded me of the first day of the January sales, and I kept to my room away from the noise and purpose. However, I slowly realised that, despite the throng, there was an anonymity to the place. Busy people missed the silent soul among the thousands. I accepted a job at a bakery to pay my way. An old guy and I arrived at 5:00 and baked for when the store opened. We left when the other staff turned up, then I attended my lectures.

I kept up with my running. Another jogger from the athletics club took a shine to me. Charlie wasn't a particularly nice person and became a nightmare when drunk but we became some sort of couple. I think she enjoyed bossing around the club's fastest runner. The coach encouraged me to attend national try-outs, but I sought no glory.

Then a strange thing happened. Christmas came. You could sense the change in mood over everyone and everything. Trees and tinsel appeared. A palpable buzz grew as the big day approached. I'd avoided the fresher parties – people were more in your face under the influence of alcohol – but I succumbed to the end-of-year Christmas bash.

Charlie's family were rich. She bought me a tuxedo and I felt like James Bond. It was heady. She suggested I cut my hair short and called me Action Man, and I liked it. The figure of him she bought as a joke even had the same expression I wore when I ran. Her beauty reflected well against my cool distance. It brought us status. Nice clothes brought me compliments.

To my amazement, the party flew by. Everyone seemed to want to talk with me and listened when I spoke. They interpreted my standoffishness and distance as drive. Many stopped and explained that they respected my commitment. They admired my focus on running at the crack of dawn. They were unaware I was running to work.

Sometimes, I'd put my trainers on and disappear late at night. Exercise silenced the voices; the ones telling me I didn't belong. But with Charlie by my side, I fitted in, and she resembled a movie star that night. I basked in the reflective glow.

Later, she dragged me back to her room.

'Fuck me. Hard!' Rank brandy breath wrinkled my nose. I gulped, not having had sex at that point.

Buttons popped as she tore the shirt from my back. Sharp nails scraped down my chest. It hurt, but the intensity was intoxicating. Perhaps that was the appeal for Barney with my mother. I'd never felt so alive. She pushed me onto the bed and straddled me.

'God, God, yes, yes.'

My thoughts strayed to my mother.

'Screw me,' Charlie demanded, frantic eyes boring into mine.

Her language shocked me more than the naked proximity of our bodies. That was what dragged my mind into the present and made me respond to her requests. As a person Charlie was shallow, but as a teacher she was very effective. I wasn't completely naïve, I'd seen porn before, but I followed her instructions.

I enjoyed the workout. The power I possessed over her during certain moments pleased me more than the climax itself. I owned her. Those occasions with Charlie showed me that, by training my body and focussing on a woman's needs, I could become something else. For the first time in my life, I felt I belonged in a way that I previously hadn't. I had become a participant as opposed to an observer.

For the last few weeks up to Christmas, the world and I were synchronised. I relaxed and looked others in the eye. I enjoyed the simple pleasures of hot chocolate in front of a pub fire and buying gifts to place next to a tree.

Until, one day towards the end of term, early in the morning when I left for work, I froze as I caught one of our senior lecturers sneaking out of Charlie's room.

4

THE SOUL KILLER

I followed him out to the exit and scowled as he cycled away on his rickety bicycle. I followed at a distance, which wasn't hard. He didn't go far, only back to one of the buildings that was near to the university. Perhaps his home came with the job.

Afterwards, I sprinted through the streets, but I was unable to still my mind. Anger bubbled at the periphery of my thoughts but, initially, it wasn't aimed specifically at her, or him even. After all, we hadn't made a commitment to each other. She had been more like a training buddy. But I knew I'd miss the recent feeling of involvement, of being part of something.

As I finally tired, I saw that they'd disrespected me. How dared they? Was I nothing? Would my university life mirror my school life? All these years, I'd turned the other cheek. To my mother, to bullies, to all. It had gained me nothing. Finally, I headed to work, happy in the knowledge that, if necessary, I knew where he lived.

That night, I returned to the lecturer's house and stood waiting under a tree in the distance as it rained. When he returned home, he kissed a middle-aged woman at the door and retreated into a cosy glow.

The truth of the matter became even clearer to me in the run-up to Christmas Day. Having a beautiful partner had grounded me and made others look at me in a new light. Charlie wouldn't figure in my future. However, I was sure such a girl did exist. I would train, get my degree, and find a good job until we met. Then I'd hang on to her and live the perfect life.

Nobody and nothing would come between us. It would be us against the world, to the end of the world.

Luckily, I hadn't given Charlie the necklace I'd bought for her. I decided to give it to my mother instead. It would be a secret acknowledgement that I wouldn't lose my soul mate when I found her as my mother did when she let my father slip through her fingers.

I returned to Wisbech late on Christmas Eve to a silent home, regretfully with no place else to go. Obviously, there was no wreath on the door. Inside it was so dark, cold and still that it oppressed all life. Even the clock seemed to struggle to tick. I knew I'd have no presents again. My room remained the same and I crept up the stairs so as not to wake anyone and slipped under the duvet. I imagined the black mould on the walls rapidly expanding, covering them completely, and then engulfing me. Stealing from the bed, I turned on the light and took some deep breaths. Gentle snoring came from the landing.

I walked towards their room and stood next to the bed. My mother looked frailer than I recalled. My eyes scanned the room for personal items, but there was nothing. I realised she had chosen this non-life. It was up to me to choose something different.

The following morning, I came downstairs in a mischievous mood. My mother and Barney ate cereal in silence and the overriding impression I had was of grey lives. Their days were featureless landscapes where breathing was automatic, but actually living was not.

What was the point to it all? Even if you were focussed on the next life, couldn't you do something in this one while you waited? I was determined to. I planned for a life full of drama and excitement. I'd laughed the first time someone called an old people's home *God's waiting room*, but that was where my mother spent her days.

Imagine wasting your entire existence with one foot in the grave. Why not live before you die? You can take risks, do what you like. In fact, if you believe in the safety net of heaven, then eternal happiness is yours even if you make the ultimate mistake. What a perfect truth. If life is a game, play it with purpose and enthusiasm. At least try to enjoy it.

'Merry Christmas,' I said.

I received a grin from Barney. My mother stopped chewing. I gazed around the spartan room. I knew I shouldn't give her the necklace, but I thought of everything I'd missed out on in my life. The people I'd left at college were elated, laughing and boisterous in anticipation of Christmas, ensuring the drabness of my childhood became blisteringly evident. I'd returned to a scene from a Charles Dickens story.

'Here you go, Mum.' She hated that word. 'This is for you.'

I reckoned on her throwing it straight in the bin, and my mouth dried as she took her time with the unwrapping. Barney slowly placed his spoon on the table as though he were a western gunfighter lowering his pistol for the sheriff. There was just the dreaded tick from that infernal clock as she opened the box and stared inside.

I sometimes kid myself that I saw tears. If they were present, she'd been blinded by wrath. I was surprised the clock didn't blow up with the tension. She eased the box lid shut and hurled it in my direction. Somehow, I caught it one handed.

Her righteous sneer still triggered a tremble in my legs. I backed away and clambered up the stairs. A few seconds later, a step behind me creaked. The urge to flee overwhelmed me, but I had only my bedroom ahead. She followed and stopped at the door.

'Where are you going with that? It cannot stay in this house.'

Without thinking, I looked at the wardrobe, which held the collection of my possessions, and I knew immediately where the necklace belonged. It also dawned on me that she couldn't hurt me any more. Her punishments were over, her power gone. She might own this house but I could take my belongings and use my wages if she threw me out.

My serene face must have betrayed my intentions because suddenly the doorway dwarfed her. Perhaps only then did I see her clearly.

'Looking for your stash, son? Your horrible little things are gone.'

Blood rushed in my ears as I yanked the wardrobe door open and searched for my secrets. With relief, I spotted the box in its normal place but it was too light when I picked it up. Placing the necklace inside the empty space, I turned with a smile. My mother retreated from my expression. She understood at that moment what her nurturing skills had created.

As she stepped down the first stair, I returned to her the hearty shoves she'd bestowed on me, backed by decades of interest. It's no lie to say she flew. Those stairs were steep. She made no sound until there was an almighty wooden crack as she hit the bottom. It could have been a floorboard, or her neck. Death was instantaneous, judging by the direction of her stare.

A falling body makes a shocking clump, and Barney ran to investigate. That was the strangest thing about the whole experience. Barney rang for an ambulance in the same casual manner as one orders a taxi. We didn't speak until the sirens sounded.

'I've been telling her to put a rail on those stairs for years. I'll sort it tomorrow.'

Did he suspect I pushed her? My mother was a strange woman. It made sense that she would have unusual friends. I listened to Barney inform the police about the terrible accident and explain that I'd been in my room. Our matter-of-fact responses must have been convincing. I think it's normal to be stunned by such an abrupt end to a life.

The police weren't daft. Many a disagreement finishes at the bottom of a flight of stairs. The sergeant directed his questions at me.

'Did you argue? Was she upset?'

'Not at all. She seemed exactly the same as always.'

His stare almost disarmed me, like my mother's. He glanced at my scruffy college clothes and smiled.

'I know what students are like. Did you come back at Christmas and get drunk with your friends? It's easy to argue at this time of the year. The holidays can literally be murder.'

Clever guy. It was like a game. Who's the cleverest?

'Not in our house, sir. We don't celebrate Christmas.' I gestured to our bare walls.

The paramedic approached and checked me over. I recall her warm and gentle hands, motivated by more than just doing her job. She enjoyed her role, it was her vocation, and I thought one day perhaps I would relish a career I could love. I wanted to excel at something and be known for it.

Once they removed the body and everyone had left, Barney

and I sat together. I struggled to find suitable words. Probing into whether or not he'd intentionally lied to the police didn't seem wise. I'd also had an epiphany. My life would be different now I understood the world, but a few things remained unclear.

'Barney, why did you stay with her? She can't have been easy to live with.'

He shrugged and his eyes rose to the ceiling and their bedroom above. 'We connected, if you know what I mean. I wanted to marry her, but she despised what she called pagan rituals. Her words. I suppose I have weird taste in women.'

'Couldn't you have found someone a little more normal?'

He slumped onto his seat and exhaled loudly. There's little difference between despair and defeat. He pulled his T-shirt down to cover his pot belly and ran a hand through his lank thinning hair.

'There wasn't a queue forming. I'd only gone to church because I was lonely. I knew she was looking for a replacement for your father, and I never filled the role, but we had a life of sorts, although I found a drawer full of their things. You know, old photos of them together, jewellery, even an old letter that I couldn't bring myself to read. I never mentioned it to her, because sometimes she'd cling to me at night and it was good. Certainly better than being alone. She cooked for me and washed my clothes. You know, it was company. I had our trips in the van to look forward to, and I enjoyed the allotment. It's been okay.'

'You didn't mind being second choice?'

'Not if the alternative is coming in last. She treated me well enough.'

It was an interesting insight. Some people lead unexciting lives but they aren't necessarily unhappy. Barney looked serious for a moment. He spoke slowly.

'It was you who I worried about.'

'How so?'

'Your mother had some strange ideas and views. She was always preaching to you and some of what she said was dark.'

'I tended to ignore most of what she said.'

'Yes, I know, but you listened more as you got older.'

'Is that so bad?'

'It depends. If you're told the same thing over and over again, it can eventually sink in, even if it first sounded wrong.'

Before I had time to consider his words, he changed the subject. 'Anyway, she loved you, of that I'm sure.'

'She treated me badly.'

He reached over and patted my hand.

'Your mum struggled with affection and love. Were you aware she went to a convent school?'

'No, she never mentioned it.'

'It was extremely religious and very strict. I think they punished the children in ways that are unacceptable now. That affected and influenced her, and, well, she enjoyed some unnatural things. I don't think she knew how to respond to authority or religion after that, nor how to be a good parent. She was completely convinced that this life was for suffering so that you could receive heaven as your reward. They'll take care of her there.'

I found myself whispering, 'Amen,' but my eyes rose to the ceiling, too. I wished I hadn't asked because I struggled to look him in the eye for a long time after that, even though he'd done me a huge favour. As I grew older, I understood that you hold on to someone you belong with, whatever the consequences, or however hard it becomes. But you protect your soul, even if that means breaking the law.

Barney gave me his debit card and PIN, and sent me down to the corner shop for a turkey, just like in *A Christmas Carol*, except I only found Bernard Matthews chicken slices. It was run by a Sikh shopkeeper who opened for a few hours for others who didn't celebrate the day. I bought a bottle of whisky, some beers, and a few bags of crisps as accompaniments.

When I returned, Barney had put the radio on and we listened to various songs intermingled with Christmas classics. We ate a Chinese takeaway later. All in all, I enjoyed a pleasant day.

Just before we retired, Barney handed me a plastic bag.

'Your mother put it in the loft this morning. I like to think she would have returned it to you instead of throwing it away.'

Opening the bag, I revealed the contents of my secret box. I considered the motivation for what I'd done and shrugged. There were few regrets because my mother, who never fitted into this world, was now at peace. What I did was hardly a crime. Hadn't I delivered her to where she'd wanted to be? Her mortal worries were over now, and her soul was free.

5

DI BARTON

The funeral

Detective Inspector John Barton began to surface from a dream filled sleep. His mount had just jumped the last fence and galloped up the home straight in the Grand National to cheering from the heaving crowds. The images faded to the presentation ceremony where the giant trophy loomed before him.

'Here you are, John. Now, get moving, or you'll be late.'

He sat up, rubbed his eyes, and focussed on the cup in front of him. It said, 'Anybody who says the police are corrupt can kiss my Rolex!' His wife, Holly, scowled at him. His head dropped back on the pillow, as though full of cement.

'Do I have to go?'

'Everyone's expecting you. I don't understand what's got into you lately.'

He watched her leave in a sombre suit and admired the tight but sensible trousers. Was that an acceptable thought to have on such a sad day? He considered her words and agreed. He didn't know what had got into him lately either. The death of his colleague Alan 'Ginger' Rodgers had shocked him to the core, but other worries trickled into his mind too. Besides, there probably wasn't a single person in the city that the acts of the Snow Killer hadn't affected. As a policeman, he always assumed he could cope with anything.

He knew that his team would look to him for guidance over the next few months. An officer killed in the line of duty would drag down morale. He'd have the tough task of reminding them they had a job to do, however brutal the murder of one of their own was.

The coroner had released the bodies over a week before and, after a month, the shock of his colleague's demise had lessened, but the gloom remained. Ginger had no close family, and when no distant relative or friend had stepped forward to organise the funeral, in the end, Barton's wife had said she'd do it.

That was Holly to a T and was one of the reasons why he loved her. She had tolerated Ginger's friendship with Barton. Ginger had enjoyed a joke and a drink, so most partners had considered him an all-round bad influence. They'd double-dated with Ginger and his long-term girlfriend in the distant past after Ginger's second divorce, but the Bartons had ended up with three children, and John had been promoted. Life had changed for them and their other couple friends as they'd aged and their families had grown, but no one had told Ginger. When Holly had finally reached his partner to ask her views on the funeral arrangements, Debbie had explained that they split up years ago. Ginger hadn't said a word to anyone.

Holly and Debbie had chosen a simple service by a celebrant instead of a religious figure. After all, Ginger's only spirituality had come in a bottle.

Barton heaved himself out of bed and gazed into the mirror with a smile. At well over six feet tall and eighteen stone, he'd make an unlikely jockey. It would need to be some horse. Nevertheless, his colourful dreams contrasted with the dark thoughts that circled him during daylight. His mother had told him that his father had suffered from depression, so, by acknowledging the risk, Barton hoped it wouldn't become a problem.

By the time he clomped down the stairs in his dark grey suit, Holly was at the door with her arms crossed. Barton smiled but a cracking came from under his foot. He stared down at his five year old son's lorry, that now resembled a Ferrari.

'Lock up. I'll drive. We'll go in my car,' she ordered, shaking her head.

The kids were at school. Only the fifteen year old, Lawrence, remembered Ginger, and he hadn't seen him for a long time. Barton had overheard Lawrence asking Holly questions concerning the recent killings. She'd given him the same explanation as Barton had: sometimes sick people got angry and lashed out.

He stepped outside and grimaced at Holly's tiny car. While he waited for her to unlock the door, he glanced around at the area where the Snow Killer had operated. There was an oppressive feel to the air, as though there were too many big white clouds for the sky and they'd tumbled towards the earth. Perfect funeral weather, he mused.

Even the wind didn't know what to do. Winter was over but no one had told spring to arrive. Perhaps it was waiting until they'd buried his friend.

Barton squeezed in next to his wife.

'Don't you think my car would be more comfortable?'

She couldn't help a smile sneaking onto her face.

'I didn't know if you'd still be over the limit?'

'I only had four beers last night.'

'It's hard for me to keep up, what with you drinking every evening.'

Barton kept his mouth shut. Management had allowed him a week off work after the end of the serial killer case. When he'd returned, he'd found himself distracted by things that had never bothered him before. It made him unfocussed and forgetful during the day, and, with gathering gloom, he struggled to drop off at night. A couple of cold ones helped with that. In the past, he'd confided in Holly when the brutal nature of policing had threatened to swamp him. He grasped, at that moment, that he had stopped doing so.

'It's the job.'

'I thought you said it was slow.'

'Not present work.'

She studied his face as she pulled up at some traffic lights. They would arrive at the crematorium in minutes. He waited while she decided whether or not it was the time to delve into a deep conversation, which they might not be able to finish. She concluded it wasn't.

'Don't exclude me, John. We'll get through this together.'

'I know, it's just my brain processing things.'

'Don't worry,' she said with a grin. 'Peterborough rarely gets a serial killer. We should have plenty of time before the next one.'

6

DI BARTON

Holly's forehead creased as she drove in circles around the full parking bays at the crematorium. Despite her fretting, they'd still arrived ten minutes before the start. Barton spotted DS Kelly Strange and DS Shawn Zander laughing at him in the little car as they did loops hoping for a space to come free. They eventually parked on a grass verge near the entrance.

Zander opened the door for Barton. Before he could struggle out, Zander crouched and waved at Holly.

'Will madam need the toolbox to get this creature out of the passenger seat?'

'Hi, Shawn. You okay? He pops out if I tickle him.'

Barton shook his head. Everyone on the planet called Shawn Zander plain Zander except Holly. Zander had lost his son over a year ago through CO_2 poisoning. His marriage disintegrated in the aftermath, so Holly often asked after him and invited him around, with little success. Zander had finally emerged on the other side of his pain, but experiences like that darken you forever. He was big. Similar in height and proportion to Barton, but grief had stolen his appetite. Barton used to compare him to Muhammad Ali due to his rapid banter. He regretted the loss of humanity in his friend, but who could blame him?

A large hand hauled Barton out. They stood next to each other and smiled. The case of the Snow Killer, Zander's loss, and years of working together had strengthened their bond.

'I'd prefer it if you two made out after the funeral, lads,' said DS Strange.

Barton chuckled. Strange hadn't been out of hospital long, and he'd kept away from her house so she could get her head sorted. He'd learned that she preferred to process life's blows alone. Strange reached over and gave his hand a meaty shake. She punched Zander on the arm. Barton suspected romantic tension between them, but it was just a detective's hunch.

They were the linchpins of his team, even though she'd only transferred up from London last year. Strange had tolerated some bullying in the capital and this had given her a tough edge. She was perfect sergeant material. In the short time she had worked in the department, she'd provided valuable insight on many occasions. Her serious nature discouraged most from flirting, and Barton admired her sparks of genius. The impressive efficiency and resourcefulness of Barton's unit had remained the only positive to come from the shocking murders.

The Snow Killer's end had resulted in a devastating loss for Strange, too. Ginger had saved her life by sacrificing his own. However, the trauma had caused her to miscarry. Events like these recent ones could rip a team to shreds if officers concentrated on the price they might have to pay. As they waited for the doors to open, Barton knew he wouldn't let that happen. First, though, it was time to remember Ginger.

Police funerals were strange things. Ginger had been far from popular. His biting wit had riled many and he'd possessed an ability to find a nickname for someone that shredded them. One such victim came to talk to Barton as they waited in the spring sunshine for the earlier service to finish.

'Detective Barton. Good to see you again.'

'Chief Superintendent Blake Lafferty. Or may I call you Bloke on such a day?'

'You can call me whatever you like if you fancy three years in Traffic afterwards.'

'They will bury your nickname with him, sir.'

Lafferty stared at him without expression, before cracking a grin. 'That cackling bastard pushed me to distraction. It drove me on, though. I wanted to get promoted so high I would never have to see his spotty face again.'

'Are you here to make sure he's gone?'

'Not officially. I was visiting the station anyway, but I'll definitely be raising a glass to him later.'

Still a dick, thought Barton, as he laughed inside at the memories. Lafferty had irritated everyone from the very beginning. He'd been desperate to climb the ladder, and his ruthless ambition had progressively worsened. One weekend, Ginger had altered his locker name card from Blake Lafferty to Bloke's Lavatory and kept sticking home-drawn pictures of turds underneath it. For years, Lafferty had borne the brunt of puns about having stuff dumped on him. Nostalgia threatened to swamp Barton as he thought about jokes from twenty years ago.

The crematorium doors opened and he found Holly's hand in his. People often fill the seats at the rear first, like at weddings, but Barton strode to the front. Navneet Naeem, his old DCI, and her sons and husband joined him. The Snow Killer had damaged their lives, too. Any staff that Thorpe Wood police station could spare filled the surrounding spaces and the place was full.

Barton couldn't see any strangers, and it was only when he stood to say his words that he recognised Ginger's ex-girlfriend, Debbie, standing at the back in between DCs Whitlam and Malik. He placed his written notes to one side; he didn't need them. He spoke from the heart, even getting in a few toilet jokes just to upset Lafferty, until a subtle cough from the celebrant told him to wind it up.

'DC Alan "Ginger" Rodgers won't be remembered as the best copper the force has ever had. He won't go down as the most reliable person to work with, either. Yet, we solved many cases because of his intelligence and experience. I was proud to call him a colleague and a friend. I'm glad he became part of my life. He died a hero.'

7

THE SOUL KILLER

I returned to my mother's old property and lived with Barney after graduating from university, but I would often make excuses to leave the house or find myself wandering from room to room. My emotions were conflicted. Mother had truly believed in her actions as she'd cocooned me from the world. She was dangerous, yet never deadly. Instead, it turned out that crossing me was her last mistake – but then she should never have touched my things. Any minor feelings of regret had long since faded.

I struggled to find well-paid work in Wisbech. I worked in a bakery again for a while, but I wanted a serious job.

The biggest city nearby was Peterborough. Shared living like at university did not appeal. I found a row of strange, tiny terraced houses along a decrepit, dead-end track. One big bedroom upstairs and one large lounge-diner downstairs sounds weird, but it made the place feel bigger than it was. Reasonable rent and plenty of parking near disused railway yards made it appealing, even though the dwellings did remind me a little of hobbits' homes with thin walls. Number three became mine and, apart from the bloke two doors away from me playing his music too loud, I loved it there.

After finishing my studies and applying all over, I got my dream role. Shift work never bothered me, and I took advantage of any overtime. I thought of my mother often with a new-found appreciation. She wasn't the only one who thought this world was a practice ground for eternity and no rules applied. My job showed me the damage humans did to one another. People died, few cared, they were quickly forgotten. My job meant people held me in some esteem. It never failed to give me a buzz.

I joined a running club but didn't meet a new Charlie. Many of the members were much older than me, meaning I failed to settle. Instead, I bounced from gym to gym to keep in shape. My body changed little despite my strength improving. Rarely did I arrive at a machine and need to lower a weight, but it seemed my muscles were fine as they were. That said, the world was changing and so was what people found attractive. Celebrities ate little and exercised constantly. People admired that look.

Long years passed and I feared I'd never meet my soul mate. Sometimes, I woke at night bathed in sweat; the point of life evading me. My thoughts strayed back to Charlie and the lecturer. It became a sore that I'd itch. I hated my history. All those people that had treated me badly and showed me disrespect tempered my enthusiasm for living. My past, left as it was, ruined my future.

Dating websites gained in popularity at the time. Those Internet pages seemed beyond the normal rules of society. You didn't need the dark web when you had social media in its present form. People assumed new identities and the witless and feckless paid the price. I dabbled but decided I would not meet my soul mate that way. However, I used Tinder mercilessly. When I was a young boy, no one wanted me. When I became an adult, finding out people had swiped right at my picture became an addictive pick-me-up.

I chose normal individuals, having found the truly attractive people over-confident and mildly threatening. The meetings with them tended to make me feel angry as opposed to horny. I dated women until they slept with me. Sometimes that was for weeks, other times only minutes. Them wanting more fed my growing confidence. I would cut all ties after that first coupling.

But it wouldn't be long until I searched for the next one, often because I needed someone else in my life.

I felt sure I would know the moment I met someone perfect. It wouldn't be through a grubby hook-up site. My mother said she knew the moment she met my father. It would be a chemical reaction – I suppose I expected a thunderbolt.

The change began eighteen months ago with a sense of

being watched while browsing at the supermarket. I'm a man of routine, shifts permitting, so I guess it wouldn't have taken Claudia too long to work out when I shopped.

Every Friday night, I bought one of those rotisserie chickens and chunks of gammon from the deli. I'd get a selection of fruit and vegetables, and that would last me the whole weekend. Two weeks in a row, I came away with an itch between my shoulder blades. The next visit, I caught a young girl staring at me. I didn't recognise her, but the moment our eyes met, she smiled. A few seconds later, our trolleys bumped while she grinned up at me.

'Hey, don't we know each other?' she asked.

She was about five feet tall and pear shaped. Faint freckles glistened on her red cheeks. Her tracksuit had damp patches under her arms while unkempt hair hung heavily down her neck.

'No, I don't believe so.' Her attire disconcerted me, but it was her wide eyed enthusiasm that made me step back. 'I think I'd have remembered someone like you.'

'Very smooth. Are you chatting me up?'

'Erm...'

'Just kidding, although I am single. Look, they gave us these at work this week.'

I read the glossy business card embossed with *Claudia Birtwistle, Property Lawyer*. I shook my head. 'Name doesn't ring a bell.'

'You used to go to the Virgin gym. We flirted a little, you know, through the machines, but then you left before we spoke. Give me a call. I see you're still in good shape. Where do you work out?'

'I'm at the Holiday Inn leisure club. They installed new equipment but haven't put the prices up yet.'

'Perhaps I'll check it out. We can grab a coffee now if you like?'

I didn't want to be rude, but I couldn't believe she was the person I had been waiting for. Regardless, the first date with my wife-to-be wouldn't happen in a Morrison's supermarket restaurant surrounded by feral toddlers and pushy pensioners.

'I can't. I'm off to the gym now. Have you just been to yours?'

If her moistness wasn't through exertion, it could only be due to illness or drugs.

'I've been to boxercise. It's great. Another time, then.'

She did that annoying pretend phone hand gesture as she backed away and mouthed *call me*. I chuckled at the prospect but, as I wandered off, I realised the inane gesture was the only thing I'd found irritating. She wasn't especially pretty, but I'd detected none of the bitterness that drunken Charlie had been unable to keep out of every conversation.

* * *

I was surprised to find that Claudia dominated my thoughts, and I almost rang her. I'd run imaginary calls through my mind but always felt daft. Work distracted me, and soon the weekend came around again; the time for my weekly shop. I arrived in new jeans and my best shirt. She wasn't there. I dawdled like a fool in every aisle and clanged into other shoppers with my eyes on the horizon. Perhaps I'd read it wrong. Huge queues swarmed at the checkouts, and I nearly deserted the trolley in frustration.

I joined the self-pay line, which moved faster, and waited with sagging shoulders. A stony faced woman with a black ponytail turned round after I accidentally nudged her hip with my shopping. Mascara darkened blue eyes drilled into mine.

'I thought you were going to ring me?' said Claudia.

There it was. More lightning bolt than thunder. My startled brain managed a dodgy excuse as I grinned at her.

'I wasn't sure whether you wanted a workout buddy or a boyfriend.'

'Maybe I haven't decided yet.'

She was unrecognisable from the sweaty shrimp I'd met the previous week. Expensive looking clothes and high heels had turned her into something striking. Beautiful women always disarmed me and I mumbled rubbish as we queued. But, unexpectedly, I learned something else life altering. It doesn't matter what you say if the other person is genuinely interested or thinking positive thoughts, as long as you talk or, better still, listen. She'd known of me but didn't know anything about me. I bet she created an idea of what I was like. People desire something more if they can't have it.

I considered whether her current look was just an illusion and not what I'd be getting, until I concluded something amazing. I would have them both. It'd be like having two girlfriends without the hassle of maintaining different lives. As she giggled at the strange things I'd put in my trolley while I searched for her, I knew, without a shadow of doubt, that I had found the one at last. We would be together, forever.

8

THE SOUL KILLER

Last Christmas

It was my first Christmas with Claudia and I wanted it to be memorable. She came to my little house in River End on Christmas Eve. Claudia cherished this time of year. She had told me that she traditionally opened presents with loved ones the night before Christmas, so she could focus on the celebration and all the great food the next day. I wondered if it was a habit from an earlier boyfriend. I said nothing, but my stomach rolled at the thought of it.

She spent every Christmas Day at her dad's house with her twin sister. Her mother had died in a car accident many years ago, which meant the remaining family members were a close unit. They visited her mother's grave after lunch as part of the ritual of Christmas Day. She had been a religious woman and instilled the fear of God in her children. They kept her memory alive with weekly flowers. I prefer to let the dead rest in peace.

I didn't have anyone else to buy for, except Barney, and I'd been getting him cheap whisky for years. He'd found a new relationship with the bottom of a bottle and discovered it less judgemental and demanding than my mother. Did his habit start the Christmas she died? Did my actions drive him to drink?

Christmas Day became the only time I saw him all year. He had retired from a career I don't recall. When I asked if he was okay for money, he said he never spent all of his pension. I don't think he left the house much. I enjoyed Christmas with Barney.

It beat being alone. He smiled a lot on those few days. If my mother's ghost haunted the house, it kept quiet when I returned.

I smiled as I watched Claudia bustling around my house that first year. To think that it was the first of many was comforting. I knew it'd be a special day now for Claudia as it was for me. She was more materialistic than me and enjoyed coveting things in shop windows when we were out, or admired items on TV adverts when we were in, and so I had assumed she was dropping me hints. I had kept a list so I wouldn't forget. When it was time for us to exchange gifts, she went outside to get my presents, while I grabbed her boxes from the loft. I arranged them under my big plastic tree and all over the sofa. Her face was a picture when she returned.

'Wow, so many. I wasn't expecting that.'

It was just like her to be so modest. What kind of boyfriend would I be if I didn't get her the very best? I poured her a sherry.

'Not for me. I need to drive first thing. I don't want to become a statistic.'

I smiled, but I'd imagined her giggling and resting her head on my chest as we watched a festive film. I knocked mine down in one go when she turned to fetch what she'd bought me.

'These are just some little things to open. I thought I'd take you for a drive to the coast in a few days and treat you to a walk and some fish and chips.'

A brief flash of annoyance threatened to sour my mood. I'd thought she'd wear a dress as opposed to jeans, too, but I soon removed them and she said she'd never received so much attention. She promised it was the most intense experience of her life.

Claudia left first thing in the morning without drinking the expensive coffee I'd brewed for her. Alone, I held her gifts again. She had got me the boxset of the American series *The Wire*, and a tie and cufflinks set. The DVD looked interesting, but I didn't wear ties and my shirts were button sleeves. None of that mattered though. We were a couple.

I went to the loft again and brought down the box that I used to hide things from my mother in. The tatty Easter basket and Charlie's necklace were the only items I'd kept from my childhood and university. The rest of the bits just reminded me of unhappier times and were best forgotten. The two remaining pieces were important as they reminded me of the two women who tried to ruin my life. I nodded as I believed that Mother paid the necessary price, but my mood spoiled as I recalled Charlie. That wound still festered.

Never mind, I had Claudia now and she appreciated me. Claudia's father, Donald, celebrated Boxing Day with a party for the wider family and we were both invited. Claudia relished the prospect. I'd have been happier on a rack with a spotlight shining in my face, but he was important to her.

I'd only met Donald briefly a handful of times, each a torturous occasion. He observed me in the same way a doctor stared at a sick patient: wondering where the faults were. He had an overbearing, blusterous manner, which made me nervous. I was never sure whether his challenges to play badminton and squash were real or his poor attempts at humour. Her sister, Annabelle, was more polite with her scrutiny than him, but her allegiance would never be to me.

On Boxing Day, we pulled up outside his house. There wasn't much parking at the best of times on the old British Sugar site despite the eye watering cost of the houses, and we parked a two minute walk away near the estate playground. I shivered as I stepped from the car and helped Claudia into her coat despite the short distance. My eyes had bulged at the price of his favourite bottle of wine. Even so, I hoped my choice would impress him.

Claudia and I held hands and wandered past the playground to his house. I forced myself to breathe slowly and distract myself by staring at the swings and slides. They trigger strange emotions in me even though I only recall going on them once. It must have been when I was very young as the memory is hazy. Yet, if I think hard enough, I can feel the breeze on my face as I swing higher. My mother pushed me for a while, and I turned and laughed at her, knowing she loved me.

At that moment, it was difficult to comprehend that I'd ended up killing her. I focussed on her being beyond help by the time I did that though, and I needed to concentrate on myself. That was what she taught me. Heaven was her goal, and she got her reward.

Claudia noticed my melancholy looks at the empty playground, so she linked arms with me. 'They always look sad with nobody in them.'

I agreed. 'The kids will be back soon.'

'Maybe ours one day?'

My heart soared at those words. Not that I wanted offspring. The world would be better off with no continuation of my family line, but at least she saw a future with me. I'd persuade Claudia later that we didn't need children in our lives.

Music flowed down the street from her father's house as we approached. Outside, the ripple of conversations and laughter spilled from an ajar window. They were the sounds of happiness and belonging. I steeled myself for the task ahead. Winning over the important people in her life would be essential.

I'd been online and found sites with ideas for people who found social situations hard. I had always wondered if some people were just born being able to chatter away. I had known many who didn't like silence so they'd spout any old rubbish to avoid the possibility of a few uncomfortable pauses. My pocket contained a list of topics to prevent that occurring. People liked talking about themselves. I just had to get them started.

Claudia and I stopped at the door. I pressed the bell. She leaned over and kissed me on the cheek as I took a final deep breath and straightened my shoulders. A whole party of normal happy people were expecting us, while the perfect girl on my arm was planning our future. It was the highlight of my whole life. I thought that things could only improve, but reality differs from dreams, and hope can vanish like smoke.

9

THE SOUL KILLER

Claudia's father opened the door. He seemed different from how I remembered him; smaller, older or thinner, and he'd grown a weak beard. His joy at seeing Claudia, though, was always evident. I received a small frown while he guided her into his house, as though I shouldn't follow. There were about twenty people dotted around the rooms downstairs. The kitchen extended into a conservatory and gave the place a lovely feeling of light and space.

Claudia kissed him on the cheek.

'Dad, beer for me. You two have met before, so I'm going to find Annabelle, while you boys chat about how great I am.'

She bounded up the stairs and away.

He glanced at the bottle I'd passed to him. 'Not bad,' he said with a raised eyebrow and held my gaze. I remembered the golf clubs near the door and searched my memory for conversation starters.

'You like golf?' I ask.

'I keep them there in case of burglars.'

I shuffled on the spot. 'They'd regret breaking in here.'

'It was a joke. I love all sports. How about you?'

'Some.' I considered trying to blag him, but my knowledge on the subject was poor. I'd played twice, and I agreed with whoever said they called it golf because all the other four letter words were taken. I gestured to the clubs.

'I have played, but I found it tricky. A couple of times a week, I run, keep fit, that sort of thing.'

'Shame. Tall, strong fella like you should be good at golf. I suppose running is something. Do you want a beer as well?'

'No, I don't...' I was going to say *drink much*, but I knew he would think less of me '... drink when I'm driving.'

'I wouldn't have thought one would kill you?'

'It tends to make me sleepy. We see a lot in A & E who've only had one or two. Besides, I have a valuable cargo.'

That got his attention. We had reached the kitchen by then. An elderly gentleman nodded hello and left us alone next to the Aga.

'I guess you must see some sights at work.' He pondered the rest of my comment. 'Your cargo is not just valuable, it's priceless,' he said, after stepping close. 'You look after her, or you answer to me. Seeing her happy and content is the only thing that matters before my time's up.'

'Let's hope that's a long way off.'

His eyes searched mine for a few moments. 'I guessed she wouldn't tell you. I'm ill, and it doesn't look great. A man with nothing to lose can say what he likes, don't you think?'

'I suppose so.'

'I wondered if I'd find anyone good enough for my daughter. It'd need to be someone very special. Do you fit the bill?'

'I believe so.'

He opened the fridge door and passed me a still water. His expression told me he didn't agree. 'Orange squash is in the cupboard. I'm afraid we're all out of straws.' He attempted an unconvincing smile. 'Feel free to go and mingle. Most people don't bite. Have a good time. There'll be food in an hour or so.'

I wandered around, trying to fit in, but most of my conversation topics fell flat. It became clear they were more suitable for first dates than as ice breakers with elderly strangers.

I did recognise one guy there due to his thick blond hair and red face. He wasn't dissimilar to Boris Johnson. We sometimes bumped into each other running or cycling next to the river. He noticed me at the same time I did him. We were similar heights, but he possessed the heavyset body of a retired rugby player. I often overtook him and I guessed he exercised for weight control rather than for pleasure. I meandered over to talk to him. It'd be nice to chat to a familiar face with a shared interest, but just before I reached him, his jovial expression faltered. He sneered in a manner I'd seen many times from drunks, turned his back on me and sauntered away.

I caught Claudia's dad and her sister, Annabelle, deep in conversation, and judging by their averted gazes when they spotted me looking over, I was their topic. It looked as if they weren't singing my praises.

A little later I watched as Claudia's family brought all the dishes out for the table. It was a Christmas feast, the likes of which I hadn't seen before. They all laughed and dodged around each other as they worked, the guy I knew from running helping them too. It turned out he was Annabelle's husband, Malcolm Somerville, and the whole group were so obviously comfortable and trusting with each other that a nasty thought occurred to me. While these people dominated Claudia's life, I could never compete.

10

DI BARTON

Ginger's Wake

Barton surveyed the thinning crowd in the conservatory at Orton Hall Hotel where Holly had booked the wake. He spotted retired DCI Naeem talking to her successor and his new boss, DCI Sarah Cox. Barton's application for promotion had failed at the interview stage, but he held no malice towards Cox. He believed they had chosen the right person for the job.

Her nickname had been Apple when she first joined, but as she rose higher the jokes got left behind. Barton thought she looked a little like Jennifer Aniston, but he'd never felt comfortable enough around her to mention it. Naeem had been a brilliant boss, and he missed her greatly.

Behind him sat a large collection of full bottles of wine on a table alongside a virtually untouched buffet. He observed a few more faces escape out of the back door.

'John, come here for a minute.'

He stared around. Cox and Naeem summoned him over.

'We're both away now,' said DCI Cox. 'Work beckons for me, and Nav's garden for her. Why don't your team have the rest of the day off? I'm not sure those two will be much use in an hour, anyway.'

Barton spotted Strange and Zander exploring the wine stash. At that moment, DCs Whitlam and Malik appeared and Barton gave them the good news.

'It's your lucky day, fellas. The boss has given us the afternoon off to send Ginger up the River Styx in a way he would have enjoyed.'

'Sorry, sir,' said Malik. 'But he was rude to me most of the time. Anyway, I've got loads to do and can't afford to waste the time.'

'I came with him,' said Whitlam with finality.

Both men nodded at him and marched out in their fitted suits. They could have been twins if they'd had the same skin colour. Barton puffed the air out of his cheeks as they left. His wife and Debbie walked towards him. He could hear their conversation as they approached.

'I did love Ginger. He just wouldn't grow up.'

'I know. He made his choices though.'

'Perhaps I should have toughed it out. Did I give up on him?'

'Don't do that to yourself. I don't think he'll be too upset. He's had a good send-off.'

Holly and Debbie glanced around at the emptying room. Debbie began to cry, and Barton's wife pulled her into an embrace. An attractive Greek lady called Sirena, one of a few Crime Scene Investigators who had paid their respects, tapped Barton on the arm.

'I'm very sorry, John. I liked him. He made me laugh.'

'Are you staying for a few drinks, Sirena?'

'No. I have too much to do. Another time. I know days like these are hard.'

She gave him a big hug. Holly cleared her throat.

'Sirena, this is my wife, Holly.'

He glanced at their faces as they shook hands. Barton detected a touch of tension between them that he couldn't work out, followed by an imperceptible nod from Holly. Sirena rested her hand on Barton's shoulder, while looking at Holly.

'John is great at his job. You must be very proud. Lovely to finally meet you, although I've got to dash away now as I have an appointment. See you all soon, I hope.' She gave Barton a huge grin and departed.

Holly froze Barton with a look. 'She seems nice.'

Barton nodded, feeling as if he were in a sharpshooter's crosshairs. 'She's one of the best CSIs I've worked with. Zander reckons she has a crush on me.'

Holly raised an eyebrow. 'I'm going to take Debbie home.'

She gestured to Zander and Strange. Each had an opened bottle of wine at their elbow and a full glass. 'Looks like it's the three amigos leading the charge.'

'I'll just have one more.'

'Nonsense. He'd burst out of his coffin if you left all this booze behind. You lot have had a difficult few months. This will be a good opportunity to put that period to rest. I'll pick the kids up. Remember where snoring drunkards sleep?'

'Sir, yes, sir. On the sofa, sir!'

She kissed him on the cheek and waved to the other two, then fetched Debbie. Debbie had recovered enough to inspect the buffet. She grabbed some serviettes and filled her handbag with enthusiasm. Barton sat with the sergeants.

'Red or white?' asked Zander.

'Both?' he replied with a grin.

'I knew that. I was wondering if you'd like them in separate glasses.' Strange laughed and poured him a glass of the claret she held. 'It's been a rough time.'

'You can say that again. At least the Snow Killer has gone. Ginger didn't lose his life in vain,' said Zander.

Barton stared out of the open conservatory doorway at the warming spring day. A young woman pushed a pram with a blinking toddler gazing amazed at a vivid world. He hoped they were signs that it was time to move on.

'Would you be happy, going like he did? Look at his wake. An hour and a half since we buried him and everyone's disappeared. It's depressing,' said Strange.

Strange reminded him of his wife, diminutive and feisty, but she had a more negative view of the world. A career in the police would do that, he mused. Barton didn't want to focus on Ginger's life before he died, but Zander picked up the thread.

'Everything's changing. A lot of people don't drink any more. Ginger was old school. Shit paperwork and a vodka bottle in his drawer. He was left behind. Kelly and I were just talking about it. Life can be over just like that, and I've been wasting it hiding away. It's time for me to rejoin planet Earth. I miss my boy, but it doesn't mean my life's over.'

Strange took a deep breath. 'I lost something I never knew I wanted so much. Maybe I gained some understanding about the kind of person I am. Aryan refuses to talk about our loss, but I reckon he's a little relieved. Even so, he says he wants us to be together still. If we have a future, I need to go for it. I don't want to leave anything out there.'

Barton smirked at the clichés peppering the maudlin conversation. 'How much have you two had to drink?'

They replied in unison. 'A lot!'

He took a moment to consider. 'You're right. What better time to analyse things? I've been drinking more than is healthy. I'm at risk of turning into Inspector Cliché. You know, the hard-boozing hungover detective. I'll start playing Mozart in my car if I'm not careful. There will always be an element of danger with our jobs, but it's reminded me of what's important. That's family and health. You two have suffered more than me, but I still lost a friend and a colleague, and I think I was already losing my mojo. Something good will come of Ginger's sacrifice. I might even get serious about shedding a few pounds.'

Barton reached over and unscrewed another bottle of red. He raised his glass.

'To Ginger.'

They echoed his toast.

'Excuse me. Should we tidy away?' The waiter pointed towards the buffet table.

'What time is the room booked until?' asked Barton.

'It's yours for as long as you like.'

The three of them laughed when Barton answered, 'We'll give you a shout, then.'

Zander paused until the hotel staff moved out of hearing range. 'They usually have a big tree in here at Christmas.'

'We almost had the Christmas party here last year, but it got cancelled along with the rest of the cuts,' said Barton.

'Great. I turn up and the party's cancelled,' said Strange.

'That's probably the end of them. Christmas parties are HR disasters nowadays. You're guaranteed at least one claim of sexual harassment,' said Barton. 'Or perhaps not, with Ginger gone.' Barton thought of his old colleague. 'Ginger hated Christmas. He loved the staff party though. Many years ago, he turned up to the company do dressed as Rod Hull and Emu.'

'Yes! I remember that,' said Zander.

'Cool, did they used to be fancy dress?' asked Strange.

'No, it was black tie. No one was safe that night. I doubt we'll see another like him in the force. Weird to think he's gone,' said Barton.

'Let's make a pact,' said Strange. 'This Christmas, we'll meet up here and whoever's made the least progress in improving their work-life balance over the rest of the year settles the bill.'

They clinked their glasses again.

'Hopefully there won't be a lunatic running around killing folk next winter,' said Zander.

Barton agreed. But the world was full of dangerous people. Somebody somewhere teetered close to the edge.

11

DI BARTON

Present day – A month before Christmas

Barton returned from his third appointment of the day. He slouched in his chair, wondering whether he should tackle the paperwork that kept getting interrupted by impromptu meetings that he didn't need to attend. The open plan office stretched out in front of him. Strange and Zander had assumed a similar pose to himself. A police station shouldn't feel like an insurance admin centre, but that was the impression it currently gave.

There'd been no recent cases requiring the whole team to pull together. It had just been a succession of nasty assaults of all types that had been growing in popularity of late. Cambridgeshire tended to catch London's maladies and the latest virus was knife crime. Luckily, A & E had been winning the war of late, or at least keeping it at a draw.

At 19:00, Barton had just decided to call it a night when the phone rang.

'Barton.'

'John, it's DCI Cox. I need a favour.'

He listened and wrote down the details.

'And there's no one else?'

'Sorry.'

He hung up, grabbed his jacket and stopped next to his sergeants.

'I'm sure you both have a busy evening's entertainment arranged for tonight, it being a Friday and all, but I don't suppose either of you fancy a drive to Cambridge. Dinner and a beer's my shout on the way back, or a twenty-four hour McD's if we run out of time. Any kind of burger you like,' he said with a wink.

'Yeah, I'll come,' said Strange.

'It'll be about a four hour round trip.'

She knew that it could be less or probably more than that, but clearly had nothing planned.

Zander stood to follow, then said, 'Wait a minute. I'm not too proud to admit that I've got nothing better to do with my time, but why aren't Cambridge dealing with it?'

'They've got an inspector off on holiday and another with flu.'

'Ah, so it's serious,' said Strange.

'Murder,' replied Barton.

They strode out together. Zander signed for a pool car with blues and twos. The A14 road between Cambridge and Peterborough was notoriously bad, but sometimes flashing lights made it worse as people panicked and got in the way. He suspected they might be okay as Cambridge was the booming university town. Workers lived in cheaper Huntingdon and Peterborough and commuted in. At this time of night, the bulk of the traffic would be going the other way.

Zander drove with Barton in the passenger seat. Strange was tiny compared to the two men. Recently, a drunk had asked her if she was a cheerleader and pulled her blonde ponytail. Zander's laugh had fallen from his face as she'd taken the inebriated man down with a sweeping kick. But it made sense for her to be in the back if she wasn't driving, so the men had more leg room. Barton turned the radio down.

'Right, guys. I was hoping to have a chat with you about team morale. Now that you're a captive audience, what can we do to improve it?'

'I've tried. I arranged a night out but no one could agree on what to do. What's wrong with bowling?' said Zander.

'Malik and Whitlam didn't mind the bowling, but Zelensky and some of the other youngsters wanted to do something like the parkrun or a mud run. You know, some exercise and a bit of competition,' said Strange.

Barton knew that the parkrun was five kilometres around a

park and the other was a longer run through a mud-filled obstacle course. He was with Zander. 'Isn't bowling a competitive sport?'

'No, of course not. What next, darts? Dominos? Checkers? Armchair aerobics?' said Strange.

Barton was about to say he liked checkers, although he called it draughts, when his phone rang. It was Cambridge with the details.

Strange leaned forward as Barton finished his call.

'What's the score, then?' she asked.

'Initial reports state a man has been stabbed outside his house during a robbery. The wife found him when she was going out. He'd been dead a while.'

'No suspects or witnesses?'

'No, nothing.'

'Are we keeping the case?'

'Nope, we hand it back tomorrow. They're holding the scene until I arrive.'

A scowl emerged on Strange's face. 'Wait a minute. Cambridge has loads of experienced sergeants. Some are even as old as Zander. Why aren't they dealing with it if we aren't keeping the case?'

'Their DI is back tomorrow. There's no point in us travelling to Cambridge from Peterborough every day if it's straightforward.'

Strange's expression indicated she still didn't understand.

Zander chuckled. 'I may be marginally older than you, Kelly, but I am wise. Let me guess, it's something to do with the university.'

Barton gave a grim nod. 'Yes, it's outside one of their buildings. The victim lived in that building.'

Zander looked in the back of the car. 'The university has a lot of clout in the city. They will be demanding that Cambridge Police send the best they've got. A weathered sergeant won't do the trick. They'll want at least an inspector.'

Strange sat back. 'Ah, I see. Cox sends you, John. She makes it look like we're doing everything we can. This way, if any mistakes are made, she's covered.'

Barton didn't need to reply that if there *were* mistakes it would be his reputation at stake. Were there worse words than *I need a favour*?

'The university passes a brick every time a student dies. It doesn't look good if you want to attract the best to study there,' said Zander.

'Actually, it's worse than that,' said Barton. 'Someone's killed a lecturer.'

12

DI BARTON

They made good time. The journey back would be a nightmare judging by the queues on the other side of the road. It started to rain, too, frequent heavy showers that would snarl everything up. Zander used the lights to clear his way through the crowds of students when they got near the incident. They took a couple of wrong turns, which added to Barton's annoyance. He'd worked in Cambridge as a constable for six months, but since then they'd expanded the one-way systems and even installed rising no entry bollards.

'Blimey. Look at this lot,' said Zander.

A huge group dressed as vicars and tarts staggered into the road in front of them. Some of the tarts had hairier legs than Zander, which was saying something. A couple of them were bigger, too. A group of American ex-presidents went past, two hookers seemingly from Pretty Woman, unless of course they were hookers, and a multitude in Bart Simpson masks. Barton reached over and stopped Zander giving the siren a blast.

This lot would have been drinking since noon. He didn't want them turning their ire on them. Even when faced with uniform, the odd one might start shouting 'Nazi baby killers' and guffaw in a cut-glass accent. If you nicked them, they had a surprising habit of getting released in the morning without charge. Daddy could be anyone. Back in the day it had been quicker and more educational to give them a solid whack and send them on their way. That way, you had no paperwork and they learned a valuable life lesson. CCTV and mobile-phone videos had put an end to that style of policing.

Finally, they saw the cordon ahead. It was on the edge of a row of old buildings. The police had done a good job. The road was secure and there were bodies in high-viz all over the place moving people along. A man with a clipboard, who looked younger than the revellers, came to the window.

'What's your business, gentlemen?'

Zander popped his large black head out of the window. 'Crime solving.'

The man stepped back and crouched. His eyes widened at Barton. 'I know who you two are. Wait while I raise the barrier.'

'There's a Sergeant Strange in the back, too,' said Zander.

The constable obviously couldn't see past the men or through the condensation on the window, but didn't want to check. He smiled and raised his hand to a man in a dark-blue poncho. The barrier was raised.

Zander parked up. It was obvious where the incident was as two police vans had their lights pointed at a stone archway. An ambulance sat behind them. Two female officers with grim stares stood together under the arch, preventing access. They parted to let out a stooped guy wearing a battered leather jacket. He had a grim expression too, but Barton knew he woke up looking like that.

'Tapper! Long time.'

The man limped over. 'Battering ram Barton. It's been a while. Zander, you still driving this lunk about?'

They all shook hands with gusto. Tapper Turner had been the one to show Barton the Cambridge ropes all those years ago. The Tapper nickname was due to him tapping his fingers on his head while he thought.

'What happened to your leg?' asked Barton. 'Did you hurt it chasing students?'

'It's a touch of gout, you cheeky sod. I'd still leave you for dust though.'

Barton laughed, thinking it was probably true. 'This here's Strange,' he said.

Tapper smiled at her. 'You'll get on well in Peterborough.'

Strange gave him a cold smile. She'd had grief over her name her whole career.

'CSI are finishing up through there. They'll have a look out here over the next few hours, drains, bushes, you know the score, but this looks like a professional hit.'

'You think a hired assassin did it?' asked Strange.

Tapper turned to Strange and widened his eyes. 'That's right. There was a box of Milk Tray on the victim's back. The perp's probably inside in his dinner suit drinking a Martini. Shall we go and get him?'

Barton grinned. The sergeant had spoken to him like that since he'd first met him twenty years ago. He was sound, though. A man you'd trust with your life.

'Follow me,' said Tapper. 'You don't need to put covers on.'

They walked under the arch to see a prone body in a dated suit lying in a small puddle of blood. A CSI was next to the tent with his arms crossed. Tapper beckoned him over.

'CSM Tim Jones, this is DI Barton and his team. The inspector has driven here from Peterborough with his top guys so we can tell the university we're doing everything we can. His ass is on the line, so even though you and me have been through it all already, I'll run through it with him again. You add anything at the end.

Barton could only see Jones' eyes behind the mask, but they definitely rolled.

Tapper began. 'The wife was in all afternoon. Her husband was late, but that wasn't unusual. She was going out herself at 19:00. That's when she found the body.'

'What time of death did the pathologist give?' asked Barton.

Tapper chuckled. 'Our pathologist doesn't like the rain. Not keen on most weather in fact, especially out of office hours. The doc who confirmed the death said he'd been dead hours.'

Tapper crouched and pointed at the neck wound.

'As you can see by the puncture in the side here, he's been stabbed by something very sharp. This, in fact.' Tapper passed them an evidence bag containing a six inch spike with a wooden handle.

'Is it an awl?' asked Barton.

'Correct. Garden variety leather or carpet tool. Looks well used. Highly unlikely we'll get any prints off it as this looks professional. Professional thief, that is.' He winked at Strange.

'It's a bit brutal for a thief, don't you think?' she replied. 'He's clearly been hit on the head as well.'

'English thief, yes. Russian, Albanian, maybe not. We had one similar a few years back. This man has had a big gold ring and a full wallet taken, but his phone was left. It was in the inside jacket pocket, so maybe it was missed.'

'Maybe they just took the other things to make it look like a robbery,' said Strange.

'That's true. Everything is possible at this point.'

'Wife not see or hear anything?' she asked.

'Heard the bin move about 17:00. They have a cat, she thought it was him. She looked out the window but it's dark out here at night. She wouldn't have been able to see the body from there. No other witnesses, no obvious evidence. You've seen the crowds on the way in. It's the last big party night before the students go back for Christmas. Twenty thousand people could have done this.'

'CCTV?' she asked.

'None on this street, some around. Unless he was walking around beforehand, holding the awl and grinning maniacally, he will be hard to spot.'

'I agree it's likely to be a him, especially because of the small amount of blood.'

Tapper's eyes narrowed. 'Go on.'

'Neck wound like that would spurt blood. There aren't any splatters. I'd say the awl was inserted and held there while the man died. He'd struggle, maybe take a few minutes to die. He'd be weak but still have to be pushed down, so a man or strong woman is likely. They may have knelt on him, so there could be fibres passed over. Whatever, it's a cold, ruthless, unnecessary crime. He could have left him knocked out, or groggy at the least. Maybe it was personal as well as financial.'

'Very good. That's what we thought, although a hammer is less easy to hide, so maybe a cosh of some kind. The victim's right hand has also been trodden on. That might have happened as he struggled for his life. The killer knew what he was doing, maybe ex-military but it could be anyone with how helpful Google is nowadays. It's a gloomy unlit area with no CCTV. I would say the victim had been seen with the ring or the wallet earlier, maybe on a few occasions. His wife said he always carried plenty of cash as he disliked using cards. The people in this city and university are richer than ever, and that attracts predators. I don't hold much hope, but we'll jump through the hoops.'

Barton squatted. 'Is that finger snapped?'

'Yes. But his ring was on the other hand. Maybe he grabbed his attacker.'

'Or maybe he did it just to hurt him,' said Strange.

Tapper chuckled at her insight, genuinely pleased. 'Excellent. I bet John here has you doing all the work. Tim, anything to add?'

The CSM pulled his mask down, revealing a large smile. 'Nope, we're just going to move the body, but that's it, folks. Good work from all of you. It's funny, because he was just saying you Peterborough lot couldn't find a fox in a chicken coop.'

They stepped outside with Tapper.

'I was expecting the Vice-Chancellor or someone similar from the university to be causing trouble.'

'He's inside comforting the widow. He's okay actually, but you'll love the wife. She's a right piece of work. No laughing when you notice the age gap. Her name's Charlie.'

13

THE SOUL KILLER

The Golden Pheasant is heaving. I don't mind meeting Claudia even though I'm tired, because I wanted an alibi, just in case. Although, if they connect me to the murder, I suspect an alibi won't cut it. Never mind. I'm pretty sure I'll get away with it. Claudia's also been hard to pin down of late. Work are taking advantage of her at the moment. Perhaps I should have a word. What I do regret doing is booking this place.

It's a been a busy stressful day. It was only forty miles to cycle to Cambridge each way, but it was cold and the wind was in my face on the way back. Even though I often cycle much further nowadays as it's kinder to the knees than running, the last few miles were hard. I can barely keep my face out of my overpriced soup.

Claudia's grinning at the guy next to her. Turns out they work for the same company. How sweet. His table is so close, we might as well be eating together. He's grinning at me now. I bet he wouldn't be doing that if he knew what I'd been up to a few hours ago. Still, I return his friendly gesture. If he's talking to her it means that I don't have to. I love being with Claudia, but she does waffle on about that job of hers. It also gives me time to think about my actions.

The lecturer itch wouldn't go away. Now I've found the woman of my dreams, it seemed my brain wanted something else to focus on. If I'm honest with myself, I was a little bored, even though Claudia is amazing.

I watch the waiter respond to her huge smile as he places

her plate on the table. He loves her, too. I see other men watching her laugh, and know they want to be me. But I have her. They wonder what I've got, why she chose me, and wish they were as lucky. Well, she's fortunate too.

She's chosen pasta for the main course. I should have suggested the salmon instead. It's my own fault, I should have ordered for both of us. I'll say I have a bit of a headache so we skip dessert.

It was my third trip to Cambridge today. I went on the train the other times. It was easy to find him because he still worked at the same university. I hesitated as to what to do. After following him home, it was pretty clear he had regular routines. It was money that made me act as I did. Claudia and I deserve the best, but it's not cheap. I don't make good money. The wallet had nearly two hundred pounds in it, and it looks a nice ring. He owed me after what he'd done.

I thought about it as I cycled. My job is important to me but I deserve to be paid more money. Not everyone could do what I do. It's a disgrace. Those who help people get shafted while those who help themselves get rewarded. It's time I was rewarded.

I didn't plan to kill him, just a blow on the back of the head with a stone. That and robbing him would have been ample payback. Seeing Charlie looking through the window was a real shock. It's been a long time since my pulse raced that fast. Probably not since my mother's little trip.

So, I realised Charlie and her lover ended up together. I'd taken the awl for protection. Not from him, of course, just in case I was disturbed by the university wrestling team or others who might have slowed me down. An awl's a deadly weapon but fairly explainable if caught. I crouched there for a few moments wondering if she'd ring the police. When he groaned, I shut him up by sliding it inside his neck.

I hope she's devastated, although, knowing her, she probably has the life-cover documents out already. It still grates that she treated me as she did, but the heat will be on. It's best I stay well clear.

'You're quiet tonight,' says Claudia.

'Yes, I've got a bit of a migraine.'

'Oh, you should have said. Do you want to go?'

'No, it's okay. Finish a little bit more of your pasta, then we'll make a move.'

We still have plans tonight. I intend to up the ante a little on the sex front. Not that it's rubbish, just a bit samey. I thought a bit of role playing would be fun. Handcuffs, naturally. Maybe even a blindfold or some gentle choking.

14

DI BARTON

Barton and Zander had to bend quite low to get through the door of the old building. When they straightened up, both of their heads touched the ceiling. There was a lightshade between them. They stepped down to a comfortable lounge. All the furniture had a worn but expensive appearance to it. Oak sideboards sat on either side of the room. There were few pictures – none of them were of children.

The Vice-Chancellor hurried to greet him and gave them a robust handshake each. He had a similar jacket to the corpse outside.

'Terrible business. Vincent had been with us for over twenty years. Awful shock, Inspector. Glad you could come. I'm sure you'll do your best. Anything you need, please get in touch with my secretary. Must dash. Gala ball.'

Barton watched him leave at a canter. His focus returned to meet the steel eyes of a woman who wasn't much over thirty. His instant analysis was ex-student. The dead guy outside was pushing sixty. Her answers would be interesting but she wouldn't have done it herself, and only a fool hired someone to kill their husband.

She stood as he approached but didn't offer her hand.

'Am I a suspect, Inspector?'

'Of course.'

'Sorry to disappoint. I can't say it's a complete devastation, but I did still love him. To be honest, I loved the ring that got stolen more. It was a family heirloom, priceless.'

'Priceless, or priceless to your family?'

'Five grand, tops. Priceless to me. It was my father's.'

'I'm sorry to hear that.'

'Ask your questions, please. I'm going to the ball, too. I have an award to present.'

Barton disliked few people. He found it unhelpful to form emotional opinions of those he was trying to help. Besides, this act would most likely be a coping mechanism. She might even seem fine with others later, but the tears would eventually fall. This night would haunt the rest of her life. Completely heartless people were rare.

'I think they'll understand.'

Her eyes wandered to the door. 'I suppose so.'

'Charlie, isn't it? Please take a seat. I understand the sergeant has taken a statement. Is there anything you'd like to add now you've had time to process what's happened?'

She shook her head and blinked back tears.

'If we're going to catch him, it's more likely we're going to do it in the next few days than at a later date. Anything might be important.'

She opened her handbag and removed a packet of Sobranie cigarettes. She had expensive tastes. After lighting, she blew a thin stream of smoke towards him. Her shoulders hunched and shook for a few seconds, but she kept eye contact.

'He hated me smoking inside. Vincent wasn't a particularly good man, and neither am I a good woman. I agreed to stop drinking five years ago, if he agreed to stop shagging the students. We've been reasonably happy since. I can't think of anyone who would want to kill him. He doesn't inspire that much emotion in people, well, not any more. It looks like a brutal robbery to me.'

'How long have you been married?'

'I came to university here and never left. A detective should be able to work out what happened. I've given a detailed statement to your sergeant and don't feel like repeating it.'

'I thought there are rules on tutors dating their students?'

'There are now.'

'Is there anything we can do for you?'

Charlie put the cigarette out, and then crumpled in on herself. Strange sat next to her and put an arm around her shoulders. Barton stepped out of the room and found Tapper pacing in the small courtyard. The body was gone.

'I take it the neighbours' doors have been knocked on.'

'Of course. It's all in hand. These brutal crimes are starting to get the better of me. Modern criminals are so cold and ruthless, it chills me to the bone. I think my days are numbered.'

'Really, retire?'

'Do you remember my quote?'

'Too much death will kill you?'

'That's right. Maybe it's time. You remember that desk sergeant, Cobbler? He's started a company advising on security. They're doing well and expanding. I'm thinking about it. He always rated you, so there might be an opening up your way.'

Barton heard things like this all the time. Eventually the job chewed you up and you got out. He didn't think he was there yet, but each person leaving left him feeling more and more melancholy. New officers joined, but it wasn't the same. He considered what had happened this evening and involuntarily shivered.

'I'm glad you're keeping this one,' Barton said.

Tapper grimaced. Neither added anything, but they both knew that whoever did this would kill again.

15

THE SOUL KILLER

Christmas Eve

For the six months following her father's Boxing Day party, my relationship with Claudia remained strong, but her dad began to get in the way. I put everything I had into making her happy, including all my money. We enjoyed trips abroad and weekend breaks whenever we found free time in our schedules. I hoped to buy a bigger place, but it was tough making sure Claudia had a good time as well as saving for a deposit. I suggested we rent together, but she wanted no upheaval while her dad fought with cancer.

Claudia proved to be one of those women who insisted on maintaining closeness with her friends, too. She'd forgotten them as a teenager in the first throes of young love, and when that relationship had ended, she'd struggled to reconnect with them. I used to tell her not to worry; we wouldn't split up, but she replied that the future is never set in stone.

I steered clear of her family as much as possible. At one point, Claudia considered moving back in with her father. Luckily, the proud old fart saved me from that by insisting that his children would never become his carers. Occasionally, their close circle of friends and family, partners included, met for a meal and Claudia expected me to attend. Sometimes I blagged it and invented a nasty car accident at work, saying I couldn't just leave. Other times, she'd get her diary out and nail me to a date.

Some of their friends enjoyed running, so I'd focus on that. I would sit and smile, comment on the food, and look forward to the evening finishing. I struggled to connect with her sister. All I could fixate on was her judgemental stares from before. After those social occasions, I encouraged Claudia to stay at mine. Her closeness reassured me that I had passed the test again. I also preferred knowing where she was – reassuringly safe at home with me. Her father's illness distracted her though, and she often returned with him.

My strange upbringing prevented me from fully understanding her situation. However, my work involves dealing with people as they struggle with bad luck. There are no specific answers. What they need to know is that you're supporting them. Claudia made the mistake of trying to push me away. Facing it together as a team should have been the way forward.

In her defence, she was working long hours at the same time. She hoped to make partner at her law firm. But something had to give, and the time between our dates gradually lengthened. Free time became my enemy, and I thought too much. We drifted apart. Books in the library or articles online offered inconsistent advice. I talked it through with a colleague when we visited the outdoor swimming pool together in the summer, and he suggested splitting up until her dad either recovered or died.

I didn't say so, but I assumed he was mad. I'd never give up on us, or her. The vague information Claudia shared on her father's condition meant his chances were slim. I would be there when he died. However, as he sickened, so did our relationship. In a way, he and I pulled her in different directions. I'm not a stupid man. I can read people's thoughts.

The day before Christmas, I took her ten pin bowling. Claudia hadn't wanted to play, but she needed distracting. I pumped my fist as all the pins went down. She gazed into the distance while on the phone and ignored my high five. After leaping to her feet, she removed her bowling shoes and hauled on her coat.

'Dad's had a fall.'

I turned and stared at the score board; so close to my highest score. The worry came off her in waves as we got in the car and pulled away. It was the first time she'd ever encouraged me to drive faster. As I undertook a slow moving caravan, a sliver of me wished him ill. I pushed it away and put my foot down on the accelerator.

When we arrived at her father's house, we found him lying at the bottom of the stairs.

'Dad, are you okay?'

She sprinted over and helped him sit.

'Yes, I'm fine. I slipped and didn't have the strength to get to my feet. My arm feels very tender.'

'I'm ringing for an ambulance.'

'No, don't worry. Help me up. A cup of tea and some rest should do the trick.'

I stepped forward and he shoved out his supposed bad arm to stop me approaching.

'Just Claudia will be fine.'

'Dad, you don't have to be brave.'

'As long as you're here, I need not be.'

I looked away to hide my disgust. She didn't realise he was manipulating her. A few awkward moments dragged by before she uttered the words I'd come to hate.

'You go. I'll sort things out here.'

'Shall I pick you up later?'

'No, no.' Dark bags hung under her eyes. 'I'll ring you.'

The old man wasn't as quick at hiding his emotions as I was and I detected a definite pleased sneer. I stood there woodenly for a moment, floundering for words.

'Okay, I hope you get better, Donald. If you need anything, Claudia, please get in touch.'

I leaned over to kiss her goodbye, but she was checking him over, leaving me to press my lips on the top of her head. I stepped outside. My legs struggled to keep me upright. The sensation in my stomach was something I've never encountered before, even under my mother's rule. I wondered if he'd be well enough for his annoying party on Boxing Day. I stayed on the doormat until my breathing returned to normal and my legs recovered their strength. A neighbour's car roared into life and made me flinch.

I went to leave but couldn't stop myself. Crouching down, I gently lifted the letterbox. I heard muffled talking, so I nudged the second insulating flap open. Their voices reached me so clearly that I could have been in the room.

'Are you sure you don't need to see a doctor?'

'No. In the scheme of things, a bruise is nothing.'

'Do you want me to stay?'

'Your weirdo isn't expecting you later?'

'Dad! You never have taken to him, have you? In fact, you've disliked all of my boyfriends.'

'That guy you dated after your A levels was great.'

'Yes, but we had three meals and he dumped me, remember?'

'I only want you to be happy. This guy's way too serious. You need to have someone you enjoy a joke with. You'll know when you meet the right one because you'll have fun doing mundane things.'

'We were bowling.'

There was a pause, then a definite chuckle from them both.

'I bet you were a little pleased to get away.'

The laughter returned. 'He can be overbearing. I should have been clearer with him about my priorities at the moment.'

'Dump him, bury me, then play the field. Enjoy yourself. You're only young once.'

'Dad, you're so funny. Let's get you that drink. I'll stay for a while but I've got a full load of washing to get out.'

The voices and laughter faded as a door shut.

She found him amusing, but I did not.

16

DI BARTON

Present day – Christmas Eve

Barton sneaked a peek into the lounge on his way out of the house. His son Lawrence was fifteen years old, but the magic of Christmas shone in his eyes as he gazed into the tree lights. He was Holly's from a previous relationship but Barton considered him his son. Lawrence had been quieter of late and Holly worried about him, but Barton suspected he was just growing up. In all honesty, he needed to. The Snow Killer's rampage in the local area had affected his age group the most. They were the ones who had ventured out on their own at night. Their carefree days had ended abruptly.

Tonka Truck Luke snuffled on the sofa, the anticipation of the day finally exhausting the five year old. Even ten year old Layla had stomped downstairs. She burrowed in the Christmas chocolate tin as if she expected to find gold until she spotted him looking over and scowled her finest *you are evil* look.

'Hey! Who's eaten all the hump-backed ones?'

'I don't think you need to contact the Major Crimes Team for that one.'

In the corner, Holly lifted the newspaper to cover her reddening face. Barton smiled. We all had our poison. Holly's came in a purple wrapper.

Layla turned back to her father. 'Do you have to go out? *Jumanji* with Robin Williams is on later. We want to watch it so we can see the new one with Dwayne Johnson at the cinema. I'll even eat the strawberry creams.' She pretended indifference, but Layla still cherished Christmas together.

'I'll tell you what. Finish the coffee creams, and I'll take my coat off now.'

The glare returned. 'Have a good night, Father.'

Lawrence grinned at him. 'You look a bit like a pasty Dwayne Johnson. Fatter obviously, but a similar size.'

'You're too kind.'

'Don't drink and eat too much at the pub. Or you might get stuck in the chimney later.'

Barton waggled a finger at him. 'Shush, you. Non-believers get nothing. I won't be late, so we can all kick back then. If I see Santa on my travels, I'll update him on your recent behaviour.'

Before he left, he popped over and gave Holly a kiss. He pecked Luke on a hot cheek and ruffled Lawrence's hair. Layla got up and wrapped her arms around him, giving him a huge hug. 'Love you, Daddy.'

Barton stepped from the house and almost bumped into a middle-aged man walking his terrier.

'You must be the detective.'

'Maybe. Who are you?'

'Ernie Hobbs. I've just moved into number nineteen.'

'Excellent.' He wondered if the man knew about that house's history.

'I know what you're thinking. Does he know what the Snow Killer did? It's just bricks and mortar to me. I might even quite like the drama. I'm a heating engineer by trade. Pop over if your boiler breaks and I'll call you if there's any more murders. Merry Christmas.'

As he strolled down the road, Barton acknowledged he was destined never to have normal neighbours. The area was changing. The other houses that were left vacant after the recent deaths had been filled with people younger than Hobbs. How long would it be until Barton was one of the oldies? He pushed the thought away because he had much to be grateful for. Not everyone gets a family Christmas and he hoped for many more ahead of him. His mother, the sole remaining grandparent, was due to arrive the following morning and it pleased him immeasurably that they all knew her worth. Even Holly had stopped trying to do the lunch her way and left her mother-in-law to her own devices.

His youngest, Luke, continued as his usual innocent boisterous self, but the other two changed almost daily. Layla couldn't decide if she loved her father, or hated him, and mentioned both on regular occasions. Lawrence had become serious and sensible, which was a little concerning. Barton wondered if he'd finally noticed girls. He had wanted to buy Lawrence a 'birds and the bees' book but Holly put the kybosh on that, saying embarrassing the boy wasn't the answer. Barton joked that it would be funny, until Holly suggested they should also get Layla a copy. Luckily, the local criminals weren't generally as clever as his wife.

Barton generally avoided going out on Christmas Eve, but it had been insanely busy since Ginger's funeral. Any plans for a Christmas party had never got off the ground and he'd hardly seen anyone away from work. Strange was still dating DCI Naeem's son, Aryan, on and off, but Barton had stopped asking about it of late as she clearly didn't want to talk about it. Zander was seeing the Slovenian woman he had met near a suspect's house, and Barton had his family.

No one had enough time for socialising away from those commitments. However, they had agreed to keep the arrangement they'd made after Ginger's funeral. Tonight had been the easiest night for them all. Barton had resisted initially, but Holly said not to be silly and to go. She'd spend the whole day cleaning anyway, and if he was out of the house, then he couldn't make a mess inside it.

Sweat stood on his brow by the time he arrived at the Ramblewood Inn, which was the pub attached to the hotel where Ginger's funeral was held. Two men smoked cigarettes outside in nothing more than T-shirts. So much for a white Christmas. He had more chance of heatstroke.

The pub catered for the hotel traffic and the higher-end market. The prices reflected this and it was never insanely busy, even on Christmas Eve. He saw a few men he knew at the end of the bar and nodded. Barton sensed the collective anticipation of the imminent celebration.

The others hadn't appeared yet, so he got them all a pint and carried them to the end of the bar. He reckoned he'd lost the bet they'd all made after the wake. A few days ago, he'd accused Holly of washing his jeans on too hot a wash. That could only mean one thing. And to think he was supposed to be getting fit.

Zander scowled when he arrived. Strange came in a minute later with a long face. Barton had requested the day off as he had volunteered to be on call on Christmas Day, whereas the other two had been at work.

They sipped their pints. 'Merry Christmas,' Zander said, without enthusiasm.

The others looked as if they could do with a seasonal moan, so Barton teed them up. 'Good day at the office?'

Strange could barely control herself. 'It's been a nightmare week. So many Christmas parties have ended in brawls this year. I was forced to buy all my presents on Amazon.'

Barton gave her a puzzled expression. 'Is there any other way? They even arrive wrapped if you pay extra. How about you, Zander?'

'I'm taking my parents out to The Boathouse for dinner tomorrow. That's my gift. They don't care about presents at their age unless they can eat it or drink it. They're just glad to have me back to normal. Not that I'll be much company.'

Barton and Strange shared a look. Barton tried to make light of it.

'Are you on Santa's naughty list?'

'Katrina, the woman I've been dating, dumped me last night. Said I lacked commitment.'

'Do you?'

'A little, but it's been mental at work. You know that. She told me she's hooking up with the postman.'

Strange choked on her lager. 'Words you hoped never to hear.'

'Damn right.' Then Zander laughed. 'Ah, my pride's more wounded than my heart. I enjoy Christmas. Both my parents have been ill, so I'm happy that they're still here. I can't believe we haven't been out for a few since the funeral. Do my tales of woe mean it's me paying tonight?'

'I put on over a stone in the last year,' said Barton. 'You could slice my chest up and sell it off as memory foam. The only exercise I've done is carrying weighty takeaways from the front door to the lounge. I spent thirty quid on a new cap and running sunglasses to go jogging in and forgot about them. I noticed Lawrence putting them on yesterday. Reckons he's been wearing them for months. Kelly?'

'I joined a fitness club and failed to attend the induction appointment. Maybe I've got that new sickness, gymtimidation. I argued over nothing with Aryan and never rang him. He didn't ring me, either, and that was a month ago. Two weeks back, I knocked a tin of paint over on my lounge carpet and haven't got round to replacing it. I'm looking up at rock bottom hoping it doesn't drift higher. My only achievement was to increase my body weight by twenty per cent.'

'Few winners here. Shall we buy rounds?' asked Barton.

'No way,' joked Zander. 'You two have done much worse than me.'

Barton enjoyed the craic and they managed to grab a free table. It's hard to beat the atmosphere of a British bar in the early evening before Christmas. As it got to eight o'clock, the place emptied. Sensible people avoided a hangover on the big day. Many, such as Zander, had car journeys in the morning and didn't want to be over the limit. Others, like Barton, had families waiting.

'Right, guys. I'm off.' Zander kissed Strange on the cheek and Barton fended him off from doing the same to him.

After he'd gone, Barton pondered on the lives of those remaining in the pub. He sensed many of them had nothing to go home for. Tonight, the bonhomie of a warm bar represented the highlight of their festive experience.

'One for the road?' asked Strange.

He smiled at her. 'Sure.' When she returned, Barton probed her arrangements.

'Going to your parents' for Christmas?'

'No, I offered to be on call at work.'

'I thought you usually saw your folks at Christmas?'

She fiddled with a beer mat but didn't reply.

'What happened?'

'They've gone on a cruise.'

Barton failed to prevent a chuckle sneaking out. 'Northern lights?'

'Caribbean.'

'Nice. But I bet it's not as warm as here. If you've got no

plans, come to ours. Twelve o'clock. Please bring earplugs and eggnog. We have everything else.'

'No, John. I'm okay. My family have never been big into Christmas.'

'I insist. If Holly found out you were on your own and I didn't ask, I'd be another yuletide domestic statistic.'

'That doesn't roll off the tongue after a night in a bar, but great, okay, I'll be there.' She blushed at her fast answer.

'I want you to come, too. Besides, I'm also on call. Hopefully there won't be any major dramas.'

'Someone's bound to have something sad happen to them.'

Barton drained his drink and put on his coat. 'Let's make sure it isn't us.'

17

THE SOUL KILLER

Christmas Day

It's a bright, sunny dawn. The odd cloud drifts by in the sky. It's not Christmas weather to encourage fireside gatherings. But it also isn't the type of morning for ultimatums. However, after what I heard yesterday, I'm forced to act. When I returned to River End, I analysed my options and a plan formed. Luckily, I had the item necessary and practised for hours. It's risky. I must be careful, but perhaps I won't need it – he still has a chance.

I cycle along the River Nene. Even the ducks know it's Christmas and a time for family. They take turns honking in a line as I pedal past. The British Sugar housing estate heaves with cars from people home for the holidays. They cover the roadsides and verges. What kind of company builds five bedroom houses and gives them a single drive? I resist the temptation to smack the wing mirrors as I pass the vehicles lined up on the pavement. Once, as a teenager, I did just that to a van, not knowing it contained three blokes. I had to throw my bike and myself over a wall to escape.

This particular street is extremely popular with young parents. The windows shimmer with sparkling lights and heavy wreaths adorn the expensive doors. I bet the houses are already full of excited kids but outside it's peaceful at this early hour.

Donald told me that he and his wife bought this big place because they wanted the extra rooms for when their two beautiful daughters come to stay. He'd laugh and say there were extra ones for grandchildren if anyone was so inclined. Then he'd pause, as though he didn't want to give me ideas, because he prayed that I wouldn't be part of that. If he craved grandkids so much, he should have kept his nose out of my business. I pump my legs faster as I recall his mocking face.

I glance around for potential witnesses, find none, then scoot to the rear of the property. Quietly, I unlock the rear gate by reaching over the top and easing the bolt across. After a peek to see if Donald is in the conservatory, I wheel the bike in and lean it against a wall. He's in his knocked-through kitchen. Even I have to admit it's an amazing space. His children tend to enter his house through the back as he often reads on one of the comfy sofas and he's sitting there now with a newspaper. I slip my shoes off, knock on the window with a gloved hand, and watch him frown with recognition. He turns the key and opens the door but stands in the way to prevent access.

'What are you doing here? Is something wrong?'

That's a charming way to greet someone. Don't I deserve a 'good morning' like everyone else? 'I'd like a word, please.'

The stupid sod wages an internal battle. But his entrenched manners win over the urge to throw me over the decking and into the ornamental pond.

Obviously, he couldn't do that now. The man is a complete shadow of his former self. He frightened me when I first met him. His intensity and lust for life made me doubt myself. Trust the woman I love to have a father who retired and took up squash and golf because football had become too much for him. He riled me and provoked me. He belittled me in front of her, often in subtle ways so it was hard to notice his undermining quips. He reminds me of the boy at school who did that to me before. I will not tolerate it again.

'Of course. I am sorry. Please, come inside. What with my health, I'm wound tight.'

I leave my shoes at the door as he shuffles backwards to allow me entry. It's incredible how fast a sick person can deteriorate. A sixty year old boasting a golf handicap in single figures, with a slimmer waist than a hula girl and shoulders from a swaggering rodeo bull, has been reduced to this little man. He must only weigh six or seven stone now, including his walking stick. This makes my task easier.

It's cosy inside and the perfect place to drink percolated coffee and read thick broadsheets. I wonder what the girls will do when they inherit the house. Claudia should move in. We could definitely raise a family here, or preferably a nice bouncy puppy.

'Would you like a cappuccino, or an espresso?'

'No, thanks, this isn't a social call as such.'

He bares his teeth as he lowers himself onto the sofa. A little grimace sneaks out, which he tries to hide.

'How's the pain, Donald?'

'Terrible at times, bearable at others.'

'Good, good.'

His eyes narrow. 'What do you want?'

'That kind of depends on your answer.'

'Get on with it.'

'I hope to marry Claudia.'

I can see my news is an even bigger shock than when he was told his diagnosis. His cough turns into a choking splutter. There's blood in the spit that dribbles from his mouth.

'Over my dead body.'

'That doesn't sound unreasonable.'

'You'll have your wish shortly, you piece of shit. Unless I persuade her not to marry you, of course. I'll give it my best shot; you see if I don't. There's still time.'

'I suspected you'd say that. Therefore, you'll just have to die today.'

'I've got a month, or more. There's fight left in these bones.'

'No, you misunderstand. It's happening now, and I'm here to help.'

He blinks rapidly, then glances at the phone on the kitchen worktop. There is no chance of him making it. The house contains no security: no CCTV, no alarms, because Mr Big Time here said if anyone broke in, they'd regret it. Obviously, that was before lung cancer robbed him of a future.

'Good. Take your best shot.'

I bark a short laugh as he rolls up his sleeves and staggers towards me.

'Don't you want to know why I want you dead?' I say as I slip past him.

He emphasises every word of his message. 'Because you are a sick, weird, little weasel. You're not worth even half of her.'

'Wrong, it's because you are an interfering busybody.' I step to his phone and slide it in my pocket. 'You dislike me but, so far, you've had the good sense to keep your distance. However, lately, you are constantly in Claudia's ear. That staged crap yesterday didn't fool me, either. No one intrudes on my happiness. Claudia and I belong together. It simply isn't possible for her to do better than me.'

'She can. You are a waste of space.' His shout fades into a wheeze. Even that little effort is almost beyond him.

'I take it that's a 'no' to the marriage, then.'

'If you're here to execute me, I'm ready. Do it.'

'Oh, very courageous, and dramatic. Do you think I'm daft? I know how your mind works. You're dying anyway. I murder you and get banged up for twenty years. Your daughter is then free to find someone who ticks more of your boxes. So, I think not. I want to get away with it. You, Donald, are going to kill yourself.'

I take off my backpack, remove the noose I carefully made, and drop it over his head. He picks it off and stares at it in horror, before throwing it on the floor. 'Never,' he says. 'That's the coward's way out.'

I nod. 'Here's the deal. If you don't do it, then I will. To you, that is. You couldn't fight off a moth at the moment. But if you make me do it, there'll be signs of a struggle. Unlikely, but it's possible I might get caught. Prison is definitely not for the likes of me. I wouldn't last five minutes. However, I belong with Claudia in this life, or the next. Perhaps she and I could have a pact. A suicide because of your suicide. Poetic, eh?'

'Never. Even you aren't that sick.'

'There is another daughter, isn't there?'

'You wouldn't. She's trying for a baby.'

'I don't suppose the baby has to die. You have an easy choice.'

He collapses onto the sofa with a gasp and shakes his head. He doesn't look at me, but his voice is loud and clear.

'You know what? I believe you'd do it. That's the reason I dislike you. I've always recognised that something is missing in your make-up. The rest of us can all see it. It's tragic Claudia can't.' He looks up then. 'I believe she's finally realising, though. You're a busted flush.'

'Rubbish. Maybe she sees qualities in me that you and your pretentious friends can't.'

'They'll know you've been here. Everyone knows I'd never kill myself.'

'No one will think I was here. If someone has seen me, I can say I popped around to make peace before the party. You were in such unbelievable agony that you'd reached your wits' end. You hoped the doctor could increase your morphine dose, but it had become unbearable.'

'Wouldn't you rather see me suffer?'

'You misunderstand. I don't care one iota about you. Your happiness or pain are irrelevant to me. All I'm interested in is Claudia and me having a happy life. More time with you would be priceless to her. But I recognise determination when I see it. You've bitten your tongue too long concerning me. Your dying wish to her will be that she promises not to marry me. You'll poison our relationship in the same way that cancer has destroyed you. From inside. I won't allow that, so time's up, Donald. Follow me.'

I pick up the noose, put a hand under his shoulder and drag him to the stairs, leaving him clinging to the last step while I ascend to the first floor. The oak balcony looks down on the hallway and the Christmas tree. I tether one end of the rope to the bannister. It's fairly easy to learn to tie a noose. I researched it online. Seems I'll have to get rid of my phone. I wouldn't want anyone finding that on my browsing history.

He struggles to breathe at the bottom of the stairs. I wait, for over a minute. He stares up. It's the face of a man resigned to his fate. I wonder if he's also a little bit grateful. Surely, it is better this way. But then his expression changes. His eyes narrow and he shifts faster than I expect. He's at the door and fiddling with the lock in seconds. By the time I've got down to him, he has one foot out of the door. I put an arm around his waist and pull him back inside.

'Don't fight it,' I whisper in his ear.

With the other arm clamping his arms to his chest, I lift his frail bones and carry him up the stairs to the balcony. He groans, but his attempt to escape has taken the last of his reserves.

I place the noose over his head and bend him over so he looks down. I place my lips next to his ear.

'There's one final question.'

'What?' he gasps.

'Short drop, or long drop?'

He slowly shakes his head. Blood pours freely from his mouth.

'The long drop will break your neck. The short drop will mean you hang around.' I smile, he doesn't.

'Long drop,' he whispers.

'Get your leg over.'

'I can't.'

'You will because you must. I'm giving you the chance of the ultimate sacrifice. You exchange your life for theirs. Now, what father wouldn't take that trade?'

'I can't. I could never end it this way.'

'Don't you understand? It's over. I can't leave you alive here, not after this.'

He still won't do it, so I lift him as I would a fallen child. I stare at him with contempt. His chin juts forward. 'Spare my girls.'

'I'm not a monster.'

'Do I have your word, as a man?'

'I thought I was less than a man?'

'Swear, by God.'

'I thought your religion was family. Do you wish to be saved?'

'I don't believe in that rubbish. Promise!'

It dawns on me that this isn't the same as my mother's demise. It's not just his life that will finish this morning, it's also his future, because he doesn't believe. Perhaps that's why he clings to life, because only oblivion awaits.

'I promise,' I say, and our eyes meet. 'Any last words?'

He takes a deep breath. Tears drip off his chin. It's clear that he's considered this moment – the end – already. It's the only positive about a slow death. You can prepare and put your affairs in order. There is time for the last goodbyes, and time to tell family and friends that they are loved. In some cases, that is.

'Please, tell Annabelle and Claudia that—'

I rest him on the bannister and give him a gentle shove. He teeters, balancing almost impossibly for a few seconds, then he's gone. 'Time's up.'

I walk downstairs and peer up at him. His eyes bulge in my direction as he sways. He kicks out at the tree next to him, but there's no venom left. It's quiet, just a groan from the wood above at the unexpected strain.

'I'm sorry, the balcony wasn't high enough for your request of a long drop. I read online that from such a short distance, the result can be unpleasant. You will dangle alive at the end of that noose for as long as your neck muscles allow. That could be up to half an hour.'

To his credit, he swings another foot at me, and I have to acknowledge his bravery. I'd planned to taunt him, as he did me in life, but it doesn't feel right. In fact, at this moment, I can't think of too many occasions where he was outwardly hostile, but I'm not stupid. What he didn't say was just as important as what he did. It's a shame. We should have been close. In time, maybe I could have called him Dad. An unpleasant smell reaches my nose and the struggles have stopped.

'Goodbye. Don't worry, I'll let myself out.'

I'm starting to sweat in my gloves and hat but had better not remove them. The plain socks that I bought from the supermarket slide on his clean floor. He has a similar pair on himself. As planned, I remove the back-door key and leave it on the kitchen table. I take the family picture off the wall and place it beside the key. I rest his mobile phone there, too.

Using a different part of the handle, I open the door, step out, and swing it back so it closes of its own accord. I cross to the rockery and retrieve the spare key from under a stone. After locking up, I return it to its hiding place.

The streets are still empty. I'll knock on my neighbour's door when I arrive at River End to cement another alibi. I believe I've done Donald a favour, in the same way I stopped my mother from suffering in this world. It's a good feeling, helping others and helping myself at the same time. My life with Claudia stretches out ahead of us. No one shall get in our way.

18

DI BARTON

Cries of ecstasy woke Barton. Cries of ecstasy that could be heard in every household with kids under ten.

'Father Christmas has been.'

Barton lay there listening to the crinkle of plastic followed by the thud of gifts as his youngest, the only believer left in the house, upended his stocking. Footsteps thundered across the landing. Luke had inherited his father's grace.

Lawrence's door opened first. Luke repeated the same words until Lawrence told him to clear off. Luke received a similar, but ruder, response from Layla. His father, however, sat up, ready to play the game, despite him realising, when he looked at the bedside clock, that it was a little after four.

'Daddy, Santa's left me loads of presents.'

'That's a big surprise. I thought you'd been too naughty.'

Barton received a stern look as Luke puffed himself up. 'This means I've been good, and you've been naughty for saying I haven't. He isn't as strict as you.'

Holly rolled over. 'Is that Santa now?'

'No, Mummy. He's long gone. He'll be in Africa now, I think. He's ever so busy. There's lots of little children in the world, you know.'

Experience had taught parents everywhere that there would be no going back to sleep now but life had also taught them to enjoy every second of this innocent stage.

John and Holly had come into the marriage with slightly different traditions at Christmas and repeating them became part of the big day. Holly's childhood experience had been waking to a stocking next to the bed, then rushing downstairs to look under the tree. Delayed gratification was unheard of.

They had cooked the turkey together with a glass of port the night before to reduce the time stuck in the kitchen. The first Christmas they did that, Barton queried if reheating the meat would cause it to dry out, but Holly had explained that's what gravy was for. She wanted to be in the lounge with the children.

Barton ambled bleary-eyed to the kitchen and nuked the bacon, which had covered the turkey as it cooked, in the microwave. It came out with the consistency, texture and colour of large toenails from an unhygienic giant. Nevertheless, Lawrence and Layla made it downstairs within seconds of the ping. Present opening started at 9:00. Luke drove them crazy a long time before that.

It was 6:30 when Holly couldn't stand it any longer and said, okay, they could open one each, but she would choose which one. The kids glanced suspiciously at each other and couldn't detect a ruse. Holly winked as she passed the two packages that contained two new tablets to the older children. They opened them, exchanged glances, and vanished to the dining room to use them while they charged.

Luke opened a train set to great fanfare.

'Look, Santa got me just what I wanted. I knew I'd been good enough.'

He pulled the top off to reveal what looked to Barton like a thousand pieces of fiddly track and scenery. His heart sank as he understood that even today, he was about to be outmanoeuvred.

'Daddy, set it up, set it up!'

Holly yawned, patted him on the head, and winked as she left the room. 'You boys will be able to play that for hours. I'll just nip upstairs and make the beds.'

Holly woke up at 9:00 and they all returned to the lounge. By 10:30, wrapping paper completely obscured the carpet, and the two older kids had escaped back to their rooms with their new stuff. Barton felt as if he'd pulled a double shift at work.

'Where's Luke?' he asked.

Holly lifted up a blanket to reveal Luke, cuddled up with his new fluffy Meerkat toy, fast asleep. Barton grinned as his phone rang. Holly pointed at him on the way out.

'No sneaking out until you've carved the bird.'

Strange's name lit up the screen.

'Kelly, let me guess. Fat man with beard suspected of reverse burglaries?'

'Eh?'

'Leaving things instead of taking them?'

'Oh, sorry. Bit slow on that. Last I heard, he'd faceplanted a jumbo jet and Christmas was cancelled.'

'That's the spirit.'

'I've just spoken to Control. It was an uneventful night. No majors in the cells. They have found a body this morning though.'

'What?' Barton's ninth chocolate of the morning attempted to go down the wrong hole.

'Uniform are with it. It looks like suicide.'

'Couldn't you have started with that bit?'

'Sorry. The house is on the British Sugar estate. I'll go on my way to your house. If it's clear cut, I might still be with you on time.'

'Okay, no worries. Ring me if you're going to be late.'

Barton glanced at his watch. It was a little early for drunken domestics. Saying that, Holly must have had three sherries already. Christmas was an unusual time of year for the police. Extra tensions kept it a busier time for certain crimes but not for others. Quiet roads meant fewer accidents and incidents, closed shops didn't let in thieves or distracted shoppers who were easily robbed. Most people would be at home, so burglaries were rare, too. Maybe, for the sake of the kids, everyone tried to get along in the morning, until the alcohol came out.

Barton had checked the log last year. There'd been eight domestic incident calls, four complaints of people being rowdy, six cases of concern for someone's welfare, four assaults, two minor car collisions, six reports of 'suspicious activity', one missing person, two antisocial behaviour incidents, a theft, a burglary and two hoax calls. As DI, he hadn't needed to show his face at any of them. Zander, as DS, had attended some, but there had been nothing bad enough for Major Crimes.

Usually, one terrible incident occurred over the two big days. Barton hoped that this year wouldn't average out for last Christmas's relative quiet. He decided he'd better get showered and changed, just in case.

19

DI BARTON

There was an air of inevitability when Strange rang at midday. Barton picked up.

'Please, not a homicide!'

'No, boss. Well, I don't reckon so. Uniform agree, but it's kicking off here. There's a man hanging from the bannister. Very dead and has been for a few hours. A neighbour came over for a tipple and looked through the letterbox when no one answered the door. Seems straightforward to me, but the daughters have arrived. One's screaming because he hasn't been cut down, and the other's demanding a murder investigation.'

'I hope you're out of earshot.'

'Yeah, I'm outside. Another crime scene van has just appeared. There's no sign of a break-in, well, apart from uniform using the enforcer on the front door.'

'Okay, tell the sisters that the big cheese's arrival is imminent. I'll be there in fifteen. Is the out-of-hours doctor there?'

'No, he's on the other side of the county. Paramedics have said the victim's been hanging there a while. The deceased's GP is on his way though. Apparently, he's a personal friend.'

That would save them waiting for the official confirmation of death, but family GPs tend to be focussed on the relatives and that could be trouble.

'Is the scene secure?'

'It is now.'

Barton cringed and put the phone down. If a call came on Christmas Day, he preferred to be with an experienced sergeant.

Uniform, on the other hand, had more of a give-the-bad-shifts-to-the-youngsters policy, especially at Christmas. Who knew what a couple of rookies might have done to the scene?

Holly folded her arms in front of him as he stood looking at her. 'I suppose I can't complain too much. At least we got the entire morning.'

He smiled. The present opening was the special part for her. She could cope with him missing the rest, even dealing with Barton's mother's imminent arrival.

'It sounds clear cut, so hopefully I won't be long.'

She gave him a big hug and a slow kiss on the lips. 'I've heard that before.'

'Keep a leg for me.'

'You've got no chance if you're not here to claim it. The only leg you'll be getting is if I'm still awake when you get home. Merry Christmas.'

20

THE SOUL KILLER

I arrive home around 9:30. Our little row of three houses on River End doesn't look at all festive. It's as though Christmas hasn't reached down here. I have Christmas Day and Boxing Day off. I take them off most years in exchange for working long shifts on New Year's Eve and New Year's Day. New Year is often bedlam, but I've never been too bothered about celebrating it, so I might as well be at work helping others.

I knock on my neighbour's door. He is a geeky, glasses type that looks as if he works in a computer room with no natural light. I only ever pass the time of day with him, so have no idea what he actually does. Mostly we moan about the music from the guy next door. His deafening tunes reached my bedroom the previous weekend, so it must have been even louder for Robin.

'Hi, Robin. I thought I'd let you know I'll be away until tomorrow. I've just packed.'

He always looks pleased to see me. As always, he is well dressed and clean shaven. I even asked him who his dentist was as his teeth are so white and uniform.

'Okay, that's great. Have a lovely time. Off anywhere nice?'

'Only a friend's. You got anything planned?'

'My friend is cooking dinner on Boxing Day. He lives in Ailsworth. I usually go for a long walk in the afternoon around Ferry Meadows, and it's not too much farther onto his place. He'll drop me back if it gets late.'

I reckon his mate is his boyfriend. He is a handsome guy who I sometimes see leaving after I've endured deep moans through the walls. That sort of thing doesn't usually bother me, although occasionally it goes on for a ridiculous length of time. It's up to him if it's a secret. I bring the conversation back to safer ground.

'I heard knobhead's music a few nights ago.'

'It's driving me crazy. I asked him to turn it down, but he told me to "F" off. I said that even you could hear it, but he just laughed.'

'I don't get it. He isn't having parties. He lives on his own.'

'That man is rude and thoughtless. There's good news though. He reckoned he's going to a friend's in London and seeing a show on Boxing Day. Says he might not even come back.'

'Okay. I doubt I'll be here either. I'll be at a party.'

Robin is one of those who likes to air his house. The windows are always open, the doors sometimes too. Especially on a Sunday, as though he spends the weekend trumping and needs to let it all out.

Still, he's harmless, and I tell him to enjoy himself. I make a big fuss of putting my stuff in my car and even honk my horn a few times as I leave shortly after. Music man has the cheek to appear at his door and give me a dirty look. He should be more careful. I'm not in the mood for any attitude.

21

DI BARTON

Barton parked on the neighbours' drive, blocking them in. Police tape surrounded the house with the body, and a young officer manned the cordon at the entrance.

'Afternoon, sir.'

Barton smiled until he spotted the state of the PVC door.

He put shoe covers and gloves on and crunched through the glass into the hall. He checked behind the front door and saw the key in the lock. Expensive UPVC doors were notoriously tough to break down. Barton glared at the officer, who reddened.

'Why didn't they just smash a window?'

'I'm not sure, sir.'

Barton wrinkled his nose at the smell. Crying and loud voices echoed from upstairs. He could hear Strange's calm voice as she explained something. A uniformed sergeant by the name of Dunning stared up at a dangling body with bulging eyes. A short man in a snowman Christmas jumper stood next to him.

Barton examined the face of the corpse. Strange was right. He was well beyond medical intervention. Barton cleared his throat.

'I'm Detective Inspector Barton. Sergeant Dunning, are you in charge?'

'Yes, sir. This is the family GP, Dr Roe.'

Barton shook the GP's hand and turned back to the sergeant. 'Were you first officer attending?'

The man gestured to the constable at the door before he

replied. 'The other one felt faint. He's lying down in the ambulance. First time they've seen a swinger. They panicked a bit.'

'It appears so.' Barton didn't judge those reactions. He'd blanched at his first suicide too. 'Who's that upstairs with Sergeant Strange?'

'The family arrived just before I did. Apparently, there was no preventing them entering. Having met them, I can believe that.'

Barton took a deep breath. Normally he'd keep the next of kin well away from a scene like this. It was guaranteed to haunt them, maybe even break them.

'Bring me up to speed.'

'Right.'

'And try not to use the word swinger,' he added under his breath.

'The neighbour found a man hanging and rang it in. Our guys arrived in a response van and, thinking they could save him, knocked the door down. But when they entered, it was clear he was dead. His face was chalk white; eyes cloudy. They grabbed him to support him but, even though it isn't cold in here, the body was already stiff and cool.' He pointed to the black liquid dripping from the body onto the presents. 'It's shit from his trouser leg, not blood. The ambulance arrived a minute later. They did some checks but left him in case we didn't want him moved yet.'

'Anything suspicious? Any signs of a break-in?'

The sergeant's eyes strayed behind Barton to the damaged front door. 'The back door and all the windows are still locked. There's no sign of a disturbance. No blood on the carpets, overturned chairs, nothing like that. It looks as though he hung himself.'

Barton squinted at the protruding wrists. 'He's very thin.'

The GP nodded. 'Yes, Donald Birtwistle had advanced terminal lung cancer. Bad luck for a non-smoker in excellent health. He had no more than a month left.'

'I assume that's a painful end?'

'Not necessarily, but his cancer had spread. Every organ contained growths. Tumours in themselves aren't usually painful. Most cancer pain occurs by them growing and pressing on bones, nerves or other organs in the body.'

Barton grimaced. 'Bad enough for someone to want it to stop more than anything?'

'Without a doubt. Chemotherapy at this point kills you as fast as the cancer. It also causes aches and mouth sores. Diarrhoea is a normal side effect. Donald was a man of character, though. I find it hard to believe he'd do this.'

'It's difficult to put yourself in another's situation. He didn't have long to go, why linger?'

'Because he had us, Detective.'

An attractive, full-bodied woman who looked in her late twenties descended the stairs in dark leggings and a white jumper with a flashing-nosed reindeer on it. Behind her was a shorter, but otherwise identical looking woman, in similar attire. They both had black hair in ponytails. The only unmatched thing was their faces. The shorter one's appeared red and puffy, no doubt from crying.

'We're twins,' said the tall one. 'I'm Annabelle, and this is Claudia. That's our father.' She pointed at his shoe, but her eyes didn't follow her finger.

'I'm very sorry. This must be tough for you.'

'He did not kill himself. You never met him. He just wouldn't. Especially on Christmas Day.'

Barton said nothing for a few seconds to release some of the tension.

'I'm sorry for your loss. I'm here to decide the next steps based on the facts so let me catch up. How did the neighbour discover the body?'

'She popped over for a sherry. When he didn't answer the door, she looked through the letterbox.'

'And there are no signs of forced entry. Both the front and back doors were locked. Your father was experiencing terrible pain and didn't have long to live.'

'He wouldn't have done this to us.'

Barton shrugged. It seemed clear to him.

'People who attempt suicide can make the decision very quickly. Christmas in particular causes emotion swings. He could have wished to save you from seeing him suffer. What other explanation is there? That he allowed someone in his house, let them put a noose over his head, then they threw him over the bannister without a struggle. Does that sound like your dad?'

Annabelle's eyes narrowed. 'I appreciate your candour. No, that does not sound like my father. But where did he get the noose from? Planning that takes more than ten minutes.'

Barton acknowledged her astute comment with a nod. The kitchen door swung open and Sirena, the crime scene manager, came in with another white-suited investigator carrying a camera. She gave Barton a pleasant smile but remained professional.

'We've taken photos and prints. Nothing to my eye appears suspicious at this stage. There aren't any mysterious footprints as such, but as you can tell the scene has been compromised. The floor is otherwise spotless. There are no weapons or items which look out of place, although there isn't a letter. The tree was leaning a little when we arrived, which could have occurred due to a number or reasons—'

'In an effort to save himself,' said Annabelle.

'If he wanted to change his mind, yes. Or it might just have toppled over.'

'What about the blood drips and the spray on the wall?'

Barton turned to Dr Roe, who smiled kindly at the sisters.

'I'm sorry, Annabelle. It's not unusual for blood vessels to break in the nose during such an event. It may have come out of his mouth or even his ears. There'd be choking and convulsions. He was considerably weakened, meaning that kind of thing would be more likely.'

'He'd have told us if it was getting too much,' Annabelle said, but was losing her conviction.

Sergeant Dunning spoke up. 'If you look on the kitchen table, there might be a pointer. A picture of the family has been left on it. I've seen it before. It's like a note; where someone can't find the words.'

Tears trickled from Annabelle's eyes but she gritted her teeth. Sobs came from behind her as Claudia broke down again. Strange had been listening from the top of the stairs.

'Is anything missing in the house? Any valuables?' she asked.

'I don't know. We haven't had time to check,' managed Annabelle.

'Did anyone want him dead?'

Annabelle stepped towards the body with shaking shoulders. 'Of course not.' She reached up for a hand and stopped mid-air. 'His ring. His ring is gone.'

'What ring?' asked Barton.

'After my mother died, he wore her wedding ring on his little finger. He never wore jewellery before she was killed.' She finally broke down.

Barton raised an eyebrow. 'Was her death recent?'

The other daughter, Claudia, came forward. She visibly calmed herself with a deep breath now that her sister was weeping. 'A car accident, twelve years ago. He swore he'd never take the ring off.'

Barton inspected the skeletal hand. A ring would slide off any of those fingers. He imagined Mortis, the pathologist on call, tucking into a big plate of Brussels sprouts with a yellow paper hat on. Mortis, real name Simon Menteith, loved his job so much that he would attend any suspicious scene and had done for decades.

'I'm sorry, but this has all the markings of a man taking his own life. I'll request a post-mortem for you, even though your GP should be able to write the death certificate, but it won't be immediately.'

Barton stared at the swaying corpse. It was time to take it down. Claudia must have read his mind because she put a hand to her mouth. He wanted to save the victim's children from seeing that, but they might not want to leave the scene.

'Why don't you look around with DS Strange and check if there's anything else missing?'

Claudia set her face. She clearly felt it was her duty to be present when her father was brought down, so Barton considered again how to get her to leave.

'If you think your father's death is suspicious in any way, that would make this a crime scene. Please give us a few minutes to complete our investigation.'

Strange escorted the twins upstairs with a tiny smile and Barton went to find Dunning, who was inhaling through his nose out of the back door.

'Sergeant. I hope you heard all that. Ring it in as a suspected suicide. Better safe than sorry though, so we'll need a post-mortem done when possible.'

'Yes, sir.'

Sirena instructed the photographer to take photos of the side of the body that had been against the wall.

'You arrived quick.'

'My turn this year. I've no family in the UK anyway.'

Barton shook his head at the body. The ripple effect of a suicide was sometimes as devastating as the act itself. The people affected would never be the same again. Sirena cleared her throat.

'That was the right call, John. Sadly, I've seen a lot of these. Especially at this time of year.'

He hoped he'd made the correct decision. Whatever he decided though, the day's festivities were over for him. At least he'd have more Christmases. This family would never enjoy another normal one. Each year would be a vivid reminder of what they'd lost. Barton shook his head at the ruined gifts. Was there a sadder sight than presents that wouldn't be opened?

22

THE SOUL KILLER

The roads are empty and I make good time to Wisbech, arriving at midday. I park on the drive behind Barney's campervan. Four flat tyres indicate he takes care of it in the same way as he does of himself. I have a key, but I knock so Barney can let me in. The door opens slowly and a balder head than I remember looks cautiously around the edge of it. Barney looks about as healthy as the guy I left hanging earlier. But instead of cloudy eyes, his have a tinge of yellow to them.

'Happy Christmas, Barney.'

'You too. I'm so glad you're here. Come in. I've got a big juicy turkey this year. You won't be calling this one roadkill. I put it in an hour ago. I'll microwave some vegetables later. Do you fancy a drink?'

'What have you got?'

'Whisky, a bottle of wine, and, erm, water. Tap water.'

'I tell you what, a glass of red wine. I'm celebrating the solving of a little problem I had.'

Barney looks troubled. 'Is white okay?'

We watch *Ben Hur* on the small portable and old DVD player that used to be in his campervan. He only opens the whisky bottle twice but still falls asleep. That isn't a good sign.

I check the turkey and it is huge. The vegetables, however, comprise of two unpeeled carrots, four tiny Brussels sprouts, and a tin of processed peas. Locating gravy proves impossible. I wake him when it's ready and we eat in companionable silence at the dining room table. My mind wanders to the space underneath my feet where my mother used to shove me. At least that bloody clock has gone.

He's back on the whisky after picking at his plate. I've not eaten much either. I keep checking my phone, but Claudia still hasn't rung. They must have found him by now. After a slice of frozen cheesecake, I can't wait any longer. I take some deep breaths as adrenalin circles my body. My call goes straight to voicemail, and I hang up.

A vein on my head throbs stronger as each call goes unanswered. Hours pass as I stare unfocussed at the TV for a few minutes before scrutinising my phone. By 19:00, I decide I should leave a message or it might look weird. I turn the TV off, as Barney's crashed again, and step outside to the overgrown back garden. A smell of smoke wafts over from another garden and I hear distant laughter.

I should be having fun. My frame of mind isn't right for a natural call, so I stretch and take some deep breaths.

'Hi, Claudia. Happy Christmas! Hope you're having fun. I'm stuffed myself. Couldn't eat another thing. Ring if you can, or I'll catch up tomorrow. Can't wait to see you.'

I return inside and find Barney still snoring. *Ben Hur* is on again. He must have woken up, restarted it, and fallen asleep again. The chariot race is at its climax but concentrating on it proves impossible. Hoping I'll sleep, I climb the steep stairs using the handrail that's now there.

I close my eyes, but my brain rages behind them. This wasn't what I expected. She ought to be ringing me and confiding in me. I should be comforting her. She can't suspect I had anything to do with it. Does that mean she doesn't need me? She must be with that bloody twin of hers. How do I come between two sisters?

23

THE SOUL KILLER

The unseasonably warm weather continues on Boxing Day morning. I lie in the musty sheets, having tossed and turned all night. Barney won't have changed them since last year. My mind can only hold one worry, though, because nothing else matters. Why hasn't Claudia called me?

Barney had the right idea with that whisky. Then I could have passed out and woken much later, having not clock watched, or mobile-phone watched in this case. The silence in the house breaks at last with a beep from my phone announcing a message. My hands tremble as I open the text.

I'm afraid my dad has died. We're in pieces. I'll ring you soon, X.

A warmth floods through me so thoroughly, it almost feels as if I've wet the bed. I hop from the sheets and knock out fifty press ups. I pull on yesterday's jeans. They hang heavy as though they absorbed the room's turgid atmosphere during the night. I dread to think about the condition of Barney's shower.

I patter down the stairs with care. I smile, as I usually do when I reach the bottom, because it feels as if I'm treading on my mother's chest. Barney's snores inform me of his location, and, judging by the smell in the lounge, warmth flooded through him while he slept, too. The TV flickers with an old *Top of the Pops* programme. It must have been on all night. Slade are telling everybody to have a merry Christmas. That tune was always too upbeat for me.

I prefer the maudlin ones like that East 17 one where he sings about suicide. I bet the twins won't play that for a while. Shame there's no party. It'd be fun without Donald. I celebrated after my mother's fall, but I imagine the sisters will huddle together and crumble. Although, they should have been prepared. After all, all I did was bring forward the date of his departure.

Claudia said she'd ring me later. That's not the warmest of messages. I focus on the big X; two would have been better. She also didn't apologise for not getting in touch yesterday. Barney's snoring escalates. I pick up the empty bottle from his lap and walk out to the kitchen. The fridge resembles an arctic scene of bulging ice and a barren landscape. The bin, on the other hand, is heaving with empties and hums of stale alcohol. I can't see any used food wrappers other than yesterday's. The cupboards have a couple of boxes of cereal inside them. One of those has droppings next to it and a mouse size hole in the side.

I think of the Sikh minimart at the end of the road that I went to yesterday. I wander there and detect thickening clouds overhead. I walk past a family in posh outfits leaving their house and clambering into a taxi. They're full of high spirits. I wonder what amazing place they're on the way to, while an empty day stretches out ahead of me.

At the shop, everything's overpriced but not so outrageously that I refuse to entertain buying it, and in the end I spend over a hundred pounds. Even carrier bags are a penny more expensive than in the supermarkets. The shopkeeper gives me a big grin when I leave. At least someone's enjoying Boxing Day.

I fill the cupboards and fridge to bursting. There's a load of washing up from yesterday, so I start on that. Keeping busy is passing the time and helping me not think about Claudia's message. I'll go mad if I spend another day looking at my phone. After tidying the kitchen, I analyse the lounge with a shake of my head. I bet my mother was the last person to clean this place.

The hoovering doesn't stir Barney. When 'Fairytale of New York' plays on the TV, I turn it up. He chunters in his sleep but that's it. I sing along to the lyrics when it gets to the bit about him spending Christmas Eve in the drunk tank and not seeing another one.

It occurs to me then that Barney is unlikely to partake in next year's celebrations. A surprising regret comes over me as I process that fact. He's like I was: one of life's victims. Well, no more, my failing friend. This time, victory will be mine.

I debate cleaning upstairs, but the thought of tackling Barney's bed is unappealing. I'm not a saint, so instead I wake him up with a cup of overpriced instant coffee. He beams. There's real affection there, and I realise I don't experience that much. My mind returns to Claudia. I need to get home to change in case she rings and wants my company for support.

Barney leans against the doorway when it's time to leave. His stubbly chin trembles. 'Come back soon, won't you?'

'Sure.'

'I mean that. It's been great having some company. We'll go out somewhere when you come again.'

'Hey, maybe in the campervan?'

He replies in a monotone. 'I've not used it for quite a while.'

'Yeah, I noticed when I arrived. Those things go forever though. What else have you got to spend your money on? Just take it to a garage and tell them to get it sorted. They might only need to pump up the tyres and charge the battery.'

He bites his lip. 'And you'll come back for a trip?'

'Of course. Where do you want to go?'

He touches his cheek. 'I miss the sea. I'd love to feel the breeze one last time.'

'We can go plenty of times.'

He smiles, but his eyes remain dull. I haven't got time for this. I bet he's forgotten the conversation by nightfall.

'Stay for another coffee. I'll make it,' he pleads.

I stare at him as he holds his breath, and nod before returning to the lounge. His splotchy damp face shines when he returns. He places the cups on the clean table and snivels. Eventually, I can't stand it.

'The place looks much better with a wipe. You should stay on top of it.'

'Thank you. I know I'm a mess. How about a New Year's resolution, eh? I'll lose some weight, get down the allotment, keep this place tidy, buy a pet or something. We can take it with us on our trips.'

I notice he doesn't mention stopping drinking.

* * *

It's mid-afternoon when I arrive back in Peterborough. The pedestrians I pass glance up at the funereal-grey sky and lengthen their strides. Robin's vehicle's parked up, but his house is dark. I assume he persevered with his hike, regardless of the forecast. When I crack open my car door, the idiot's music booms from his lounge window. I check my mobile and see a missed call. Typical, she rang when I was on the country roads where the signal is poor or absent.

I hit return call but her number rings and rings. I'm about to smash my phone on the floor when she picks up.

'Claudia. Hi, how are you?'

'Hey, you. Bad. I don't know what to do with myself. We're going to go to the cemetery and see Mum. Perhaps the thought of them together will give us some peace. I don't even seem to be able to cry. I can't believe he would do such a thing.'

'How did it happen?'

'He hung himself. It's just so unlike him to do something like that.'

'What?' I cringe as I say it. 'Why?'

'His cancer was spreading like wildfire. The only thing I can think is that he gave up when it became too much.'

'I didn't know it had got that bad. I knew he'd lost a lot of weight.'

'He convinced himself it was beatable and hated people's sympathy. It was only a few weeks ago that they said there was nothing more they could do.'

'He must have been in serious pain. Did he leave a note?'

I don't worry about probing. Nobody behaves the same with grief. I've even had people laugh when told their loved one has died.

'No. He removed a picture of Annabelle and me from the wall. That's something.'

'Yes, that should be a comfort. Who knows what was going through his mind? You should have told me what happened yesterday.' I am your boyfriend, after all.

A deathly pause occurs. I need to speak to her face to face to convince her that we should deal with this together. 'Shall I come over?'

Another lingering nothing has me fearing the worst.

'I really hope you can understand, but I need to be with Annabelle.'

I choke back the surge of anger but can't stop a hard reply. 'Aren't I family? Didn't you say it was us against the world?'

A further pause triggers high alert. I've pushed too far. Am I about to get dumped?

'I'm sorry, but I'm feeling stressed with everything. We haven't been seeing much of each other as this is a time for family. You must have realised I'm not present even when I'm with you. I can't think straight. I'm going to stay at my sister's for a while.'

Damn. I didn't realise she was actively keeping me at arm's length. I'm on thin ice. There's no chance they'll allow me around there. Backing down is the only option.

'That's perfectly understandable. I'll be here when you're ready. Sure you don't need me to get you anything?'

'Malcolm's not due back to work until early January. He'll look after us.'

Fucking Malcolm? Her sister's husband is such a snake. He's as bad as her father for interfering.

'Okay. I'm thinking of you. You take your time and call me when you're ready.'

'Thank you. I'll ring in the new year.'

'Love you.'

'You too.'

The line goes dead.

I get out and take my things from the back seat. Slowly, Claudia's words sink in. New year could mean any time in the next few months. Why can't anyone be on my side?

The beat discharging from the house drives me further up the wall. I could cope with 'White Christmas' or something similar, but the deep bass grinds away at my last nerve. When I slam my front door shut, there's still no escape.

I step back outside and walk over to the source of my fury. He opens up in a short-sleeve, off-white dressing gown but wears a gaudy gold watch. It's an unusual combo.

'Yeah?'

'Hi, I live at number three.'

'I know.'

'I planned to have a nap, but your music is pretty loud for lunchtime.'

'God, you're as annoying as the poof next door. He's always complaining.'

I gasp. His front is incredible. 'There's no need for insults. You should consider your neighbours. Why do you play it so loud? Are you a bit deaf?'

'That's how I like my tunes. It isn't against the law.'

I rub the back of my neck. He's chosen a poor time to irritate me. 'You are breaking the law, in fact. I'll ring the council.'

'Like they'll be answering the phones on Boxing Day. Face it, there's not much you can do. Besides, it's not that bad.'

'I hear you're moving out soon.'

His eyes narrow. 'Who said that? Oh, him next door again. No, I'm just going to a gaming conference in Huntingdon and staying at a lovely hotel, but I'll be back. I told him a load of bollocks to shut him up.'

That's enough time wasted on this moron. I breathe through my nose and run my hands through my hair to calm myself. 'I'd prefer you to play it quieter.'

I haven't been this close to him before. He's a short, ugly, wiry thing. Like a piece of gristle. I struggle to decide if he laughs or leers. He has too many teeth in his mouth. I could help sort that out. I have a strong urge to slap his face and smash his watch but instead I give him my don't-mess-with-me look – the one I use at work when I've had enough.

'Okay, chill out. I'll turn it down.'

'Thank you.'

I'm halfway to the end of his path when he turns the volume up further. My skin prickles and I stop. Stalking back to the house, I knock on his door again. After all, with no party to attend, I have time to teach him a lesson.

24

THE SOUL KILLER

He smirks when he opens the door, but not for long. My frustrations burn and I hammer out my fingers, which spike his Adam's apple. Stunned and choking, he falls towards me, and I catch him. Self-defence training at university helped with that one. Charlie made me go with her for a taster session and I enjoyed it so completed the remainder of the term after she quit.

I stand him up in front of me and it suddenly dawns on me that I could lose my job if he reports me. I'm not sure what to do next. He's wobbling and wheezing, so I escort him to his sofa. What am I doing? He slumps sideways on the low seat but gathers his composure. The sneer returns with his senses.

'Prick. You won't be so full of yourself when I ring 999 and scream assault.'

An unplanned attack isn't sensible. I search inside for a reason to let his comments go. He's just another person taking advantage of my better nature. Why should he walk all over me? Why am I always the victim? My eyes refocus, and a grin creeps onto my face. His brow wrinkles as I lean forward to explain.

'You don't need to ring the police. They're already here.'

I can't help but smile at his confusion. What a satisfying moment. Why do people like him think they can do and say what they like and have no comeback? The scorn in his expression softens to terror. I would be afraid, if I were him.

He whispers, 'No fucking way.'

I slowly remove my warrant card from my pocket and show

it to him. His face whitens, he stutters, and I taste the fear in the room. Maybe this is what the bullies at school fed on, because it is intoxicating.

He knows it's over for him now. He feebly attempts to dodge past me. With a violent barge, I batter him into the door jamb. He hits the floor for a second time, but desperation stops him from giving up. He crawls towards the front door, until I grab his ankles and pull him back into the room. Kneeling on his shoulder blades, I reach my hands around his throat and crush the life from him. A burst of energy flows through me. My eyes close tight.

There's a part of me shouting 'stop', yet I know I've gone too far for that. I carry on squeezing, teeth gritted and bared, for what feels like minutes, as I finish my gruesome task.

Gasping, I finally loosen my grip as he stops moving and scrape my hands through my hair. The omnipotent euphoria fades into the horror of what I've done. What the hell was I thinking? It was his fault for provoking me. He deserved all he got, but I doubt the Crown Prosecution Service will see it that way. I stand and stare around the room. There are only a few splatters, but it's tricky stuff, blood. Hard to get rid of and easy to spot. It's lucky I've had involvement with how CSI work.

A burst of annoyance hits me and I'm tempted to kick his head. How dare he make me lose control like this? I'm a detective, and a beat copper before that. Few escape justice after impulsive crimes. This mustn't happen again, not unless there's no risk.

My mind whirs. I need to take care of the body and any evidence. I touched very little except him. I'll wipe the doors, and I should clean the floor. My breathing speeds up as the seriousness of my rage registers. I could go to prison for the rest of my life. My mouth is bone dry, but I still detect the touch of joy, a thrill perhaps, that coursed through me. And, something more. It's the sensation of being centred. Life has become these seconds. I release a slow breath. That's all very well, but I have a corpse to dispose of.

I bet those mindfulness types weren't thinking of this when they said to live in the moment. Luckily, time isn't my enemy. No one comes down our lane apart from us three. Robin is away for the rest of the day and most of the night. This joker was supposed to be elsewhere, too, so nobody will be coming to visit him. The lack of urgency enables me to pause and think. I see his packed bag on the bottom of the stairs with an envelope on top.

I empty it out on the floor. Inside is the paperwork for an open-return train ticket to Huntingdon and a room at the Holiday Inn for Arnold Stone. There's also a ticket for a toy soldier show tomorrow at nearby Hinchingbrooke.

I look at the corpse and dismiss him with a shake of my head. What a lying muppet. He's been swaggering around with a name like Arnold. And he mentioned a five star hotel and games convention. He really was a pathetic creature. Nevertheless, my actions were reckless and stupid. I should have ignored him. I wonder though. I can still feel the fading rush. I suspect that what I felt then might not go away. It's me in control. My job gives me gravitas and I love that, but it pales compared to how I feel right now.

It's not easy to hide a body, never mind get rid of one, but an image of a hiding place appears in my mind. We had a training course on decomposition rates a few weeks back. Apparently there's a field in America full of donated dead bodies, where they study them as they rot. Certain conditions accelerate the rate, others slow it. Barney's allotment contains a compost heap. I'll bury him in that, for a short time at least. Barney won't sober up and get back into gardening despite his good intentions. I can throw away this guy's things. I doubt he'll be quickly missed because I haven't seen many visitors over the years. Once he's gone and the place is sterile, I'll form a new plan. One that means the world forgets Arnold without a care.

That said, my DNA, skin cells and the like, could be everywhere. I have a Tyvek suit in my car, which we're sometimes required to wear at crime scenes, so at least I won't add any more. The street is still empty, so, after collecting the suit, and some Marigolds and cleaning materials from my house, I slide Arnold, minus that nasty watch, into some large heavy duty bin liners and tape them shut. It's always surprising how cumbersome dead people are. I check the road again and consider whether to put him on the back seat of my car or in the boot. I place him in the boot on a blanket, which will need to be disposed of as well.

The bin liners will stop the little blood that came from his mouth spreading, and it'll be at least twenty-four hours before any fluids start leaking out of him, but there must be chances of DNA moving with the body. Let's hope they never get to the point of letting a cadaver dog stick his nose in my boot. If they suspect foul play, I'll just have to dispose of the car altogether. It might not even be safe selling it, which is annoying. I can't really afford a new one.

I pop back to his house with another bin bag. Everything of value he owns fits in it, including his old laptop. I hold his cheap mobile under the tap for a minute and drop it in the kitchen swing-bin. I've only touched it with cleaning gloves and he's never rung me on it, so there's no connection. They'll think he dropped it in water accidentally and will stop ringing it. With modern technology, they might even get the messages downloaded. Hopefully he'll have been arguing with others by text.

I scratch my head and try to relax. It now looks as if Arnold has deliberately vanished from the house. If he's behind on his rent, and he seems the type, that will help. I drop the bin bag into the boot next to the body. I'll find a commercial bin for it as they tend to be emptied faster.

I return to his house and get out a pot of Vanish oxy cleaner. Bleach cleans blood splatters from the human eye, and ruins DNA, but it'll still show up under luminol. Oxy cleaners ruin the test. If there's anything left for them to find after all this cleaning, it'll be marginal. Sneezes and coughs cause blood traces to enter the air, as well as unhealthy gums.

It was a crazy thing to do. Imagine twenty years in prison while someone else screws my girl, or, worse, impregnates her. I couldn't protect her from other men if I were on the wrong side of some bars. The thought of being so weak and vulnerable causes me to shiver. That will never happen to me. How would Claudia cope if I was gone, especially after what she's been through?

My heartbeat returns to normal. I'm pleased my mind functioned perfectly, even under all that stress. It's why I'm good at my job. Now, how should I cover my tracks further? I stand outside in the spitting rain for inspiration. Looking next door, I see curtains billowing from the top windows of Robin's house. My brain connects the dots. Robin was always at risk of burglary. I can help myself to whatever I want, or, I realise with a grin, I can leave whatever I please.

25

DI BARTON

DCI Cox had settled into DCI Naeem's role smoothly. Barton couldn't enjoy a laugh with her as he used to with Naeem, but their relationship remained professional and efficient. She accepted he knew his job and more or less left him to it. She liked her meetings, though, and called one for the day after Boxing Day.

Strange attended, but Zander was still on his break. Strange and Barton hadn't got away from the scene until late afternoon on Christmas Day, and she had decided to go straight home. Some people like company after seeing the dead, others prefer to get their head together, and Strange was the latter. Barton invited her for Boxing Day instead and she spent most of it helping Luke with his new Lego. Luke told Strange she was better at Lego than Daddy because Daddy had too-big sausage fingers. The rising smile on her face let Barton know that comment would come to haunt him.

His phone remained silent, and it was a time he wouldn't forget. No one left the house all day and the rain encouraged them to put on the fire. He could have done with a few more days like that. It was a day immersed in his role as a father and husband, and nothing else.

The next day in the office, Barton observed the others in the room. Two of the new DCs, Ewing and Zelensky, pulled a Christmas cracker in the corner. Someone dropped a cup, to everyone's amusement. Barton nodded at DCs Malik and Whitlam, who arrived just before Cox entered.

DC Clavell, a secondment from the Wisbech office, had come in for the meeting even though he didn't officially start until the New Year. He looked like a farmer; blond-haired and ruddy-faced, but he was getting experience before his sergeant exams and was on the fast-track. Barton wondered to whom he was related. His advancement was unlikely to do with excellent policing.

'Morning, team,' said DCI Cox.

'Morning, ma'am.'

As she stated her expectations for the new year, Barton pondered on why he called her 'ma'am' and the old DCI 'Boss'. As a consequence, he missed his name being mentioned. He refocussed on a sea of curious faces.

Strange whispered in his ear. 'It's your turn to sing.'

'Eh?'

'She asked you to tell us about the suicide, if you've snapped out of your Christmas stupor.'

Barton recovered fast. 'Sorry, I was considering what to get you lot for Easter. A smart officer thinks ahead.' He smiled at the chuckles and groans. 'A sick man, near the end of life, hanged himself. It looks clear cut.'

'Thank you, John. I received a call from head office saying this needs prioritising. I want to hear the post-mortem results immediately once they're available.'

'Okay, that might not be for a few days.'

'A little bird tells me it will be this morning. Now, it's been a slow festive spell, which is as well with how busy we've been of late. This is a chance to catch up on your outstanding paperwork and revisit colder cases. If I see anyone taking it easy, I'll find something for them to do. Something unpleasant. It will be business as usual before we know it. End-of-year appraisals are first week of January. Come prepared with the paperwork complete, or it will delay me. Any questions?'

Barton recalled Ginger not being able to resist throwing a few jokes in when they had these meetings. This current crop of detectives was too law-abiding. He pondered on whether, if he'd got the promotion, he would have appreciated snide comments from the back of the room. And he couldn't help wondering who had an interest in the case of the hanged man. The GP was probably a mason.

Despite DCI Cox saying it had been slow of late, Barton had a lot to do and when his phone rang at eleven, he felt he'd made no progress.

'DI Barton speaking.'

'John, it's me.'

'Morning, Mortis. I assume you have the results for me. Very prompt.'

'I'm not sure I had any choice. It's rare that I get calls asking for a favour from on high. You understand it isn't who you know, but who owes you. I told them I was mega busy and had some out-of-town work, but I'd push them to the front.'

'Very sneaky.' Barton took a deep breath and concentrated. 'Okay, fire away.'

'The cause of death was asphyxia and venous congestion.'

'Whoa! My blood is 50 per cent brandy sauce at the moment, so I take it that's starvation of oxygen, and what?'

'It's the blocking of veins, jugular in this case, caused by the rope. Then cerebral circulation stops – no blood around the brain – which causes cellular death. Ligature marks indicate a classic hanging. The rope provided matches the marks and is sufficiently strong to hold the weight and long enough to do the job. The noose seems poorly tied but would have been adequate. The knot ended up behind the right ear as the abrasions are deeper on the other side.

'There is blood present on the face, but that's normal, not the result of foul play and will have come from burst vessels. That could occur regardless of his illness. There's pooling of the blood in the legs and hands, which you'd expect as he was hanging and liquid flows down. But there is more in the back and buttocks, which indicates you cut him loose within four hours of the event. Therefore, you can work out the time of death. The hyoid bone is broken, which, judging by how wasted this poorly man was, would have led to a speedy death. No cartilage mobility in the neck and no elasticity of joints makes the likelihood of him experiencing a lingering death unlikely.

'As for foul play. There are no fresh bruises as such on the body or marks to indicate any kind of struggle. There is a contusion on the arm, but it looks like it didn't occur the day of his death. With the condition of the deceased, his body would bruise easily and apart from a few minor red marks there's no sign of that. Fingernails are clean and clear, clothing isn't ripped. I see from the report there was no disturbed furniture. In any case, homicidal hanging is extremely rare. A victim's desperation to live makes that difficult unless someone drugged the target, or they were unconscious from other means. Tox screen results should confirm that line of enquiry.

'It was clearly not a post-mortem hanging. I'd put money on it being a classic suicide of a dying man. He wouldn't have suffered for long. With such a weak neck, he'd have experienced some confusion and loss of logical thought. Once unconscious, there would be convulsions adding to the blood splatter.

'His face remains livid. The rope forces the tongue up the throat, which is displayed by the tip of it sticking out of his mouth. Respiration stops at that point, but the heart may continue to beat for another ten to fifteen minutes. Unlikely though, in his debilitated state.'

'Brutal and informative as always, Mortis. But no sign of criminality?'

'No, not at all. With such a cancer ravaged body, I'm amazed this man was still able to walk around.'

'Could he have been thrown off unconscious?'

'It's conceivable. You'd need to be very strong though. He still weighed over seven stone. I found traces of the rope on his palms, so it looks as if he put it on himself.'

'Perhaps he was at gunpoint?'

'Everything is possible, John. You know that. But I don't see the point. It would have been obvious to all that this man would be dead in a few weeks anyway.'

26

DI BARTON

Barton decided to ring the daughters straight away. He considered which one to call first. He decided on the shorter one. She seemed the most upset of the two and he knew his call would sound more heartfelt the first time around.

'Hi, Claudia Birtwistle speaking.'

'Hi, Ms Birtwistle. DI Barton here.'

'Good morning, Detective.'

He considered correcting his title, but decided it wasn't worth it. She wouldn't need much of an excuse to lose her temper.

'We have the results of the post-mortem. It's as we expected.'

'Suicide?'

'Yes.'

'I see. Nothing suspicious?'

'There's a bruise on his right arm, but it doesn't look like it occurred the day he died.'

'No, he fell on Christmas Eve. I should have known he was struggling.'

'If you want a full copy of the pathologist's report, you can request it from the coroner's office, but there's usually a fee. Your GP should be able to interpret the terms for you. In the light of the results, we'll be closing the case. I rang to explain.'

'Thank you. We'll get the report. To be honest, I've calmed down a little since the initial shock. I can accept he may have taken his own life. Our GP explained what a rotten time he was having. He told me about the pain pills he'd prescribed. They could have affected his mind. Made him angrier or impulsive, or even depressed and suicidal.'

'I'm sorry. It must be a tough period for you. I lost my father too young.'

There was a pause, then she whispered, 'Does the shock ever go away?'

Barton paused. He himself had struggled with moving on afterwards, but it wouldn't help telling her that.

'It's only human to want the pain to vanish, but that's not really the answer. If the grief faded too quickly, then we wouldn't have cared enough in the first place. There are many stages, but eventually you'll be capable of looking back fondly. Keep your loved ones close. Talk to each other. I found nature helped, so long walks and big silences. My mother, admittedly a straight-talking woman, asked me if my father would want me wallowing in despair, or would he prefer I wrung every last moment out of life. Everyone deals with it differently. In the beginning, to be honest, it's sometimes a case of just enduring it. Try to get out. Spend time with your sister or your partner.'

There was a longer gap in the conversation while she absorbed his words.

'That seems wise advice. We're getting away for a week after the funeral. The fact it happened at Christmas is hard to bear. I – we – appreciate your efforts and the way you've handled this.'

'Thank you. I planned to ring your sister next.'

'Please, don't. She isn't handling it at all well. I'm at her house, and it will be better if I give her the news.'

Barton finished the call. It had gone better than he'd expected. Strange had signed on to the computer next to him.

'Was that one of the Birtwistle family?' she asked.

'Yeah, Claudia. I thought she would demand line-ups and thumbscrews, but she seems to have accepted it.'

'Suicide is always a shock because it's often impossible to understand. What did Mortis say?'

'He nailed it. He said there was no point in killing someone that close to death.'

They worked in companionable silence for a while until Barton's stomach growled.

Strange's head jolted up from her computer, and she cocked an ear. 'What foul beast made that sound? Are we safe?'

'Let's offer it a sandwich as a sacrifice.'

'How about some carrot dippers, or maybe celery and a pot of Light Philadelphia?'

'Hmm. Unless the creature is a killer rabbit, I can't imagine he'd be happy with that. A couple of slices of pan-fried elephant would hit the spot.'

'We can try Sainsbury's, although I believe they are ethically against illegal game meat. We can discuss your protein requirements on the way.'

Most officers ate at their desks, Zander included. But Strange, like Barton, thought getting out of the building was good in many ways. Barton drove as Strange brought out the big guns.

'Being overweight is linked to depression.'

'You don't say.'

'People who exercise are always happy.'

Barton laughed. 'I never knew that.'

'My gym, the one I haven't been to yet but pay the monthly charge, is doing an induction morning on Saturday. No joining fee for those who sign up.'

Barton glanced over at her. 'Now who's got the thumbscrews ready?'

'Come on. They offer a discount for police so you'll be among friends. We'll be the leanest team in the country.'

'I doubt that, but I'll give it ago. The second of January is the time to do it.'

'That's the spirit. This is going to be a great year.'

27

THE SOUL KILLER

It's the fourth of January, and the twelve days of Christmas will be over soon. I saw my neighbour, Robin, after his Boxing Day excursion, but I try to keep out of his way. I resisted fabricating a story about Arnold getting picked up with all his stuff. It's better left unsaid. Robin already thinks he was leaving, anyway. If anyone comes around looking for him, I'll know nothing. Every time I walk past his house, I imagine him under a metre of compost.

I must return to the allotment and move the remains at some point. It's been surprisingly warm for January. Those conditions should cause a faster decomposition, but it'll be slower until spring. Then, after three to six months, I should be able to put my hand in and pull out a skeleton, like in a cartoon. There's no need to hurry. He's not going anywhere, and I can't think of a better place. Disturbing his remains if the process is unfinished would be a gruesome task.

I place the Christmas tree in its box and carry it upstairs to the loft. So much for relaxing in my lounge with my woman. Claudia has rung twice. She mentioned her holiday and I commented that I had plenty of days left to take – at which point, she fell silent. She feels like a stranger when we talk. That's hard to handle when you know you're supposed to be together. She said she'd ring this morning before work, but it's gone eight now and still nothing.

At times like this, I reconsider my actions. Arnold probably deserved to die, but I knew so little about him. He didn't seem a religious man. Did I send him to hell, or does his life just end? It's hard to recall what my mother taught me about such things. Even the Internet can't give me answers. It seems everyone has a different take on things. She taught me to look out for myself. That I do recall.

I've kept things going professionally, despite the guilty moments. I almost threw it all away with a lack of control. One colleague mentioned my quietness, but I'm not the most outgoing at the best of times. My life has reverted to what it was before: empty. I can't even be bothered with turning the TV on, never mind exercise. Everything seems pointless. I hate the thought of splitting up with Claudia. There doesn't appear to be an upside in continuing life without her.

I don't know how I've stopped myself screeching round to her sister's house and pulling Claudia into a huge hug. She hasn't gone back to her own home yet. I know that because I drove past on a few occasions. It made me feel like a stalker. That means her brother-in-law, Malcolm, has influence. He'll undermine me every chance he gets.

My phone ring volume is on maximum, and I jump as it lights up.

'Hi, Claudia.'

'Hiya. Sorry. Crazy morning sorting out the last few funeral arrangements. It's on Monday, 10:30, at the crematorium.'

My eyes widen and I have to check I'm understanding what she's saying. 'You want me to come as well?'

'Of course. I'm sorry I've been distant. Thank you for your patience and understanding. I've just stayed at Annabelle's and done nothing. A kind man told me to go with the flow and take each day as it comes. He said to stick to the people I love. I think I pushed you away as I can't believe he's gone. Will you travel in the limousine with me? My dad fell out with his brother a long time ago, so the only relatives left are my sis and me. She'll have Malcolm, and I'd like you to be there.'

'No problem. I can take the day off. Shall I come to your house, or Annabelle's?'

'I should be back at mine by then. The car will pick us up, then collect the other two. If you arrive at my place around 9:00, we can have a coffee beforehand.'

I can't resist a little fist pump but try to keep the pleasure out of my voice. 'I'll be there. You'll get through this, Claudia. With my help.'

'We're going on holiday afterwards. My dad loved cruises, so we thought about scattering the ashes off the back, but I think he'd like to be buried with Mum.'

'I agree. They should be together again.'

'Sorry you can't come. This is just for family. Malcolm and Annabelle paid for it.'

I might have known. 'No problem. It'll be good for you.'

'That's okay. We'll grab a break later this year. I'll see you next week. Take care.'

I say goodbye. I add *I love you* as an afterthought, but only to a disconnected line. The holiday aside, it's a fantastic result. We're back to having a future.

* * *

I sail through my shift at work. The energy that lay dormant reignites with a vengeance, and although I prefer to jog early in the morning while it's quiet, the late evening can be as good, especially in the winter. At ten o'clock at night the chance of seeing anyone at Thorpe Meadows or Ferry Meadows is slim. They are only a few miles from the town centre, but both are green, quiet areas: the first along the river and a rowing lake, the latter around some bigger lakes that are used for sailing. I decide to use the former. I pull my beanie with the built-in LED light on and sprint down Thorpe Road. This life has potential again.

The rowing lake has a path surrounding it but no streetlamps. Occasionally you'll get cyclists who brave the dark in the winter, but apart from the odd homeless person wandering along there, it's usually devoid of life. It's a thousand metres end to end, so I can gauge approximately how far I've done, but gone are the days when I checked my times.

It's a cloudy, wet evening without a moon. I spot no one else until my last circuit when I notice a cyclist up ahead. Whoever it is seems large on the bike. A hood obscures their head, but they aren't going fast because I'm catching them up. Judging by the proportions, it's a big man. He wobbles as I overtake him. I can't help a glance behind and I stumble a little as I recognise

Annabelle's husband, Malcolm. It isn't a complete shock because I've often seen him running or cycling along the river and the rowing lake to work and back, but I've never seen him here at this hour.

'All right, Malcolm. You're out late.'

He pulls the brakes and judders to a halt. A light breeze wafts a hint of alcohol over me. I also detect a lighter, fragrant smell. It's possibly aftershave, although it could be perfume. Finding out Malcolm is a cheat wouldn't be the greatest surprise in the world. I've noticed the odd glance between him and Annabelle, and once she pushed his hand away.

'Work situation. Carried on late. Schmoozing partners at business functions is all part of my role. You wouldn't know about that sort of thing.' He's drunk plenty, but he isn't steaming. He's breathing hard, though. 'Didn't realise it was so cold or dark down here, or I would have left the bike.'

I can't be bothered with this chump's arrogance, but I need us to get on, or it'll make things tricky.

'Yeh, it's really gloomy this evening. I'll see you at the funeral.'

His lip curls. 'Sadly so. I hoped she'd shaken you off.'

I hide my scowl with a hand. You can't beat alcohol for loosening tongues.

'And why would that be? Why don't you like me? I've only ever been polite to you.'

He snorts through his nose. 'You aren't like us. There's something off about you, and I don't enjoy having you around. Clear off and give the poor girl a break?'

'She rang today. Said we'd go away later in the year. That doesn't sound like the actions of a person who wants to be left alone.'

'Ah, yes. You won't be coming on our little cruise though. That'll give Annabelle and me plenty of time to persuade her to find someone new. I'm sure there'll be lots of rich bachelors looking for beautiful women.'

Arguing with inebriated people gets you nowhere and there's been enough unplanned violence already, so I turn and jog away. That's when he laughs. It's a drunken chuckle that has me gritting my teeth. On instinct, I stop, return, grab his handlebars, and lean into him. My clenched jaw prevents me talking, meaning I can only snarl.

'See. There is something off about you. Don't think I won't be telling Claudia about this. And get off my bike.'

I notice the white around his iris. To my amazement, he reaches out and grabs my throat in a painful grip. I know big men can swiftly do some damage. My years in uniform taught me that. Before I have a chance to break the hold, he swings a punch at my head with his other arm. It's a huge, lazy, swinging haymaker and I only have to shift back a few inches for it to miss. The momentum of his swing unbalances him and the bike between his legs. He lets go and falls to one side and hops to get his balance. Lurching and staggering, he practically runs off the path, down the slope of the bank, through the reeds, and into the dark. There's an almighty explosion of squawks and flapping wings. Malcolm roars as if he's fallen into a pit of vipers. A tremendous splash, like the sound of a hippo charging into a river, erupts from the lake.

The swans charge out in my direction. I remember my mother saying they could break a man's arm, but I'm pretty sure they're all bluster. It's too early for nesting, anyway. They flap around me and disappear into the dark. I expect Malcolm to come crawling up the bank, but instead there are faint choking noises and hand splashing from out on my left.

The murk prevents me seeing well, so I walk along the path and hold up my hat so the beam plays onto the lake. He's somehow drifted farther out.

'I can't swim!' he splutters in panic.

I can just make out his head going under after he shouts out. Two steps over the stones and water reaches above my knees. It's freezing, and I catch my breath. Even though it's a rowing lake, it's much deeper than a man's height. Malcolm reappears, spitting and gagging. I dread to think what is in the water.

I edge forward and am soon out of my depth. The brutal cold has me gasping and panting. He's splashed towards me, so I only need to swim a few strokes to get to him. Panicked chokes implore me as I approach. His giant arms pound the surface as he attempts to keep himself afloat. If I'm not careful, he could pull me under, too. I consider what he just said to me. Would he have offered a hand if I was shouting for help? I don't think so.

I try to stare through his wild eyes at the soul behind. It's easy to see he means me no good, and so there's no need to show mercy. It's an impulse decision. But as I reach out, I realise no one will know.

I place my fingers above his forehead and press him under the water. It only takes five seconds before his struggles stop and his hands sink from sight. Stepping back, dripping onto the path, I listen to the sounds around me. The swans have settled, and all I can hear is the traffic from the parkway in the distance. I turn off the LED in my hat. There are no moving lights in either direction in the surrounding dark. If they don't find Malcolm's bike here, they won't know where to look. I pick it up, switch his lamps off and cycle towards town and from where he came.

My trainers squelch on the pedals. It's pitch black. Heavier rain is falling. My jogging bottoms swing lazily on my legs, but they'll soon lighten up. I walk the bike through the meadows next to the riverside. There's no chance anyone will see me here. I'm careful as potholes and rabbit burrows abound. When I approach the main path that runs under the bridges near the edge of town, I turn on the bike's lights. The gears are a little oily, so I pull the chain off and wedge it between the cogs. With a nudge, the bike plops into the water. My gloves are ruined again. I run hard when I get to the bridge over to the Asda supermarket and the town centre but I meet no one.

Back now, I stagger inside my house, remove all my clothes, and flop on the sofa with a tired grin. I remember my mother's words, repent in this life, rejoice in the next, and I wonder if Malcolm had repented his sins.

28

THE SOUL KILLER

Last night's run and excitement wiped me out. A beeping at nearly 8:00 interrupts my slumber. I never sleep in and feel disorientated. There are four missed calls, all from Claudia. I hit redial. She picks up on the first ring.

'I've been trying to get hold of you. Where have you been?'

'In bed, then having a shower. My phone was downstairs.'

'Malcolm's disappeared.'

'What do you mean he's disappeared?'

'He had a business dinner early evening and didn't come home last night. Annabelle's beside herself with worry.'

I drank a herbal tea just before bed last night and role played this scenario. I knew she'd ring me.

'He could be anywhere. What was he doing last night?'

'His company were entertaining a big account at that posh restaurant, Prévost. He mentioned it might run late, so Annabelle went to bed. When she woke up, he still wasn't back and isn't answering his phone.'

'I bet he had a skinful and slept at one of his workmates' houses.'

'He would have been in touch by now though.'

'Perhaps he stayed at a woman's?'

There's a very slight pause before the rebuke. Interesting.

'He wouldn't stay out all night and not call this morning.'

'Has Annabelle spoken to his work colleagues?'

'His boss said he left around ten, and that he'd cycled home.

They ribbed him about it, but he claimed it was only a fifteen minute ride.'

'Odd decision considering the time and weather. Do you know which route he used?'

'They believe he cycled towards Oundle Road, but Annabelle thinks he usually cycles along the river and past the rowing lake.'

'I've seen him do that before, but not so late.'

'Can't you do anything? You're a policeman.'

'I work in Major Crimes. I'm not sure this qualifies.'

'What's wrong with you? This is my brother-in-law! Do something!'

Damn. She's right. That didn't come across as caring. Time to backpedal.

'Sorry, Claudia, I'm still half asleep. Calm down and let me explain the procedure. The team aren't going to be very interested with him missing for ten hours. He's bound to turn up, possibly with some drunken story.'

'I thought if they didn't find someone within twenty-four hours, the chance of them being found alive is really low?'

'That's abducted children, not six feet tall solicitors.'

'Can't you get someone to search now?'

'I'm in court all day, and this is a uniform case. Here's my advice. Stay with Annabelle and support her. Unless there are suspicions of a crime, they won't divert resources to it yet. Get Annabelle to write down all she knows about what he was doing, where he was going, where he went, and who he was with. Get an up-to-date photo of him ready and a detailed description of his clothes, weight and height, and state of mind. Malcolm's been under pressure lately. He might have got drunk to let off some steam and staggered into some bushes or down a slope. She'll need to ring the hospital.'

'Oh my God. What if he's been run over, or toppled into the river?'

I pause for a few seconds to allow those thoughts to crystallise. Staring in the mirror as I wait, I notice a scratch on my neck. It's long but shallow, and must have come from Malcolm. Could they pull DNA from his fingernails after he's been in the water for ages? I'll need to check that out.

'Are you still there?'

'Sorry, I lost the signal for a bit. You know how it is down here. If he hasn't turned up by midday, she can take the information to Thorpe Wood police station. You stay at her house in case he comes home. If she gives them all that information straight away, they should be able to get a special or a support officer to look along the route.'

I hear her take some calm breaths. 'Okay, we can do that. Thank you, I really appreciate it.' She starts to cry. 'I'm sorry. I don't bother to ring, and then something goes wrong and I'm straight on the phone demanding help.'

'Hey, that's all right. Try not to worry. I'm sure he'll pop up soon.'

29

DI BARTON

It was nearly evening when Barton got the message to see DCI Cox in her office. The intense stare from Zander, who took her call, suggested he do so immediately. He knocked on her door. Chief Inspector Frank Brabbins from uniform sat next to her.

'Afternoon, John. Take a seat. You know CI Brabbins.'

Barton shook his hand. He knew him well. Brabbins was time served and knowledgeable. He'd been offered further promotion last year but declined because he enjoyed his current role, but rumour now had it that the lure of extra money and status had finally proven too great, and he was leaving for the capital.

'Afternoon, ma'am. Sir, good Christmas?'

'I think we've known each other long enough for you to use Frank in this environment. And Christmas proved excellent, you?'

'Can't complain, Frank. Very slow workwise, so loads of time with the kids and wife. It was the Christmas most non-service people enjoy every year.'

Cox cleared her throat. There wasn't an offer to call her Sarah.

'John, we've had two cases arrive within a few minutes of each other. There's been a hammer incident over in Paston at the John Clare pub. An ambulance is on its way. Who's in the office with you?'

'Zander, Strange, Malik, Clavell, and Whitlam.'

'Send DS Strange, Malik and Clavell to the pub. Also, a

woman rang 999 over in Upwell saying that her husband kept her hostage for a week. Uniform are in control of both scenes, but we'll need to attend. Send DS Zander and Whitlam to the latter.'

'Which would you like me to attend?' He hoped it wasn't the Upwell one. That was right in the middle of nowhere.

'Neither for the moment. Let's see how it pans out. We may have a different case. Frank, give him the spec.'

'We've had quite a few mispers over the holiday period. That's not unusual. One looks like a transient person, the other two left debts. However, last night, we had another. This is a local, professional man. Waved goodbye from a restaurant late and biked home. Wife wakes up to an empty bed. He still hasn't shown up. First reaction?'

Barton smiled. 'Drunk, stayed at a mate's, possibly a girlfriend's.'

'Apparently, he had quite a few bevvies and had been drinking more than usual lately. Although, the other diners think he cycled along the river opposite Railworld. His colleagues saw him go off in that general direction.'

That sounded interesting. Railworld was a volunteer organisation run by rail enthusiasts. It sat on the edge of the town centre. There were often drunkards and worse there at night.

'What time was this?'

'Ten o'clock.'

Barton rubbed his chin. 'With a chilly night like that, you wouldn't get many people, nasty or otherwise, hanging around there. What was his destination?'

'Orton Waterville.'

'That's about three miles. Anything could have happened. If he was drunk, he could have fallen in, or been robbed and his body dumped in the water or in the shrubbery. That's a lot of river and bank to look in, and you've got the rowing lake, and even the lock at Orton Staunch. The current is much faster there.'

'Our thoughts exactly,' said Brabbins.

'Is it still a misper, or are you asking us to take over?'

'We'll manage it for the moment. He might turn up yet. Murder is usually the last explanation. I've arranged for the underwater search team to arrive tomorrow at midday. If he hasn't turned up by then, we'll get started. I'd like you to work with us if the body turns up, assuming that's okay with your department?'

Barton didn't even bother to look at Cox. That conversation would have been held long before he'd entered the room. 'Of course. Isn't it a bit early to be calling in the big guns for a misper case?'

Cox's face pinched but not in Barton's direction. Brabbins had the grace to redden.

'The missing man carries some heft around town.' He quickly moved on. 'You worked that situation with the body in the River Ouse a few years back. The dive team came to that, didn't they? Can you talk me through it?'

Barton recalled the incident. A lad had cycled home from St Neots town centre, again drunk, and never arrived. They found him at the bottom of the river four days later.

'It sounds similar to this. A guy disappeared after a night out. The divers began searching about thirty-six hours later. It was a comparable time of year too, so I know it's going to be hard work. Visibility is very poor, and the water's freezing. There's less daylight to use, too. It took them two days, and they had a much, much smaller target area. They can't go too fast because they're hunting for evidence as well as the body.'

Cox tutted. 'That doesn't sound promising with the size of our search zone. Did he float down the river too before he sank?'

'Do you want the detailed answer, or a simple one?'

'I think we have the time for a thorough explanation.'

'I got all this from the dive sergeant. The human body is slightly heavier than fresh water, more so if it's clothed. It sinks pretty quickly once the lungs fill up with water. That's likely to be near where the person went in. And it will go to the bottom, however deep it is. The sergeant told me that even if the current is strong on the top, it's entirely different on the riverbed.'

'No suspicions when that body was recovered?' asked Frank.

'No, the body was unmarked, and the toxicology indicated high blood alcohol content. Basically, he cycled off the path and drowned. So, you'll need the exact make and model.'

Both the chief inspectors stared blankly at him.

Barton explained. 'Of the bike. It was the first thing we found.'

30

DI BARTON

Barton left the changing room of the Holiday Inn leisure club, nodded to the friendly chap at reception, and self-consciously entered the gym. It was obvious his clothes were brand new. The induction with Strange a few days beforehand had been interesting, and he'd really enjoyed it. Inevitably, he'd signed up on the spot, weakened by the rush of endorphins. They'd even let them stay and use the machines afterwards. Barton had been so keen, he'd visited the next morning at 6:00 and pumped some weights for an hour.

It felt different this time. In the past, working out had proved an arduous experience, requiring great willpower just to get through the doorway of the gym. Upon arrival, he'd struggle to get going, especially with the lure of a sauna or steam room. The visits would slowly space out and eventually stop altogether, leaving him feeling unfit and guilty. Not to mention poorer. Holly had rolled her eyes at him when he'd mentioned he'd joined a gym again. She'd seen it all before.

Maybe that motivated him. He wanted to prove to her he could do it. Since having children, getting in shape had become one of those things he'd do in the future. But when was that going to be? The years were ticking by. When he retired? Ginger's demise, and decades of policing, had taught him that time waits for no man. Balancing work and family life proved tough for everyone, rich and poor. Yet his health had to be a priority.

As he pushed the doors open and checked out the scene, it

was almost like being in the office. Half the department sweated before his eyes. He spotted DCI Naeem and her husband on the rowing machines. The new guy, Clavell, posed with free weights in front of a mirror. Barton joined Strange at the water cooler.

'You didn't say you were coming down,' she said.

'I thought you lot would be out for a while. What happened?'

'The hammer incident turned out to be a carpenter doing maintenance in the pub. A local got the hump because he couldn't hear the horse racing on the TV. He threatened the carpenter, who had been nailing down some architrave. There was some pushing and shoving, and the instigator tripped over a toolbox. We took a few statements, but the CCTV showed it was handbags.'

'And the incident at Upwell?'

'Zander attended the false imprisonment case. It was a domestic. They weren't even drunk. Neighbours believe they love the drama. They both got a warning for wasting police time.'

'Does Zander come here?'

'No, he said he was already perfect.'

Barton laughed, he could imagine him saying it.

'Cox told me about the missing guy. What do you think?' asked Strange.

'One of the officers door-knocking the flats overlooking the river got a lead. A bloke's wife won't let him smoke in the flat, so he has to go out on the balcony. He said he heard a splash some time around 22 30.'

'Ah. Case solved, then.'

'Yeah, appears so. The divers will search tomorrow when it's light, but it doesn't bode well. A couple of constables have a long, cold night ahead of them patrolling the scene. That family are having some terrible luck. The guy who hanged himself on Christmas Day was the missing man's father-in-law.'

Strange took a while to get her head around the new information. 'Wow, that's got to be hard for her.'

Barton was distracted by Malik and Whitlam sprinting hard, side by side, on two running machines. They ran in unison. Being light and slim, they resembled robots.

'Do you reckon I could look like that?'

Strange looked him up and down. 'Easy. You could do that now.'

Barton rubbed his chin. 'Really?'

'Obviously I'd have to cut you in half.'

31

DI BARTON

Barton decided to go into the office next morning, as opposed to the scene by the river. If they were hoping to pull a dead body out, he didn't need to be there until later. He sent DC Malik down to keep him informed. Malik rang him at 11 00.

'Barton speaking. Any news?'

'No, turns out there are a lot of bikes in here, and trolleys. We had a nasty shock when we found a slimy dolly in the mud, for obvious reasons. It's slow going with the weather, too. The water's so cold that even in dry suits they can't dive for too long. Hang on, they've got something.'

Barton listened as he heard Malik walk towards some raised voices in the background. 'Yeah, it looks like the bike.'

'Okay. Ring me when they find him.'

Malik returned to the office in the late afternoon looking frozen. Barton cringed as he'd meant to swap him with one of the others and forgot. Malik gave Barton a dirty look and shook his head. Barton steepled his fingers. They were difficult conditions out there, but he suspected they would find a body soon.

Barton finished on time and rushed home, hoping to find a full dinner plate with his name on it, but it was eerily quiet in the house. Trying to be silent, he crept upstairs, thinking that Luke must be in bed. He brushed his teeth to get a day's instant coffee off them and checked behind the closed doors. Lawrence was studying in his room. Layla was gazing at her tablet in hers. Luke's room was empty.

Feeling uneasy, he descended the stairs, opened the lounge

door and found Luke immersed in a comic on the floor. The fire glowed and a candle flickered on the windowsill. Holly read the paper on her lap. Only the flame near the window moved.

When Holly looked up, Barton whispered, 'Apologies, I seem to have come to the wrong house.'

'Nice, isn't it?'

'Unusual is what it is. What happened to Lawrence? Is he being bullied?'

Holly chuckled and made room for Barton to sit next to her. He gave her a quick peck on the cheek. She was free of make-up and her was hair was pulled back, but he preferred her looking natural and chilled. She was usually relaxed when the kids were all accounted for.

'Some ex-students returned to talk to them a few days back and he's been stewing on it ever since. One guy came in and admitted that he never tried at school. Said he's struggled ever since and currently works as an industrial cleaner, whatever that is. The others had stories about trying hard and it still not being easy. We had a little chat. He's worried it's too late to change but he's doing his best.'

'After all the talking-to we gave him, it's a cleaner that gets the message home. Whatever it takes, I suppose.'

'How was your day? The news said that the missing man hadn't been found.'

'No, I'm going to ring Mortis.'

'The pathologist?'

'Yes. While they dredge the river, I'll drain his brain.'

'Okay, I've relished a peaceful early-evening with a glass of wine. There's some crusty bread if you want a sandwich. Or do you fancy a pizza after Luke's in bed?'

'Meat feast?'

'Spinach and ricotta.'

He wrinkled his nose. 'A sarnie will be fine. I might go to the gym for a bit later too.'

'Again?'

'Yeah, I feel pretty good. I've lost a few pounds already.'

'You do realise that you won't end up looking like David Gandy.'

'Who's he?'

'A male supermodel.'

'I know that. I just don't want to be one of those dads who can't keep up with his sons.'

Holly squeezed his leg. 'Men and their testosterone, eh. You need to face up to the fact you're an older father. You'll be fifty soon enough. Beating their old man in a running race or dribbling by him at football is a rite of passage for all boys. You're supposed to lose and be proud to do so.'

'Don't you yearn to be married to someone with a six-pack?'

'If I wanted that, I'd have dumped you years ago.'

* * *

Barton grabbed a chair in the kitchen and rang Mortis.

'John. I assume you've found the misper?'

'Nope. I was hoping to pick your brain. Missing persons are a nightmare for resources as there are so many possibilities. As you know adults can do what they like, so you can't just send the police after someone because they disappeared. He could have staged his death for all we know and then run off to see his Australian pen pal.' He paused, realising Mortis knew all this already. 'Anyway, I was wondering, if the dive team don't locate him, what are the odds of the body turning up?'

'You mean will it float to the top?'

'Yes, and how long would that take?'

'An intact dead human is guaranteed to rise to the surface unless it's trapped, which is unlikely. Gases form as decay advances. The torso distends and *thar she blows*.'

Barton imagined a bloated corpse with a harpoon in it, breaking the surface like Moby Dick.

'You paint a nice picture, Mortis.'

'I do my best. Now, the deceased, fat or thin?'

'Beefy.'

'Bigger bodies can bloat faster because there's more to feed on. That said, the temperature will greatly affect the rate of decomposition. In warm water, they'd rise in a couple of days. In present conditions, someone like that would probably resurface much later. I'd guess around day ten. It's an extremely interesting but far from exact science.'

'And they float up near where they sank?'

'Yes, you need to spot them quickly once up though, as, fully distended, you'd struggle to sink them with weights, and they may then drift.'

Barton thanked him and hung up. The river ran through the town centre, so there was little chance of anyone missing a dead body floating along it. He climbed the stairs and got his exercise clothes together, and his thoughts turned to the poor woman who'd lost her father and her husband in the space of a few weeks. Life could be so cruel.

32

THE SOUL KILLER

In the light of recent events, Claudia remains at her sister's. The funeral of their father is going ahead, as I don't suppose you could just keep him on ice until a more convenient time. We've agreed I'll be at Annabelle's when the hearse arrives.

It's been four days since Malcolm vanished. There has been no sight or sign of him, except his bike. Uniform have kept the case seeing as there are no grounds for suspicion at this point.

This is the first occasion I will be seeing Claudia or Annabelle in person after everything that has happened. I steady myself at their door. I need to focus and not say anything that doesn't make me look like Mr Supportive. I'm looking forward to winning her over. She'll be looking forward to seeing me, despite the occasion.

It's been a while since we had sex, but that might be pushing it. She wasn't super-enthusiastic when I suggested we spice things up, but she seemed to relax as we got going. I grin at the memory, but remove it as I see one of them advance towards me through the glass after I ring the bell.

I can't quite make out which of them it is but I recognise Annabelle's grim eyes close up: they turn vacant as she lets me in. After a perfunctory hug and the briefest of kisses on the cheek, where I can feel bones that I couldn't feel before, she thanks me for coming and guides me into the kitchen.

Annabelle's suit hangs heavy. There appears no substance to her body. It's as if she's melting away. Her once full cheeks are now jowly despite thick foundation, as though the goodness has leached from them. Make-up has run down her face, and she looks a little too Gotham for a church service. Claudia notices.

'It's just us three leaving from here. I'll sort her make-up out. Can you carry our handbags to the door so we don't forget them, please?'

I nod and smile. Black suits her. The stairs creak as they disappear up them, so I wander around downstairs and admire the decor. What a lovely house: very spacious. They love their photo canvases. There must be more than twenty all over the walls in the lounge, dining room, and stretching along the hall and landing. Malcolm peers down on me from wherever I look. If he could see me now... It's probably easier to spin in your grave if it's a watery one.

A solemn knock on the door reminds me again that I shouldn't smile today. A tall, grey haired gentleman offers his hand. 'When you're ready, sir.'

'Ladies,' I shout next to the bannister.

Claudia shrugs as she descends. It's unclear what she did to Annabelle because to me she looks exactly the same, but I suspect it was an impossible task. I pick up the handbags. The twins link arms, and I do the same on Annabelle's other side to support her. Her eyes are so watery, she must be struggling to see anything. I lock the door behind us and put the key in Annabelle's handbag.

We slowly step towards the vehicle. The sisters huddle next to each other in the back of the limousine, and I sit opposite. The funeral director walks along the street. The hearse and our car follow.

'I didn't lock up!' shouts Annabelle.

'It's okay, I did. The key's in there.' I pass them their respective handbags.

'Thank you.' Claudia reaches forward and squeezes my hand.

Annabelle stares at me. 'Any news?'

'They wouldn't tell me if there was, I'm afraid, as I'm not assigned to the case. You'll be the first person to hear if they find anything.'

She slumps in her seat. 'He must be dead. His phone and

bank accounts haven't been used. We should get a discount with the funeral parlour for being regular customers.'

She laughs: a strange high-pitched cackle. Claudia hugs her in tight. Her eyes soften at me, and she touches a finger to her lips. I give her my most reassuring glance. It's okay, I'm here now.

33

DI BARTON

Barton was cycling in the gym next to Sirena, unaware his phone was ringing in his locker. She had arrived shortly after him and, with a raised eyebrow, offered to spot him. He'd asked whether he should be spotting her, but they'd ended up going around the machines taking turns. They'd even had a sauna together. It felt strangely normal. It was a far cry from his youth, where the out-of-hours socialising occurred in pubs and bars. Ginger would have hated the weights but he'd have enjoyed the steam room, he ruefully thought.

Barton agreed to a coffee afterwards in the hotel lounge and had just ordered when he noticed the missed calls. He listened to the messages and turned to Sirena.

'They've found a body.'

'Whereabouts?'

'Some rowers hit it on the rowing lake.'

'That'll help with the forensics.'

'I should go.'

'Finish your drink, he's not going anywhere.'

They chatted for a bit, but Barton couldn't concentrate. She stood up and kissed him on the cheek.

'Leave. I'm off today, so you'll have to fill me in the next time you see me. We won't get much from the crime scene, anyway, I wouldn't have thought.'

Barton wandered back to his car, thinking it was also his day off. After texting Zander to confirm receipt of the message, he drove there, even though he could have walked in twenty minutes. He parked in the rowing club car park and grabbed his thick coat from the boot. A harsh wind blew along the kilometre lake and heavy, funeral-grey clouds raced overhead. The police vehicles lit up the area on the far side of the lake about two hundred metres from the near end. Barton spotted the tent that no doubt covered the body. He spotted Mortis staring into the water, then returning to the tent.

Zander stood out on the edge of the scene, and Barton headed for him. CI Brabbins and DC Clavell huddled next to him. Neither was saying anything.

'Morning, sir. I assume our missing guy has turned up?' Barton asked Brabbins.

'Yes. It's him all right. Sergeant, would you show him? My breakfast is still lurking next to my tonsils.'

Zander stretched his back but smiled mischievously. 'John's seen everything. This won't worry him.'

Barton followed him to the tent and shook Mortis's hand. Mortis pulled back the sheet.

'Gee,' uttered Barton. He hadn't been expecting that.

Swollen hands were the first thing he noticed, then the caved in head. The man's shirt had ridden up, exposing a vast distended stomach. That, and the face, were a foul greenish-black colour, not dissimilar to how you'd expect a large well-fed zombie to look.

'He's a beauty, isn't he?' said Mortis. 'I said it'd be ten days before he surfaced, what do I win?'

Barton remained lost for words. He had been on the scene when they'd found the victim in the water at St Neots and the boy had looked as if he could have just been swimming. This body was rotten and bloated. He'd never seen the fascination with zombie films, finding them ridiculous, but if this guy climbed to his feet, there'd be large laundry bills all round. Barton licked his dry lips.

'Has he been bludgeoned to death?'

'No. Post-mortem injury. There's still some skin on the front of that boat. Careless not to have a bow ball on the end as you can see the damage that's been done. Imagine if he'd been alive.'

Zander asked the obvious. 'A bow ball?'

'It's a ball that goes on the point of the boat, which stops it smashing the skull of unlucky swimmers.'

'Have you had a chance to check the body?' asked Barton.

'Yes. It looks like he drowned, but I won't know for sure until I remove his lungs and examine the blood.'

'Why his blood?' asked Clavell.

Before Barton could say anything, Mortis was in full flow.

'The main cause of death from drowning in fresh water is the explosive dilution of the blood with water from the lungs. Your blood becomes half blood, half water. Therefore, it can't carry oxygen. Oddly, in saltwater, it's the reverse and osmosis removes the water from the blood, which still renders it useless.

'It's a nasty death but a quick one. Once under, the person holds their breath but eventually gulps in water, which causes the larynx to spasm to protect the lungs. In stopping the liquid entering, the air supply is cut off. The spasm stops to allow in air, but more water is consumed. The spasm occurs again but for a shorter time, and the process repeats until the lungs are full of water. I usually find they are twice the normal size when I open the body.'

Barton gave Clavell a you-did-ask glance, but Clavell's eyes were on Mortis.

'Any signs of violence?' asked Clavell.

'Concrete findings after this long in water are rare. Decomposition is fastest in the torso, as the forming gas causes it to rise up, the hands and head loll down, possibly dragging along the bottom. That would dirty and damage the fingers and face. He could have bumped into the bank or branches, or other boats might have hit him without realising. From what CI Brabbins has said, I would guess he was drunk, and him and his bike entered the river farther up. He pulled himself out as it's shallower there and then wandered to the rowing lake. There are no lights – he may have got disorientated and fallen in.

'Apparently, he couldn't swim. People drown a lot quicker and quieter than you expect. You can't scream with a throat full of water, and the natural response is to extend your hands laterally and press down on the water. They struggle on the surface before silently sinking, maybe in as little as twenty seconds from first going in. I doubt there's any mystery here.'

Zander smiled. 'I'll give Brabbins the good news.'

Mortis nodded in agreement. 'I doubt we'll find where he went in after all this time. We can order DNA tests on the body, but most evidence would have degraded by now. It seems clear cut, so I'd just leave any samples in storage.'

'I wouldn't bother, but that's Brabbins' call. Apparently, the victim and his wife had been struggling to have a baby. He'd been coping by drinking more,' said Barton.

Mortis tutted. 'That wouldn't have helped with his sperm count.'

No one was in the mood to debate how illogical humans could be. Barton watched Brabbins acknowledge he'd keep the investigation while Clavell pulled a chocolate bar out of his pocket and bit the end off.

'What's your first name?' asked Barton.

'It's James, but like your man, Zander, everyone calls me Clavell.'

'That's some big boots you're hoping to fill.'

'In time, he'll fill mine.'

Barton wasn't sure if he was joking or not. Nevertheless, Clavell had impressed him.

'You handled that well.' Barton nodded.

'Once you've seen a few of them, you get used to it. I come from the Fens, remember. It doesn't matter how often you tell the kids not to go too fast on those country roads, they still end up in the ditches. And that's not to mention the farming accidents. Every few years someone falls asleep in a field and gets runs over.'

Barton strode from the scene, trying not to think of combine harvesters. He stopped at his car and stared back over the choppy water. He had a nasty feeling that today wouldn't be his last dealings with the body from the lake.

34

THE SOUL KILLER

I'm nervous about what I'm going to do, but there's something in the air today that makes me think it will go well. I step out of the front door at the same time as my next-door neighbour. He's grinning too. Spring always has this effect on me. I detect a different warmth in the direct sunshine. I can hear the birds conducting their business and the sound of a mower somewhere in the distance.

Robin reaches the end of the path and stops. He looks smart and often reminds me of how well many professional golfers dress. We talk more now the asshole, our ex-neighbour, Stone, has gone. He even invited me in for a coffee once. I wandered around and admired how he'd decorated the place. Although, obviously I'd been inside his house on Boxing Day. Once he knocked on my door and gave me a huge slice of a cake he'd baked. However, I keep him at arm's length. I don't need any more friends or distractions. Claudia deserves all my attention. In some ways it's a shame, because I find him endearing and upbeat. Still, he might be on borrowed time.

Robin stops with an excited, dramatic expression on his face, but I still detect a hint of tiredness beneath his eyes, which should be absent now the music's stopped.

'You won't guess who banged on my door a few days ago,' he says.

'Tooth fairy?'

'No.'

'Elton John?'

'I wish. No, your lot.'

'The loners' society?'

'The police! This particular officer was very dishy in his uniform.'

'Really? What for?'

He speaks in a hushed conspiratorial tone. 'It was him with the deafening beats, Arnold Stone. His mum has reported him missing.'

'She took her time. He's been gone ages.'

'Apparently they weren't at all close. He struggled with drink and drugs, and they only spoke on the phone every three or four weeks. She'd not heard from him for months. He usually went to see her once a year in February on the anniversary of his father's death. There was no sign of him, and he isn't answering his mobile.'

'That's a little odd. Did you tell the officer that Stone had mentioned he was moving away?'

'Yes, of course. He didn't seem surprised at that. People like him disappear all the time, but they have a duty to investigate. His mother lives up north and is in poor health so she can't visit herself. The policeman thought it was pretty obvious he'd done a bunk when I told him that the property owner also hoped to find him.'

'You've got your finger on the pulse. No one's knocked on my door.'

'They did, actually. Your car was there, but you must have been out. The landlord informed him that Stone paid his rent pretty erratically and fell further and further behind. He hated him as well because he was rude when he chased his arrears. Apparently, there isn't much he can do until the tenant's two months behind. Stone's missed three complete payments now, so there's a notice of abandonment on the door.

'Apparently, Stone had changed the locks. The landlord called a locksmith out to gain entry, he reckoned to ensure that Stone wasn't dead in there and to make it secure. He found cutlery, crockery, old paperwork, and a few items of clothing. There was a mobile phone in the bin, but there was a layer of dust over everything. It looks like Stone left last Christmas.'

'Looks like you and the landlord made that copper's day for him. Solved his problem without him having to do anything.'

Robin laughed. 'Yes, that's what he said. Someone new will be moving in. Let's hope we have more luck with this one. Maybe we should have a "welcome to the street" party.'

I can't prevent my lips pulling back. Robin leans into me. 'You're a private person, aren't you?'

'Yes. I had a bad experience with a neighbour once. I like to keep my distance nowadays. People can be funny about living near a policeman.'

'That's fine. I understand. Not everyone's as understanding with my lot either. See you later.'

Later that day, Robin's boyfriend arrives in a low riding, sky blue, 7 series BMW, which must start at eighty grand. This one screams to be looked at. He crawls over the potholes so as not to ground the car. Grey flecks his hair. He looks a little like Sean Penn. He's as feisty, too. They've had some real humdinging arguments lately. I reckon Robin is a bit of fun soon to be discarded. Despite that, Robin gets in and gives him a lingering kiss. The Penn lookalike pulls away when he spots me watching. Mother would have hated that sort of behaviour in public. Personally, I believe people should be able to live how they please. There's too much interfering in others' business nowadays.

The news on Stone was interesting, though. I knew most of it, of course. I'd kept an eye out on the computer for missing men and Stone's name had appeared. They don't waste resources hunting someone who's bolted to evade their debts.

I'd seen the policeman doing his cursory investigation and hidden behind the sofa when he'd knocked. I guessed that if he spoke to Robin, he'd never come back.

The law is on the tenants' side now to a massive degree and plenty of scumbags like Stone take advantage of the situation. If they can blag their references, they pay their deposit and first month's rent, move in, and then stop paying. The landlord has to wait and then go through the courts to evict them. It can take six months to get a possession order, which is more expense on top of not getting the rental payment but still having the mortgage to find. The tenant usually skips just before the final warning about imminent bailiffs, and they keep six months of housing benefit in the process.

I imagine that would make you slam a few doors. If it was my house that I rented out, I'd put the tenant's head in the way first. Only last week, a case of GBH occurred when an argument overheated between the landlord and tenant.

Barney and the corpse have popped into my mind every now and again. I've cycled to the allotment on the odd dark night, stolen compost from other plots, and turned the compost heap over. Apparently, that helps with aerobic decomposition. Judging by the foul release of gas, it's rotting fast. There's nothing to be gained from moving him in that condition. Once he's bones, I'll dispose of him. I can probably just burn them. I ought to visit Barney, but all my focus has been on Claudia. She needs me. But I mustn't forget poor Barney. I'll write him a letter.

Before I see Claudia today, I've decided to have a chat with DI Barton. I asked him if I could pop around his home at the weekend. He told me to come on Sunday morning and have a coffee. I'm not sure which of my visits is making me more apprehensive: the one to him or Claudia's.

I leave my street and arrive at the Thorpe Road junction. The Sessions House opposite was a pub I visited once. They converted it from a jail built in 1842. Such a stunning building, but the vegetables tasted as if they started cooking them back then. It's closed now, and the forecourt is a car park for the railway station. The hospital complex, which filled the surrounding land, has been demolished and replaced by toy town houses. It's a constant reminder that nothing stays the same. You need to adapt and respond or you get left behind.

I've learned that there are no handouts in this life. It's a dog-eat-dog world. Only the ruthless survive.

35

DI BARTON

Luke had Barton playing dinosaurs farm attack: his favourite game. He'd emptied out every single bucket from the playroom, and the almighty clash on the lounge carpet was about to begin. Unsurprisingly, General Barton's side were the livestock. His army lined up with a particularly large anteater, which Field Marshall Luke insisted was a farm animal, front and centre as his senior officer. The portly farmer next to him had a chicken under his arm and held second in command. Behind them, wave after wave of cows, horses, and pigs prepared to defend to the death, supported by a rearguard of three goats and a small fluffy donkey called Bernard.

Luke's premier force comprised four tyrannosaurs, closely followed by ten velociraptors. Barton had concerns over his right-flank where he had a battalion of small sheep. The opposing line up of triceratops and other giant-horned dinosaurs nearby loomed menacingly.

His son's trembling hands wielded an enormous plastic monster called a spinosaurus, which was more dragon than dinosaur. Strange how his boy couldn't remember what he'd done with the remote control five minutes beforehand, yet could recall the scientific name of more than twenty of these prehistoric beasts.

Luke shouted, 'Charge.' The battle commenced.

'Rah!' Luke bellowed with wild eyes. Amazingly, considering that he had just informed his dad that it lived in water, spinosaurus swooped from the clouds and flattened his father's advance team. The creature also savaged Barton's thumb as Barton tried, and failed, to save Bernard.

Holly popped her head around the door. She'd raised three children and seen many shocking sights but even she was lost for words at the chaos that confronted her. Barton gave her a thumbs-up with his bleeding digit.

'Are you the cavalry, come to rescue the day?'

'If I owned a gun, I'd definitely use it. Why did you have to make such a mess? I've got friends arriving later.'

Barton opened his mouth to say it was Luke's idea but knew it would sound pathetic. Still, he grinned. It was fun to play dinosaur Armageddon.

'That colleague you said was coming over is here. I've put him in the dining room. Try not to wreck that as well.'

Barton sucked his thumb. His knees creaked as he rose, leaving Luke to smash his farm buildings by stomping on them with a vengeful brontosaurus. The war was over. The good guys lost. He found the officer smiling at a picture on the wall of a very young-looking Barton and Holly when they first met. He gave Barton an easy smile.

'Morning, sir. How are you?'

'Very well. You can call me John in my own house.'

'Sorry, John. I won't take up much of your time, but I wasn't sure if I should mention this or not.'

'Sounds serious. Do I need a strong coffee to hear it?'

'No, I don't think so. Well, you know the hanging case at Christmas?'

Barton raised an eyebrow. 'Go on.'

'The man had two daughters, twins called Annabelle and Claudia. I dated Claudia for about a year before her father committed suicide.'

'Okay, I remember her well. She seems a clever woman.'

'We'd more or less separated before he died. We drifted apart. I didn't want to split up, but I wasn't sure what to do. I was devastated, but her dad was ill, so I kept my distance. When I saw he'd killed himself, I didn't know whether to say anything at work. It wasn't really my business any more, and Claudia didn't want me involved. She told the family liaison officer as much. Obviously, I would have mentioned it if we'd ended up investigating the death, but I informed Claudia we don't deal with straightforward suicides anyway.'

Barton puffed out his cheeks. 'Perhaps I will make a coffee. Wait here. You want one?'

'No, thank you, sir.'

Barton grinned at the return to formality as he filled the kettle in the kitchen. Holly chopped vegetables in the sink. He winked at her and used the time to roll the information around his head. The man sounded naïve, and earnest, even though he must be in his early thirties. Barton was sure he had never been that way himself. He returned to the dining room with his cup.

'I don't think it matters. We never took the case. Were you close to the twins' dad?'

'No, not at all. I'd only met him on a few occasions.'

'Okay, fair enough. I appreciate you telling me, but it was a straightforward suicide. Your connection wasn't important.'

'That's a relief. I'll get out of your way, then. Looks like you have a nice lunch planned. Although it sounded like there was a riot in your lounge.'

Barton raised both eyebrows at his humour. This officer rarely joked. As they stood, Barton asked him a final question. 'Why tell me now?'

'Since the funeral and what happened to her sister's husband, we've got back together. It's serious now. We've realised how much we mean to each other.'

'That often happens. Tragedies like that make you see what is and isn't important in your life. How is her sister coping with the death of her husband?'

'Badly, as you'd expect. I only met Malcolm and her once or twice, but they seemed a strong couple. Claudia rented her own flat, but she's moved into her sister's house to support her. Unfortunately, losing two people close to her has pushed Annabelle close to the edge. She's been signed off work and put on medication. She stayed in bed for a long time, but she has better days now and gets out sometimes.'

'That's a lot to deal with. Was her husband a good bloke?'

Barton noticed the man struggle with an internal battle. It finished quicker than the war in the lounge, but it definitely happened. With a sad smile, the reply was controlled and balanced.

'He wasn't especially friendly, but he was polite. I guess he came across a bit arrogant. She loved him though, and Malcolm was a big presence.'

'Hopefully she'll get there.'

'There are a couple of other things I should mention.'

'Go on.'

'I thought I'd also tell you because I'm planning on asking Claudia to marry me.'

Barton concealed his open mouth by rubbing his chin. He contemplated having a joke with the young man but decided against it. Ginger used to say, don't get married, get a motorbike. Then you can trade it in when the back end goes.

'Congratulations. It's a big commitment.'

'I know. I'm prepared for it.'

Barton ushered him out while wondering whether Claudia would be ready for it. At the door, he remembered there were to be two more points.

'What were the other things?'

Again, the man fumbled for the right words.

'It's okay. Another time. I'll see you back at work.'

Barton watched the officer drive down the cul-de-sac to turn around at the bottom. He appreciated the fact that he crawled along. A lot of kids lived in the street nowadays, and they weren't used to traffic. When the car passed, Barton gave him a double thumbs-up for luck. There was a good chance he'd need it. He returned to the kitchen where Holly was aggressively massaging butter onto the chicken. It wasn't far off performing CPR.

'What did that bird ever do to you? Isn't there a no violence policy in our home?'

'I need to strangle something.'

'You have to let Luke play, Holly.'

'I spent most of yesterday tidying this house from top to bottom, and you two have been up for a few hours this morning and wrecked it.'

Barton realised he was charting dangerous waters. 'I'll take him for a drive and keep out of your hair.'

'Good idea. Don't go to McDonald's though, or he won't eat his lunch.'

Barton had been rumbled but responded in style. 'The park will be lovely on such a nice day. Anyway, my body is a finely tuned machine nowadays and irresistible to all. No doubt you'd like to cover me in butter later too.'

'That won't be happening, I'm afraid. I'll be exhausted from repeatedly cleaning up after this family. Despite your tempting pert bottom.' She whacked him on the behind with a wooden spatula. 'That officer was a solemn young man. Did I hear him telling you he was asking a girl to get married?'

'Many of the younger officers in the department are serious types. It's almost like they're scared to have a joke in case it offends someone.'

'Don't all jokes insult people?'

Barton shrugged. 'I guess. Although, I've found it more enjoyable to go through life not being so easily offended. I reckon he's pushing his luck. That poor family have had a lot to handle, what with the brother-in-law's drowning on top of the father's suicide.'

'Are neither suspicious?'

'No. The post-mortems ticked all the boxes. Both died of asphyxiation but in different circumstances. We didn't get involved. It's tragic, but these things happen.'

Holly slammed the chicken into the oven and washed her hands. 'Shall we all watch a movie after lunch?'

'Yeah, although I hoped to pop to the gym later. I haven't been for a few days and don't want to let it slip.'

Barton's skin prickled as he left the room. She tapped the spatula on the table, causing him to stop in the doorway.

'Remember, we enjoy your company, and we don't care how big your belly is as long as we can still see the TV.'

Barton decided to mention what had been on his mind for a while.

'Do you mind who I work out with, even if it's a woman?'

Holly's eyes narrowed. 'I assume you mean Sergeant Strange?'

'Her most of the time, but also that lady from CSI, Sirena.'

'The young one I met at Ginger's funeral? I don't think I have too much to worry about with those two.'

Barton returned to the apocalypse in the living room. Perhaps Sirena was too young and attractive to be interested in an old bloke like him anyway and he had nothing to worry about.

36

THE SOUL KILLER

I decide to drive down Barton's cul-de-sac and turn round at the bottom. It's hard to comprehend this peaceful street housed those killers. But that's why I'll get away with it. No one thinks to look under their noses. Killers live in semi-detached houses and nod greetings to you as they pass, even in these nicer areas. The Snow Killer surprised us all.

I admire places where no cars are on the road because everyone has their own driveway. This place fits the description. DI Barton has done well for himself. Those lovely kids and a beautiful wife must be a joy to come home to. I deserve the same, although I bet it isn't cheap to live around here.

It's a shame Barton is involved with the cases. I'd be confident otherwise. We all know his reputation for tearing apart alibis and exposing the facts. Modern forensics might be the undoing of me. Mortis will have taken fingernail scrapings from the deceased at the rowing lake, and even though they didn't send them for testing, they'll be on file.

When people join the police, they provide elimination DNA and fingerprints. Modern forensics is so efficient now that even hairs from officers at the scene can blow onto evidence and then appear during testing. Obviously, they need to disregard those on most occasions, but I am walking a tightrope. Once the finger of suspicion points in your direction, it can take some removing. Still, despite what you see on TV, no one has ever been convicted on just DNA evidence.

It's becoming a strategy game. Not a child's puzzle but a battle. Barton is Napoleon to my Duke of Wellington. I need to plot one step ahead. More, actually. At the end, I will be victorious for my Queen.

Barton has left the house and leans against his gate. He gives me a thumbs-up as I pass. I like him and think he's a good man. It was him who suggested to Claudia that she look to her friends and nature to help her through this. That's why she suggested going to a farm this afternoon. I don't care what we do, as long as it's together. It's time she accepted that we belong with one another.

Hopefully there will be no further lines of enquiry about Malcolm and Donald and we can put it all behind us. I hope our paths don't cross. Barton might be old, but he's a big unit. I'd have to take him down quick. Perhaps I should refresh myself with those martial art videos.

I turn out of Black Ermine Street and marvel at the impressive vista of the bigger homes on the village road. The houses rest on huge plots and are set back. Thatched roofs abound. Claudia deserves something like this. I can imagine her pulling up to one of the houses in a little convertible.

The traffic lights change and I turn left to the next village along – Orton Waterville – where Claudia now lives with Annabelle. It's only a few minutes' drive and has the same country feel to it. Instead of Claudia moving into her father's place on the British Sugar estate, they've put it up for sale. I suppose it would be hard not to picture the hanging body every time you went up or down the stairs. I imagine my mother's corpse when I see where she died.

Four hundred grand is a lot of money, so the twins will be rich when the house is sold. Maybe Claudia and I could afford something in these villages with her deposit and our combined wages. Finally, it's all coming together. It's no less than we deserve.

I honk my horn when I pull onto their driveway. We agreed to save her sister having to see visitors if she wasn't feeling great. That suits me, as there is a strange atmosphere in the house every time I visit. Annabelle needs to pick herself up. Her dad was living on borrowed time anyway, and she's better off without that pecker, Malcolm. A few of the blokes from work are single – she could do worse than them.

Claudia appears at the doorway in a summer dress. The breeze rustles her hair. She looks so beautiful that my breath catches in my throat. Both sisters have lost weight, but Claudia had more in reserve. Still, her legs actually look a little too thin now. Understandably, trips to the gym and fine dining have little appeal when death visits your family.

It's strange to see how it's affected them so much. I wonder if my life would have been different with supportive role models. Such strong bonds create advantages and shortcomings. Despite the loss of their mother, the stability their father gave the twins through money and love made them free. They could branch out and try new things. Risks weren't so scary with a safety net, because ultimately, they had a home to which they could return. There was always a safe place. But once that sanctuary and security have gone, like now, they are weak. They doubt themselves. They've never learned to depend on just themselves.

Annabelle, in particular, can't see that she should be pleased that she ever had that safety. All she can focus on is her loss.

At some point, people realise they need to put down new foundations. Add extra ballast to their existing relationships. To be fair, Annabelle is all at sea because she's lost both pillars to her life. Maybe it's no wonder she can't get out of her pyjamas.

Claudia gives me a peck on the cheek when she gets into the car. It's soft and almost not there, but she lingers close to my face and gently kisses me again. I stare out of the windscreen and grin. You see, that's where I come in. Annabelle might be wallowing in self-pity and shock and the only person she has is her sister, who is grieving as well. Claudia, though, has me. I will give her strength. Carry her if necessary.

We arrive at Sacrewell Farm after a twenty minute drive out of the city. I pick up a leaflet in the queue. Apparently, there's a whole range of animals, from traditional farm stock such as pigs and sheep to the more unusual alpacas. I show her the peacock on the front. She leans in, hugs me and smiles.

'Let me pay. You spend too much on me as it is. I don't expect presents and gifts when I see you. Just your company is enough.'

I shake my head at her and nod at the lady at the till.

'Fourteen pounds, please.'

I scramble in my pockets and settle the entrance fee. It's a little expensive to stroke a few creatures. We wander around. It's not quite what I expected. The entrance fee is working out at about one pound per animal until we get towards the fields behind the water mill. Nevertheless, Claudia is relishing the distraction.

'Look at the size of those horses,' she says.

The paddock contains four of the biggest horses I've ever seen. The sign says they are Sussex Punch draught horses. An older mare wanders over and makes a beeline for Claudia. Claudia and the horse gaze at each other and I find myself edging away to take a photo. She'll love that. It's as though she's drawing strength and happiness from those huge brown eyes and shiny muscles. After ten minutes, we stroll over to the donkeys and sneak them a polo each.

The picnic area is empty at this hour, and we tiptoe through the grass towards the bird hide. We watch the swans, herons and moorhens for a while, and, holding hands, meander along to the rickety bridge over the stream. There's nobody in hearing distance, but I wouldn't care if there were. It's perfect. This is our destiny.

I stop strolling and gently tug on Claudia's sleeve. She turns with a contented smile and I drop to one knee. My voice doesn't waver. 'Will you marry me?'

Her eyes fill with tears. She wipes them away and stares across the tilled fields. It's spring, and birdsong fills the air. Why is she pausing? Her soul should soar and readily accept the inevitability of our union. Finally, she turns to me with a sad smile.

'Yes.'

37

DI BARTON

Three months later

Barton grinned as his daughter, Layla, jumped higher than anyone from the rebound and snatched the netball. He reflected on the gobby mare who had been giving him backchat only a few months ago. What had happened? He'd expected Layla's new attitude would escalate, and so would the door-slamming and screeching, but instead she had come back to him. Holly said it was the calm before the storm of the teenage years.

He recalled the little girl who loved spending every moment she could cuddling her 'Dadda', as she used to call him. She'd only been about nine when she'd first called him horrible. His wife had prepared him for the hormonal onslaught but it had arrived earlier than they'd expected. He'd laughed it off and chastised himself for being stupid, but it still hurt. As usual, it was Holly who pulled him through.

'We don't want her staying a little girl forever, do we?' she said.

Life moved on, he knew that, but he mourned that innocent stage. It was only last season that Barton had offered to support her team in a cup final and she'd looked at him as though he'd said he was planning to turn up naked. 'Erm, no, thanks, Dad.' Dismissed, he hadn't mentioned it again after Holly had let it slip that they got thrashed. A year later, they'd reached the final again, but this time, Layla asked him if he'd come.

Strange used to play at a good level in London and offered to tag along to see if she could offer any hints or tips. Again, the younger Layla wouldn't have been having any of that. Yet, here they both were, cheering her on. The two teams were evenly matched and both edged ahead at various points, but the opposition boasted two willowy girls in attack. As the match wore on, Layla's team slowed from all the leaping and blocking, and the chances of victory slipped away.

She came off at the end smiling.

'You were great,' Barton and Strange said.

'Well, we were better. At this rate we'll beat them when I'm sixty.'

They drove Layla and her teammate, Terri, home afterwards. Barton offered a fast-food treat as he neared Boongate – the area where Pizza Hut, McDonald's, Frankie & Benny's, and all the other places of temptation plied their trade – but the girls said not to bother. He exchanged a glance with Strange but didn't comment. Lawrence had asked for healthier meals recently as well.

Holly always told Barton not to make jokes about fat or thin people as the children grew up. She was painfully aware of Instagram and Facebook's impact on adolescents, and she uncomplainingly cooked them dinners from fresh and accommodated both of the older children's short-lived vegetarian phases.

Terri and Layla laughed in the back seats.

'Terri said you can donate that money to a homeless person.'

'No problem. Perhaps you'd like to spend Saturday outside the supermarket with a tin collecting for them?'

Barton glanced in the rear view mirror as they pouted at each other and then burst into giggles. He stopped at Terri's house on London Road and double-checked that her mum had agreed to drop Layla back after they'd eaten.

After Terri had got out, Layla reached into the front and squeezed her dad's shoulder.

'Thanks for coming, both of you. I really appreciate it.'

'How come I'm flavour of the month?' he asked.

'I've finally grasped that you only get one father. You might be a little useless at times, and reasonably smelly at others, but you mean well.'

Strange choked next to him.

'Very kind of you to say so. Will you be doing more chores around the house now to help out?'

'No way! Should I waste the best years of my life on menial tasks?' Her voice dropped to a whisper. 'Terri's dad moved out a while back. Her parents are divorcing, and she wishes she hadn't been such a cow recently. I reckon she thinks it's her fault. I want you to realise I appreciate everything you do for me. You know, the lifts, cooking, tidying. Please maintain that level of service.'

Strange couldn't help herself from guffawing this time, and Barton good-naturedly joined in. His mobile rang as he started driving again. He reached into his pocket and passed it to Strange. 'Who is it?'

'Control.'

Barton checked the time on the dashboard: 20:00. 'Answer it, please.'

Strange spoke on the phone and took the details, and it was clearly an unusual call, judging by her frown. They were at Strange's place when she hung up.

'Someone's uncovered some remains.'

'Great. I knew I shouldn't have mentioned being on top of my workload. Is it a murder?'

'It might be hard to tell.'

'Why's that?'

'It's a skeleton.'

38

DI BARTON

Strange waited while Barton rang DCI Cox. After he'd finished, he slowly turned to her as he processed the facts.

'This is going to be different,' he said.

She nodded in agreement. 'Too right.'

'Let's summarise what we know so far. A man took over an allotment recently. It hadn't been worked for years, and he spent ages clearing it ready for planting. He put a fair number of cuttings and the like on a huge compost heap and turned it over with his pitchfork. It stuck in something heavy. He reckoned on a branch. Instead, his prongs had wedged in a ribcage.'

'Gross. And quite a moment, I would think.'

'Yes, I bet. Uniform said all the bones are visible and it could have been there years. Anyway, it's our investigation. There isn't any point in going tonight. They posted some poor sod to protect the scene. Cox spoke to Mortis, and he'll be there at eight in the morning. As you might expect with a nickname like that, he is overcome with enthusiasm. CSI will attend at the same time.'

'You know we could go and have a look now?'

Barton laughed. 'Looks like it's got your interest, too. It's in Wisbech, so not worth the effort of a two hour round trip.'

Strange had just completed on a small house in Stagshaw Drive and, although he'd forgotten the exhilaration of owning your first home, Barton was pleased to see Strange in such good form again. The best he'd seen her for ages, in fact.

'We haven't had anything juicy to get stuck into since the Snow Killer,' she said.

'Is a skeleton juicy?'

'Okay, we can be like dogs with a new bone.'

'Gross, but it doesn't have to be murder.'

'What? Hiding a body in a compost heap?'

'Funerals are expensive nowadays. It might be a DIY one.'

'Is that legal?'

Barton squinted for a moment. 'On an allotment, no. You'd need permission from the freeholder. I think we can agree they wouldn't consent. A Certificate of Authority for Burial is necessary, too. It has to be done before the burial takes place.'

'So, it's definitely a crime. Shall we go together tomorrow?'

'Sure. Actually, take Zander. I'll bring the new lad, Clavell. It's his turf, so he could come in handy, and having two cars is helpful.'

'Good idea, although I've found Clavell hard to warm to.'

'Yeh, he's a bit shy, I think. I usually get a read of people within moments of meeting them, but this guy puzzles me. I didn't want to ring his old boss to get the lowdown as that's not really fair. Tomorrow will give us a chance to chat to him properly and see what all the fuss is about.'

Strange opened the car door. 'Do I need to bring my wellies?'

'Definitely. There's the risk of rain tonight.'

'No problem. Catch you tomorrow. My money's on murder.'

Barton liked to keep an open mind, but tomorrow looked set to be an interesting day.

39

DI BARTON

Barton rang Clavell when he got home and told him to be ready for a dawn pick up. He was waiting outside his house in a pair of walking boots when Barton pulled up at 7:15 the next morning.

'Morning, Clavell. Not too early for you, is it?'

'Farming stock, sir.'

Barton had given up asking people to call him John by that point. Some of them did it naturally, others kept things formal. He suspected Clavell preferred the latter. A car journey was a great opportunity to get to know someone, so Barton had turned the radio off when he arrived at Clavell's place. How would Clavell handle the silence?

After ten minutes of quiet, Barton broke first.

'You have an unusual surname.'

'Suppose so.'

Barton waited for him to continue, but he didn't.

'Where does it originate from?'

'I'm not sure.'

'How are you enjoying working in Peterborough?'

'I like it.'

'Why?'

'It's busier.'

'How much busier?'

'Wisbech had four hundred crimes last month. Peterborough had two thousand.'

Barton thought for a moment. 'Doesn't Peterborough have

five times the staff, though? By that rationale, you'd be just as busy in both places.'

'I suppose so.'

Barton was about to put the radio back on, when Clavell began to double-check the facts about the uncovered remains. He listened intently to Barton's replies, then sat quietly as they left Peterborough. It was dual carriageway up to Thorney but single roads the rest of the way. Weak June sunshine already lit up the scenery. This part of the world was so flat that you could see for miles. Peterborough sat on the edge of the Fens, but Wisbech nestled in the centre. The view of lush green fields stretched beyond sight. He'd always imagined there'd be loads of people buried out here, especially with all the recent migrants who were ripe for exploitation.

The Fens produced over a third of the UK's vegetables. In their search for cheap labour, the companies brought in thousands of Portuguese, Polish and other Eastern European workers. Most barely spoke a word of English when they first arrived. Such a massive influx had led to a big jump in violent and sexual crimes. Barton decided to have another go at opening up Clavell.

'Any ideas on what we're about to find?'

'A murder victim.'

'What makes you say that?'

Clavell paused for a few seconds. 'I went back into work last night and I've been running through all the likely scenarios since I heard the details. You haven't told me anything new. It's a strange place to bury a body. Bodies decompose fast out here anyway, so to put it somewhere like that means they've thought about it. Looks like foul play to me. It will obviously depend on the condition of the corpse. There might be bullet holes in the skull.'

'Eastern European?'

'Certainly possible. Although allotments tend to be out of the way, so I'd more think of someone who lived nearby and knew the area.'

'Perhaps the new owner is our perp?'

'Didn't he ring it in? So that's unlikely. I'd bury my body in a different allotment if I was going to kill someone. Even then, it's too close to home. Organised crime deal with the migrant workers. We've had a couple of cases of missing people or strange suicides. This is the kind of case I want more experience of. I'm looking forward to it. My old boss always said murder is a messy business, mostly committed by amateurs. If the bones are recent, I bet they'll match someone who's disappeared. If they don't link to anyone, my guess would be one of the pickers complained too loudly about being ripped off. Either way, the perpetrator won't be a criminal genius. We'll solve it.'

Barton smiled at his incorrect assumption about Clavell being shy, even though a tractor had pulled out in front of him.

40

DI BARTON

Clavell directed Barton when they reached the town centre and Barton recognised Mortis's car when they parked. The CSI van was also there. A sergeant from the Wisbech station had arrived as well and greeted them warmly. He guided them through the allotments. Barton didn't know much about gardening, but even he could appreciate the earthy smell in the air. The place heaved with people considering the hour. Barton approached the sergeant.

'Are these places usually this busy this early?'

'It's mostly retired folk, and there's plenty to do this time of year. A lot of them come every day, even at Christmas. It's a nice little community where they look out for each other.' He spoke with a typical Norfolk accent and had their talent for deadpan delivery. 'I should think it being on the radio this morning might have had an impact, too.'

'What?'

'Yes, it featured on the local breakfast programme. Looks like someone spilled the beans.'

Barton shrugged and analysed the large plot that was contained by police tape. The ground was cleared, but nothing appeared to be growing. He had a discussion with the scene guard at the outer cordon to warn him that the press might try to get inside. They walked down the row of stepping plates that had been put down on the path to protect the scene until he spotted Mortis in a blue CSI suit rubbing his hands together. Sirena didn't even glance his way. Barton suspected that in their line of work, this particular body was the holy grail.

He cleared his throat and introduced Clavell to them in case he hadn't met everyone. There were assorted crime-scene bags and boxes all over the place.

'I take it you arrived early?'

'Just a little,' said Mortis. 'Would you like to meet our new friend?'

'Do I need to get suited and come inside?'

'No, you can see from there.' Mortis stepped to the side.

Barton crouched and stared at a perfect Halloween decoration. Only the lower legs remained covered by compost. The grinning skull, arms and ribcage seemed intact, not even showing signs of damage from the pitchfork.

'I assume this has been here a fair while?'

Mortis grinned. 'Not necessarily.'

'Please try to keep your explanation to less than ten thousand words.'

'Sirena has finished splitting the scene into sections, so we can uncover the legs. Assuming there are no surprises, it appears the skeleton is complete. We'll get the bones analysed by an expert, but I have some knowledge in this field.' He paused to take a deep breath. 'A compost heap is a great place to dispose of a body. There will already be bacteria present in such warm and moist conditions, and there'd be oxygen when the corpse was first left. That's an excellent environment for microorganisms to thrive. Combine that with the bacteria inside his body, the gut in particular, and it's an efficient system.'

'How long would it take to strip a body like that?'

'Three months if turned over. Otherwise six months. Perhaps less.'

'You think someone might have come back to encourage it to decompose?'

'It's possible. After all, the individual was buried naked. The perp knew what they were doing and undressed him. Aerobic decomposition is faster than anaerobic, so allowing oxygen in accelerates the process. Rats, foxes and mice could help in that regard too. Maybe snakes feeding on them could have added oxygen. The necrobiome is an underappreciated ecosystem.'

'What's a necrobiome?' Zander, who'd just arrived, gave Barton a smile.

'It's the community of organisms associated with a decaying corpse. Bacteria, other living things such as fungi, nematodes, insects and larger scavengers all play a part. If the death is recent, research is progressing where they can analyse the bacteria to see how long the body has been decomposing as different organisms are present at different times. And—'

'Thank you, Mortis. Anything else?' interrupted Barton.

'There's no ID or jewellery, glasses or shoes.'

'You said he was buried naked. Aren't they clothes?' Barton pointed at what he quickly grasped was scraps of remaining skin. 'Ah, I see. Could it be years old?'

'It's hard to state an exact date for obvious reasons. The skeleton is in very good condition so I would guess it's fairly recent. Whoever disturbed the remains should be able to suggest the length of time since the earth was last turned.'

'I was expecting the skull to have hair.'

'That's what Indiana Jones films teach us. Our hair is attached to the skin, not the bone. There's still a little on the back of the head.'

'Straightforward identification?'

'You've probably been lucky. We'll easily collect DNA from the victim, but how about dentistry?'

'Of course, we can check dental records.'

'There are a few fillings, but you might not even have to do that. Look at the top row of teeth.' Mortis used a pencil to point. 'They are quite bunched. This man had a very pronounced grin.'

Clavell laughed. 'I said it would be easy. All we need to do is find out who's missing and ask whoever reported them about his smile.'

'A quarter of a million people vanish every year, so it isn't that simple,' said Strange.

Clavell rolled his eyes. 'You're right, of course, but most of them turn up quickly. Many reported mispers are not, in fact, missing at all, they are just adults who are thoughtless or need some time to themselves, and we can narrow it down by looking locally. Also, two thirds of those who disappear are children.

These remains are adult and complete. Mr Mortis here will give us his height and approximate age through bone condition.'

Mortis clapped Clavell on the back. 'Spot on, young man. Definitely mature as wisdom teeth are present. Bones fuse together as we age. Later life causes bone loss, which doesn't look advanced. Ossification, otherwise known as thickening, is complete by your twenties. The teeth are in good order, too. I would suggest at least twenty years old, probably not as old as forty. I've checked the bones for breaks. Remember the hyoid bone we discussed. If it's a strangulation, that gets broken in about a third of cases. It's intact here. He broke his arm at some point, but not recently, which will help with identification.'

'And it's definitely a man?' asked Barton.

'Oh, yes. Females have a more rounded pelvis. The jawbone tends to be larger, and the brow higher. Male skeletons display longer, thicker bones in the arms, legs, and fingers.'

'Looks like that narrows our search,' said Clavell.

One of the scene guards returned at that moment with a sprightly looking gentleman with a full head of grey hair.

'This is the owner of the allotment.'

Barton shook the man's hand. 'This is your compost heap?'

'I rent it from the council. I don't own it.'

'It's not one of your friends in there?'

'A mate of mine ran off with my wife, but he'll be suffering enough without me having to kill him.'

Barton smiled. A dry sense of humour was common in these parts. Barton had plenty more questions but thought he'd see who was on the ball. He caught Clavell's eye. 'Anyone else like to ask anything?'

Clavell stepped forward. 'How long since you took possession of the allotment?'

'Only a few months. I've been on the waiting list for years. It was overgrown when I first turned up. The previous bloke can't have used it for a long time. A bloody tree grew in one corner.'

'Do you know who had it before you?'

'No idea. The council will be able to tell you that.'

'Have you seen anyone suspicious here since you've been working it?'

'No.'

Barton picked up on the growing frowns at the bullet questions. Flattery often helped. 'You've obviously done a lot of work here.'

The old fellow stood taller. 'That's right. Broke my back turning this place round.'

Clavell cut in. 'Any other bones turn up?'

All those present raised their eyebrows. It hadn't occurred to them that it could be a multiple burial site. The gardener shook his head.

'Maybe you haven't found the others,' pressed Clavell.

'It would be time consuming to have to start poking around the entire allotment,' said Zander. 'What about looking in all the compost heaps? There must be fifty plots here. Sirena, had you considered that?'

Sirena blushed. 'To be honest, I hadn't. We taped up the immediate area. That's a bit of a schoolgirl error, but we don't have the manpower for that kind of thing at present. This plot looks well worked and it's exposed to the elements over a long period, so we won't get much from it. We will fingertip-search the inner cordon. The senior investigating officer can make further decisions. Is that you now, John?'

'Yes.' Barton nibbled his index finger. 'God, imagine if we found remains in more than one plot.'

Clavell tutted. 'Well, I would say that's unlikely, so you'll probably get away with not looking. Serial killers are rare. I think Joe Bloggs here will turn up as a missing person. Sir, if you'd instruct the team to question these other gardeners. I suspect that there are a fair few nosey parkers who miss nothing. They'll know who worked the plot in the past. They may even know where he or she lived. I'll ring the council, where I've got a contact, and find the address that way. Perhaps someone can check who's on the misper list.'

Clavell grinned at Strange. He took his phone out of his pocket and scowled. 'Poor signal here. I'll try at the road.' With that, he trudged off up the path.

Barton watched him leave. 'I like him.'

'I don't,' said Strange.

41

THE SOUL KILLER

The station is awash with talk of the skeleton. I've really messed up. Barney worked that allotment for as long as I've known him. I thought he'd never give it up until he died. Perhaps that's what happened. It's a poor reflection on me that I don't even know either way. There's no one else to blame but myself. It wouldn't have taken much effort to check on Barney, and I should have removed the teeth.

Work's been busy, and Claudia's been hard work. We've seen each other, but it's hardly quality time. She's thrown herself back into her career, using it as distraction. Her demanding sister seems to have gone completely off the rails. I asked Claudia a million times if she wanted to look at dresses, or churches, or locations, or rings, and I've been brushed aside each and every time.

If Barney's still alive, it might even be worse. He didn't tell the police anything when my mother died all those years ago, so he may not now. And I can't believe for a minute that he'd imagine I'd been burying bodies in his compost. But if he and I are linked, I am screwed. I tried to imagine other options, but it's simply impossible to cover everything. Once he began to decompose, it made sense to leave him. I suppose I knew it might only be a matter of time, but clever people make plans for when their plans fail. I am prepared.

About 90 per cent of missing person cases reported to the police are closed within forty-eight hours; 99 per cent of all cases are solved in a year. This one made it to six months.

They'll check the database and link the skeleton to Arnold Stone sooner or later. Let's hope what I've put in place is enough. Someone's going to get a nasty shock.

I wonder now whether Claudia and I are meant to be happy in this life. I hoped, with time, there'd be no more need for drastic actions, and we could lead a simple existence. But I fear my days might be numbered.

Zander instructed us to sort out the special property cupboard, which looks as if it hasn't been tackled in a while. However, Barton will have the bit between his teeth. We'll be pulled off this and dragged into that case and I'll be investigating my own crime.

Sure enough, DCI Cox approaches with purpose.

'Malik, Whitlam. You'll have heard what's going on. I've no doubt you'll be pleased to get out of that cupboard. We've been checking the mispers for the county. We reckon the skeleton is of an adult male between the age of twenty and forty. The system has provided eighteen names for you to contact. All missing within the last year but not as recently as three months. The details are on the computer and my request emailed to you, but I'll summarise. The teeth of the individual were unique. There's a picture taken by DI Barton showing how bunched they are. Speak to the people who reported the lost persons and see if you get a match.'

She scans a printout. 'Our victim also broke his right humerus years ago. The pathologist said it looks like a nasty break which had to be pinned.'

'Remind me where your humerus is again?' I ask.

'Upper arm bone. Breaking it is a common injury for children falling when running. A parent would remember, a partner maybe wouldn't. The teeth are the clue though. We can revisit the calls with height and other factors later. However, if we identify the victim fast, it will save an enormous amount of resources from pouring in the wrong direction. Report to me when you've finished.'

We retreat to our desks and my colleague splits the list in two. Nine people each. My eyes scan the names and there he is, fourth down, Arnold Stone. I'm surprisingly calm and begin the calls. The first one tells me her son sent her a postcard saying he was okay. The second goes to voicemail. I leave a message asking him to ring back to enable us to keep our files current. The third explains that her husband's body washed up in a coastal inlet not far from Redcar a few weeks back.

I listen with interest while she tells me the story of how he grew up there but couldn't find work. They both moved down south and settled in Peterborough, where he found a job at Perkins as an engineer, which is a subsidiary of Caterpillar. I comment that it's a good company. She agrees and cries.

She was proud of him. He always worked hard and never complained. He took further qualifications and planned to stay for the rest of his career. But they made him redundant. He couldn't find work and he was stuck at home, eventually turning to alcohol. Soon, he rarely left the house. One day, he left a note stating he was going home to be with his family, despite his parents being dead. She talks factually, as though reading from a book. It will be real soon enough.

Next is Mrs Stone. I read the report. There are no details of too many teeth in the description. Probably, like any other mother, she thinks him handsome and normal. There's no mention of a previous broken arm either. I guess they wouldn't have thought they'd need to identify him from his bare skeleton at that point.

I punch in the numbers.

'The number you have dialled has not been recognised.'

I know it's only a reprieve, not a pardon. But I still release a long, slow breath.

42

DI BARTON

Barton felt he had the situation under control as he left the allotments. He'd left Strange and Zander to direct operations and he'd talk to DCI Cox about widening the search. The immediate scene was protected, and the nearby allotment holders had been questioned or were in the process of being talked to. There had been no need to track them down as they'd all turned up as news spread. Clavell's contact came through and gave them the details of a Barney Trimble, who lived at 499 Norwich Road in Wisbech.

Barton decided to take Clavell to visit him as Clavell knew the area. He'd amazed Barton with his analytical thinking. It was no wonder that the top brass thought he was destined for great things. Barton pondered how long it would be before he called Clavell 'sir'. Still, he didn't mind. He'd met a few high flyers before, and there was no stopping them. Cynically, he understood that if you helped them on the way up, they might provide favours later on.

He gave the car keys to Clavell so he could concentrate while the other man drove.

'Impressive work back there. How do you know so much about that sort of thing?'

'I've wanted to be a detective since junior school. A lot of it is common sense, the rest is experience. Some of which you can pick up from TV programmes. We have loads of individuals disappear around here, particularly in the summer. Migrant workers and criminals, poor people too, live on the land in tents and barns. We find quite a few bodies. Obviously, the murders are dealt with by Major Crimes, which is where I want to be permanently.'

'Where do you see yourself ending up?'

'I hope to go all the way. Right to the top.'

Barton considered his next question for a minute as they weaved through the busy Wisbech traffic. Clavell bobbed in and out of lanes as though he'd done it a thousand times before. If Barton could encourage him to look at his behaviour now, it might save plenty of anguish further down the line when the man had more power.

'Would you like some advice?'

'Of course, your opinion is well respected.'

Barton choked down a laugh. Cheeky little twat. 'I'm impressed, but do you realise you upset people with your brusque ways?'

'I've found suspects generally respond to my direct manner.'

'I was talking more about how you spoke to your colleagues.'

Clavell cracked a smile. 'That may have popped up in my last appraisal. I've been working on it. It's greatly improved.'

Barton grinned. It was no wonder Wisbech station were keen for him to get experience elsewhere.

'Policing is dealing with the public. Promotion is politics. People have to respect you, even like you, or they won't perform for you.'

'Be nicer?'

'Not necessarily. Tone down your ambition. If you're too serious, you're no fun to be with. Nobody likes over-confidence or to feel as if they're doormats for your own lofty hopes. A wise politician once spoke some appropriate words. He warned about choking on your aspirations.'

Clavell nodded with understanding. 'Thanks for the advice. Who said that, Margaret Thatcher?'

'No, it was Darth Vader.'

43

DI BARTON

They arrived at a terraced property with a huge pool of thick black water on a cracked, crumbling driveway. They skirted the puddle with suspicion. The peeling windowsills and yellowing curtains gave the impression of a similarly unloved interior. There was no bell. Barton lifted the rusty knocker and let it fall. He half expected the door to split in two. No one answered. A passage at the side separated it from the neighbour's house. They stepped over abandoned tools and pots to the rear.

The overgrown garden resembled wild countryside. Dirt covered the windows, stopping anyone from seeing inside. Cobwebs hung around the top of the door. Paint peelings littered the floor. They returned to the front.

'Perhaps he died,' said Clavell.

Barton rattled the knocker again. The lounge window opened next door, and an elderly man scowled out of it. Barton's glare and size removed that expression quickly.

'Does Barney Trimble still live here?'

'Yes. I saw him a week ago going to the shop to get supplies.' He mimed putting a bottle to his mouth.

'Thank you.'

At that moment, a bolt clanged across inside and Barton was reminded of a dusty tomb in a horror film being slid open as the warped and ill-fitting door moved away from them. A small guy in dirty clothing peered at them with the yellowest eyes Barton had ever seen outside animation.

'Yes.'

'Barney Trimble?'

'Yes.'

They showed their warrants. 'I'm Detective Inspector Barton. We have some questions for you – can we come in?'

'Yes.'

The officers exchanged a glance. Clavell stepped in first. Barton glared at the neighbour until he removed his head from view. When Barton entered the lounge, Clavell stood against the fireplace. The room smelled strange. There was a hint of sweetness to the stale odour Barton had expected. Barton understood why Clavell hadn't taken a seat on the sofa because there was every chance he'd have been sucked into it and not seen again. Clavell took his notebook and pen out.

'Take a seat, gentlemen.'

'It's okay, we won't be long,' said Clavell.

'Do you mind if I do?'

'No, of course not. Make yourself comfortable.'

Trimble slumped into a chair. Barton expected a thump, followed by a billowing of dust, but neither came. It was as if the man were a ghost. Barton nodded at Clavell to begin the questions.

'Mr Trimble. You had an allotment until fairly recently on the road out to Leverington. Can you tell me why you returned it to the council?'

Trimble's breath wheezed out. Barton knew plenty about death and could tell when it was getting near. The old man moistened dry lips with his tongue.

'The council took it back, saying I hadn't been using it. They'd been threatening to do it for years.'

'Why did you stop going?' asked Clavell.

'Why do you think, son? I'm old. I'm ill. They told me I should go into one of those hostel places soon.'

Barton blinked. 'You mean hospice?'

'That's what I said, didn't I? It doesn't matter much. I'm ready.'

'Do you live alone?' Barton continued.

'It seems everyone has forgotten me. I've lived here a long time, but I don't speak to anyone for weeks on end. My partner died over ten years ago.' He tried to rise from his seat. 'Excuse my manners. Would you like a drink? I can't vouch for the milk but it's probably okay.'

Barton's eyes widened. 'We're fine. When was the last time you worked on the allotment?'

'Who knows? Christmas rings a bell.'

'The last one?' asked Clavell.

But Trimble was miles away in his head. 'Yes, I recall that earthquake had just happened. Loads of people died.'

'The Indian Ocean one on Boxing Day?'

'No, don't be daft, not back then. The one in the Caribbean. A bloke I know told me his daughter was there on holiday. I've always remembered that. Must have been a terrible time of worry.'

Barton couldn't help himself. 'Was she okay?'

The man chuckled, temporarily lighting up his face. 'Yes, the stupid old fart had the wrong island. She visited Cuba not – now what was it – Haiti?'

Clavell took his phone out. Ten seconds later, he read out the information. 'Haiti earthquake. Catastrophic, magnitude seven, twenty-five kilometres south of Haiti's capital Port-au-Prince. 12 January 2010.'

'That's the one. That's when the council noticed I hadn't kept the allotment shipshape. I popped over there to see what state it was in. My other half had been dead a while, and I'd given up on it. I felt lonely and lost, I suppose. Gave up on a lot of things. I don't know why. It doesn't make sense as I could have been with my friends down there.'

Barton rubbed his temples. 'You haven't been since your partner passed a decade ago?'

'That's right.'

Clavell frowned. 'Is she buried around here?'

Trimble grinned. 'If I'm honest, I'm enjoying the company, but why so many questions? Is it about the skeleton at the allotments?'

Barton jerked his head back from gazing at the swirling dust above the TV.

'Yes. They found it on your old plot.'

Trimble shrugged. 'You don't say. Well, it wasn't my partner, if that's what you're thinking. We cremated her years ago. Have you asked the new owners? I can't explain it.'

Barton's mind raced while he checked out the room. This might be their last chance to speak to this guy. No pictures adorned the walls or fireplace. That was unusual if Trimble had lived there for years.

'No kids or grandchildren, Mr Trimble?'

'No. I'll die alone.'

Barton shook his head. 'Okay, we'll get going. Is there anything we can do for you?'

'Let yourselves out. It'll take me a while to escape this chair.'

* * *

Barton asked Clavell to drive again on the way to the station. Clavell was silent and clearly not one for idle conversation. Barton recalled the young detective's style.

'You can take this any way you like, but I'd have said you were a little abrupt back there. I know you want to be super-professional, but we're dealing with real people. You must always remember that. We could have stirred up some bad memories for him back there, and then we've left him on his own.'

'We all have our ways. You might like to keep things lighter, but I prefer not to let mistakes slip in. Look at DCI Cox. She's serious.'

Barton frowned, feeling outmanoeuvred. 'She can be charming when she wants to be. If people are relaxed, they talk. You could argue that getting suspects and witnesses to open up is one of our most important skills.'

Clavell nodded but didn't look convinced.

'When we get back,' said Barton, 'make sure you update the system. I'll check and see if the missing persons search has found a match.'

'No problem, sir. I type fast.'

Barton picked up his phone and rang Cox. He wondered if Clavell would prove too smart for his own good. He had a lot to learn about people.

44

DI BARTON

Barton headed for DCI Cox's office when they returned. He knocked and received a beckon through the glass.

'Any fresh news?' he asked.

'The incident room is ready. You'll have a HOLMES operator by tomorrow morning. The nationals have been given enough rope so that most of the country will be gossiping about it. We've released a phone number for those with more information. No hits yet from the mispers, but they've only contacted half of them. We'll try again tonight.' She flexed her fingers. Barton noticed a white stain on her suit jacket. It was probably from one of the yoghurts she loved to eat. He'd seen it on the suit the day before, which was unlike her. She seemed to visibly steel herself to concentrate.

'So, definitely not the man who had the allotment prior to the current owners?'

'If Mortis is right about the age of the skeleton, he couldn't have done it. Not without help. I believed him because he looked like he's been ill for years. I don't even think he'd have been fit to assist someone, never mind do it himself. That said, a person close to him might know that he didn't use his allotment, and therefore the remains wouldn't be disturbed. If Trimble knows anything, he'll take it to the grave. He's very poorly.'

'Hmm. What's your plan?'

'I intended to chat to the team today, but they have interviews, statements, exhibits, you name it, to sort out. Let's get all the paperwork entered and everything on HOLMES and the other IT systems. We'll have a meeting tomorrow at midday. Hopefully someone will contact us in the meantime. Mortis' post-mortem might shed some light on the circumstances. Although, he said getting a specialist to look at the bones will take much longer.'

'Good idea. Initial thoughts?'

'Seeing as it's out in the Fens, it could be anyone, but I'd put money on it being a foreign national. However, the body hasn't got any signs of damage on it, except for an old break. That muddies the water because it rules out guns, knives, RTCs and fatal beatings. I suppose it's possible he crawled in there to keep warm and suffocated.'

'I didn't think of that. Maybe not a murder.'

'No, but unlikely. Let's find out who he was. Then we'll have something to go at. If we know where he lived, we can see how near it is to the allotment, speak to his friends and neighbours, talk to his work colleagues. I reckon it'll be straightforward then.'

'They chose a clever place to hide the body. Do you reckon that narrows down the culprits?'

'Again, it almost creates more suspects. Gardeners understand how fast things decompose in a compost heap, but so would a scientist. Maybe they planned to conceal it there the whole time. Just as likely, it could have been a person who lives nearby who had an inspired moment. I'll sleep on it. But I reckon we met the killer or a person who knew the killer today. Someone somewhere will be shitting themselves now we've found the remains. Allotments don't figure in most people's worlds. It might be one of the gardeners or a relative, or even someone who walks past, but the night they buried him wasn't their first night in there.'

'Clever, you're right. Talking of which, how did you find Mr Clavell?'

'Impressive, ambitious, and abrasive.'

'Yes, he reminds me of someone.'

'Hannibal Lecter?'

'Very funny. Although, his last boss described him as being rather serious to the point of darkness. Think closer to home.'

Barton scowled at her. 'Surely not me?'

'Of course not. I'm referring to me. I possessed that same

drive. Work with him, please. He can be your project. Shave down some of those rough edges. Results are everything and, if he is as good as I'm led to believe, our chances of success are much higher with him involved. I'll be at your meeting tomorrow.'

DCI Cox turned, stared at her computer and began typing.

Barton had seated himself at his desk by the time it registered that she'd insulted him. Strange and Zander returned a few minutes later. They dropped into chairs near him.

'Anything?' asked Barton.

'We've got a lot of information and I'm not looking forward to sieving through it. Those old folk love to chat. There's nothing obvious though. No one knows of anyone that went missing. There are plenty of gangmasters in Wisbech with a lawless approach to HR, and it isn't easy getting much out of that community.'

'Okay. No problem. Let's get it typed up. There'll be a wash-up meeting at midday tomorrow. We'll pool what we have so far then.'

'What are you doing tonight?' asked Zander. 'Fancy a beer?'

'I'm going to the gym at eight, if you'd rather?' said Strange.

Barton stared from good to evil, and back again. 'I don't know what it is about a tricky investigation that makes me want to drink neat alcohol, but I'm going to resist. I'll see you on the cycling machines. We can go out on the booze when this has been solved.'

Strange laughed. 'I'll put it in the diary for Christmas.'

Zander growled at Barton. 'You've changed.'

45

THE SOUL KILLER

I closed my eyelids last night but didn't sleep. I don't think it was anything to do with Stone being found, because I've made my choices in that respect. If the police are better, well, I bow to their superior skills. It's Claudia. She's back to not replying to my calls or messages: three of the latter yesterday and nothing in return.

This morning I lay in bed and remembered when I knew, without doubt, we were the perfect match. Her sister had invited her to an end-of-season hockey awards presentation. Annabelle had been voted players' player of the season. She wanted her father and sister to be there. Seemed fair enough to me. I guess it's a big deal to be admired by your fellow players. Claudia wanted me to come. I heard her arguing with Annabelle, who was saying it was just close family because it was a small hall. Claudia stood her ground and said she wouldn't go otherwise.

It was a warm night, but Claudia's hand shook as we walked towards the Bull Hotel in town. She stopped before the function rooms and pulled me into the quiet bar area.

'Wait a minute, let me prepare myself.'

I didn't recognise that version of Claudia. Nothing else seemed to faze her. She took so many deep breaths, I was concerned she might be struggling to breathe.

'What's wrong?'

'Get me a vodka, straight.'

When I came back from the bar, she was sitting in a quiet corner, but she'd calmed down. It's a pleasant upmarket place and the carpeted floors and wood panelling gave a secluded feel. I sat next to her and waited.

'I know all these girls from school. They were the popular ones who were good at sport. Annabelle was brilliant at every game she played. I tried out for the team but wasn't good enough. They put me in defence and I kept making mistakes. Annabelle was on my team and she shouted out, "For God's sake, Blobbia," and the name stuck at school for a bit.'

'What a bitch!'

'It was kind of her pet name for me when we were growing up, because I was a bit chubby, well, fat's probably closer. She said it just slipped out because she was frustrated at losing.'

I sipped my drink, unsure what to say. There had always been a barrier between her sister and me. It sounded as if Claudia would be better off without her, but I needed her to work that out.

'I hate bullies.'

'Me, too, but we were only twelve and it only lasted for a few years, but I never felt comfortable around that group. It didn't matter as we got older because I was much more studious. I wasn't always this much fun, you know!'

She reached across and intertwined our fingers.

'I'm here for you. It'll be fine.'

'I know, I'm just being silly. For a moment, I just felt a bit like a thirteen year old girl being called names as I waddled around the field or the dinner hall.'

'Didn't Annabelle stick up for you?'

'We weren't always as close as we are now. She's struggled since we left school. Everything came so easily for her back then, but life can be hard for people like that when they leave full-time education. They haven't learned how to really work for things, so don't think badly of her.'

I looked away to hide the sneer on my face.

'Come on, let them see what you've blossomed into. No one will be mean tonight.'

She downed her drink with a grimace and we linked arms, arriving at a function room. There were plenty of spare chairs and tables. I watched Annabelle get her reward and thank her father, but that was it. Claudia chatted to everyone there, and they loved her. We had a couple of slow dances where she made me feel as if I'd had my prayers answered. I must confess to struggling to relax as I kept looking for insults. Nobody seemed to come close to us when we were together.

Claudia chatted to her sister and congratulated her. I didn't bother because she seemed to be pleased enough as it was. There was a strong bond between them, but the healthiness of it concerned me. Deep down I've always understood that it would come down to a choice between her sister and me. The odds were stacked towards her twin, but I think Claudia and I saw Annabelle for the person she really was that night. I was pleased as I knew it might help with tough decisions in the future.

Recalling that night makes me want to take action to keep things heading the way I want, but today is a pivotal one. I do some stretches to find some peace and drive to work without managing any breakfast.

I walk into the incident room early and find a seat in the corner, which is perfect. I'll need to see who, if anyone, is a threat. Despite what the papers tell you, the police solve most serious crimes. We don't have time to deal with burglaries and petty thefts, and cannabis prosecutions are a joke. But as the office fills up I comprehend why murders are different. It is the ultimate crime.

When you kill someone, it's decisive. Once you've taken that person out, there's no coming back. My mother, the lecturer, Donald, Malcolm, and that arsehole, Stone, can never interfere again. I've beaten them. They cannot harm me any more.

People recognise that finality. Everyone's here with determination in their eyes, unable to step back from the irresistible lure of the drama of death. Sure, rape is a terrible violation. Offences against children are worse, but it's not the end. Lives are ruined by such actions, but they aren't over. Only a person who is prepared to kill invokes the strongest emotions, but catching me, one of their own, won't be easy.

DI Barton arrives and heads to the front of the room. I can't help but respect him. He's an officer with a sense of fair play. I think that deep down he'd empathise with my actions, even if he wouldn't condone them. There's a strong team here. Zander is not a guy to mess with. He's been to the bottom, just as I have. We could have been friends under different circumstances. I love Strange's peppery personality, too. She sometimes reminds me of that feisty Charlie from university.

The temperature of the room slowly rises because of the amount of people present and I notice that upstart, Clavell, is sweating like a cheap burger. Barton clears his throat.

'Ladies and gentlemen. Thank you for getting here on time and for your hard work yesterday. I'm here to tell you we've received a lead. An hour ago, a woman in North Yorkshire rang the helpline after seeing the BBC news about the body found in Wisbech. She thinks her son vanished in the New Year. DCI Cox has the information. Ma'am.'

'Thank you, John. I also appreciate all your efforts and first class work. DC James Clavell, in particular, impressed. Mrs Cynthia Stone reported that her boy in Peterborough disappeared without a trace. He was never much for keeping in touch but would visit once or twice a year. She feared the worst when her mobile phone stopped working in February, because he paid for it so they could stay in contact.'

'And the teeth?' asked Strange.

'Confirmed. He had an unusually narrow upper arch, meaning there wasn't enough space for all the teeth to come through. She said the schoolkids picked on him mercilessly about it. I called her. She paints a picture of a bit of a sad loner. Even though an earlier assessment proved inconclusive, she suspects he had Asperger's. Arnold Stone, age twenty-eight, had no friends at school as far as she could tell, and this continued into adulthood. He was awkward with people he didn't know.

'This meant he kept away from others for fear of being misunderstood. As if the poor man didn't have enough problems, he also struggled with deafness. The schoolkids were cruel about that, too, meaning he hated anyone knowing. He owned hearing aids, but was extremely adept at lip reading and often didn't wear them. When he listened to people talking, he would always stare at the speaker's lips, which some people found unsettling. His last known address was 1, River End.'

Things have moved faster than I expected. I raise my hand but Malik beats me to it. 'Hey, Whitlam. Don't you live at River End?'

46

THE SOUL KILLER

The whole place turns to me in unison. I will need a Robert-De-Niro-standard performance, but I'm ready.

'Yeah, I'm at number three. Did you say Arnold Stone?'

The room stares back to DCI Cox, and I take a deep breath.

She looks my way and takes a step towards me. 'Correct. Do you know him?'

'That's weird. He was on my list yesterday to ring and the name looked familiar. The telephone bit tallies as well because the number she left had been disconnected. A bloke who lived two doors away from me left abruptly at Christmas. I think I only ever talked to him three or four times. I went in his house on a couple of occasions to carry a delivery in for him but never visited socially.'

'Is the property still empty?' asked Barton.

'Not any more. It's been empty for a while as a couple backed out at the last minute, but a new family moved in a week or two back.'

'There goes the crime scene. What was Stone like?' said Cox.

'I don't really know. He seemed odd the few occasions I talked to him. When I took the last parcel around, he was on the phone. He told me to bring it in and put it on the sofa for him. Not asked, ordered. When I spoke, he stared hard at me. I thought he was rude. But if he lip read, that would account for that. Actually, the guy who lives in-between us was always complaining about the music from next door. The walls are thin, so the sound passes through them. I often found myself humming along to it in the street.'

'There's a possible motive there,' said Clavell. 'Looks as though we ought to be having a word with your neighbour.'

A hubbub of chatter broke out as people discussed the case with those sitting near them.

'That's a valid point. I don't suppose the guy who lives between you is a shaven headed psychopath?' asked Cox wearily.

'Robin? No. He's pretty quiet, but the music drove him to distraction. Not long before Stone disappeared, Robin said he couldn't stand it any longer.'

47

DI BARTON

Barton clapped his hands twice.

'Okay, everyone. Calm down. This clearly sends the investigation in a new direction. We'll need to visit this Robin Rowe asap. Does he work, Whitlam?'

Whitlam appeared very relaxed for someone whose neighbour had been found dead in a compost heap. Saying that, he wasn't a man who got too excited or emotional about anything. Barton didn't know Whitlam that well. He was very much the type who came to work and did a professional job but had little interest in most social activities. That said, Barton knew he could rely on him if they were dealing with the more shocking cases.

'Yes. His car is usually back by the time I get home at six.'

'Do you know where he works?'

'No idea.'

'And the family who've moved in?'

'I've only seen a woman and a baby. The houses are small. I'd guess at her being a single mum with one child, so she should be there during the day.'

'Right. Jobs, people. Arnold Stone's mother is in a wheelchair so she won't be coming in to see us. Whitlam, go with Sergeant Strange and talk to her. Liaise with North Yorkshire's family liaison team and see if they'll meet you there. It's a sparsely populated area, so please do the visit yourselves otherwise. You both know what you're doing. I want to move fast because the person responsible might be panicking.

'Don't tell her that you were neighbours, but we need as much background information as possible. Ask for an up-to-date photo and take a picture of it. If he didn't have friends, he may have had enemies. Clavell, ring CSI, and send them to River End. Malik, check Stone's social media footprint. Zander, grab a DC and return to Wisbech and the allotment. Maybe the gardeners will remember someone who looked like that. A current photo will help with questioning when it's available.'

'We won't get much from his house after so long and especially now another family has moved in,' said Clavell.

'That's what I'd have thought, but I had coffee with Sirena, the crime scene manager, and—'

Barton waited for the good-natured cheers to die away. 'Quiet, children, please. I talked to her about just that. Apparently, you'd be surprised. CSI techniques advance daily. The team can enter a house years later and pick up minute traces of DNA from people who've been in the property in the past. It's called low grade or low template DNA.

'This is where the problems with DNA stem from. It's too good in some respects. If I shook your hand and then got a pistol and shot my wife, they'd probably be able to match you to the handle of the gun. Maybe even put you at the scene. Therefore, it isn't always admissible. Having said that, it helps with the big picture.'

Barton noticed that Clavell nodded appreciatively. He wanted to learn.

'Let's get to it. We'll all meet back here tomorrow at the same time unless you hear differently. By then, we should have pictures of the victim, an idea of his social and working circle, have spoken to the landlord, and checked out what the neighbour has to say. Perhaps he'll confess, and I'll bring in cakes for everyone.'

Barton observed them as they filtered out. Most had been fired up by the news. Clavell had also held back and watched the others leave. As the last person left, Barton realised Clavell observed Whitlam with narrowed eyes. He would discuss that with him later.

48

THE SOUL KILLER

Strange and I are off to a place on the outskirts of Skipton in the Yorkshire Dales to see Arnold Stone's mother. Strange has volunteered to drive, which is fine by me. She has an unusual style. Even though it's one of the older pool cars, she accelerates rapidly with fast, firm gear changes. There's a hint of rally driver about it. It's another tick in her box.

The family liaison officer couldn't make it until the morning, so we'll deliver the news. Most officers are well used to giving such bad tidings. For many it's the worst part of the job. I don't mind doing them because someone has to do it. It's usual to go in pairs, one of each sex. Compassion is called for, but there's no point in being vague or delaying. The facts won't improve.

As death messages go, delivering one to a mother is always difficult even if, as in this case, they are expecting the worst. Even though Arnold was nearly thirty, his mum would see him through the prism of being a parent. She'd remember him as a baby.

How much time is spent raising a child? It's a lot of lessons over decades: so many hours, so much commitment. For most mothers, obviously not mine, losing your children is like an artist having their life's work ripped up. There's no starting again. It's simply too late, and impossible to comprehend. People like Zander, who learn to function again, are to be admired.

It's interesting what they said about Arnold being deaf and a person with a disability. It explains a lot, and I do regret killing him, but I think that's more because my time as a policeman is coming to an end faster than I envisaged. The developments in the case mean I'll soon have to play one of my final cards.

Strange eases back as the traffic thickens on the A1. I pretend to check something in a folder on the rear seat and sneak a peek at her profile. She's understated and cool, much like myself. She has the same detachment and bearing as if she's not quite being involved in the world. She'll make someone a good wife. The kind you could drive to the seaside with, park up, watch the tide come in, have chips out of paper, enjoy an ice cream, and not have to say a single word. Because you'd know.

That's what Claudia and I had. Yet, it slips through our fingers. Is she the one after all? I'd be surprised if I was wrong about her. In some ways, she feels like my life's work. I don't want to start again. She's been strong up to now, but I suspect this latest news will break us apart. I hoped never to have to admit to what happened, but I may have no choice. Better to confess than for them to come for me when the evidence points in my direction.

I pick up my phone and give her a ring, not expecting her to pick up, but she does.

'Hi.'

'Hi, Claudia. I'm free for a chat if you've got a few minutes.'

'Sorry, David. I've just got Annabelle settled back at home. One of the neighbours rang to say she'd been walking around the street in her nightie. He said she'd been looking in people's bins.'

I can't help a little chuckle at the thought of Annabelle looking for her family amongst the trash. She really has begun to crumble. 'Perhaps it's time for her to get serious medical help.'

'I won't give up on her. It's just so hard when I'm so busy at work. I can't be here for her.'

Admirable sentiment but foolish. I've found a lot of women lack basic common sense. Sticking with evil men, letting thieving junkie children back in the house, and sometimes just doing the right thing. Life's simpler than they make it.

'Perhaps you could get someone to live in until you're home from work. A carer.'

'No, she wouldn't tolerate a stranger in the house.'

I smile again. I knew that. 'How about a stay in a residential place? It wouldn't be for long.'

I enjoy the silence, knowing full well that it's simple to enter those places, but not so easy to leave.

'I'll think about it all. Work have given me a few days off, but I can't keep expecting them to do that.'

Claudia should stop thinking. Her default decision should be to accept whatever I say. I'm rarely wrong. Let me take these choices from her and take the strain. It will be for the best.

'What can I do to help?' I ask.

'Nothing. It just needs to be me and her for the moment. I'm sure you understand. I've got to go. I can hear her crying again.'

I attempt to distract myself with the fantastic scenery once we leave the main roads. It's the kind of place where you could disappear, or easily hide a body. Perhaps I should have thought of somewhere like this. There's a heavy drizzle making the roads slippery, but we meet little traffic as we follow the signs. It's weird to see the houses built on hills, especially coming from somewhere so flat.

'Okay, turn the satnav on. We can't be too far away,' says Strange.

We pull up outside some retirement housing. A dirty plaque announces it as Happy Memories Court. It's not too shabby, but it's getting old, and there's an unloved feel to the place. Even though many people must live here, we don't see a single soul.

'Let's be courteous and go to the reception,' says Strange.

We walk through a deserted outside seating area, which is reminiscent of Chernobyl. I open a sliding door to what looks more like a kitchen than an office, but there's no one around. I stare at the poster pinned on a cupboard.

> Happy Memories.
>
> Non-resident management staff and Careline Alarms service. Lounge, laundry, garden. Whole site accessible by wheelchair. Regular social activities include: weekly coffee morning. New residents taken from 55 years of age. Cats only accepted but not replaced when gone.

It should say welcome to hell. Bring your happy memories because you won't make new ones.

A purple haired lady shuffles in on a walker. 'If you're looking for the manager, let me know when you find the useless git.'

I laugh. 'Okay, we're after a Mrs Stone. Shall we just go to her apartment?'

The woman chuckles a surprisingly dirty chuckle. 'If you mean her poky bedsit, it's down there on the right.' Her smile slips away. 'You're here about the son, aren't you? He was an odd bugger, but this'll devastate her. I'll wait here. Let me know when you've told her.'

We wander down past some small units. The final one has a wheelchair parked on a narrow porch. Strange taps her car key on the glass. A shaking hand pulls back a curtain, and I catch a glimpse of grey hair. The door slides open and we hear, 'Come in.'

'Ladies first.'

Strange puts her palm on my shoulder and shoves me in. 'I'm no lady.'

We enter a reasonable-sized bedroom with a tiny kitchen attached. A slight whiff of tobacco hangs in the air.

'Take a seat, please.' A lady with only wisps of hair on her head points to what might be a rickety sofa but could just as easily be something the Spanish Inquisition designed. The woman sits on the edge of the bed. 'Was it him?'

She's staring at me, so I nod. People react in various ways. This woman is a weeper. We sit quietly and try not to fidget on the uncomfortable seat.

She's still looking at me when she recovers. Old school. She thinks I'm in charge. 'How did he die?'

'His skeleton was found in a compost heap in Wisbech. We believe someone hid the body there. The post-mortem has come back inconclusive. There's no noticeable damage apart from the historic upper-arm break you spoke about over the phone. No knife or gun wounds. It's still possible he died of natural causes.'

The woman gasps but her expression changes. 'I only talked to him on Christmas morning. How comes he's already a skeleton?'

'Organic material decomposes fast with heat and bacteria.' I pass her a photograph of the teeth in the skull. It's brutal but best all round if we're sure immediately. 'His smile is unique.'

She's more rueful than upset. That happens. The journey of acceptance can be a short one if life has been tough. 'Yes, they're his all right. He didn't have the best start in life. In some ways, he never stood a chance. His disadvantages made him spiteful and aggressive. He hated sympathy.' She wipes a fat tear from her cheek with her arm. 'Arnold tried to be good to me, though. He loved Amazon. I'd get gifts and things sent from them regularly.'

'Did he have any enemies?'

Her mouth twitches with a hint of a smile. 'He annoyed everyone he met but not enough to be killed. Well, I don't think so. I'll be no help to you. The only thing I know of him recently was that he found a group he connected with. It seemed they were strange people, too.'

'Are we talking loners or some kind of cult?' I say.

'That's what I asked him. They were just a bit odd. Fancy being interested in wizards and things at their age.'

I nod with respect at her stoicism.

'Is there anything you know that might help? You haven't given us much to go on,' asks Strange.

'You'll need a picture. Hang on.' She patters to the fridge. Strange and I exchange glances. With trembling fingers, the old woman pulls a photo off the side of it. 'It's the only one I have of him smiling. He was going to his first war battle or something. He couldn't wait. And there, he has his father's gold watch on. Jim didn't leave much behind apart from six bottles of undrinkable home-brewed brandy and that watch. He had it engraved to Arnold. On the back it simply said, "My Boy".'

Strange stands and passes her business card to Mrs Stone.

'Someone will call tomorrow morning from the family liaison team. They'll help you with all the necessary arrangements and will be your point of contact. But if you think of anything that might help, then please ring me.'

'Thank you.'

There is little else to say. I shake her hand with the thought forefront in my mind that I killed her son. The woman doesn't release her grip. We look into each other's eyes and I wonder if, on some level, she knows. I avert my gaze and see a crucifix hanging on the wall.

It reminds me of my mother. She believed in God, Jesus and

heaven, or at least her version of it. What exactly do I believe? I recall her lessons. She taught me to repent to save my soul. If you've erred from His lessons, you must seek forgiveness before the end. And the end is coming.

'What do I do now?' she asks.

'Pardon?' I forgot where I was for a moment.

'Now what?'

'Oh, I see. Your liaison officer will arrange for you to be picked up and escorted to the hospital for a formal identification. The remains, your son, will be released shortly so you can bury him. That might take a while, depending on the focus and direction of the investigation. We'll get this photograph copied and returned as soon as possible.'

'No, I meant with myself. He was all I had. I lived for his gifts and funny texts. This isn't a life in here. I wish I'd died in the accident with his father, and that happened twenty years ago.'

That's a damning indictment of our care-home system, and also a resounding echo of what my mother believed with regard to being separated from her soul mate. There's little I can offer to ease her pain.

'We're sorry for your loss. Here's some leaflets on bereavement and there are charities such as Cruse who will be able to listen. We'll get to the bottom of this for you. If you want to ring us, of course you may. Can we do anything for you now? Perhaps drive you to a friend or family. A resident in the office said she'll visit you after we've gone.'

The woman shakes her head. She seems to shrink as she closes the door on us.

I knock on the window of the office and watch the old lady shuffle down the path towards Mrs Stone. Strange gawps at me as we get in the car. Her bloodshot eyes blink away tears.

'Didn't that affect you, David?'

This world is full of suffering and sadness, but many deserve it. If that old lady had done a better job with her son, then things might have been different. Strange doesn't want to hear that. The truth would chill her, even though deep down she may well agree.

'I try not to focus on the emotion while I'm doing the job. It tends to bother me later, when I've had time to dwell on it.'

She raises an eyebrow at me. 'You're a cool customer. That was brutal, even for me.'

'Older people prefer their facts straight.' I think back to what the woman said and shrug. 'I kind of agree with her. If you've lost everything, what is there to hang around for?'

'You have to start something new. Learn to live again.'

'Very poetic, but really? At their age and in that place? People quit when they've had enough. Did you see the crucifix on the wall? If she has faith, then she believes something better is waiting for her. Some young people are prepared to die as martyrs knowing paradise awaits. Mrs Stone's future on Earth looked bleak to me. Anyway, she didn't give us much except the watch thing. A big, flash item such as that might have caught someone's eye.'

Strange drummed her fingers on the steering wheel. 'It sounds as if Arnold was hard to be around. Modern life is a bit like a pressure cooker. If he was continually antagonising people, being rude, playing his music too loud, perhaps it was only a matter of time before someone snapped.'

I bob my head in agreement. It's nice to hear some common sense. That was exactly what happened. This will be like a four piece jigsaw to Mr Barton.

49

DI BARTON

Barton trundled down River End. He tutted at the state of the road. Right at the bottom, he found three small houses in a row and stopped. A woman opened the door of the first one and stepped outside. Even though the sun had made an appearance, Barton thought it wasn't warm enough for that much skin to be on show. She wrestled a pram through the doorway. Judging by the shaking, he hoped the baby wasn't inside. He got out of the car and walked over.

'Allow me,' he said.

Heavily made-up eyes glowered at them. 'Who are you?'

'DI Barton and DC Clavell. Are you Chantelle Bowden?' he said as he lifted the pram up high and guided it out.

'That's right. What's he done now?'

'Who?'

'I've told you idiots before. We're not together any more. I don't speak to him. That's why I've moved here. To get away from that clown.'

Clavell tensed next to him. The younger man pressed forward.

'We're here about the person who lived here beforehand. We wondered if any of his things are still here, in the loft maybe. Crime scene investigators will need to have a look around and take some samples. I'd also appreciate you not calling me an idiot.'

Barton shook his head as Clavell and Bowden glared at each

other and debated if it was the start of World War Three or the beginnings of a beautiful relationship.

'You should have said. Sorry, but I'm going to a new mothers' coffee meeting with Saffy. I don't know anyone here. Without friends, I'll struggle.' Her shoulders drooped. 'Wait there a moment.' She nipped back inside and returned carrying a sleeping baby. 'Look, my ex was a thieving little prick, so I know the score. Come back at five, and you can come in and do what you want.'

She locked the door behind her and, with an exhausted expression, set off down the street. Barton called out after her.

'I don't suppose you discovered a big bloodstain on the carpet when you moved in?'

She finally smiled. 'It was extremely clean and totally empty. The landlord's due at half five to fix the tap. He should be able to help.'

'Nice question,' said Clavell, when she had gone.

Barton knocked on number two without any reply, so they returned to the car.

'There's nothing to do for a while. A few hours aren't going to make any difference to anything. If we come back at five, we chat to her, then the landlord, and finally the neighbour. It'll make us a bit late tonight, so I can drop you at home for a while.'

'Sure,' said Clavell. 'Although I don't mind working through.'

'I'll drive you back. This job will burn you up if you let it. Try to keep some outside interests and stick to them. Do you have a girlfriend?'

'No. I kind of focus on work. There was a girl at school. We dated all through the sixth form. I did a degree, then got a job while I waited for vacancies in the police. She travelled through America for a year, but I stayed as they said they were going to advertise for staff. It wasn't easy being apart so much, but we stuck at it.

'While I trained, she completed her last term at college in Bristol, so we saw each other even less. The next time we met, she seemed different. We struggled for things to say. She said she wanted to focus on her exams and we should take a step back, but she'd catch up with me after the term finished.'

'Cool.'

Clavell turned abruptly, and Barton noticed the memory was still raw to him. 'I meant, as in frosty.'

'Yeah. You can probably just about remember what training was like. It's full on and exciting. I was swept away with everything. Before I knew it, six months passed by without contact. Next time I met her was the following Christmas. She happened to be in the same pub. When she stood up to leave, she had a bigger belly than Santa himself. I think she has three kids now.'

Barton pulled up at Clavell's address. He'd moved into a room in a big old Victorian house for his secondment. Landlords loved them for homes of multiple occupancy. 'What's this place like?'

'All right, but there's a lot of noise and it can be tiresome getting in the bathroom.'

'You should be able to grab a shower now. I'll pick you up at quarter to five.'

'Thanks.'

'You know you can always talk to me, about anything. On or off the record.'

'I know.'

Clavell looked as though he was about to add to that, but then leapt from the car. Barton watched him fiddle with his key at the door. He had the same defeated air that the young mother had displayed earlier. That was the first time Clavell had mentioned his past. This job ruined relationships, that was for sure. He remembered Ginger again. That man had lost everything. Barton hadn't thought of him for a while, yet in the immediate aftermath he'd often been at the front of his mind. Once you're gone, you're soon forgotten.

A light came on in the top floor. A cigarette butt sailed out of the window underneath. Barton had warmed to Clavell. It sounded as if he'd sacrificed a lot to get where he was. He hoped it'd be worth it.

50

DI BARTON

Barton pootled home. A shadow of gloom had descended, as it often did when dealing with others' personal lives. The children would be back from school and some Holly-time would raise his spirits. An amazing smell greeted him as he took off his shoes. His mouth watered as he stepped towards the kitchen and discovered the three kids and Holly scraping their plates clean in companionable silence. Wrappers from the local fish and chip shop littered the work surface.

'Uh-oh, we're in trouble,' said Luke.

'That's strange. This man looks a bit like your father. Perhaps it's a hologram or something,' said Holly.

'I hope there's a big plate for me in the microwave.'

Lawrence took an apple from the fruit bowl in the middle of the table and polished it on his T-shirt. 'What kind of family would we be if we hamstrung your efforts at weight loss by dangling this fatty rubbish in front of your nose after a hard day of protecting the innocent?'

With that, he handed Barton the apple. Lawrence, Layla and Luke all rose and departed in a well-practised move in an attempt to escape any washing up duties. Holly collected their plates and plopped them in the bowl. She threw a tea towel at her husband.

'You can dry.'

'Not on your nelly. It'd be like the final insult.'

'You said you wanted to eat healthily.'

'I meant we all should be good, not sneak around having takeaways behind my back. I feel as though I've come home and found you in bed with a neighbour.'

Holly laughed. 'No, you missed him by a few minutes. You know the retired postman from number nine. What did you used to call him?'

'Hairy Harrison.'

'That's it. He's my lover.'

'So that's why I keep finding furballs.'

Holly snuggled between his arms. 'It's lovely you're back early. You home for good?'

'No, just an hour. I've got some visits tonight.'

'We barely see you these days. Why don't we go and have a few drinks down the road later? Lawrence can listen out for Luke.'

'Because I'll wake up tomorrow with a mini hangover and want to eat my bodyweight in processed pork products. I can't consume calories when I'm working out.'

'Really? I imagined you on the rowing machine leaning forward with Kelly firing Ferrero Rocher into your mouth with each stroke. How about the cinema? I'll take some fruit.'

'Okay, I'll try to get away in time.'

They caught up as they tidied. 'Lawrence's form tutor rang to say she was really impressed with the extra effort he's been putting in. The other teachers have also commented. That's why we bought fish and chips. It was his choice for being serious about his future.'

'Excellent.' Barton blew out a breath and wondered whether he had his own priorities mixed up. He should talk to Lawrence. Holly pushed him into a seat and sat on his knee. She chuckled as she pretended to look in his ear.

'I've got everything covered here. We'll catch up properly soon, when you're not running at full pelt. A few hours tonight away from it will do you some good, maybe some distance from it will help.'

He squeezed her in, happy that she understood.

'Thanks, sweetie.'

'I assume this guy in the compost heap was murdered.'

'It looks likely. Although, it could be something else, like the prevention of the lawful and decent burial of a dead body. Anyway, I've got an up-and-coming detective on secondment. We'll have this solved in no time.'

51

DI BARTON

Barton collected Clavell and arrived at River End in bright sunshine. Clavell said nothing at all in the car, as though the earlier conversations hadn't occurred. Barton put his new sunglasses on as he stepped out of the vehicle.

'Very Brad Pitt. Are they Ray-Bans?' asked Clavell after pressing the bell.

'They were a quid from Poundland.'

'Come in,' said the tenant. She'd removed her make-up and looked about seventeen years old. Barton peered over her shoulder at a clean house with little furniture. He and Clavell put on some boot covers and gloves but he detected a strong smell of bleach, a sure-fire DNA killer.

'I notice you like the minimalist style,' said Barton.

'Yeah, I find it suits seeing as I don't have any stuff. You want a coffee?'

She turned the kettle on while she gave them the tour. They were finished before the water boiled.

'You've been here two weeks?' asked Clavell.

'That's right.'

'Where did you live before?'

'Nottingham.'

'Your boyfriend got a record?'

'Correct.' She tilted her head at Clavell. 'My ex-boyfriend. Is he always this nosey?'

'He's usually worse. I think we can put you to the bottom of our list of suspects.' He made a mental note to discuss Clavell's direct questioning again. Barton found the occasional smile produced far better answers.

The landlord arrived looking harassed. Barton asked him to step outside to answer the questions seeing as there wasn't really room for four adults in the lounge.

'I'm going to talk. You stop me if I have it wrong. Arnold Stone owed you rent. He was a little behind all the time, but not enough for you to chuck him out. Then, he disappeared. There's nothing you can do for a while, apart from come around and keep knocking. The guidelines state you can't enter legally if you believe the tenant still occupies the property. The rules are greyer on abandonment. After a while, you leave a note on the door and let yourself in a week later. If the authorities query it, you're making sure it's safe.'

'I wouldn't like to agree completely with that. My tenants are treated with respect and dignity.'

'I'm not the council. Your tenant turned up dead. Maybe you rowed about his arrears and cut his head off. Then drove to a friend's allotment and hid the remains.'

'Don't be ridiculous. I've got twenty properties and am well used to people doing a runner when they get too far behind. Decapitating them would be satisfying but running the business from prison would be tricky.'

'Were there any signs of a struggle?'

'No. It looked like he'd just got up and gone. Most of his stuff was missing. There was nothing of value anyway. I cleared the remainder out. I'm only required to keep it for a short time, but being a reasonable man—' he glanced from Clavell to Barton, 'I kept them for a couple of months. Then I painted the walls magnolia, hired a cleaning company, and let it out again. I've still got a bin liner of what he left. It's just clothing, old paperwork, and a mobile phone.'

'Show me,' said Clavell.

'It's back in my shed. I tried turning the phone on and charging it. Neither worked. Some water leaked out after I picked it up. I bet that was why he didn't take it.'

They peered out of the door as a red hatchback trundled past. A thin man with a pasty complexion and the beginnings of retreating hair jumped from the car and scuttled by with his head down. He didn't look over at the three men on the path next to him. Barton spotted Clavell's jaw bunching.

'Don't go anywhere for thirty minutes. We might have more questions,' said Barton.

'I've got things to do. That tap for a start.'

Quick as a flash, Clavell replied, 'The tap can wait until our crime scene people have had a look. Would you like to wait in our vehicle or your own, sir?'

The landlord strode to his car. Barton and Clavell pressed the bell at the adjoining house.

The door opened slowly to reveal a worried man who bit his bottom lip as he waited for them to speak. He stared directly between the detectives. Barton shifted his position so the man's eyes were in line with his. The man lowered his gaze.

'Robin Rowe?' asked Barton.

'That's me. How can I help?'

Heavy eyebags indicated a lack of sleep. There was something very off about his behaviour. Barton guessed this man would crack with minimal pressure.

'Can we come in? Your neighbour has been found dead in suspicious circumstances. You need to answer some questions.'

52

DI BARTON

Twenty minutes later, Clavell peered down at his notes with a furrowed brow. The story didn't add up, but Rowe hardly seemed capable of extreme violence.

'In summary,' Clavell said, 'you spoke to the victim on Boxing Day morning and argued about his music. You describe him as a horrible, homophobic person who called you a shirt-lifter to your face. In fact, he's been the bane of your life ever since he moved in. You stayed out late that night but would rather not say where, even though what you were doing wasn't illegal. However, you know nothing about Arnold Stone's burial.'

'Exactly.'

Barton took over. 'Tell us where you were. If we are able to confirm your alibi, then you'll be ruled out as a suspect.'

'I'm under suspicion now, am I? Look at me, Inspector. Do I seem the body burying type?'

'I admit that you don't fit the typical mould, but homophobia causes all manner of extreme reactions, as can loud music. Especially if it's over a sustained period. Angry confrontations can easily escalate. You clearly aren't telling us everything. Did he provoke you? Did he do something else to anger you? We could take you in for obstruction. Then you'd have to tell us.'

Robin tittered. 'Or what? You'll fine me, or lock me up for a few weeks? I had nothing to do with his disappearance. So, there's no need to say who I was with. You haven't charged me.

England isn't a totalitarian state yet, I believe, and I have my rights.'

Barton laid out the stark facts. 'This crime could be murder. It doesn't get more serious. Your strange behaviour makes me believe you know more than you've said. I agree with you completely. You seem an unlikely killer, so who are you protecting?'

'I won't say another word without legal representation.'

'Fair enough. Come to the station to assist with our enquiries. You can call a solicitor there if necessary.'

'You still haven't accused me of anything. I'm not going anywhere.'

'I have reason to now suspect that you're assisting an offender. I could arrest you for that if you want, but it's a serious offence, punishable by years in prison. Think hard now, as you don't look like someone who would enjoy being locked up.'

Rowe's face whitened so fast that if he'd been a pensioner, Barton would have called an ambulance. Then Rowe crossed his arms. A minute later, Barton had cautioned him, guided him out of his house, and placed him in the back seat of the pool car. Clavell was spinning his handcuffs behind him when the door closed.

'Did you want to book em, Danno?' joked Barton.

Clavell frowned. 'Eh?'

'*Hawaii Five-O* – TV police series?'

'Oh, sorry, don't watch it. I was trying to get my head around it all. Why don't I know what to do first?'

'You do. This is an unusual case, but you don't need to worry about that at the moment. Think back to your training. Where are we now?'

Clavell scratched his chin and then recovered. 'A potential crime scene.'

'Is there a danger to life? Civilian or police?'

Clavell didn't bother answering. They could both hear Robin crying.

'What's next?'

'Preserve the crime scene.'

'Correct. Ring Control. Get uniform here. Inner cordon off both houses and Robin's car and get an outer cordon up the street in case someone else comes down here. It's a dead end, so there'll be minimal traffic. Send the landlord to fetch that phone. I've got no idea what's happening but something is. Book the neighbour and her baby into a hotel for the night. Uniform will help with that, too. I'll get CSI to do what they can with her house and she can return tomorrow. As for Rowe's house, let's get him back to Thorpe Wood and question him. We can arrange a search of his place and his car in the morning. We might get an unexpected break.'

'What do you mean by that, sir?'

'That man's guilty of something, but I've got a feeling it might not be to do with our dead body.'

Clavell nodded. 'Either that or he's more afraid of the person he's protecting than he is of us.'

53

DI BARTON

Barton moved the meeting to ten o'clock the next morning after a fruitless discussion with Robin Rowe. There'd been no chance of the cinema with Holly the previous night. It had been near midnight when he'd arrived home and, when he'd got into bed, he'd literally got the cold shoulder. He'd muttered to himself, thinking she should understand, until he'd remembered he'd forgotten to ring her. Breakfast was an equally chilly affair.

DCI Cox entered the incident room with two seconds to spare. She'd requested an immediate update in her office, but Barton hadn't wanted to have to repeat himself. Zander, Clavell, Whitlam, Malik, and two junior detectives were present: Ewing and Zelensky. Zander had affectionately nicknamed them the EZ (ee-zee) Crew as they worked well together. The HOLMES operator also attended.

'Right, ladies and gentlemen. This is what we know. Arnold Stone went missing last Christmas, assumed vanished with debts owing. He was a person with additional needs. I believe that's the correct way of saying it nowadays. The details are on the file, so please read it. The only suspect at this point is Robin Rowe. His nervous behaviour makes me uneasy. He knows what's going on, or he's done something else dodgy. CSI are on the scene searching his house and garden. Sergeant Strange is present, so I'll update her later. Let's roll some ideas around. What do you think?'

Zander spoke first. 'It sounds like the guy in custody is protecting someone. Charge him with murder. Explain the Peterborough Ditch Murders case to him.'

Barton surveyed the younger officers in the room and wondered if they would know the details of the case and the implications. 'Refresh our memories on that, please.'

'Joanna Dennehy murdered three men in the city and tried to kill two others in 2013. She received life with no parole. Two men assisted her. One man helped select the victims and received nineteen years. They found the other only guilty of perverting the course of justice and two counts of preventing lawful and decent burial. His sentence: fourteen years.'

'I agree, that should shake him up. Whatever he's done, it's unlikely he's the dominant force. Yes, Clavell?'

'I thought about it last night. The victim only disappeared six months ago. With the right authorisation, which I think is Superintendent for over ninety days, we can check the Automatic Number Plate Recognition cameras. If there was an argument and a kill at the home address, then the body had to be transported to the allotment. If his car went all the way to Wisbech, it will have triggered the cameras en route.'

Zelensky, who hadn't been out of uniform for long, put her hand up. Barton pointed at her. 'The fact he's been to Wisbech and back doesn't mean he drove there to bury a body.'

Clavell gave her a hard look. 'No, but it proves he has been there. At the moment, Robin has been refusing to give us details but is answering questions. I believe that if we ask him a simple question about his movements, we might get him to deny it. If he does, and we know he's been there, we'll also know he's a liar.'

Barton smiled as Zander raised his eyes next to Clavell.

'Good work, all of you. Clavell, that's your idea, so that's your task. Use Zelensky for any legwork. Perhaps we can also request a cadaver dog for the car and he may then crack. Zander, we'll have a further chat with Mr Rowe.' He pointed at Ewing. 'Get down to Strange at the scene, and keep your radios on. We might need to be quick when Rowe breaks. If his car has been to the scene, then get CSI to examine it.'

'Malik, check HOLMES and the PNC with the operator here to see if Rowe or Stone turn up on any other cases. Whitlam, visit the girl at the hotel and check out the background of this ex of hers. If you ring Strange, she'll let you know when she can return to the property.'

'Actually, sir, I need to talk to you and DCI Cox.'

Malik let out a small cheer. 'Whitlam's the Compost Heap Killer.'

The cheers died down at Whitlam's serious face.

'Does it need to be right away?' asked Cox.

'Yes, ma'am. I have a confession to make.'

54

THE SOUL KILLER

I follow them into interview room two. They sit opposite me. Cox scowls, whereas Barton seems more puzzled. I've noticed she's been in a worse mood than usual of late.

Cox leans forward. 'What is this?'

'There was an investigation a while back where I knew something, but I didn't mention it.'

Both pairs of eyes harden.

'Which case?' says Barton.

'The man who drowned in the rowing lake.'

'Okay,' says Barton. 'I recall you talking to us about that. He was your girlfriend's sister's husband?' He speaks the last few words slowly, then clicks his fingers. 'That's right. I remember. You were going to ask her to marry you.'

'Yes. You're aware I run a lot to keep fit. I'm always jogging through the meadows. A couple of times a week at least, I would say.'

I detect a vein throbbing on DCI Cox's forehead. 'Go on.'

'I was running along there and heard a big splash around the time the witness in the flats said he heard one too. When I looked in the river, there was Malcolm Somerville splashing about. He slurred that he needed help. I didn't even see the bike and assumed he'd staggered in. When I tried to save him, he lost his balance and dragged me on top of him. For a moment, I thought he was trying to drown me. When I climbed out and then pulled him up, he calmed down.'

Barton raised an eyebrow. 'Then what happened?'

'I offered to get him to a taxi but he told me to piss off. He'd been acting strangely so when he staggered away along the path towards Thorpe Meadows and the rowing lake, I decided, screw him. I was freezing in only my running gear by that point. He lives in that direction, so I just hoped he'd experience a horrible walk home. He was a big man with a thick coat, so he wouldn't have frozen to death. I turned around and ran off.'

Barton twirled his pen. 'Why didn't you say anything?'

'I couldn't believe it when Annabelle reported him missing. Claudia, my partner, and her sister are incredibly close. When she rang me, I panicked and said nothing about seeing him. My first concern was preserving our relationship. If she finds out I dragged an inebriated Malcolm out of the river and didn't help him, then she'd never forgive me. Honestly, I expected him to crawl out of a bush and turn up, so I kept quiet.'

'You still had plenty of opportunities to come forward,' stated Cox.

'As time passed, I felt less able to mention it. Besides, it wouldn't have affected the operation that much. You would have still searched the river and not the rowing lake. It was selfish. I didn't feel like I could say anything after it had gone on so long. When he turned up, I wished I'd mentioned it. I wanted the twins to know what happened. When I spoke to you, I almost told you.'

'I thought you had something else on your mind. Was this it?'

'Yes. Claudia rang me for help, and I lied to her by saying I hadn't seen him. If she found out, she would never have agreed to marry me.'

Cox looks incredulous. 'You asked her to get married, despite not informing anyone you were the last person to see her brother-in-law alive?'

It's unnecessary to act disappointed in myself. I am. I should have declared all this at the time. It would've seemed much more genuine.

'I'm almost afraid to ask. Did she agree?' asks Cox.

'To marry me? Yes.'

'Bloody hell. How do you sleep at night?'

This is the tricky part. I need to be convincing. 'That's it. I don't. Our relationship isn't the same because my lies are poisoning it. She's going through a traumatic time, and I can't help. I know I should have told the truth.'

Cox slams her hand on the table. I jump in my seat because I guess that's what she wants, but my nerves are solid.

'You underestimate the seriousness of your actions, or inactions. Why tell us now?' says Cox.

'Our engagement is heading for the rocks, anyway. I needed to report the facts and get it off my chest. Hopefully, she'll forgive me. She knows how Malcolm acted after a few brandies. She'll understand that he wouldn't have accepted help from me when I found him looking stupid.'

'John, what do you think of all this?'

Barton shakes his head. 'I wish he'd told us next week because we'll miss him. You're a good copper, David, but you've made a serious mistake. The implications are far reaching. There's only one route we can take.'

'I agree. Go home, David. We have no choice but to notify Professional Standards. I wouldn't be surprised if you lose your job over this.'

'Will you tell Claudia the truth if she asks you?' I ask.

Barton gasps. 'Of course, we'll have to. You're in a lot of trouble. I hope for your sake you belong to the Police Federation.'

'What will happen now?'

Barton stood. 'I'll walk you out. You'll need to leave your warrant card so you can't come into the building. We'll talk to HR and Professional Standards. They'll want statements about everything we discussed today.'

'Do you really think they'll kick me out?'

'I'm not sure. You have an exemplary record for nearly ten years. That's got to count for something. One thing I do know is that the whole process takes ages. I don't predict you being back at work before Christmas.'

'I'm sorry.'

Barton shrugs. 'We all make mistakes. Are you feeling all right? Don't do anything drastic. The Fed are good at looking after their own, so they might be able to save your job.'

I shake his hand and leave. The Fed is the nickname for the Police Federation. They're like our union, and they aren't that good. Driving out into the harsh sunlight of what's looking to be a very warm day, I allow myself a smile. All said, that could have gone much worse. The changing situation forced my hand. Let's hope that Claudia is as understanding as Inspector Barton was, or the consequences for her and Annabelle will be deadly serious.

55

DI BARTON

Barton returned to his desk, cursing at the man's stupidity, and more importantly his loss of manpower. Someone had stuck a note on his keyboard asking him to ring Strange.

'Kelly, what's up?'

'John, it was proving a nothing search of Rowe's property until they found a gold watch hidden in one of the cupboards.'

'What's the significance of the watch?'

'Didn't Whitlam tell you what Stone's mother said?'

'Whitlam's been suspended.'

'What? Why?'

'Long story, but basically he saw Malcolm Somerville fall in the river the night he died. He didn't help him home, and Malcolm is related to his fiancée, so he kept quiet.'

There was a pause on the line. 'Right. I need more coffee to connect all that. My point is that the mother said Arnold cherished this watch and never took it off. The words "My Boy" were engraved on the back of it, as they are on this watch.'

'Rowe has the victim's watch hidden in his house?'

'That's correct.'

'Excellent. It's not looking good for him. Anything else?'

'No, both houses are immaculate. I'm not sure if Rowe's a clean freak or he hoped to hide any evidence, and the other house won't reveal much after all this time either. There's the possibility of DNA from hoovering the carpet for hairs and skin, but that's it. But the presence of the watch says he knows more than he's letting on. It might even be enough to get him to confess. Perhaps he kept it as a memento.'

'Yes, or maybe to sell.'

'Well, he wouldn't have made much money. The only thing gold about this watch is the colour.'

Barton laughed. 'I've got one of those myself. Okay, come back in when you're done. There's no rush. Clavell is getting authorisation to check ANPR for hits from Robin Rowe's car. If he gets it today, we'll present all the evidence to Rowe in one blow. He'll talk, or we arrest him for murder. We can have him in front of the magistrates before lunchtime tomorrow and locked up in the local nick by teatime.'

'Still think it involves someone else?'

'Without a shadow of doubt.'

Zander was listening in. 'A break?'

'Yeah. Stone's watch turned up in Rowe's cupboard.'

'Kerching!'

'Yep, the way forward looks clear. We'll wait until Kelly's returned with the evidence before we talk to him again.'

Clavell returned to the room. 'Any joy?' asked Barton.

'I was right. Cox signed the ANPR request, but it needs a superintendent's authorisation because it's over ninety days.'

'DCI Cox, you mean?'

'Didn't I say that? The super's PA said he'll be here at three. She'll have it sorted and back to us the moment he gets in. We should have the information by five.'

'Great stuff. You're making this look easy.'

'I'm finding working under you inspiring, sir. Thank you for your time explaining things to me yesterday. I appreciate it.'

Barton ignored Zander's look of disdain.

'My pleasure. I'm sure you'll go far.'

Clavell hung around at the door before adding, 'Is Whitlam off the case?'

'That's correct.'

'May I ask what he's done?'

'You can ask, but I won't tell you. I wouldn't be surprised if the rumours had reached the canteen. Why do you ask?'

'It was just the way he said he wanted to talk to you. It sounded important. When he spoke earlier, he reminded me of someone, or there was something vaguely familiar about him. I couldn't put my finger on it. Thought I'd chat to him, see if I could pin it down, but it looks like it might be a while before I get the chance to do that. Professional Standards can be strict.'

Barton's jaw dropped open at Clavell's cheek as he strode from the room. Zander broke into a wide-mouthed chuckle. Clavell, the bold sod, had already heard all about the suspension and was just double checking. Barton tutted at his deviousness. He really would go far.

56

DI BARTON

Barton and Zander shared a look as they sat down early that evening in front of Rowe and his solicitor. The solicitor's name was Burke, which Barton thought was entirely appropriate, and his reputation preceded him. After they completed the formalities, Barton held up the watch in the plastic bag.

'I'm showing Mr Rowe evidence bag 44-e containing a gold watch. Is this your watch?'

Rowe glanced at it without emotion. 'No, it's not.'

'Can you explain how it came to be in your house?'

'I don't know anything about it.'

'It belonged to your dead neighbour, Arnold Stone.'

'I haven't seen it before.'

Barton put the watch to one side while Zander continued.

'Did you visit Wisbech in the last six months?'

Rowe's eyes narrowed. 'I visited in March for the first time in years. A friend was interested in seeing the display on anti-slavery at the museum. I certainly wasn't there at Christmas in an allotment.'

'Do you know what Automatic Number Plate Recognition is?'

'No.'

'It can tell us in real time or historically where a car was on a certain date. It identified your vehicle in Wisbech.'

'I went in my boyfriend's car.'

'On Boxing Day?'

'No, in March. I told you that was the only occasion I've been there in years.'

'Mr Rowe, we flagged your car at various points between here and Wisbech on Boxing Day. There are no mistakes with this system.'

'But I was at a—'

Tears began to flow down Rowe's face and his solicitor decided he'd had enough. 'My client is getting upset. Please stop the interrogation for a moment.'

Zander coughed. 'We prefer the word interview but, regardless, Mr Rowe has been having a running argument with his neighbour, Mr Stone. That man disappears around Christmas last year, and then his skeleton appears in an allotment in Wisbech. We estimate it's been there since he went missing. Your client denies having been there then, but his car has been traced to that location. When we searched his house, Mr Stone's watch was hidden there. There's motive and evidence.'

'Circumstantial evidence. Do you have images of my client driving the car?'

'Not yet.'

'I'm sure I don't need to tell you that the ANPR system records movement of cars. It doesn't reveal who drove them. Any pictures found on CCTV of a moving vehicle on a dark night are unlikely to stand up in court. Even if you can locate such images.'

'And the long-running arguments and insults?'

'Circumstantial.'

'And the watch?'

'Explainable. Perhaps he found it. You would have charged my client with murder by now if you believe he did it.'

'We think he knows more than he's letting on.'

Barton noticed the solicitor's eye twitch at his comment.

'Will he give us his passwords for his phone and laptop?'

Rowe snorted at the prospect.

'Not at this point,' said Burke.

'Who is his alibi? Why doesn't he reveal his identity?'

Finally, the solicitor crossed his arms and exhaled. 'We'd like a break. Let me talk to my client. I'll let you know when we're ready.'

Zander stood. 'We'll return in our own time.'

The solicitor also got to his feet. 'Your twenty-four hours to charge him are up. If you're requesting an extension, I will need to be informed.'

Barton and Zander stepped from the room and Zander shook his head. 'I don't like this Rowe for it, but, without his alibi, I say we have no choice but to charge him. He's guilty of something. I reckon his lover came around and got into an argument with Stone. Sounds as if Stone could be combative. Rowe isn't the fighting type, but maybe his boyfriend is, and Stone dies. Perhaps it was an accident; one of those head-hitting-the-kerb incidents. They panic. Someone knows about this allotment. Before they have time to think it through, they've stuck the body in the back of Rowe's car, driven to the compost heap and buried him. Then they dream up this story about him saying he was moving out.'

'That's plausible. Why stick up for the other person, though, when we have the car's movements and the watch?'

'Well, I suppose Rowe could be a knife wielding maniac who's trying to cover his tracks.'

'It will have been a while since I was that surprised.' Barton sucked his teeth. 'That smart-git solicitor's not helping. Problem is, I'm not convinced either. There's something else we're not seeing. I'll ask Cox to sort out an extension. If he doesn't give up his boyfriend in the next few days, we probably have enough to charge him with murder, although we have nothing concrete. Perhaps time under lock and key will weaken his resolve.'

'We've got his laptop and mobile phone. The details of who he's protecting will probably be in one of them somewhere.'

'You know we struggle to get into these new iPhones. We'll have more luck with his laptop, but he'd need to reveal his passwords if we want to read his emails, and he's already laughed at the suggestion. The old fashioned route is the quickest and strongest.'

'You mean threaten him until he confesses?'

'I wouldn't say threaten. Convince him that honesty is the best policy.'

Zander smiled. 'Any angles that we might have missed?'

Barton considered what they knew. 'It's weird that Whitlam lives next door.'

'Yeah. I wonder if he knows who the boyfriend was. What a mess.'

'They wouldn't pay us the big bucks if it was easy.'

Barton smiled. 'It's never simple. Let's sleep on it. Another night in the cells will help. If he refuses to talk in the morning, we'll get started on the other routes. If we can track his phone to Wisbech as well as his car, it'll confirm his movements, but we all know how long that sort of thing takes.'

'Can't they rush it all through?'

'You'd think, but look at it from their point of view. We have a skeleton with no damage to it and a lot of circumstantial evidence. There doesn't appear to be an imminent risk to anyone else, especially with Mr Rowe enjoying our facilities downstairs. It's always the same. Neither Rome nor cases are built in a day.'

Zander bobbed his head in agreement. 'Let's hope time is on our side.'

57

THE SOUL KILLER

I don't want to show myself at my house in case they haven't finished with the potential crime scene next door. There's no point reminding them how close to the scene I live so I spend the afternoon walking around the new Tesco Extra shopping centre at Hampton. My latest credit card bill prevents me from buying anything so I have a cheap dinner at the Mulberry Tree Farm pub. By accident, I sit beside the toddler play area, only to endure screams and shouts with my food.

Afterwards I head to Claudia's office. She's supposed to finish at six o'clock but she often works late. The reception closes before that, but the cleaners have opened the door in the past. A harried looking young lady is leaving as I arrive, so I try to slip past her.

'Can I help?' she asks.

'I wanted to catch Claudia before she leaves for the day.'

The woman pauses. A range of expressions passes over her face. I spot pity and sympathy, possibly even a hint of fear. She knows who I am, that's for sure.

'She's been working out of our Huntingdon branch for the last few weeks. It's quieter and more relaxing. You understand how she must feel.'

I think I'd feel better if she'd told me personally. 'Of course. My mistake.'

My poor attempt at recovery is more degrading than not knowing in the first place. I decide to go to her house, even though I'm perhaps not in the best frame of mind. I have no choice. It has to be done.

If Barton plans to tell Claudia about my lack of disclosure about seeing Malcolm the night he died, I'm better off delivering the news myself. I frown as I consider our future. There's no good reason why she wouldn't tell me of the office move. The breadcrumbs of missed calls, texts and dates beforehand have lessened the shock, but it's still a blow.

Claudia won't be home from Huntingdon yet, so I meander back down Oundle Road to the petrol station. I decide to venture into the British Sugar site opposite and cruise past Donald's old house. Expecting it to look the same, I slam the brakes on when I spot children's curtains hanging in the windows. There's a 'sold' sign lying flat in the grass out the front and a shiny people carrier fills the too-small driveway. I get out and peek through the glass into what was once his study, which now appears to be a playroom, filled with more toys than I've ever seen before. I can't help wondering if the new family know the history of the house. Mind you, lives are worth less nowadays. They probably don't even care.

I return to the car and park up next to the playground that we wistfully stared at what seems a lifetime ago. There are children playing now, even a dad in his suit, no doubt just back from the office. That should be my future. I stare down at my clenched fists and force myself to relax. Driving usually calms me, so I drive around the estate. It seems everywhere I look there are families. Part of me wants to mount the pavement.

I nip to the parkways and let off some steam in the fast lane, before heading to Orton Waterville to explain my actions. Claudia's back as both of the twins' cars are parked outside. Perhaps I should talk to them together. At least I'll be able to take note of their reactions at the same time. I wonder how furious they're going to be. It'll definitely be a shock, but it's not as though they'll think I murdered him. But I suspect Claudia will use it as an excuse for us not to see each other any more. She won't get rid of me that easily.

Her sister stares through the glass after I knock. She's a wraith in a mauve tracksuit. I open my mouth to talk but she hollers up the stairs, 'It's him,' and doesn't open the door. Bitch.

Claudia arrives, moving as if she has a concrete coat on. She opens the door slowly, as though she'd rather not have to.

'Hey, David. What are you doing here?'

'I came to explain something.'

Her mouth droops but she maintains eye contact. 'I've been planning to speak to you for a while. I just don't seem to have a second free at the moment.' She takes a deep breath. 'Now is as good a time as ever. Come to the kitchen.'

I follow her. Her jeans are baggy. We meet many anorexics and people with eating disorders in our line of work. There's also contact with drug addicts, who often waste away. But it's the misery that comes from grief that depletes people the fastest.

'Tea, coffee?' Claudia asks.

'No, thanks. Can you fetch your sister, too? What I need to tell you is relevant to both of you. I hope you'll understand why I never said anything at the time. It concerns Malcolm.'

Puzzled and curious now, Claudia shouts to Annabelle. Finally, they sit opposite me at the big kitchen table. Claudia appears ready to cry; her sister looks demonic. Claudia has lost a lot of weight, but Annabelle's arms are the thinnest I've ever witnessed on an adult. She might not be long for this world at this rate.

I start my tale at hearing a splash when Malcolm fell in, and finish with feeling guilty the next day when I heard the news. I explain the poor decision not to tell anyone. It was a big mistake and I'm so sorry. The news takes quite a few seconds to sink in. Longer, in fact, than it took Malcolm to sink under.

The silence is almost a physical presence in the room. The pressure builds on their faces. Claudia shakes her head from side to side. Annabelle's face forms a mask of such pain-filled hatred that I want to look away.

'You pulled him out and let him walk home in that state!' roars Annabelle.

'Why didn't you say straight away?' asks a wide eyed and disappointed Claudia.

'I thought you'd both react like that. I offered to get him a taxi, but he told me to clear off. You know how he was.'

Meanwhile, Annabelle has circled to the pans hanging on hooks. The frying pan flies closer to Claudia than me, but it's thrown with real venom.

In the melee I can see Claudia staring at the table, trying to process the information, but there's too much for her to get it straight. The only thing she can focus on is the worst part. 'You lied to me, to all of us.'

'You might as well have killed him yourself,' screams Annabelle.

I dodge the saucepan and egg poacher, which both hit the wall next to my head with a clang. My knuckles are white as I pick up the saucepan. My shoulders open up as I feel its weight. How dare she? I came around so they could hear it from me. I step towards Annabelle and she gasps with incredulity. Then bares her teeth. She's as mad as her father. She wants to die. I manage to change the expression on my face just before Claudia looks up at me. I place the pan on the side.

A snarl from Annabelle snaps my head back towards her. It's time to leave as she heads towards the knife rack. Claudia follows me out. She slams the kitchen door behind us and something sharp-sounding ricochets away. The next sound is a thud and a point of metal pokes through the wood.

I step outside the front door, which Claudia closes before turning the key. She stays on the other side and through the glass I see her shake her head again. There's sorrow and regret, but worst of all is the expression of acceptance. The decision she'd made earlier, without me, was the right one. Annabelle flies into view, bangs her fists on the glass, and tries to get out but Claudia pulls her into a hug. Then they collapse on the floor and Claudia strokes her sister's hair.

I stride to my car and get in. The whole car rocks as I slam the door shut. With a quick reverse, I bump off the drive and zoom from the street. I'm in a rush to get away but, deep down, I know what I want is back there. Annabelle is such a drain on poor Claudia. It's up to me to help.

58

DI BARTON

Barton left Robin Rowe sweating in his cell and he weakened overnight. Perhaps it was the pressure of the evidence, or maybe his solicitor talked sense into him. Whatever it was, the pair of them faced Barton and Zander across the table.

'My client would like to make a statement. I will read it.'

'Go on,' said Zander.

'My client denies any involvement in his neighbour's death and any knowledge of the watch you have as evidence. Mr Rowe was with his boyfriend at the time that car was being driven to Wisbech on Boxing Day. His partner is on holiday at the moment and can't be contacted. However, my client is prepared to give you his partner's email address to enable you to receive the alibi.'

Barton glared at Rowe. 'Do you think this is a game? That email address could be your mother's, for all we know.' He moved his frown to the solicitor. 'We need the name of the person who is giving the alibi. We will want to question him in person. Who is he? Tell me his name. Or I'll have your client in front of a magistrate this afternoon.'

The solicitor whispered in Rowe's ear. Rowe nodded but didn't look up.

'My client is trying to protect his boyfriend, who is a pillar of the community and married to the mother of his children.'

A slow grin crept onto Barton's face. 'That makes more sense. No dice. I want him back from his holiday and in here today, tomorrow at the latest. In fact, I'll have his phone number and location immediately.'

'My client's boyfriend is not contactable by phone because he is abroad. The only method of communication is electronically.'

'Where the hell is he, Antarctica?'

The solicitor rubbed his temples. He turned and rested his hand on Rowe's arm, whose head bobbed twice.

'Cambodia.'

'Don't mobile phones work in Cambodia?'

Zander was much faster off the mark. 'Visits Cambodia a lot, does he?'

He stared hard at Rowe. 'For the benefit of the tape, Mr Rowe has nodded.'

Barton caught up. 'I assume he hasn't gone for the cocktails and palm trees?' When no response came, Barton growled and pushed further. 'Ah, now we see why Mr Rowe didn't want to mention it. These prostitutes he visits. I trust they're over eighteen.'

'Of course! He just likes to party with young men.'

Rowe's head drooped lower. Barton could see his eyes flickering from side to side. The solicitor cleared his throat.

'It's legal over there, Inspector. And he knows nothing about any murder.'

'I think you'll find it is illegal over there, just that the law is ignored. When is he due back?'

Rowe finally raised his head. 'I don't know. Sometimes he goes for a fortnight, other times he stays a couple of months.'

'Doesn't his wife care?'

'They're only together for the children and for the sake of appearances. I think she prefers it when he's not there.'

'When did he leave the country?'

'A week ago.'

Barton and Zander watched the sweat trickle down both sides of Rowe's forehead. It wasn't even hot in the room.

'The evidence points to murder. You're the one currently in the frame,' said Barton.

Zander inhaled sharply. 'You've been with your partner to Cambodia, haven't you?'

Rowe's gaze returned to the floor so Zander pressed his advantage. 'Tell me!'

'Once, I did it once. All those bodies, it was disgusting. I said I wouldn't do it again, and we fell out. It was never the same between us after that.'

His solicitor jumped to his feet. 'This is all total conjecture. You don't have a single speck of proof. Not to mention this has absolutely nothing to do with any murder.'

Zander jolted to his feet too, leaned forward, planted his hands wide on the table, and glowered at the panicking man. 'Now, what else have you only done once?'

59

DI BARTON

Barton and Zander stepped outside.

'I didn't see that coming,' said Barton.

'No, what do you reckon?'

'Let's speak to the boss. I suppose we take the email address and send this married man a message, saying we need him back. Although if he receives that, he won't be in any rush to return home.'

'No, I shouldn't think he'd want to answer any questions about his friends here or over there.'

They found DCI Cox in her office. Barton updated her, and she jotted down the pertinent details. 'The plot thickens. One day we'll have a straightforward case.'

'Do we charge him?' asked Barton.

'Yes. He's involved in something underhand. He's lied to us and is clearly a flight risk. Get his phone unlocked and everything on it downloaded. Ensure the team complete the paperwork for the telecoms records and see what's recoverable from his laptop. The report from the forensic anthropologists will be back soon, but that's probably not going to tell us much. Let's hope we match some DNA from the crime scenes.'

'Done,' said Barton. 'Now, what are we missing?'

'Who's in the incident room?' asked Cox.

Barton scratched his head. 'Just Clavell and Malik.'

'Get them in here and update them. We'll run a quick meeting.'

Zander fetched them and Barton observed their faces as he

mentioned Cambodia. Cox hadn't batted an eyelid at the mention of sex tourism, but newer detectives often couldn't hide their revulsion. Barton knew they would harden in time.

Clavell seemed particularly perturbed. 'That little weasel lied to cover up their orgies?'

'All mere conjecture at this point. We're going to have a brainstorm.'

Cox pulled over the flip chart she kept behind her desk. 'Throw stuff at me. Think out of the box.'

Clavell visibly brightened. 'It was a love triangle. Rowe had been sleeping with both men. They fought over him. Stone lost.'

Malik grinned. 'Stone was a drug addict. The dealers came to collect. He failed to pay, and they took him in Rowe's car, murdered him, and dumped the remains in the allotment.'

'Why would they use Rowe's car?' asked Cox.

Malik shrugged. 'Oh, yeah.'

Clavell almost shouted. 'It was a brothel. They were all involved. Stone got taken out for being indiscreet.'

'There could easily be someone else involved, maybe connected, maybe not,' said Malik.

'What about Whitlam?' asked Clavell.

'Good point,' said Cox. 'You're tight with him, Malik. He must have seen some of their movements. Give him a ring and ask him what he knows about Rowe's love life, or Stone's for that matter. See if he remembers a lot of different cars turning up. We'll be able to find out who the boyfriend is from all these sources; it's just going to take time. Once we spring the name on Rowe, he'll have to talk.'

Barton tapped his finger on the table. 'We could still just charge him with murder. I've enjoyed these other ideas but, at the end of the day, the gold watch and car trip to Wisbech put Rowe right in the middle of it. Once he's locked up, he can't get in touch with his boyfriend as he won't have email. If he wants to ring anyone, he has to fill in a form. We'll ask prison security to monitor that and inform us of his requests.'

Cox nodded. 'Even if we had an extradition agreement with Cambodia, it's a long, drawn out process. Better Rowe's boyfriend knows nothing of this, and we nick him when he arrives back in the country.'

'Agreed,' said Barton.

'We'll need to put this guy on an ACCT after breaking the news to him.'

'Well remembered,' said Barton. ACCT stood for Assessment, Care in Custody, and Teamwork, and would guarantee that Rowe would be observed regularly while in custody. If any man was at risk of suicide, it was Rowe. If he'd been up to no good in Asia and participated in a murder, his immediate outlook looked bleak in the extreme.

'Do you know what I actually meant?' said Clavell.

The others stared blankly at him.

'What if Whitlam's involved? He only lives two doors down. He could have had a fight with Stone.'

Malik laughed out loud. 'You mean instead of a love triangle, it's a love square. Perhaps Whitlam killed Stone, then broke into Rowe's house when he was out, hid the watch, drove to Wisbech in Rowe's car, left the body, and then parked it back up without Rowe knowing.'

Zander smiled. 'He's not the warmest guy we employ, but that might be pushing it. Isn't he engaged to a woman, so probably not using male prostitutes?'

'I heard his fiancée's related to the bloke who drowned,' replied Clavell.

Barton strode to the door and opened it. 'You seem to have your paws in many pies, Mr Clavell. You're aware what gossip does?'

Clavell shook his head.

'It steals reputations. Whitlam's a careerist. Talk like that will finish his. Besides, I've met a lot of dumb cops in my time, but not one daft enough to murder their neighbour.'

Barton blew out a big breath. They hadn't asked for DNA analysis on Somerville when they'd dragged him from the rowing lake because it had looked like an accident. That was a mistake. It was time to get it done.

60

THE SOUL KILLER

I've parked at the cinema intending to go in, but everywhere I look there are couples. I know my angry thoughts shouldn't be directed at them, but I bet they don't appreciate what they have. My eyes burn into a laughing pair who hold hands as they saunter past. She looks a little like Claudia did, before all this madness began.

'What you looking at, freak?' He slams my bonnet with his free hand.

I'm out of the car before I even realise it. He and I stand eyeball to eyeball. I want to bury my thumbs in his sockets. My teeth grind as I strain to stop my hands raising.

His girlfriend recognises the danger and pulls on his arm. 'Terry, please, leave it. Come on.'

Incredibly, a sneering Terry leans back and spits in my face. I can't help smiling, laughing even. My shoulders shake. His arrogance drains away but it takes me showing him my homemade warrant card before he fully appreciates his mistake. I was in civvies in the one I returned but the public only look at the picture, and this one is of me in police uniform. He stutters as my arm reaches around and I squeeze his neck tight from behind. I lean into his ear.

'Where's your car?'

He points to a yellow hot hatch, to which I drag him over, leaving his snivelling partner stricken with fear.

'Unlock it. Open the door.' I ram him into his seat and grab his ear. 'I know your car, and soon I'll know where you live. If you break the law again, you will die.'

I twist his earlobe. He doesn't fight back now, just winces in pain. His girlfriend weeps as she clambers in next to him. He drives away swiftly, but I notice with a smirk that he doesn't speed.

Blood pounds in my forehead, but as quickly as it starts the tension fades and stops. By the time I return to my car, I can barely remember what the fuss was all about, although my face smells faintly of popcorn. Malik's name lights up on my phone. I contemplate ignoring it, but can't stop myself answering.

'Yes, Malik.'

'David, I cannot believe you didn't tell them you pulled Somerville out the water that night when he became a floater. What were you thinking?'

'Clearly not very straight. You know how I feel about this girl. I didn't want to mess it up, and now I've done just that.'

'Hopefully Professional Standards will only give you a warning.'

'Yeah. What's up? Are you going to work out at the gym later? I reckon it might be weird for me to carry on with Barton and Strange in there.'

There's an unpleasant pause as Malik considers whether he'd like to be seen working out with a suspended officer. I can't recall the rules, but suspect he'd have to report any contact. Instead he chooses to ignore the question.

'Anyway, I'm not ringing about that. Cox told me to ask what you remember about Rowe's and Stone's visitors.'

'Why's that?'

'They searched Rowe's house and found a watch that belonged to Stone.'

'No way. Case closed, then.'

'Yep, and the ANPR system tagged Rowe's car going to Wisbech at the time we reckon the body was placed there.'

'It must be Rowe, then. To be honest, I'm surprised. I didn't think he had it in him. He'd been moaning about the music for ages, but I never expected him to act on it.'

'Well, Barton and Zander still aren't sure. They reckon there's someone else involved. You are not going to believe this next bit. Rowe was dead cagey when it came to being questioned. Turns out he and his boyfriend have been up to no good in Cambodia.'

'What?'

'Yep. Rowe reckons he visited his boyfriend's house in Ailsworth the night his car was in Wisbech. When they asked him, why not drive to Ailsworth, he said he liked to have a walk on Boxing Day.'

'Yeah, right.'

'Exactly, anyway, so far, he hasn't given up who the boyfriend is. We're struggling to get it with his devices being locked. Zander questioned Rowe's colleagues at his work, but no one knows him very well. He's on Facebook, but he doesn't use it much. Cox wondered if you remember seeing anyone, or a particular type of car, or even remember a number plate from someone visiting him.'

'Hang on. My phone's dying. Let me plug it in.'

'Sure.'

The battery is fine, but I need a few seconds. This news is manna from heaven. The Lord is looking out for me. How do I use this gift to my advantage? What always shanks up an investigation? It comes to me. We all hate red herrings.

'Hi, sorry about that. It's charging now. What did you ask?'

'Can you remember any cars or visitors?'

'I did see a few nice motors arriving, actually, and a couple of people on foot. I thought it was weird as the men looked well dressed. Some of them weren't there long. I spotted a black Porsche more than once. I'm not a big car fan, but even I couldn't take my eyes off it.'

The pause at the other end roars in my ears. Come on, Malik. You can do it.

'Shit, Rowe might have been a rent boy?'

'Wow, you're right. Have they checked his bank statements, or found any cash? You can't judge anyone at face value nowadays.'

Malik laughed down the phone. 'This will make you laugh. Clavell reckoned you could be involved. He said it was a bit suspicious that you live next door to Stone and Rowe, and saw that Malcolm Somerville just before he drowned.'

'I can assure you I haven't been paying for sex with male computer programmers.'

'Sure, of course not. Look, I better report back. Take it easy, yeah? I'll see you at the gym.'

I breathe deeply and still my mind. A mistake has got me into the mess I'm in. I won't make another. If I hadn't touched Stone, I wouldn't be under suspicion at all. And there's me thinking Barton was the one to watch out for. I have a new enemy. There is something familiar about that Clavell, too. I'd better keep an eye on him.

61

THE SOUL KILLER

When I woke this morning, I lay in bed for hours, processing Malik's news. It was clear that my days in River End were numbered and my career was finished. I considered giving notice on both, but I know the rules regarding tenancies, and I'll squeeze every last penny out of my job.

I'll simply stop paying the rent. It'll take them six months to evict me. I'll leave my mobile attached to the charger and my car parked up. If anyone comes to visit, they'll assume I'm out or asleep as they'll hear the phone ringing.

I'll control the timings of the meetings from now on. There are only guidelines around answering your phone for hearings. My plan is to disappear shortly. If things go bad, they won't be able to arrest me if they can't find me.

The Major Crimes team's investigation will be floundering at the moment and hopefully I've sent them racing in the wrong direction. I wonder if some poor sod nearby has a black Porsche. If so, he or she could be in for a tough few days. But I know eventually I'm going to make an appearance in their investigation, whether it's sooner or later. When they search Rowe's car, they are likely to find a trace of me so I need to put myself in there before that comes back. If Barton doesn't connect the dots, Clavell will. I don't relish a hand on my shoulder when I'm not ready. Only the rich escape prison.

Currently, the police have insufficient evidence to prosecute me if they decide to look in my direction, unless something else turns up, but I don't want them picking me up willy-nilly and taking me in for questions. I've got my first interview with Professional Standards in a week, but after that, they'll discover I'm a ghost.

I decided to visit Barney and hopefully stay with him. I need to find out what he said. It's safe to assume that he didn't mention my name, or I'd already be sharing a cell with Rowe. I caught the last train tonight and brought some of my things. Wisbech railway station closed years ago, so I changed at Ely and went to King's Lynn.

I had no choice but to get a taxi. The meter shows over twenty pounds as we pull up around the corner from the home I grew up in. That level of expense is unsustainable. I'll need transport soon, but it must be untraceable.

I pay the driver with cash and yank down my baseball cap. There's no one nearby, so I stride along confidently. Barney's campervan gleams in the glow of the streetlights. Even in the dark, I can tell someone's cleaned it. The tyres are pumped too, all of them. I'm tempted to get in and check the interior, but there's plenty of time for that.

The house looks empty at this late hour. I can't see a light on in any of the rooms. The main bedroom is upstairs facing the street, but the curtains aren't closed. I have keys, front and back, so venture towards the rear. The stiff door feels as if it hasn't opened since I last visited.

I check the bin under the sink and note there's household rubbish but no whisky bottles. Maybe Barney has been born again. A quiet rasping echoes from farther into the house. I tiptoe towards the sound. It's a slight rattle, coming from upstairs. The stairs creak as I ascend. I turn into Barney's room. I suppose it was my mother's room, too.

Moonlight streams through the window and shows Barney lying in state. He has his hands clasped on his chest, as though in prayer, and his head slightly raised by the pillows. The cobalt mottled skin appears lifeless. I've seen livelier looking corpses, yet his chest rises. I perch beside him.

'Barney.' I whisper louder, 'Barney.'

His breathing alters, but his eyelids don't move. I walk to the windows and close the curtains. There's a thin eiderdown on the bottom of the bed, which I unfurl and place over his small body and tuck under his hands. Despite the pallor, his face is crease-free. I can only assume he hasn't got long. I'm leaving the room when I hear him gasp loudly. It's dark, so I flick on the light switch. His eyelids are half open now.

'Is that you, David?' A hand moves towards me.

'Yes, Barney. It's me.' I sit next to him but avoid his outstretched fingers.

He smiles, which makes his cheek twitch. 'I knew you'd come. Would have put money on it. I fixed the van. We can go for that ride now.'

I'm not sure I've ever cried properly before, but my eyes empty as though they're releasing thirty years of pain. I take his hand and squeeze tight.

'That's what I came home for.'

'You're a good boy.'

'How are you feeling?' It's a lame question, and it croaks out.

'I'm dying. Either that, or I have some hangover.'

My laugh is a snivel, and I wipe my nose.

'How long are you back for, David?'

'Until the end, Barney. Until the end.'

62

DI BARTON

Barton stared out at the sea of faces in the incident room. He hadn't asked for silence, but all the conversations were hushed. Even though most of those present didn't know the sum of the information that had come in, they appeared to sense it. Naseem, DCI Cox's predecessor, had preferred morning meetings as cases came to their conclusion. That way, everyone left motivated and had a whole day to act.

It'd been a week since they'd charged Rowe with the murder of Arnold Stone. Rowe had remained silent as the magistrates had remanded him in custody and as far as they knew, he'd said nothing since. The prison security team had reported that he'd made no application to make any telephone calls.

Barton also noted that Rowe had only lasted three hours on main location before someone had asked him what he was in for. It wasn't surprising. Each standard wing held eighty prisoners at HMP Peterborough. Your average prisoner would have looked at him with suspicion the moment they saw him. It would only take one to shout something out. The prison officers had struggled to get him out alive. He'd spent the last week on the VP wing, with the other vulnerable persons at risk of being battered for their crimes, appearance or sexuality.

Cox moved to the front of the room. She had a new suit on and appeared energised by the fresh intel.

'Listen carefully. I have a lot of information to dispense and frankly, repeating it would be inconvenient.' The muted chatter died down instantly. 'First, and most importantly, we paid the premium for the GrayKey and unlocked Rowe's phone.' A small, cautious cheer erupted. 'For those who don't know, Grayshift sell an ultra-expensive plug-in called the GrayKey, which gets you in despite Apple's best efforts. We had little choice because Rowe's laptop, workplace, friends, and family gave us nothing. Before you celebrate, Rowe's phone wasn't used in the Wisbech area the night his car was there, but neither was it in Ailsworth. Text messages between him and someone named Franco went back a year. We found texts agreeing to a meet last Boxing Day.

'That number belongs to an Alun Franco, who is a businessman with some gravitas. Married, fifty-four, three kids, lives in Tunbridge Wells, which is south of London, and who has a bolthole cottage in Ailsworth when he visits his factory here in Peterborough. UK Border Force checked and revealed he has made numerous trips to Vietnam, Cambodia and the Philippines over the last few years. There's no evidence he's there for the sex trade, but it's unlikely he just enjoys long flights.

'The Border Force also warned us that he was due to arrive at Heathrow late yesterday evening. I can confirm we have him in the custody suite below.' Much louder cheering echoed around the room. 'Steady on now. I doubt he'll confess. We need to find more proof of any involvement. A DNA swab has been sent for testing, but that takes up to five days. We can't hold him that long, so we'll have to release him unless he gives us anything. John?'

Barton acknowledged the silence. 'That's right. The only case we have at the moment is on Rowe, and I don't think he did it. Not on his own anyway. We triangulated Franco's mobile, and it was turned on and taking calls near Ailsworth on Boxing Day. Nothing in Wisbech. His car; a 7 series BMW, was not picked up by number plate recognition.'

'They obviously used Rowe's car,' said Zander.

'Maybe. Who's to say there wasn't someone else involved? We've managed to find four grainy pictures of Rowe's red car from CCTV that night. Two are useless, from the rear. One is from the side and shows a man in a white baseball cap. The final shot is head-on from distance. It seems there was only one driver.'

A few swear words and the odd groan rumbled through the room.

'That's right. Rowe could have had help to lift the body into the boot, but, unless his accomplice hid on the rear seats, he'd have had to remove Stone on his own. Zander, visit Rowe in his prison cell and check if he has a hernia.'

Cue groans, mostly from Zander, and laughter this time.

'Team, we're almost there. A cadaver dog – apparently some prefer the term *human remains detection dog* now – indicated that Rowe's boot has had dead remains in it, but we need more. Keep thinking about this case. There are more twists and turns, I can feel it. We have most of the DNA evidence back and it brought up another oddity. Forensics and pathology taught us little we didn't already know, but some low-copy DNA identified someone else. Any guesses?'

'Alan Titchmarsh,' joked Malik.

'Charlie Dimmock,' from Ewing, whom Barton noted had come out of his shell recently.

'Yeah, baby,' shouted Zander.

'Isn't she ginger?' said Malik.

'Too wild for you, boy?' replied Zander.

Barton shot Cox an apologetic half-smile. 'Very good, everyone. I get it as well: allotments, famous gardeners. You all really are wasted here. No, you're all wrong. It has nothing to do with the allotment. The DNA gathered from Stone's house matched a sample extracted from the fingernails of our drowning victim in the rowing lake.'

63

DI BARTON

Barton smirked at the confused expressions on his team's faces.

'Ewing, talk us through it,' he said.

Ewing rose to his feet. 'Yes, sir. Right. I'm sure I don't need to tell you professionals this, but DNA under the fingertips usually signifies either an attack or defence against an assault. Rape victims often scratch their attackers, and it puts the case beyond doubt if the DNA from the fingernails matches the DNA of the accused.'

'Correct. Go on.'

'That means that the person under the fingernails was also in Stone's house.'

'Yes. What does that mean?'

'Stone drowned him?'

Barton pointed his finger at those who made Homer Simpson 'Doh' noises. 'Ignore them, they were rookies once. We have Stone's DNA and it wasn't his.'

Clavell put his hand up. 'It's possible that whoever killed Stone drowned Somerville in the lake.'

'Pass the man a cigar, or maybe a carrot and some houmous if we don't want to get sued further down the line.' Barton stared around the office as the penny dropped for the others. 'We also got a match with DNA from Rowe's car.'

'That means the same person was in Rowe's car and Stone's house, and they had a fight with Somerville,' said Zander.

'Two carrots for the handsome fella! So, what do we do?'

Barton detected Clavell's rising arm, but he scanned the

room until he got back to him. Clavell wore an expression of satisfaction.

'We arrest them,' said Clavell.

'And who is it?'

Clavell leaned back in his seat and smiled. 'David Whitlam.'

64

THE SOUL KILLER

Barney's campervan drives pretty smoothly now he's fixed it. I've driven it to my Professional Standards meeting at Thorpe Wood police station. I drive down Thorpe Road and into the quiet well-to-do area of Longthorpe and park on Holywell Way. From there, I can sneak over the pedestrian's bridge to the station, so no one will see me in the van. It will do for transport over the next few months while I decide what to do. The fewer people know what I drive, the better.

I wear my only suit. Detectives tend to be pretty casual. I like one for funerals and weddings, even though I haven't been invited to many of either. This is a nice fitted dark blue one. It'll do for my own wedding, although Claudia will probably want everything new. The road towards the station is quiet. I suppose most people have already gone to work. They'll be sitting at their desks worrying about spreadsheets and meetings, while I have concerns over my entire future.

As I stride out, I find myself relaxing. It's a fresh day and I feel good. Work had lost its sheen since I met Claudia. We could start a business ourselves with her inheritance. Barton's not too bad to work for as he's reasonably good at his job. Obviously, people like me make him look good, but taking orders from some of the other idiots they have there is frustrating.

I recognise the woman at reception. She's relatively new. Her blank face and dismissive point at the seats mean I made little impact on her. That's odd, I'm sure she was flirting with me a few weeks back. PC Leicester walks past. We worked for years on response in C Division together. He's desperate to join Major Crimes and often bugs me about how to get in. He gives me the smallest nod imaginable and disappears through the doors. A bloke from Traffic who I see at the gym walks by looking anywhere but at me.

My good mood filters away. I've become a pariah. Well, that didn't take long. These people were more than happy to chat when they wanted something, but when I need the offer of friendship, or even just a supportive smile, they walk on by. It's school again; another place where I became invisible.

I massage my head to keep cool. Is it any wonder people do bad things to others, when this is how they behave? My mother said it was a cruel world. I think of dying Barney. We had a good chat last night. He helped make things clear. I asked him straight, and he was honest.

'Do you have any regrets?' I asked him over our takeaway.

'I regret not eating more of these.'

I'd bought him a battered sausage from the fish and chip shop. They're foul things. An actual squirt of grease came out on his first bite. His chin glistened and dimpled as he smiled. Apparently, he was never allowed them when he was growing up. He forgot for all those years. We realised that as an adult you want the things you didn't have as a child.

In Barney's case it was narrowed arteries. There was a lot missing from my childhood. I tried to place one word on the thoughts I was having, but struggled. I want people to listen when I speak. Nobody should be able to tell me what to do. Claudia will realise what's best for her, but the others might need to be told. If they don't catch on, they will be made to understand.

Everything is clearer now. I recall seeing my mother as she was the night she died. The disguise had gone. She couldn't stop me from doing what I wanted then in the same way the authorities can't prevent me from doing what I want now. Unless they turn up with guns, of course.

I pressed Barney again.

'Really? You said that people dismissed you most of your life. Managers took advantage of you throughout your career. Women cheated and stole from you. Don't you wish you had stood up to them? Told them it was enough? Why should you always have been the victim?'

Barney popped the last piece of sausage in his mouth and wiped his chin with his fingers. I noted he hadn't touched the chips or mushy peas. 'My parents taught me to respect my superiors. My mother taught me to respect women. I don't have much anger in me. I never have. I've tried to lead a quiet life, taking small pleasures on the way.'

'And now what? You haven't been to church in years. Do you go to heaven?'

'I'd rather you scattered my ashes at a Norfolk beach.'

I paced the room, frustrated with him. 'I should drive you around your old boss's house now with a carving knife and you should cut off chunks. You'll feel good and it won't affect anything if you're going to cease to be.'

Barney shook his head. 'Your mother believed in eternal life, not me. She said God would cause Armageddon and only those he loved would survive. Afterwards this planet would be heaven. It all seemed rather cruel to me.'

'Was that the church where you met her?'

'Oh, I never really listened in any of those places. The people made me feel welcome, at least until it was time to leave. And look, I have you in my life, so good has come of it.'

Barney grinned at my confusion. He tapped the seat next to him with his shiny fingers. 'Sit down.'

I pulled a different chair up and faced him.

'Some people are Buddhists,' he began. 'They spend their entire existence in prayer. Others rape and pillage their whole lives. Who knows what's next? I like to think we answer for our sins, and I've lived my life accordingly.'

'And if it's nothing afterwards, you're okay with that?'

'I'll be gone. My life will be over. Nothing will bother me again.'

I stood to argue and shout down his view, but it didn't matter to me what he thought. This life isn't the end. It can't be. I haven't waited all these years to meet my soul mate to have her disappear while I die alone. My life won't be meaningless. I must be one of the chosen ones. Barney might be happy to turn the other cheek, but that's not me.

A loud voice pulls me back to the present.

'DC Whitlam, can you follow me?'

I look to the security door where a plain woman in a horrible green suit is waiting. I'm not sure if she smiles or has wind. I sense the receptionist looking at me. Our eyes meet and I detect a glimpse of pity. My glare unsettles her and she glances away.

I recall *The Terminator* film where Arnie walks into the police station and blows everyone away. He must have enjoyed it.

65

DI BARTON

Barton sipped from his cup during the shocked silence.

'Very dramatic, Mr Clavell. But yes, we need to speak to David Whitlam about this. Before you rush off and construct the gallows, let's also remember that he knew Malcolm Somerville and had contact with him the night he died. Whitlam had also been inside Stone's and Rowe's houses. He lived next door, so his DNA will be present in many areas.'

The team grumbled at those points.

'He's due in now for a Professional Standards meeting. I'll pin this on him afterwards. It doesn't mean he is responsible for either death, but he is clearly a person of interest.'

Cox returned to the front.

'DI Barton and Sergeant Zander will interview Franco after this meeting. We'll see what he says. If he's evasive, we wait until the DNA checks. Do not jump to conclusions.' She looked pointedly at Clavell.

'John, make sure you ask if Franco's been in Rowe's car.'

'Will do.'

'Shame. It could be Whitlam or Franco, or even Somerville's wife at this point. It might just be Rowe, or someone else we don't know about. Keep open minds.'

Cox allowed those facts to sink in for a few moments. 'John, after your interview with Franco, stop by my office and we'll talk to Whitlam together. I'll make sure PS don't let him go after their little chat. Zander, wait and see if these interviews raise anything new, then take Clavell to the prison this afternoon and shake Rowe up. Show him those pictures of his car with what I assume is him driving. If Franco denies everything, maybe Rowe will drop him in it to save his own neck.'

'Yes, ma'am.'

'We'll have all the tests and reports back soon, then I expect this investigation to be near its conclusion. Get to it, team. Remember, together, those who uphold the law are smarter than those who break it.'

66

DI BARTON

Barton had no time for people who used their wealth to exploit the vulnerable. Men like Alun Franco bought what they wanted and to hell with any consequences, as long as they were all right. Despite the fact he'd been plucked off a flight and retained in custody, his chinos and polo shirt still looked clean and Franco retained an air of privilege.

Barton expected nothing from the interview, though. Rowe's solicitor had been efficient, but he was Sunday League football compared to the crumpled fellow who sat next to Franco. Some top legal eagles displayed their success in outrageously expensive cars and by wearing the best of everything. But Barton worried less about them than the ones who arrived in creased suits after studying past cases until the early hours.

Barton hadn't recognised Alastair Drayton, but the receptionist told him that she'd seen the man in front of him on TV.

Clavell was desperate to be involved in the questioning, but it wasn't a time for learning. There could be no mistakes when playing in the Premier League. Zander did the introductions and statements, following protocol to the letter. Barton checked his watch.

'Interview commenced at 11 a.m. Please explain your relationship with Robin Rowe, Mr Franco.'

As Barton expected, Franco said nothing. His brief smiled.

'My client has been under some extreme conditions over the last twenty-four hours and isn't fit for questioning. I insist he's released. We will come back at a future date and help you if we are able.'

Barton almost laughed at the predictability of it all.

'I'm not in the mood to pussyfoot around the truth today. Your client will only have to answer a few questions, and then we can perhaps find him somewhere to lie down and rest.'

The solicitor picked up on the threat. Franco analysed the back of his hand. He'd learned money bought most things and wasn't unduly concerned.

'You haven't charged my client, Inspector.'

'I refrain from charging people with murder until I've given them a chance to talk.'

The man inclined his head with respect. He cupped his hand and whispered to Franco. Drayton grinned again.

'Here's a statement. That's all you'll get from us today.'

This time it was Barton who nodded.

'My client saw the news. He is aware you arrested an acquaintance of his in connection with the murder of the acquaintance's next-door neighbour. Mr Franco has never spoken to the victim and barely knows the accused. To hold him in this manner is an outrage.'

'He does know Rowe though, doesn't he?'

'Yes, he has spent time with him on the odd occasion. He met him at a local bar one evening with some other friends. They got on well. Mr Rowe seemed a troubled soul. He may even have been a little infatuated with Mr Franco. It was nothing more than that.'

Barton cut to the chase. 'Did your client see Mr Rowe on Boxing Day last year?'

'Yes. Rowe came around my client's house, had a cup of tea, and left. That's it.'

'Mr Franco didn't go anywhere with him?'

'No. Nowhere. Mr Franco kindly paid for a holiday some time ago. He hoped the young man could get his head together among the beautiful temples of Angkor Wat, but he seemed stressed for much of the trip. They only met a few times after. My client has only been inside Mr Rowe's house once or twice.'

'Would you like to tell us about their holidays? Were the locals friendly?'

The solicitor looked at them in the same way a cat disregards a stupid dog.

'That's all, gentlemen. You took my client's DNA sample to prove his lack of involvement. Release him, please. If you had more, you would have mentioned it.'

Barton terminated the interview and stepped outside with Zander.

'There's a word for this,' said Barton.

'Does it rhyme with duck?' said Zander with a grimace.

67

DI BARTON

Cox had ordered Zander to take Clavell to visit Rowe in Peterborough prison but Barton decided he'd take Clavell himself as he was keen to observe him in action again.

First things first though: Barton was due a chat with Whitlam. The two suits from Professional Standards departed without giving Barton any information about their discussion. Cox and he sat opposite Whitlam, who sat upright in his seat with his shoulders back. Barton, on the other hand, felt frazzled. He'd dressed smartly for the interviews, but his tie had now come off.

'David, we're recording this interview because some evidence has come to light linking you with the Somerville investigation.'

'Okay.'

Cox paused and scowled. 'Right. Have you been in either Robin Rowe's or Arnold Stone's house?'

'Let me think. Rowe, yes. I've had coffee on the odd occasion at his. He's a quiet lad, a little needy even. He gave me a lift into town once when my car wouldn't start, but then he got a bit too friendly. You appreciate what this job's like. I have enough involvement with the public at work. When I arrive home, I very much keep to myself.'

Barton shrugged in agreement. 'How about Mr Stone's?'

'Once, actually, or maybe twice. Both times for parcels. He used to get quite a bit of stuff delivered; said it was role-playing outfits. Not entirely certain what he meant by that. I wasn't sure if he was referring to wizards' cloaks or gimp suits. A couple of occasions he asked me to carry them in for him because he was on the phone. He was rude once actually. He was finishing a call and as I struggled with the heavy box he just watched me. Didn't I mention that at the meeting when we realised Stone was the victim?'

Cox squinted at Barton as she tried to remember. He nodded in confirmation that Whitlam had done exactly that. She bluntly stated the facts.

'Your DNA was found in Mr Stone's house, Mr Rowe's car and under Malcolm Somerville's fingernails.'

'Really? That's weird. Well, not the house and car as I've been in both of them, but definitely the fingernails.'

Barton stared hard. Whitlam smiled back. He didn't give any sign of being a person who had been rumbled.

'It's definitely yours. You know there are no mistakes. It was poor quality and only one locus matches, but it can still only be you or someone related to you,' said Barton.

Whitlam didn't seem fazed. 'I've no idea how, then. I haven't got any living family.'

'Did you and Somerville fight?' asked Cox.

Whitlam clicked his fingers and grinned. 'Well, kind of. He could have scratched me when I struggled to pull him out of the water. I told you that he dragged me in on top of him, and it felt like he tried to drown me.'

Barton and Cox shared another look.

'You can't be serious,' said Whitlam, with a chuckle. 'You think I killed Malcolm and was involved in Stone's death? That's crazy. I'm a policeman. Why the hell would I want to hurt those two?'

Cox tapped her pen on the table. 'You had nothing to do with either of their deaths?'

'Of course not. All the evidence points to Rowe. He'd have told you by this point if I had any involvement. This is beginning to feel like a witch hunt.'

Barton exhaled deeply. 'David, you know we have to investigate every angle.'

'Fair enough, but let's not lie to each other. It's obvious that

Professional Standards will hear about this, too. Any chance of me getting my job back now is zero. Tell me that's not true.'

'This interview is now over.' Cox rose and turned off the recorder. 'Off the record, your career finished when you lied to us.'

68

DI BARTON

Barton drove Clavell to HMP Peterborough. It was only mid-afternoon, yet he was already daydreaming about pulling his duvet over his head. He wished Clavell would stop complaining about Whitlam. He was starting to feel murderous himself.

'I can't believe it. Whitlam said what? That he got his skin under Somerville's fingernails trying to save him?'

'That's right.'

'And that his DNA turned up in Stone's house from carrying parcels in for him?'

'I'm glad you listened.'

'And you don't think that sounds dodgy?'

'It's more plausible than the alternative.'

'Which is what?'

'That he pulled an aggressive eighteen stone man out of the river, dragged him a mile along a path and threw him in the rowing lake. Remember, there were no wounds on the body. After those exertions, he and Rowe then killed his neighbour and buried him in Wisbech.'

Clavell stared hard out of the window as they parked outside the prison. 'This imbecile in here better start talking.'

Barton turned off the engine. 'Listen, simmer down. If you're too wound up, perhaps you should wait until I come back.'

But Clavell answered by getting out of the car. As the two men walked towards reception, Clavell grimaced. 'I hate these places.'

'You mean the hopelessness of it all. Lives ruined and futures lost.'

'I was referring to the smell.' He smiled. 'But that, too.'

Barton spoke through the grille.

'We're here to interview a remand prisoner.'

'What's your name?'

Barton showed them his warrant card. 'Detective Inspector Barton and DC Clavell, Peterborough Major Crimes.'

'You're not on the list.'

'I should be. Control said they'd ring it in. It's for Robin Rowe.'

'Your name's not down.'

Barton rolled his neck to let the steam out of his collar. 'I'm not on the list, so I'm not coming in? What is this, a nightclub? We will wait there.' Barton pointed at two seats through the security door and scanner. 'Ring Security. Tell them I'm here, and I wish to speak to an inmate immediately. He will contact the VP wing and get them to escort Mr Rowe to the interview rooms, where I will be waiting.'

The gate staff worker didn't reply, but the door swished open behind them.

Thirty minutes later, Barton and Clavell were waiting in a stuffy room for Rowe to appear.

Clavell paced the floor.

'Why don't you sit down?'

'I think better on my feet.' Regardless, he sat in the seat opposite Barton. 'Why did they search us so thoroughly? We're the police.'

'He probably did it to piss us off. It's actually good practice. Who knows what you might have stuffed up your arse?'

Clavell shot him a dirty look but started laughing. 'It would have been a bad moment if he'd asked me to remove my trousers and squat. Crazy case, eh? I'm really enjoying it, and I've picked up loads of great practice from watching you.'

'What have you learned so far?'

Clavell stood again with enthusiasm. 'The way your brain works is intriguing. It's different. I'm looking for a result all the time. I want to know who did it, charge them, and move on to the next case. You don't do that. For you, it's more about trying to understand a story. You strive to identify everyone's part in it. Eventually, it knits together.'

'Anything else?'

'I've seen how easy it is to jump to conclusions. DCI Cox is the same as you. There's no emotion involved, it's about the facts. Franco's holiday preferences are probably not important. Solving the case is. I know detectives should be patient, diligent, have excellent record-keeping, and check every angle, but I've really observed it here.'

'Still want my job?'

'No. I want to be your boss.'

Barton smiled as a tiny female prison officer ushered Robin Rowe's solicitor into the room. Her name badge said Di Matteo, but she didn't introduce herself. The brief slipped into the chair Clavell had vacated and the temperature in the room rose with an extra body. 'Afternoon,' said Burke. 'Warm day.'

'Thanks for coming at short notice.'

'You said you had news that affects my client's defence.'

'Yes, very much so.'

'I will advise him to make no comment, you understand. Is this official?'

'We want Mr Rowe to finally reveal the truth about that night.'

'Interesting. I know it's not usual for a solicitor to say this about a client, but I don't think he did it, and, if I'm not mistaken, I would wager you agree.'

'He's all we have.'

'He has an alibi.'

'That's why we're here.'

The female officer returned with Rowe, who had visible marks around both eyes and a cut on his chin. He wore a prison issue T-shirt. Barton suspected the clothes Rowe was incarcerated in had blood on them.

'Do you require me to stay?' she offered with a blank face.

Barton contemplated the trembling individual that had slunk onto the seat next to his solicitor. 'I think we'll be okay.'

She pointed at the alarm on the wall with the merest flicker of a smile. 'In case he overpowers you.'

Barton pressed a button on his recorder once the officer had closed the door on them, and then re-cautioned Rowe.

'Mr Rowe, have you had a change of heart about what you'd like to tell us?'

Rowe's eyes narrowed. He rocked slightly in his seat.

'We've spoken to the man you said you were with on the night of the murder, a Mr Alun Franco. He returned to the country yesterday.'

Rowe's head snapped up. 'See, I told you he'd be back and say where I was.'

A wave of sadness washed over Barton. Even though Rowe had potentially been involved in a serious crime, it was clear he lived an empty life, seemingly devoid of friends. Not one person had given a damn about him so far. The news Barton had to impart would devastate him.

'Mr Franco acknowledged that he knows you as a friend, but nothing more. He also confirmed your presence at his house for an hour or two on that Boxing Day. That's it.'

'I stayed for more than a couple of hours.'

'It doesn't really matter. We suspect his involvement in the murder of Arnold Stone, but suspicions are all we have. We have nothing solid on him at the moment.'

'What does that mean?'

'That means we only have you.'

Barton expected anger or tears but, instead, a weary resignation passed over Rowe's face. 'I didn't do it.'

'Tell us who did, then,' said Clavell.

'I don't know. I honestly thought Stone had done a runner.'

'There's indication that there has been a dead body in your boot. You know it's likely that his DNA will be found there. We also found black plastic caught on an ice scraper. It looks like the victim was wrapped in a bin bag and transported in your vehicle.'

'That's impossible. I know nothing about it.'

'Is this your car?' Barton slid over the still of Rowe's vehicle showing a man with a white cap in the driver's seat.

'Yes.'

'Is that you at the wheel?'

'It's hard to say, it isn't very clear.'

'Do you own a cap like that?'

'I did. I haven't seen it for ages.'

'You don't have to answer these questions, Robin.'

Rowe turned to his solicitor, and they all jumped as Rowe roared in his face. 'How is keeping silent helping? Look where I am. A place where rapists say they'll kill me for things I didn't do.'

'This car was clocked on Boxing Day night driving to and from Wisbech around 9 p.m. Is that you in the photo?'

'If this picture is from that night, then it must be someone else.'

'Wearing your cap?' asked an incredulous Clavell.

'I was with Alun. Why would he say I wasn't?'

His solicitor cut in. 'Mr Franco is very wealthy, almost as rich as the brief he has defending him. He will distance himself from all of this. I think you can probably forget about any support from his quarter.'

'So that's it? I'm guilty of murder?'

'You'll go to trial,' said Clavell. 'What about your other neighbour, David Whitlam?'

'What about him?'

'Perhaps he killed Stone and drove him in your car while you were out.'

'Where would he get my keys, and why would he do that anyway?'

'Was your house ever broken into? Did you lose a set of keys for a while?'

'No, of course not, or I would have said.'

'Then trial it is.' Clavell considered his words. 'There's something else. We've been led to believe men visit your residence, for short periods.'

'Eh? For what?'

'We assume for entertainment.'

Rowe snorted. 'I'm running a male brothel now! Really? You're all mad. This is insane.' Rowe's eyes bulged further. 'Take me to court. Surely the judge and jury won't be as nuts as you lot.' His wild expression focussed. 'Alun Franco will have to testify if you tell him to, won't he?'

'Yes.'

'He'll have to admit the truth. I'll make him. I know things about him that he won't want told. He'll back me up.' Rowe dropped his face into his hands. The other three sat quietly for a few moments.

Barton stared at Rowe's solicitor. 'Are you going to explain?'

Rowe raised his head. 'Explain what?'

The solicitor shrugged and kept silent, but Barton thought it only fair that Rowe knew.

'Franco's solicitor is going to know everything. He will be well briefed and pre-warned. Even under oath, I expect Franco to lie through his teeth and turn it all on you. He'll accuse you of being a liar. You'll be implicated with the same things that you accused him of. The jury will be disgusted with both of you. And at the end of the day, it'll only be you standing trial for murder.'

Rowe stared at each of them in amazement. He scraped his hands down the sides of his face, drawing a thin trail of blood on each cheek. Then he burst forward, and screamed a few inches from Clavell's nose. 'Screw you.' Clavell flew backwards off his chair. Rowe leapt from his seat and hammered the yellow alarm button. His snarl turned into a snivel and he backed up against the door.

Barton slowly rose and stood in front of Rowe. No one moved until Clavell got to his feet and gingerly rubbed the back of his head. Barton expected to hear a siren blaring out. Instead, after a few seconds, they heard the patter of a light pair of approaching boots. Officer Di Matteo checked the scene through the plastic window in the door and opened it.

'Sit down, please, Mr Rowe.'

'I'm leaving. Let me out.' Any bite had gone from his words, leaving only a childlike whine.

'Okay, go and stand next to the exit. I'll be there in a minute to arrange an escort.' Rowe left. Di Matteo asked, 'Everything all right?'

After three nods, she spoke into her radio. 'QV, Officer Di Matteo, Mike eight, Legal room four. That's a false press. I repeat, a false press. Stand the alarm down.'

'Mike eight, this is QV, we need confirmation from another call sign.'

'QV, I'll get them to give you a ring if they turn up. Mike eight over.'

She released the talk button on the radio. 'I see your meeting went well.'

69

THE SOUL KILLER

After the Professional Standards interview and the discussion with my superiors, I cruised back to Wisbech with a sense of satisfaction. Barney had rallied after I returned to live with him, albeit from a low ebb. I told him to pack his things before I left this morning. It's time for a final trip. I hope his heart holds out long enough. He was confused and exhausted yesterday, despite only walking down the stairs and outside for a few gulps of fresh air.

These days, I've taken to wearing a baseball cap and sunglasses at all times so I think the bloke in the petrol station thought it was a hold-up as I stepped from the cab. I filled the tank from empty and nearly had a heart attack at the cost. Daylight robbery, and the man in the kiosk wasn't even masked.

I joked to Barney that we'd have to make a run for it, but he didn't get it, gave me his debit card and insisted that he'd pay. Funds are plentiful, apparently. Barney hadn't changed his pin number from when I used his card at Christmas and said to treat myself to whatever I wanted, but I felt uncomfortable. That said, money must mean little when you're on borrowed time.

It's lucky they suspended me on full salary because money has been tight since I met Claudia. Looking good and looking after her is proving tricky. I remember another officer under investigation being on full pay for three years. It was a standing joke. He kept cancelling meetings and missing the rescheduled ones. He changed his representation twice and his address a couple of times. Then he went off sick with stress. Kicking the can down the road is the expression and I plan to do the same. It's only August now, but I deserve one more Christmas with the woman I love. I'll need more money, though, to win her back.

We approach the turning to West Runton, so I give Barney a nudge.

'Hey, is there anything you want to do?'

He turns his face towards me, grins, and his head drops to his chin so I turn the radio on for company.

It's five o'clock in the afternoon and I've not eaten since this morning's bowl of cornflakes. I miss the West Runton turn and carry on to East Runton where the fish and chip shop was that Barney took me to all those years ago. I park outside and stare at the sign. Will's Plaice. Barney used to joke it was *our plaice*.

The guy serving would have been wearing nappies when we last came in, but he's friendly enough. Fish and chips are expensive now. Once I've bought dinner, I get in the cab and drive back towards West Runton. There aren't many happy memories from my youth, but I cherish the few I have. I head down Water Lane, which leads to the cliff tops and the sea. At this point, Barney would always say, 'Almost there.' There are even three tall sunflowers swaying in the gentle breeze at the entrance to Lavender Caravan Park, as there are when I dream of this place.

I drive up the steep slope with the caravans on the left and swing into the area for campervans and tents. I reverse into the space so we can look down the hill at the kids playing football on the field. Turning to face Barney, I see he's awake and he grins and winds down the window. He takes a shallow breath, almost as if the goodness might be too much for him.

'Hmm, sea air. I'll be back to normal after a night here. Something smells good. Don't tell me we've got sausages and chips again? Plenty of salt and vinegar?'

We eat, as we always did, in silence. He consumes more in twenty minutes than I've seen him eat in the last two days. He lobs the odd chip out of the window and laughs as the ever-scavenging seagulls swoop down with glee.

'We need an ice cream now,' he says with a contented smile.

'I'll get them. You stay here.'

'Okay. Shop's probably in the same place.' He reaches into his back pocket, and I see him flinch. His face crumples in pain, and his neck arches. Drool hangs from his mouth for three or four seconds before he recovers and wipes it away. Our eyes meet.

'Must be the damn mercury in those fish I keep reading about,' he says.

'Nothing a mint Cornetto won't sort.'

'You're right. They cure all ills.'

My smile droops, but I raise it for him. 'I always enjoyed our time here. I want you to know that.'

His eyes close for a moment. 'It sure is a special place. I brought your mum once. Even she was different here.'

'So you don't think you'll see my mother again, you know, after? She might be waiting for you.'

'I used to think she would be, if I'd been bad.' He has a little chuckle. 'She told me often enough. But I don't think so now. It's a strange concept, which makes little sense if you look at it scientifically. I'm prepared to die. I know some people have such fabulous lives that they don't want them to end. They're happy for the party to continue in heaven. My life hasn't been much of a celebration. It's been quiet and uneventful, drab even. No one will mourn my passing.'

'Barney!'

'Don't be silly. That's okay. And I'm ready now. I'm tired and worn out. Everlasting peace will be enough for me. Now come on. I'm dying for that ice cream.'

I step from the cab with a little snort at his brave joke. Although he may well find he'll be more famous than he thinks when all this pans out.

'Wait,' he yells. 'I'm coming. Please, help me. One last time.'

I walk to his side and ease him down. He's no burden. I could carry him, but instead we link arms and shuffle along the path. We stare at the ice cream labels when we get to the shop, even though we always choose the same thing.

I grab the cones and walk to the counter, where I recognise the woman.

'Marcie?'

'It's Martha, but I get that all the time. You look familiar.' She stares behind me. 'Is that Barney?'

I step back, and her smile slips away as she sees the frail old man leaning on the fridge, wracked in agony. I pass her the ten pound note and speak under my breath. 'One last trip.'

'David. It's David, isn't it?'

I nod.

'It's wonderful to see you doing so well. You were such a quiet, shy lad. You'd come in here with your spending money and stare for ages at the chocolate displays. At first, I thought you were stealing things when I wasn't looking. You were a good boy though, weren't you? Barney said you had an unusual, erm, start in life. Anyway, those ice creams are my treat.'

'Thank you. Shall I settle up for the fees now?'

'How long are you staying?'

I glance back at Barney. He's stepped out and peers up into the sky. The sun bathes his face and removes the years. He seems childlike with his baggy trousers. 'Just until tomorrow, I think.'

She reaches over and folds my hands over my money. 'No charge.'

It takes forever for Barney to get to the bench that sits on the cliff top. It's much closer to the edge than it used to be. It isn't just us that the years have worn away. Barney's thankful, though. His eyes are misty as he leans against me.

'I love it here. I always have. Thanks for bringing me, son.'

I unwrap his Cornetto and place it in his hand and we stare out into the blue beyond. I wonder if this is a good end. It's not what I'd want.

I was never meant to grow old like Barney. I can't see the point. For me, like my mother, this life is only a stage. It's a dress rehearsal before the main event. A practice, if you will, for when I'll be really happy. I consider my life and the people in it. I've played well, I think, except for a few mistakes. Sacrificing my career to avoid suspicion was inspired after the net began to close. But I've let people get one up on me and that doesn't seem right.

Barney leans forward, and I only just manage to stop him falling off the bench. His ice cream lands upside down with a splat. He's still breathing though, as I can feel it on my shoulder. But his gasps don't have the strength of someone with any kind of future. I pull the Cornetto out of the dust and throw it with mine into the bin next to me. Standing beside Barney, I pick him up like a baby and cradle him in my arms. I'm glad I came. It's made me see that I don't want to die alone either.

To save going past the shop, I stride through the long grass back towards the van. The sinking sun blinds me, but I know the way.

I place Barney in one of the beds at the back of the van and sit opposite, contemplating my future. Claudia and I should be together, but there are clever men out to ruin things. Who's the best player? Who plans the furthest ahead? It's time for me to act without restraint. They will be bound by the laws they uphold, and I know them all. They are forced to play as police, whereas I can be whoever I choose.

70

DI BARTON

A week later, all the results from the labs were in, but so was something more dramatic. Cox had left the building with little notice, which was becoming a regular habit, so Barton had to chair the meeting. The full team were present, including the admin staff. Detectives must possess extra senses, he thought. The people present knew that the DNA test results had arrived, but defeat was in the air. Barton cleared his throat.

'This is not how I would want a case to end but it will go down as case solved, even if many of us here disagree. I'm here to tell you the investigation into Arnold Stone's remains has ended.'

'Why?' said Clavell.

'Every avenue leads to Robin Rowe. The DNA gives us nothing else concrete. Alun Franco will continue his grimy life free from charges. David Whitlam's involvement remains unclear. And the only man who'll be judging the soul of Mr Rowe is the Lord above.'

'Shit,' said Clavell.

'That is what will hit the fan, yes. An officer discovered him dead in his bed this morning at unlock after noticing a pool of blood edging out from underneath his door. A shoe contained a well-made prison weapon. They suspect someone gave it to him, as he wouldn't have had the know-how to construct one. Whether he requested it, or was told to use it, we'll never know.'

'Wasn't he on an ACCT book? Surely they must have been checking on him through the night?' asked Zander.

'That's what DCI Cox asked. They only had him on one observation an hour. His duvet was covering him, so it looked like he was sleeping. The coroner's inquest will no doubt focus on that. We didn't advise the jail to up his obs after our visit.'

'Wouldn't the prison officer on legal visits have done that?' asked Clavell.

'I imagine there's many people in the crosshairs.'

Ewing put his hand up. 'What happens now?'

'We don't have unlimited resources. There's no reasonable chance of prosecuting anyone else for the case unless further information or evidence is forthcoming. So let's tie up any loose ends. Get everything inputted. Two girls wandered into Huntingdon station and said they've been kept as sex slaves. One's French, the other German. Many of you will be directed towards that. Clavell, you'll leave us on Monday to join an investigation on a series of farm robberies. You are our contact if anything changes. Enjoy your last few days with us.'

Barton smiled even though it was an effort. 'There's no satisfaction in a case ending this way, but you've all worked incredibly hard. I'd like to thank DC Clavell for his efforts, as I'm sure you all would. Clavell, you have a promising future ahead of you. Please take this present back with you to Wisbech. Your colleagues will see what a great bunch we are.'

Barton grinned as Strange handed over the large parcel. Clavell had clearly annoyed plenty of people in the office because Barton had needed to make up the money to pay for it, but the gift was perfect and worth the extra tenner. Clavell opened it to subdued cheers. He held aloft a twenty inch plastic figurine of Darth Vader. When he pressed a button on the front, the familiar mechanical breathing of the evil villain echoed around. With another press, the figure spoke.

'If you only knew the power of the dark side.'

The whole room burst into good-natured laughter. Barton admired his team. They were a strong unit with a bright future. The last person he had eyes on was Clavell. He smiled, but Barton noted his clenched fists.

71

THE SOUL KILLER

I had a visit from carol singers last night. Bit early on the first of December, but I listened anyway. Strange how time drags when you have so little to do. It feels similar to the anticipation before a much-longed-for holiday or event. This will be a Christmas everyone remembers. I'll make sure of that.

I intended to drag out my standards investigation at work, but I haven't needed to. Instead, when I showed up for my second meeting, it was cancelled due to sickness, and I haven't heard from them since apart from a call telling me the investigation is still ongoing. It's as though they aren't sure what to do with me: a bit like whether to lay on a Christmas party or not. No one wants to make a decision, so they just delay until it's forgotten.

Barney died that night in the campervan. I drove home feeling very alone. Just as he must have felt in the years since my mother's fall. When I got back to his house, I carried him upstairs and laid him in his bed. I considered arranging a funeral but decided not to bother just yet. It settles me, knowing he's still with me.

I looked in on him this morning. It made me think of the pathologist I used to work with, Mortis. I expected Barney to decompose as Stone did, but it's different. Initially, Barney rotted fast. I burned through candles and air fresheners at an expensive rate. Then it stopped. He's mummified and doesn't look much worse than when he took his last breath.

I opened Barney's bank statements and grinned at his balance. All the direct debits have continued to tick over. No one knows he's dead. I could live here forever. I've had the central heating on most days. It's one of my few treats after how frugal my mother was with it. Because of that, Barney's body has dried out. The heat made his remains inhospitable, even for flies and bacteria.

It's been a disorientating time. So much unwanted freedom, so many hours, too many thoughts. My mind rarely strays from Claudia. Sometimes, I want to race there and grab her. I wish to hold her, love her, possess her, and blow the consequences. Why can't she see how good we are together?

Sometimes, I see us getting old and giving each other knowing glances across candle-lit tables that only a lifetime together could explain. Other times I'm realistic and think she's better off without me. Maybe I should get a gun and end it all. That way our youthful love would be preserved forever. Because how could it be heaven, if I were there, and she were here? I'm not waiting fifty years for her to arrive.

I've decided to visit her one last time. Perhaps she's mellowed and remembers me affectionately. Who knows how we'll be when we talk again? Will I be able to say my goodbyes and leave her be? But no, I don't have a life without her. There are cold grey days of rocking in my seat and shouting at the walls, dispersed by warm, sweet nights of hope where I dream we're together again.

The campervan starts first time and I steer it through the streets with intent. It's as if it knows of the challenge ahead. I park up the road from Annabelle's house and stroll towards it with my head down. There's a strange car in the drive. I'd guess it's a man's vehicle, by the mud splatters up the sides. I step behind a large skip and peer around the side as the front door opens. A figure I recognise steps out with Claudia. My brain struggles to process what I'm seeing. It's Clavell and, judging by the laughter, they are more than just acquaintances. I will kill him instantly if he kisses her, but he doesn't. He gets back in his vehicle and leaves with a friendly wave.

I didn't come here for nothing, so I walk towards the door. I spot the Christmas tree in the lounge with its twinkling lights. A curtain twitches above, and I see someone flit across the window. I'm pleased it's Claudia who answers when I knock.

'David? What are you doing here?' Her expression is open, cheeks flushed, soft lips parted. But it's not for me. There's only curiosity in her eyes. Did I really mean so little to her? Was our love so easily forgotten?

'I was in the area and thought I'd pop by and see how you are.'

'Thank you, I'm okay. I've kind of accepted things as they are and am trying to move on with my life. Work's going well.'

'How about Annabelle?'

Claudia's mouth droops. Then she looks wistfully up, steps outside and shuts the door behind her. 'Not good. I'm trying to get her into a residential home called Achieve. I don't think her medication is right and she's so thin. It's over in Bedford. The fees are astronomical, but we can afford it after selling Dad's place. She's got so bad that I don't know what to do with her any more.'

'That must be tough. You probably feel a bit like you've given up on her.'

She cocks her head to one side. 'You're right. That's exactly it.'

We share a small glance of understanding for a moment. It reminds me of my dreams. She must still have feelings for me.

'I see you've hung your decorations up early. Was that to try to cheer her up?'

'Yes. I didn't think it through enough though, as it's just reminded her of what happened to Dad on Christmas Day.'

'Oh, yes. An honest mistake through good intentions.'

'It feels like something's coming; you know, on the big day. As if something horrible is imminent, despite all the terrible things that have already happened last year. Sorry, I'm being weird. How are you – doing well, I hope?'

I don't want to seem a loser, but there isn't any point lying, seeing as Clavell's been here. 'Not great. I got suspended over the Malcolm thing.'

'Do you reckon you'll lose your job?'

It's clear that she already knows. 'I guess that's likely.'

'That's a shame. You loved your career.'

We both turn to the sound of a door slamming upstairs. Claudia's eyes moisten. 'Sorry, I ought to go. I'm meeting a friend for lunch soon.'

I feel dismissed. It'd better not be Clavell. I could follow her, but I'd stand out in the campervan.

'Okay, have a good time.' I step back to leave, but my body tenses. I need to ask. 'I recognised a guy from my department leaving when I turned up. What was he doing here?'

She blushes and stumbles over her words. 'He's been over a few times. That case where your neighbour died in that allotment still bugs him, despite the fact he has a lot on in Wisbech.'

'What's that got to do with you?'

'I'm not sure I should say this, but he thinks you have something to do with it.'

'Really, in what way?'

She wrings her hands. 'I don't know. He's been asking questions about you. Where you're from, what you're like.'

'And did you tell him?'

'That's just it, David. I don't know where you're from. I never met your parents, or any of your other friends. I don't even know where you grew up. Maybe that was why it didn't work out for us.'

'I told you my parents were dead.' As I'm talking, I hear a window above our heads open. I glance up into Annabelle's rage-filled face. She screeches.

'Fuck off from our house. You're the devil. I'll ring the police, you evil bastard.'

Claudia steps back inside and gives me a commiserating look. 'I don't want to get into a row. Let's leave all that in the past. I'll box up all your gifts. They must have been expensive. I am sorry it ended this way.'

'Keep them. They were for you to have, always.'

I flinch as a porcelain ornament flies over my head. I gasp and can't help a chuckle as another one smashes into smithereens next to my foot. Claudia smiles. God, I've missed it when she does that.

'I hope next year's better for us both, David,' she says with a little wave. 'Move on and be happy. It's for the best that we're over.'

I dodge a picture frame and retreat with a bow. She may think that, but I do not. I'm starting to think she is an ungrateful liar, but I'm sensing Clavell's hand in her change of attitude.

72

DI BARTON

A week later, Barton dropped the phone into the cradle with a clatter. He absent-mindedly took one of the chocolates out of his advent calendar and ate it, grimacing at the non-Cadbury's taste.

'That's the third one of those I've seen you eat today,' said Strange.

'Correct. I forgot to eat yesterday's, and I'm not in tomorrow.'

'A little old for those, aren't you?'

'We bought all the kids one. Layla said she was on a diet and didn't want it.'

'What? She's only eleven.'

'Eleven next month, but I agree. It's worrying.'

Barton ate the tenth of December as well.

'You know, some families get such bad luck, while others sail through lives of privilege with barely a scratch,' he said.

'Who are you talking about?'

'The Somervilles.' At Strange's blank face, he explained. 'Annabelle's father, Donald, had cancer and killed himself. Her husband drowned in the rowing lake.'

'I know, she must wonder "why me". Don't tell me something else has happened?'

'Yes. That was Norfolk police. Someone reported a car seemingly abandoned at a car park in Overstrand on the Norfolk coast. The driver's door was left open despite torrential rain. When the police ran the plate, the owner was Annabelle Somerville.'

'Has she turned up?'

'No, and she might not. The police searched the area and found a pile of neatly folded clothes next to a breakwater held down by a big rock, including shoes and pants. A photo album and her mobile phone were at the bottom. No sign of her, but it had been a foul night with a strong offshore wind. The tide conditions mean that if she swam out far enough, it's possible the current pulled her out to sea.'

Strange grimaced. 'You think she killed herself?'

'It certainly looks that way. We received a call last night from her sister, Claudia. She'd been working late, and when she got home the house was empty.'

'Why'd she ring us?'

'She said her sister hadn't left the house in months and wasn't of sound mind.'

'Oh, dear. That doesn't look good, then. Why did Norfolk ring you? I'd have thought uniform would deal with it.'

'They checked the computer and found the case and my name. I said I'd go around and talk to Claudia.'

'You want me to come?'

'No, it's okay. She'll want to get involved in the search. I won't be able to persuade her otherwise. I'll get uniform to drive her to Overstrand if she hasn't got anyone else to go with her. I'd do it, but it's nearly two hours away. It's terrible how suicide can have such a ripple effect.'

'I couldn't end it like that. It wouldn't be fair on everyone else.'

'I think that's the point. Mental health issues are irrational and hard to understand. Complicated things, brains. That's why Zander's lucky he doesn't have one.'

Strange laughed at Zander, who'd just walked in. He frowned.

'That's weird. I came in here to see if my friends wanted a beer on Christmas Eve, seeing as it doesn't look like there's going to be a work thing. Yet, I see no mates, just a pair of gits. I must have come to the wrong place.'

'This git is definitely up for it. I enjoyed last year.'

'Count this git in as well,' said Barton. Holly had instructed him to invite Strange on Christmas Day again. He kept forgetting but thought he'd be better off doing it when it was only the pair of them.

'Right. I'm off to break some bad news.'

Zander sat in the seat he'd vacated. The last thing Barton heard as he left was, 'Man, you've definitely got issues if you're unable to control yourself with an advent calendar.'

73

DI BARTON

Barton dawdled on the way to Annabelle's home. He tried to think of what he could say to ease Claudia's pain, but there wasn't anything. He slowed when he turned into Cherry Orton Drive and let a black and white campervan pull out ahead of him. The man hunched over the wheel under a low cap. His speed made the tyres squeal. He'd be lucky if he didn't kill himself driving like that.

Two cars were in the driveway. If Annabelle's was in Overstrand, then hopefully that meant Claudia had a friend over. Calls like these were a part of a detective's life, but they were never easy. In some ways, this one would be even worse than normal, as there would be a glimmer of forlorn hope.

They didn't really know what had happened to Malcolm; no one did. He wondered what the twins had said when Whitlam told them the truth about what happened the night Annabelle's husband died. Whitlam must have been given his marching orders.

Barton's fist was raised for his second knock when Claudia appeared with a face flitting from concern to optimism. She paused with her hand on the lock before she opened the door and stared at Barton. A visit from the police wasn't always bad news, but maybe she had hoped for him to bring Annabelle back, like a lost child. Besides, she probably realised that if it was positive, the police would have rung straight away. Claudia crumpled to the floor. Barton could hear her sobs from outside.

A man came out of the darkened room behind her, knelt

down and kissed her head. Barton rubbed his eyes. What the hell was Clavell doing in the house? It was Clavell that opened the door.

'Boss. Is it bad?'

'We think so. Shall I come in?'

'You know where the lounge is.'

Barton sat opposite the hand holding couple feeling uncomfortable. It was hard not to focus on this unexpected relationship instead of the devastating news he had to deliver.

'There isn't any easy way to say this. We found your sister's car, seemingly abandoned.'

Claudia's snivel turned into a strange keening sound.

'Where was it?' asked Clavell.

'Overstrand.'

'Where's that?'

'It's a small Norfolk village up the coast from Cromer and East Runton.'

'And Annabelle?'

'No sign.'

'Maybe she's not dead, then?' Claudia gasped.

'We found a pile of clothes, a mobile phone, her shoes, and a photo album of your family in a heap near the sea.'

'But you don't actually know she's not alive?'

Barton paused. Hope could be an awful thing. 'No, but the prevailing conditions meant that if she had gone in the water and not come out, she may well have disappeared into the North Sea.'

'My God! Are they looking for her?'

'The coastguard is searching the area. People can drift quickly at this time of the year, or they can sink.'

'There's no chance?'

'It is possible that she changed her mind, but unlikely, I would have thought. A healthy person with some body fat might last half an hour before hypothermia set in.' Barton didn't see the need to labour that point. Annabelle wouldn't have lasted five minutes.

'I hope you understand but there are some questions I have to ask because it could help us in our search. Was your sister mentally sound, in your opinion?'

Claudia wiped her eyes with the back of her sleeve,

smearing mascara across her face. 'Are you asking if she was suicidal?'

Barton nodded.

'Yes, she was. Very. Annabelle lost her husband, as you know, while we were already grieving for our father. Our lives have been turned upside down. It's been too much for her. I got a call yesterday telling me they had accepted her at a mental health care home. That should answer your question. I've let her down, and now I want to kill *myself*.'

She banged her fists on the sofa cushions, jumped to her feet, and stomped to the door. Clavell rose to follow, but she held up her hand. 'No, talk to him. I'm getting ready for the journey to Overstrand.'

Clavell sat back down. 'When's this all going to end?'

'If you don't mind me asking, how long have you two been dating?'

He reddened but looked Barton in the eye. 'A few weeks. I came to speak to her about Whitlam, and we got along. The final time I returned, it wasn't to discuss him. Instead, I asked her out.'

'Did you see much of Annabelle?'

'A bit. She slept most of the day though, only getting up for dinner. She'd come down and rant about Whitlam being an evil demon who killed her family.'

Barton smiled. 'Isn't that what you think?'

'I'm sure he was involved. Do you remember me saying something felt familiar about him?'

'Yes.'

'I only just realised, but it might be the way he talks.'

'What, you mean his accent?'

'It's not as strong as mine, but there's a slight element of the Fen dialect to his speech. He once said tret as opposed to treat.'

'Eh?'

'She tret that man badly. People from the Fens, places like Wisbech, talk like that.'

'What's that got to do with anything?'

'It gives him a link to Wisbech. Do you know where he's from? Where he was born? His past was a mystery even to Claudia. If he came from Wisbech, or nearby, he might be familiar with the allotment. Robin Rowe had no connection at all. Could you speak to HR, find out where his next of kin lives?'

'I'm pretty sure he's an only child and his parents are dead. I thought that explained why he was so quiet and shy.'

'Just before I left, I took a sneaky picture of Whitlam on my phone. I went and knocked on the door of the guy who had the allotment until recently. Perhaps he knew Whitlam or recognised him. I've been twice, but there's never anyone in.'

'He's probably dead. He wasn't in great shape.'

'Yes, that's what I reckon. I haven't given up yet though.' Clavell stood and offered Barton his hand. 'Thanks for coming to do this. I know this isn't your remit. Don't worry about her getting to the coast, I'll take her.'

He rose to walk Barton out. Sobbing echoed from upstairs. Clavell stopped a few steps from the door and turned around.

'You're a good man, John.'

'Thanks. Don't worry, I'll look into Whitlam for you.'

Barton let himself out. Sitting in his car, he considered how Whitlam would feel if he knew Clavell was shagging his ex-fiancée. Love can make you reckless. Clavell was a brave man if he suspected Whitlam of being a killer.

74

THE SOUL KILLER

I have a plan, and now I'm really looking forward to Christmas. Only two days to wait, then Claudia and I will enjoy one final uninterrupted day together. Hopefully, when she sees that everyone else has left her, I'll be back in favour. But there's a niggle in my head. It hints that I've lost sight of things; that I've stopped seeing the world as it is. I suppose self-doubt is natural.

My thoughts stray to my mother, and her gradual detachment from reality. Am I destined, pre-programmed even, for the same fate? The question of sanity is only an opinion. At some point in our lives, we all struggle. Who knows what His plan is? My mother taught me to look out for myself. I think I understand her sermons now and must trust in my decisions.

If Claudia decides we have a future, we should move miles away. There are too many hidden crimes here and, after what I plan to do tomorrow, some that will soon be discovered. By the time they connect the dots to Cambridge, we will be far away, and hopefully at peace. I hope Inspector Barton has forgotten about me. I'd hate to bump into him and get his brain churning.

I've spent a lot of time outside Clavell's bedsit. I tried not to consider where he was at night because he wasn't home very much. I've seen his car at hers on a few occasions. Does Claudia deserve me if she's fooling around with him? But no, I can't believe she'd do that. He must just be comforting her as a friend. But that should be my job. At least when he's gone, there'll be a vacancy.

I rub my temples. There seems to be a permanently present

dull thud of late to accompany my inner critic. It stops me from thinking straight, and it makes me tetchy. I jolt awake from troubled dreams filled with my mother's rantings. Now I have time to consider her words, I'm inclined to agree with her. There's too much pain and suffering in this life. Is it all a test before something better? It's made me remember the church. A visit there is long overdue.

I stretch my body to warm it up. I'll be too strong for him, but I don't want to risk an injury, not with all my plans. I turn the engine off and look at my watch. He should be here at his place very soon. Clavell wouldn't make it in the secret service because it didn't take long for me to deduce a pattern. Leave Claudia's, or wherever he is, and come home to get dressed for work at 6:30. Same thing now for a few days. But this time, I'll be waiting to meet him.

I put on the woolly hat that Annabelle wore all the time to keep warm as her weight plummeted. I glance in the mirror. I have done a terrible job with the lipstick, but I still shudder at the realisation I resemble my mother.

I can just fit in Annabelle's jacket. She must have bought it before all this happened. I also found some big sunglasses in her room before I left. If they find any grainy CCTV of her car on the way to Overstrand, they'll see her driving. I took a train back. No doubt my DNA is present in her car. If they check that, I really am screwed.

As I watch Clavell park up, it dawns on me that I'm not bothered. 'I don't care if I die.' I chant the words a few times. Maybe I am going crazy. Why aren't I scared? Do I have so little to live for? I've lost my job, my girl, and even Barney drank himself to death. That seems a slow way to go. One thing I do know is that when I leave this unloving world, it will be on my terms.

I step out of the van. The path to Clavell's house has a big concrete ball on a pillar post. I slouch to disguise my height. Clavell stops behind me, and I turn to him. There's a satisfying huge intake of breath. Confusion reigns until realisation dawns. I growl the words to him.

'James Clavell. Or I think you used to prefer Jimmy.'

His mouth is still open as he hits the pavement. There's nothing that says *screw you* quite like a baseball bat around the head. I bench press more than this moron at the gym. Throwing him in the campervan is no problem. After taping his arms behind his back and putting a strip over his mouth, I cruise along the empty street. They'll be looking for a six foot drag queen if anyone noticed anything.

I drive out to a quiet country lane I know and stop. He's beginning to stir. A shattered right knee wakes him fully.

'Remember me, Jimmy?'

He rocks from side to side in the little kitchen area where I put him, his face pinched in silent agony, sweat beading his brow. I tap his knee again, rip the tape from his mouth, and, finally, his howls satisfy something primeval in me. He eventually stills and scowls through slit eyes.

'It's you. The weird kid from our first year at senior school.'

'That's right. You probably never knew my name. Too busy making everyone laugh. I thought I recognised you, although you've changed. You're still small, though.'

'You're sick in the head. I guessed you were involved. There's no chance you'll get away with it.'

'I'm not even sure I want to any more.'

His predicament finally sinks in. He frantically glances around for help. 'It's not too late to hand yourself in.'

I laugh in his face. 'We both understand that's not true.'

He shakes his head in disbelief. 'Please, don't.'

'It isn't easy killing people and evading justice. You'd think I'd know that. There's CCTV, DNA, witnesses, alibis, number plates, post-mortems, and good old police savvy getting in the way. I'll get rumbled at some point. Everyone does. Hopefully, I'll be gone when the time comes.'

He lets out a whimper. Whether that's from pain or self-pity, I'm unsure. Perhaps it's regret for his promise that will now be unfulfilled. Well, he shouldn't have touched my woman.

'You must be pleased your intuition didn't desert you. That'll be a nice thought for your soul to take to hell, you vicious, bullying bighead.'

I can't resist a slap across his face. I want him begging. He needs to feel real fear, just as I did at school. I punch him hard on the nose. He rocks back and his voice slurs as blood pours down his face.

'Don't, David. Think about it. Show mercy.'

I thrust my knee into his chin and he falls back. He scrabbles back to face me, no doubt hoping that eye contact will jolt some humanity loose in me.

'Please,' he gasps.

'Do I look the merciful type? And why should I be? Don't you remember your jibes, your cruel lasting taunts? You left that school but I had to stay for another six long years. You tarred me in those first few months. You made me a victim. Kids grow up, but they don't forget. From those days forward, they saw me as someone to pity and keep at arm's length. You destroyed me.'

I realise I'm shouting at him, and it's now me who wipes a sheen of moisture from my head.

'I–'

'Don't! Don't try to explain. You're too late. On my very last day, one of your friends called me Shitlam. That's the school memory I took for the future.'

I tap the bat into my hand. 'Well, there's always a price to pay for cruelty, and you will settle your account today.'

He weeps at his end. 'I was just a child.'

'Does that negate your actions? I suffered, and you must experience the same fate.'

'I'm sorry.'

They are the last words he utters as I wield the bat. I plan to kill him slowly. I don't want blood everywhere so I try not to break the skin too much, but something takes over. I wipe my face afterwards. The walls and ceiling run with red. The curtains hang heavy with moisture. I open a storage box under the seats at the back of the van. He'll fit in nicely after I've removed the blankets. I use them to clean away some of the blood and put on my old clothes.

I fire up the engine. There's no time for dawdling seeing as I haven't fed Annabelle today.

75

THE SOUL KILLER

Christmas Eve is the perfect day to wipe the slate clean and Orton Longueville church is just the place. Barton said the vicar there was a bit odd when he talked to him about the Snow Killer. Perhaps he absolved the murderer's sins before the dramatic end.

I drive over the town bridge towards the cathedral. It looms large over the city and adds much-needed elegance to it. It's too big and impersonal for me. The men who run it are no doubt busy and would struggle to find time for my affairs. I need to talk to someone who will hear me out.

Peterborough United are playing at home later. It's a cup replay. Football fans flow through the streets on the way to the ground. I smile as they stagger off the pavement, jeering at each other. Sometimes they frustrate me, but not now, not today. My life will be different soon. I will finally be able to move on. Everything seems special as I ready myself for forgiveness. I want to run my hands over life and experience it afresh.

Oundle Road is heaving and Woodston Chippy is enjoying a roaring trade. I pass the railway bridge next to the Cross Keys pub and wait at the crossing for the signal to change. Decorations sparkle in windows; lights adorn trees. It's as though they are guiding my path. I increase the radio's volume in the campervan and sing along to 'Last Christmas' by Wham. I'll enjoy this year.

Claudia and I should have some fun when this is all settled.

After all, laughter is food for the soul. Although, it's funny how the season of goodwill can bring such ill will.

I've found Christmas magnifies reality. If life is great, Christmas makes it better. If you are poorly, the day will sicken you further. Lonely, and you'll want to die. If money's tight, you'll regret your choices. But worst of all, if you're already angry, Christmas can push you to your limits. Murder becomes just a disagreement away.

I turn left at Ferry Meadows traffic lights and cruise past the Ramblewood Inn. There's no car park for the church because it's been there for centuries so I park on the verge as they must have done when they rode horses and drove carriages. The door is open, which is a good sign that there's someone who I can talk to. I need to unburden myself, or it will have all been for nothing.

First, I stop amongst the newer headstones. Both victims and perpetrators of the snow killings are buried here. There are fresh flowers on the graves. Somebody still cares, despite the brutality of the Snow Killer. To think a paid assassin lies here in God's holy ground. Can there be a sin more wicked than snuffling out others' lives for money? The inscription on one says *I will sleep in peace until you come for me*. It's food for thought.

The door of the church shutting interrupts my melancholy. The vicar is leaving. I crunch through the gravel behind him. He's so old and crooked, I doubt it would take much of a shock to loosen his grip on life.

'Father, could I have a minute?'

It's the most weathered face I have ever encountered. I've seen fresher bark. The eyes judge me though, and that's what I'm here for.

'I don't have many of those left, but you can have one.' He walks to a nearby tomb and leans against it. 'You looked at that family over there. Did you know them?'

'I had dealings with some of them, just before they died. The fact people like that lie in hallowed ground is proof of His forgiving ways.'

'It's a sad story. Not all you read in the papers was true.'

'Is it ever?'

He contemplates that for a few seconds. 'You're right, I guess it's only ever opinion.'

I follow his gaze back to the graves. 'Even killers need final resting places, but don't people desecrate their tombs because of what they've done when they find out where they've been buried? I imagined there'd be protests or something at a funeral for murderers such as them.'

'I laid them to rest quietly and without fuss. Now, what can I do for you? You seem a man with a burden.'

'I'm a man with a question.'

'Ask it.'

'Does everybody go to heaven?'

'Do you believe in Jesus?'

'I think so. My mother and other religious people taught me to respect his story, but I have deviated from those lessons.'

'In my Father's house, there are many rooms.'

I look into his wise eyes. 'What does that mean?'

'There is space for everyone who asks for forgiveness and means it.'

'Even for those who have committed inexplicable evil?'

'The requirement for entrance into the kingdom of God is only to atone and believe in Christ.'

'And what of those souls who never asked for mercy? What of those who don't believe?'

Curious eyes regard me. 'There are many views, a lot of which differ. Each person can believe in what they wish. I'll ask again. What is it you want?'

'I would like to repent.'

A cold breeze scatters leaves around our feet.

'Perhaps we should go inside for a moment.'

I follow him through the stone doorway, and he suggests I take a seat on a pew. A crucified Jesus stares down at me. I sense the eyes following me as I kneel down before him. The vicar returns wearing his cassock and holding a small black Bible. Lowering himself next to me, he makes the sign of the cross.

'I don't know what to do. Am I supposed to ask for forgiveness?'

'I'm not Catholic. Forget what you've seen on TV. If you'd like to get something off your chest, now is the time.'

I repeat for clarity. 'Anyone can be absolved, including people who've done terrible things? Maybe even those who took a life?'

His piercing glare settles on me once more. 'When we repent our sins and receive Him into our hearts, God has promised to forgive us. Completely and fully. The Bible gives us a clear example that leaves no place for doubt. Two robbers were crucified with Jesus. They even mocked him while they nailed his hands. Yet one of them saw the light. He asked Jesus to remember him when he ascended. Jesus promised entrance to heaven with Him saying, "Truly, I say to you, today you will be with me in Paradise." Luke 23. And not only that, but it was to a killer who would never do good in life, as he was soon to die.'

'I understand. All who ask are saved.'

'That's right.'

'And you won't report me to the police?'

'I think if the message got out that we blabbed to the authorities, then no one would talk to us. Not about the truth, anyway.'

'Okay.' I take a deep breath. 'I pushed my mother down the stairs and killed her because she was sick and cruel to me when I grew up. My girlfriend's father's cancer entered its final stages, and his last wish was to see us apart. I put a noose over his own head and I shoved him over the bannister.

'A drowning man interfered in my relationship with his sister-in-law. Instead of saving him, I plunged him under to a watery grave. I throttled a man and buried him in an allotment for playing his music loud and generally being annoying. Turns out he had learning difficulties and was deaf. I faked my girlfriend's sister's suicide and keep her in my basement, because she, too, got in the way.

'A detective in the police almost solved my crimes and tried to ruin my life. He befriended my girlfriend to catch me. It was the same person who bullied me mercilessly when we were at school. I bludgeoned him to death and placed his remains in a storage cabinet.

'My girlfriend rejected me, but I hope we'll run off and start a new life. I'm not sure what I'll do if she decides not to come with me. Eventually, or sooner if necessary, I want us to go up to heaven together. Two people took advantage of my better nature at university. One paid with his life and the other is due a visit. My mother said to repent in this life, rejoice in the next. I am here to absolve my sins.'

The Bible slipped from the vicar's fingers. 'You can't be serious?'

'Deadly. Let's hope he's listening and feeling merciful because it sounds terrible when you say it like that.'

'You must hand yourself in to the police.'

'Are you mad? They'd lock me up and never release me.' I let out a little chuckle. 'Misconduct in public office seems rather an understatement.'

He leans away, as though it's painful to be so near.

'What are you?'

'I'm a detective.'

He blanches. 'It doesn't matter. That is part of forgiveness. You must confess and take responsibility for your actions.'

'Hmm, not tempting.'

'Are you sorry for what you've done?'

'Yes, I'm repentant. I didn't want it to turn out like this.'

'Do you utter those words in the hope of salvation, or do you truly believe?'

'I believe I will rejoice in heaven. It's all I've ever known.'

'Even after your actions? Can't you see the conflict in your words?'

It's as though this peaceful place has stilled my mind. Only now can I think about what I've done clearly. I've broken every commandment there is, and then some. I open my mouth to blame my mother, but she never taught me to murder. If I'm to confess, I must lay it all out there. I may not get another chance.

'It's worse than you imagine.'

'Explain.'

'I knew that my victims didn't believe. I wanted to do more than end their lives.'

'I think I see. You think of yourself as some kind of soul killer.'

'I suppose so.'

'And, in a way, you thought you were doing God's work.'

'That's right. My mother told me to protect myself. Those people interfered, and I stopped them, forever.'

'I have to say it's a depressing take on things. I'm not sure that a place filled with people like you is any kind of heaven I'd be interested in.'

His honesty and evident sadness confuse me. All that time

under my mother's influence and then over a decade on my own has corrupted me. What is it I want? Can I still have it?

'What do I do?'

His gnarled hand reaches over and takes one of mine. 'You must care for others. Learn to turn the other cheek. Sacrifice yourself, not the innocent.'

I place my other hand on the top of his. 'I will change.'

'And you'll lead a good life from now on? There'll be no more crimes, no more killings.'

I consider his question carefully. It can't benefit your salvation to lie to a man of the cloth. I stand to leave. He whispers a prayer under his breath and looks to the cross above as he speaks.

'Remember. God is watching, always.'

'I know, Father. I felt his hand upon my shoulder, but it wasn't pulling me back. These were bad people. He gave me strength.'

'Stop these wicked deeds, I beg you. Trust in the Almighty. It's not too late to ask for His mercy.'

'I know. I'll return when I'm finished. When others have asked for mine.'

76

DI BARTON

Barton shaved his head and face and gazed in the mirror before he left for the night. It had been a strange year that he'd be glad to see the back of. He'd had an unsettling visit from Claudia Birtwhistle not long before he finished work. He found shaving helped still his mind. He tried Clavell's mobile number again, but it was turned off. Whitlam's phone continued to ring out.

'Another hot date on Christmas Eve, eh?' said Holly.

'That's right. I have a double date with two sergeants.'

'Bilko and Pepper?'

'Sadly not. Think *Police Academy*. I'm meeting Hightower and – who was the one with the big boobs?'

'Callahan. Although I probably wouldn't mention that to Kelly.'

'She'll be flattered. I saw her in a film last week, and she's pushing seventy and still fit.'

'Will you be wearing animal furs tonight or just talking like a caveman?'

'Ugg.'

'If you're done at eight o'clock, I'll swing by and pick you up. I'm collecting Layla from Terri's then.'

'Sounds good. I'd hate to walk the five hundred metres home.'

Of the children, only Luke remained downstairs. Barton ruffled his hair and said he'd be back in time to put him to bed. Luke had finally got his head around the entire Christmas thing and was a little freaked out about the strange bloke coming down their chimney and going in his bedroom while he slept. Holly promised she'd leave a message to tell Santa to hang the stocking outside on his door.

Lawrence had babysitting duties. He came into the lounge and sat next to his little brother. Lawrence whispered into Luke's ear, who then piped up, 'Don't eat Father Christmas's mince pie, Daddy.'

Barton strolled along to the pub with a smile. Even his son knew about his legendary lack of willpower. When he got to the church, he crossed over the road past a campervan parked on the verge.

Barton checked his phone: 17:55 on the dot. He was the last to appear. They'd bought him a pint, but there were numerous empties around them. He spied two little Sahara nut tubs. Zander only ate them when he was tipsy.

'Cheers, guys,' he said, and they clinked glasses. 'Been here a while, have we?'

'Four,' said Zander.

'You got here at four?'

'No, we had four drinks before you arrived. Remember, we took today off because we're both on call tomorrow, so you can make your sofa groan all day.'

Even though Zander spoke clearly, the banter was well advanced. A slightly inane grin settled on Strange. Drinking at the same pace as Zander was tough when you were half his size. Especially seeing as she was one of only a few women he'd met who often went pint for a pint. Barton cleared his throat.

'I know we said no talking shop, but I had an unusual visit earlier, and it's got me a little worried.' The other two slid their chairs closer.

'Clavell might have gone missing. He didn't show for a little get-together at the Wisbech station yesterday or for an arrangement with his girlfriend today. No one can get hold of him either. His car's parked at his home, too. Now, he had two days off, and didn't have to go to either event. It wouldn't be the first time he's not turned up to social stuff, but it's got me thinking. I only found out because that Claudia Birtwistle who's had all the bad luck came in to see me, distraught.'

'Why does she care?' asked Zander.

'I didn't think it was anyone's business, so I kept quiet, but he's been seeing her for a while.'

'What? He's been dating Whitlam's ex-girlfriend? Didn't Clavell think Whitlam was involved in that murder in his street?'

'Yes, I thought it a brave move, too.'

'The difference between being courageous and foolish can be a fine line. I'd do anything for love, but I wouldn't do that. Oh, no.'

They all joined in with the next few lines from the Meat Loaf song. It was a nice moment, but Barton stopped quickly and Strange picked up on it. 'You think Whitlam's responsible?'

'My rational head says of course not, but Clavell's not spoken to her for days and he was keen. There's a whole load of misery surrounding Whitlam. Robin Rowe killing himself put that investigation to bed, but Whitlam lived two doors away. If you start to look at Whitlam with real suspicion, it has to put him at least in the frame. And what if he was implicated in that drowning despite what he said?'

Zander piped up, 'And there were the two suicides. This Claudia's father and sister.'

'Yeah, I'm not sure he's involved with them though. What would be the point?'

They mused on that for a few moments. 'What if Whitlam fell out with them? Maybe they were trying to split him and Claudia up,' said Strange.

'It's bloody hard staging a suicide,' replied Zander.

Strange came straight back. 'Who better to do that than a detective? He'd understand how to cover his tracks and plan it.'

'Interesting thought. Very dark. So, he knocks those two off to get them out the way. Now he's done Clavell as well, which is actually more understandable. That doesn't explain why he'd kill Arnold Stone.'

'No, that's true,' said Strange. 'Unless he's a complete psychopath.'

She had spoken glibly, but her words hit home. Barton pressed his lips together. 'It's a stretch, but nothing surprises me any more. It's just dawned on me, too, that I don't really know anything about him. He's a good detective, and he likes the gym. That's it. If you two turned out to be homicidal I'd be surprised, but not so much with Whitlam. He enjoys a joke every now and again, but I get the feeling he said stuff like that because it's expected of him. Malik said he was obsessed with Claudia, and unrequited love makes people dangerous.'

'What's happening about Clavell, then? Are they investigating it as suspicious?'

'Wisbech station sent an officer to Clavell's house share. One of the other tenants heard him in his room first thing yesterday, so he hadn't even been missing for a full day this morning. And who's to say he has vanished? Most missing persons cases tend to be adults who are thoughtless. Maybe he couldn't be bothered with the party and forgot about the date. Perhaps one of his parents is ill. He'll only be officially missing tomorrow if he doesn't turn up or ring in for his shift.'

'That's true, but it doesn't feel right.'

'It's skeleton staff at this time of the year, so I've put out a BOLO for him. Wisbech are taking it seriously now as it's out of character for him not to answer his phone. Their chief rang me just after I found out to ask if I knew anything.'

'Did you tell them about the Whitlam angle?'

'Yes. It sounded bonkers when I explained it. The chief didn't like the sound of it either, although he's inclined to wait until tomorrow morning in the hope he shows. I placed a request with ANPR to see if Whitlam's vehicle headed towards Wisbech lately. I sent Ewing and Zelensky to River End. Both attended as who knows what Whitlam's frame of mind is? They reported that the house looks empty and, judging by its dirtiness, his car hasn't been used for quite a while.'

'Ooh, where's he gone?' said Strange. 'Perhaps he's back at the allotment? Wow. Could Whitlam *be* the Compost Heap Killer?' Strange and Zander found that highly amusing and took a minute to settle down again.

'You may laugh, but I told them to send someone there to check it out. Uniform have been briefed and I've asked for officers to drive past at regular intervals throughout the night. I've asked the EZ Crew who are on until ten tonight to travel between Whitlam's house and Claudia's house as well to keep an eye on things. They've been told not to engage if they spot him because we don't know the level of risk. Luckily Claudia is out with an old school friend tonight. She won't be back until nine.'

'He's either a man having a terrible time or a stone-cold killer,' said Zander.

'I discussed it with DCI Cox. She's got the armed patrol vehicle on notice. Not to put too fine a point on it, chances are if Clavell's been taken, he could already be dead.'

On that grim note, Barton found a spot at the bar and ordered another round. He ordered himself an alcohol-free lager this time. The others were already too far gone. They were still discussing the case when he returned. Barton picked up the thread.

'Right, what are the risks here with not scaling up the investigation fast enough? How much can we realistically get done on Christmas Day and Boxing Day? It's rubbish for morale if leave is cancelled for a wild goose chase. Most of the other departments are shut.'

'If Whitlam is the killer, is anyone else at risk?' asked Zander.

'There's no family left, and the boyfriend's gone. It seems to me that all threats have been eliminated.'

'What about Claudia? Is she safe?' asked Strange.

'I spoke to her on the phone. It wasn't a nice call, telling her that we have concerns about the state of mind of her ex-boyfriend. I didn't mention that he might have killed everyone close to her, but after talking this through with you, I realise I need to.'

'I think that's the right call. What did she say?' said Zander.

'She thinks something's not right, and her family have had too much bad luck. She'd had a visit from the family GP and they still don't think that her father would have killed himself, whatever the evidence indicates. She mentioned her dad had been trying to get her to split up with Whitlam near the end. Her brother-in-law hated him from the start.'

'God, I was joking earlier, but there's too much circumstantial evidence. Should we have seen something?'

Barton grimaced. 'We're not solving maths problems. It often takes time for the full picture to form. We might not even be right. As I said, he could turn up at the station tomorrow and wonder what all the fuss is about. The work we do will never be perfect.'

'I suppose that's right. Is Claudia on her own tonight?'

'That friend is staying with her.'

'Is she at risk?' asked Strange.

'Her friend, Chloe, has never met him. She's recently moved back to the area. Claudia is the object of his desire, so she shouldn't be in danger. Saying that, talking to you has got me more on edge.'

'Christmas does weird things to people. What if he decides that if he can't have her, nobody can?'

'That's the risk. The house has excellent security. I've told her not to open the door to anyone and ring if anything is out of the ordinary, but I'm going to go over at quarter to nine. Claudia said she only spoke to him a little while back, and he was fairly reasonable. She doesn't think he'd hurt her, although from what we've discussed, I'm not so sure.'

'We'll come,' said Zander.

'No, you won't. You're both on call tomorrow. If it does kick off, you need to have had some sleep. We're thinking worst case scenario here. All we might have is a bloke who's missed a couple of dates and isn't answering his phone.'

They sat in silence for a while and struggled to drag their minds away from the intriguing and troubling case. When an unexpected person turned up, they tried to put the issue out of their heads for the moment.

'Hey, isn't that Sirena?' said Zander.

Barton's eyebrows raised, then his eyes widened at her little black dress.

'Roll your tongues up, boys,' said Strange.

'Hi, guys. Sorry I'm late.'

'I didn't think you were coming,' said Barton.

'I know. It's a surprise.' She laughed loudly and appeared to have done some pre-loading elsewhere. 'I saw Kelly in Queensgate doing some shopping today, and we had a coffee, which was very nice.' She reached over and squeezed Strange's hand. 'She told me your plans, and I love you guys. So here I am! My round?'

Sirena came back with four sambucas as well as their orders. Barton explained he was driving later. She slid herself onto the bench between Barton and Strange, downed Barton's shot as well, and proceeded to monopolise the conversation. Her life story kept their attention. It sounded as though she'd been all over Europe.

'I grew up in a small village in Greece. It was beautiful but it could have been a hundred years ago. I couldn't be myself there. Anything different or new was frowned on. But we watched TV and YouTube. The world was having fun and we wanted to be part of it. So my friends and I left. Amsterdam was cool, France was nice. Berlin made me feel at home, even though it was so different from home.'

'Why settle in Peterborough?' asked Zander. 'Especially after Paris and Berlin.'

'I like it here. We all have to grow up. I got a job in CSI and enjoyed it, but the main reason is that I could get a really nice house for my wages. It's also nearly in the middle of the country, which is good for travelling. I enjoy working with John.' She reached over and tweaked Barton's cheek. 'There are many people of all nationalities here. You have all types, and everyone generally gets on well and is accepting.'

They continued to chat and laugh at some of her crazy stories. Barton and Zander shared a wistful look. While Sirena had been chasing adventure through her twenties, they'd been pursuing shoplifters.

Barton's phone beeped at 20 15. It was Holly. 'My chariot has arrived,' he said.

The others also rose. Zander nudged Strange's shoulder. 'Best we go home too. If a body turns up, it will be busy tomorrow.'

'I had fun, guys,' said Sirena. 'Let's do it again. I'll try not to be late next time, but I had to pick a friend up from the station, and she bought wine!'

They stepped outside into the mild evening air. It was to be a snow-free Christmas. Sirena gave Barton a huge sloppy kiss on the cheek as Holly wound down her window. She poked her head out.

'He's yours for a tenner.'

'You must feel very safe sleeping next to John.'

'Yes, his snoring would deter even the most desperate of burglars.'

Zander received the same treatment as Barton. She kissed Strange a little more head on. The kiss lasted just a touch too long. Barton got in the car and put his seat belt on with a puzzled expression. Zander crouched next to Holly's open window.

'Ring me if it kicks off. I'm great at drunken boxing.'

Barton picked up on the lack of energy in his delivery. He'd seen the kiss, too.

'I'll text you after I've spoken to her.'

Holly cruised down the village road with a big grin.

'That didn't surprise you, did it?' he asked.

'Did it you?' replied a chuckling Holly. 'Call yourself detectives. I don't think even Kelly knew. Maybe she'll be intrigued. You'd expect our prisons to be empty with you lot running the show. You should invite Sirena tomorrow as well. The more the merrier. I can sit her next to your mother, use her like a shield.'

Barton relaxed as they passed the big houses on the main road. Impressive decorations lit up the conifers many grew at the edges of their plots. Luke was waiting at the window when they got back. Barton cursed under his breath. Lawrence was behind Luke. When Barton stepped from the car, they ducked out of sight. Then both of them popped up laughing and wearing plastic antlers. He smiled and waved, feeling rotten inside.

'I've got to go out.'

'Oh, John. Come on, you promised.'

Barton explained everything to Holly.

'Can't someone else go?'

Barton opened his hands. She exhaled slowly and turned to walk away, but then stopped herself. She pointed a finger.

'Luke will be asleep before you leave and the others know the score by now. But be back for when Luke wakes up because he will not understand if you aren't there.'

Barton stood alone on the drive and, at that moment, hated his job.

77

DI BARTON

Barton awoke as his son's heavy footsteps pounded across the landing. He'd stayed with Claudia for two hours. Annabelle's paranoia had risen as she'd struggled to cope with her losses and she'd upped the security on the house before she disappeared. There was toughened glass on the windows and the front door had multi-point locks and a reinforced frame.

To cap it all off, they had a top-of-the-range alarm system with Homewatch. Short of having a couple of Rottweilers running around the front garden, there wasn't much more they could do. Claudia's friend, Chloe, was an imposing woman too. Apparently she was a member of the rowing club. Her friend had taken the knife block upstairs and put it next to the bed that they'd share. Barton had no doubts either woman would use whatever force was necessary.

Barton's already high respect for Claudia had gone up further. She must have been under incredible stress and yet she was holding it together. She'd joked with her friend and had made everyone coffee. Eventually she'd thrown Barton out at eleven, saying he should be home with his children and they'd be fine. She believed that David wouldn't hurt her.

Barton had reiterated that she should not open the front door, but he'd stared at the huge single pane window of the lounge as he'd got in the car to leave. He'd rung Control and, as it had been a quiet night, he'd asked for uniform to wait in Claudia's street between calls. Short of sleeping at the foot of Claudia's bed, there wasn't much more he could have done.

Holly had beamed at him when he'd arrived home. They'd had time for Barton to eat Santa's mince pie and enjoy a glass of port before they'd retired. He hoped Christmas Day was going to be non-eventful because he already felt shattered.

'He's been,' Luke shouted.

It was 4:45. He supposed that was progress from last Christmas Day. The morning followed as it had for many years and soon Strange and Barton's mother arrived at midday. Strange looked refreshed and festive in a snug dress that had a hint of elf about it, although his mum looked a bit disheveled, as though she'd been out clubbing last night.

'You all right, Mum?'

She beamed at him but didn't say anything. Weird.

'Anything happen last night, Kelly?'

'Not in Peterborough. I spoke to Control first thing this morning and it was relatively peaceful. The usual issues with drink but nothing of note.'

'Excellent. I rang Claudia and she practically put the phone down on me, telling me to enjoy Christmas. Wisbech have no further news on Clavell, though. Let's hope it's a day of peace and goodwill for everyone.' Strange's comment registered. 'What do you mean by not in Peterborough?'

'There's been an incident in Cambridge. Have you seen the news?'

'No? What's happened?'

'I heard it on the radio on the way over here. A woman's been found dead in Cambridge at a university property.'

Barton walked into his office and brought his PC to life. He brought the BBC news page up and the headline was *Woman Murdered at University*. The image was of a property with police tape and vehicles surrounding it. It was the same place as where the lecturer was killed.

'Shit.'

'Yeah. That's going to be trouble all over. Cambridge will have their hands full.'

'I'm going to ring Tapper for an update. Can you do me a favour and help Holly with the dinner? My mum doesn't seem herself.'

'Sure. We won't need to go to Cambridge, will we?'

'No, they'll have enough people on call. I'd just like to know the details.'

Barton rang Control again and got hold of Tapper.

'Morning, John. I hope you're having a better Christmas than me.'

'Sorry to hear that. Is it the wife of the previous victim? Wasn't her name Charlie?'

'Yes, she's very dead. I'm there now. It looks like it was done last night.'

'Another similar robbery?'

'Definitely not. It's too early to know if anything has been taken, but this is personal. A friend came over this morning and saw the body through the kitchen window. She's had a terrible shock. I've not seen anything like it in twenty-five years of policing. It's so gruesome, even our reluctant pathologist is here. That's it for me, after this. I'm out of here. I wish I'd retired before today because I will never unsee this.'

'How did she die? Was it an awl again?'

'No, she's been stabbed in the torso multiple times but with a small blade. It was still stuck in her side. He's then used insulating tape to bind her in an oak chair. Taped her good and firm. He left the rest of the roll behind. And then, he...'

Barton was gobsmacked. Tapper was one of the most hardened officers on the force. Barton knew he'd pulled dead children from a motorway pile-up in the vain hope of saving them.

'Take your time, Tapper.'

Barton heard a few slow breaths before Tapper continued. 'There's a bloody carving knife stuck through a photograph of the couple. It would be a reasonable guess that he used that weapon to decapitate her.'

'Christ.' Barton couldn't think of anything else to say.

'What the fuck is going on in the world?'

'I know. It's getting madder by the day.'

'CSI and the pathologist think the killer stabbed her with the small knife to incapacitate her. She'd have still been conscious. There's blood everywhere, thirty feet away. Tell me, John. What kind of maniac cuts someone's head off while they're still alive?'

78

DI BARTON

Holly bellowed out that the dinner was ready. Barton mouthed to Strange he'd update her after the meal. Everyone appreciated the traditional fare, except Barton, who struggled to focus on it. Then the kids ran off with their presents. Even Barton's mother seemed less acerbic than usual. In fact, he would almost describe her as polite.

'You sure you're okay, Mum?' he asked.

'Yes, John here was telling me about his exams.'

'You mean Lawrence?'

'Don't be silly.'

Holly stopped collecting the dessert bowls. 'Okay, let's get you lot in the lounge so I can tidy up.' She ushered them away after taking orders for coffees and soft drinks.

'What just happened?' said Barton when just the two of them remained.

'I meant to talk to you later. She was all over the place preparing dinner. Usually, it's her way or a hassle. But eventually, she sat at the table and told me to do it how I wanted. Nicely, too. Not at all sarcastic. I was glad of Kelly's help.'

'That's not like her.'

'I know! And I found a tea towel in the freezer. Now any number of culprits might be responsible for that, but I think I gave her that one to dry up with.'

Holly came to Barton and studied his face. 'You understand what that might mean?'

He nodded. 'Let's enjoy the occasion. Perhaps she's just having an odd moment.'

Strange was finishing a call in the hall as Barton left the kitchen.

'I rang in to find out if Clavell had rung in to confirm he was on call at midday. Not yet. Wisbech station have taken the decision to up the ante. They're door-knocking and checking CCTV. Nothing so far. We haven't been called in at this point.'

'I didn't sleep that well last night. All this was racing through my head. That comment you made about Whitlam being the Compost Heap Killer really resonated.'

'In what way?'

'Someone had to know Wisbech to hide the body in that allotment. It wasn't Rowe, and I can't see it being that older guy, Franco, either. We don't have any other suspects apart from Whitlam. His DNA turned up at Stone's place, too.'

'He said he'd been in there before, though.'

'Yes, very conveniently. His DNA was under Somerville's fingernail, too. He claimed that happened saving him, but maybe it happened killing him.'

'But he mentioned it before we knew.'

Barton waited for her to cotton on.

'Ah, he told us because he guessed his DNA might turn up at Stone's. He also realised we'd match it to what was found under Somerville's fingernails. He brought it up so he could have his story prepared. It wouldn't have been a big leap to see who connected the two people. It would have been way more incriminating if we'd joined the dots. Wow. That is clever.'

'Yes, and scary.'

'Why scary?'

'That's a level of planning and foresight beyond most criminals. We need to get to this guy, or he might prove very dangerous.'

'Or even lethal.'

Barton grimaced as his mind churned.

'What were the Cambridge details?' asked Strange.

'Someone cut off the head of that lecturer's wife.'

'What?'

'Yeah, gruesome.'

'Clean off and left it on the side?'

'No, that's the sick part. The killer took it with them.'

'I take it we're going into work.'

'Yes. I hope Whitlam doesn't have any connection to Cambridge. Something is very off here. We need to be ready to react.'

Holly came out of the kitchen, smiling and holding two cups of coffee. She saw their faces and stopped. 'I'll drink them myself. I'll need the hit if I'm going to be doing everything on my own.'

79

DI BARTON

Thorpe Wood police station was getting its first customers when Barton and Strange arrived. An officer mopped a claret coloured liquid off the reception floor. They proceeded to the incident room, sat down at adjoining desks, and fired up the PCs. Barton logged onto his email and checked to see if he had replies regarding ANPR or HR. Both were there.

'The emails are here.'

He opened them and scanned the results.

'Well?' asked Strange, who'd got up to stand behind him.

'Whitlam's been that way twice in the last year. Once last Christmas Day, returning on Boxing Day. He was back in Peterborough when Stone disappeared.'

'Interesting. Who do you visit on Christmas Day?'

He said the obvious out loud. 'Family.'

'What did HR say?'

'Hang on, they scanned his application for me. No next of kin on the form.'

'Damn, although he could have lied about that.' Strange widened her eyes. 'Maybe they are a family of psychos?'

'Let's hope not. I hoped to be back for turkey sandwiches.' Barton clicked his fingers. 'Bingo. Here's his previous addresses. Oh, no!'

Strange looked over. 'Bad news?'

Barton gawped at the screen in horror. 'One of his previous addresses is 499 Norwich Road.'

Strange blinked and then it dawned. 'The same house as Barney Trimble?'

'The very same.'

'What does that mean? Was he a lodger there or something?'

'Oh, fuck. It gets worse.'

Strange knew Barton rarely swore. She grabbed her chair and scooted it over, tucked in next to him and stared at the screen. He'd zoomed in on the previous addresses, two of which were in Cambridge.

'No way. You don't think he's responsible for those murders too?'

Barton looked at Whitlam's qualifications. 'GCSE results and A levels from Queen's School, Wisbech. He was at Fitzwilliam College, achieving a second class honours degree.' He paused while he typed into Google. 'Fitzwilliam College is a constituent college of the University of Cambridge.'

'Surely he can't be responsible for both. What's the connection?'

'He's the connection. We can deduce why at a later date. So, Whitlam was from Wisbech. Sneaky sod. All that time, and he never mentioned it.'

'He must have known he'd get caught out at some point.'

'Yes, but I think he knew that.'

'What do we do first?'

'I'll get Control to put whoever they can spare outside Claudia's house and to be vigilant. DCI Cox will want an update. It's still not concrete, but it's too many coincidences. We can't rest until Whitlam's in custody. We're going to drive to Wisbech to Trimble's address. I'll get Cox to drag a magistrate out and get us a search warrant. Clavell visited that house, but no one answered the door.

'If there's nobody there and we don't have the warrant, we'll nip to the allotments again. If Whitlam lived around that area, he would probably have known that place a long while ago, but someone might recognise his photo. Maybe he worked the plot with Trimble. Clavell said people go down there even on Christmas Day, so we might get lucky. You drive, I'll ring Tapper in Cambridge on the way.'

Empty roads made a siren unnecessary. They were there in a little over half an hour. Barton had only just finished updating

DCI Cox and DS Tapper when they pulled up at Barney Trimble's property.

'Right. I've just had a thought. If Whitlam lived with Trimble, maybe they were friends. There's a slim possibility that Whitlam's in here. If he is, he won't be pleased to see us.'

Strange nodded to show she was prepared. They left the car and approached the house. Barton knocked on the door and they retreated from it. He rapped again and cursed, realising he'd stepped in the oil slick on the drive.

'What did the boss say?'

'She's rung the ARV and sent it to Claudia's house. The tactical unit are on standby as well in case it really escalates, but there's a situation in London. The ARV was in Ely, so won't be back in Peterborough for nearly an hour. We'll go to Claudia's after the allotment. Claudia will be able to tell us more about Whitlam's movements. Wisbech are being kept up to speed.'

'And Cambridge?'

'Tapper and his team are dealing with the situation there. His guess was that if Whitlam and Charlie were at university together, they knew each other and perhaps dated. Either that or he had a thing for her. Perhaps she left him for the lecturer. To top it all off, there's been a brawl over lunch at a pub in Huntingdon. And Lincolnshire have been pulled to some kind of hunting demonstration over tomorrow's Boxing Day hunt. We're seriously down on manpower. It's going to be up to us to find Whitlam. We need to stop him before he kills someone else.'

'If this is Whitlam, he chose a good day to do it.'

Barton cursed under his breath. He'd seen films where an officer had gone rogue and not fully appreciated how dangerous it was. Whitlam knew everything Barton was going to do.

'I'm getting a growing sense of dread. Zander has the late shift on call. He won't mind coming in early for this. I'll get him to go straight around to Claudia's to support uniform and be there for the ARV. Let's have a peek around the back before we go.'

Woodworm had riddled the back door. Barton tested its weight. 'I think Baby Luke could push that in.'

Strange clucked. 'You do know he's six now.'

Barton smiled at the thought of his boisterous son and wished he were with him. 'He'll always be my baby boy. I missed a lot of Layla's early years but was on light duties with a dodgy knee when he arrived. We spent plenty of time together.'

'Shall we fetch Luke, then, or perhaps ask the neighbours if they've seen anything and then get going?'

Barton remembered the old curious fellow who'd leaned out of his window on the last occasion they were there. They tried him first. He grinned at them when he opened his door.

'It's the police. How lovely. Social calls for the lonely on this special day. Come in. I was about to have my microwave turkey dinner for one.'

'I'm glad you're enjoying yourself. I've got a few questions regarding your neighbours. Do you know them well?'

The man's smile dropped. 'Trimble? No, not at all. He's a solitary man. I don't mind that. If you rarely talk to each other, then you can't fall out. I haven't seen him for ages though, although the van keeps disappearing off the drive, so he must be about.'

'Is that what's leaving that oil slick?'

'Yes. He didn't use it for years, then did it up. Not sure why, as he's pretty much bones now. To be honest, I'm surprised he has the strength to drive it. Maybe he wanted a last holiday, before, you know.'

Barton couldn't believe it. 'Please don't tell me it's a campervan. A black and white campervan.'

The old man beamed at him. 'That's it.'

Barton got his phone out, found the right picture and showed it to him. 'Do you recognise him?'

'Yes, it's David, used to live next door when his mother lived there. Now, she was as fruit loops as they come. Always banging on about heaven and hell. I felt sorry for David. It must have been very hard growing up under her preaching.'

Strange joined the conversation. 'You said lived. Do you know where they moved to?'

'No, she died. Mad cow that she was, she didn't deserve that.'

Barton gave him an exasperated look. 'Deserve what?'

'To die like that.'

Barton stared at him and debated if it was just turkey's necks that you were allowed to wring at this time of year. 'I don't suppose it was suspicious?'

'No, a terrible accident. She fell down the stairs.'

Barton and Strange exchanged a glance. 'How long ago was that?'

'Years. Decade maybe. Happened on Christmas Day, too.'

'And David left? Where did he go, with his dad?' asked Strange.

'His mum scared his father off years ago. No, her new guy was Trimble. He moved in when David was at secondary school. David went to university and paid a visit sometimes. At Christmas, usually. I think he came here last year.'

Barton's brain tripped into overdrive. He tried to recall his previous visit. Did they ask Trimble if he had any family? He supposed Whitlam wasn't related by blood. Perhaps Trimble was in cahoots with Whitlam. Barton thought about the van. He'd spotted it racing past when he'd visited Claudia. If Whitlam was driving it, he'd have seen Clavell's car. So that was why he was driving so recklessly. It looked as though he was furious enough to kill.

'Did you see the van here today?'

'Yes, this morning, but I heard it leaving about an hour ago.'

80

DI BARTON

Barton made his mind up fast.

'We need to return to Peterborough.'

Strange jumped into the driver's seat. She was the quickest driver of the two. Well, the safest at speed anyway.

'Drive fast, Kelly. I'll ring Claudia.' They carried on talking while the phone rang and rang.

'You think he's gone to get her?'

'God knows. Who else is there for him to visit?'

Claudia didn't answer after multiple attempts. He called Control and instructed them to update the ARV that was on its way to Claudia's house. He also let the station know that Whitlam was suspected of murder and driving a black and white campervan. More than once, they drove past a van that had them pointing. Barton finally rang Zander, then sat grim faced as he ran through as many permutations as he could of what might occur.

'It's worrying that we can't get an answer,' remarked Strange.

'She could have left her phone in a different room or something, but it doesn't bode well. They sent a police motorcyclist to sit outside the front. They're chasing him for an update. Another patrol car's just finished at a traffic accident and is on its way. We need to act, but if Whitlam is there, we could have an extremely violent situation on our hands. We'll be there in a little over ten minutes and so will the ARV.'

Barton always remembered the police training about the force continuum. If you were attending a fist fight, take batons.

If knives were possible, send armed officers. Guns present, you need bigger weapons and marksmen.

Barton made more calls as they approached Peterborough. He got through to Malik, who was at his parents' in Bedford. He explained he had no idea what Whitlam did outside work apart from go to the gym. They had gone swimming together once in the summer. He said he'd drive straight to Thorpe Wood and help any way he could. Ewing and Zelensky weren't picking up.

It took Strange twenty-seven minutes in total to get back to Peterborough. Very impressive considering Barton's stomach hadn't lurched once. She parked just down the road where Barton directed at the same moment as the ARV arrived, so Barton flagged it to stop.

Alistair Smith and Jules Cureton, the two authorised firearms officers involved in the Snow Killer shootings, stepped out. They all shook hands. Barton brought them up to speed.

'David Whitlam's been killing people?' asked an incredulous Al.

'It looks like it. We have no concrete facts, but there's too many coincidences. It has to be him. I reckon he's gone off the rails. He could be capable of anything.'

Jules, the older of the two, checked up the road at the house. 'It seems peaceful enough. There's no campervan. The front door is intact. And he hasn't got a gun. You're pretty sure about that?'

'We don't know for certain, but there's no indication of him being armed. He's bloody strong though and capable of extreme violence. I've seen him in the gym. There's supposed to be a police motorcycle out the front.'

Jules shook his head and removed his pistol. He wouldn't chamber a round without an immediate threat, but Barton knew there was no safety on the pistols they used. Al did the same thing. He said, 'No one's as strong as a bullet. I say we just knock. You stay back. If he comes at us, we'll put him down. We'll do our job.'

Barton had watched TV programmes where firearms officers had said they would shoot to wound rather than kill. It was rubbish because, realistically, these guys weren't sharpshooters on rooftops. In a fluid situation, there would be little time for choices. They would shoot to stop.

Barton bit his lip as they neared the house. Jules looked behind a wall and conversed with Al for a few seconds, then approached the door. Al peered through the glass. Jules knocked, and the door opened a few seconds later.

A tall woman with her hair tied up in a towel and wearing a dressing gown stared at them with an open mouth. Jules spoke to her for a moment, then waved Barton over. At that moment, approaching sirens could be heard. It was the patrol car who hadn't got the message about approaching with caution. It screeched up in front of them. An officer in leathers carrying his helmet came from around the back of the house.

'Have you seen anything?' Barton asked him.

'No. No one said to knock or anything, just to look visible as a deterrent. I've just stood at the front. There was nothing going on, so I walked around the back to check in the garden. There's nothing going on.'

Barton saw the police motorcycle behind a low wall. There was only one car parked outside. He approached the woman from the house.

'Hi, Chloe. Where's Claudia?'

'She's gone out.'

'Where the hell to?'

'She's visiting her family.'

'I thought they were all dead.'

She rolled her eyes at him. 'They are.'

'Ah, you mean in the cemetery. Which one?'

'I'm not sure. She wrote it down for me.'

Barton couldn't help a rueful smile sneaking out at the horrified Cureton and Smith. They'd all had a very bad experience in a cemetery a year ago, courtesy of the Snow Killer. Barton followed the woman in and Smith said, 'We'll have another look around the back.'

'Why did you let her go on her own?' asked Barton as he followed her in.

'She wanted to be by herself. Apparently, it was a tradition to visit the graves on Christmas Day. They've done it since her mum died. She said her head was spinning. She refused to believe David would hurt her. I've never seen her so angry. But she lurches from furious to overwhelmed in seconds at the moment. She said that no one would stop her being with her family. I offered to go but she wanted to be alone. She said she'd be safe in the car. Besides, she'd only be gone for an hour.'

'How long's she been out now?'

After some mental arithmetic, Chloe pulled a face. 'An hour and a bit.' She peeled a Post-it note off the fridge. 'Here it is, Woodston Cemetery.'

Barton walked back outside. It didn't look good. Claudia had been longer than she said, and she'd been on her own. Whitlam would know exactly where she went on Christmas Day if she did it every year. He'd be waiting at the cemetery. Barton called the ARV officers over and told them the details.

'You're kidding me. I remember what happened last time you asked us to hunt amongst the graves,' said Cureton. 'My arse hasn't been the same since.'

Barton nodded at both. 'Don't worry. It's a different graveyard.'

81

DI BARTON

Barton instructed Chloe to ring them if Claudia returned. A domestic assault in progress came through over the radio. Barton sent the patrol car and motorcyclist to attend. Zander had just arrived and Barton thought they had enough bodies to stop Whitlam with the ARV men staying with them. After a quick conversation, Zander followed Barton, who drove after the ARV down Oundle Road. They cruised into New Road and past the entrance of the cemetery, turning right to stop behind a wall. Woodston Cemetery sat in the middle of an estate. It was nearly two hundred years old. Barton realised they'd parked behind Claudia's car and he was relieved that he couldn't see a campervan anywhere in sight.

This time Smith and Cureton took rifles from the safe in the back of their 4 x 4.

'What's the idea?' asked Barton.

'Does anyone know this place?' asked Cureton.

Zander did. 'We buried my uncle here. In the centre there's a small building, like a chapel. There's nowhere to hide.'

'It's the same plan as before, then. He hasn't got a gun, and we suspect he works alone. We'll sweep the area. With luck, Claudia will still be in there. If he's around, we'll find him. Wait in your cars and keep an eye out. I'll be back shortly.'

Barton rang the office and Cox patched Malik in to listen to the call. Barton explained what he wanted. With advances in technology, they could track vehicles in real time as long as they stuck to main routes. If Barney Trimble's campervan lit up one of the ANPR cameras, they'd have his location. There'd be no hiding something of that size easily either. Once they got the general direction of travel, they could scramble every resource. Now they all believed this was likely to be the man responsible for DC Clavell's disappearance, nobody would mind leaving the Christmas washing up to settle the score.

Cureton and Smith jogged back with their rifles pointing at the ground. 'There's no one at all in there. What do you want to do?'

Barton considered their next move. 'We're onto ANPR. If the van moves, we'll know shortly. Did you see her family's graves?'

'You want us to check every tombstone?' asked Smith.

'No, of course not. Their headstones will be new. We'll all search. The fresh plots are often close together. Donald Birtwistle will be next to his wife.'

'What are you thinking?' asked Strange.

'If he's waited out of sight for her and then attacked, the most likely time would be when she put flowers on the grave. There might be a dropped shoe or a scattered bouquet, or at least some sign of a disturbance.'

They spaced out and walked into the cemetery. Despite the armed officers saying it was safe, each face was pinched. It was eerily quiet. The new headstones appeared to be clustered in the middle on the right hand side. A lone crow perched on one, giving the searchers a wary look, before flying away with a haunting caw. A minute later, Zander shouted out that he'd found the graves. The team gathered in a circle and peered down. There was no mistaking the red splatter on the stones. Barton's phone rang before he could swear. It was Malik.

'I'm in the control room getting real-time info. The van's route has been traced. It came to Peterborough and then returned to Wisbech. Half an hour ago, it triggered a camera in King's Lynn and then near Fakenham. It's on the A148.'

'I don't know that road well. Where's he going?'

'If he follows it to the end, he'll hit the coast. That route finishes at the seaside town of Cromer. The spot where Annabelle's car and clothes were found, Overstrand, is two miles farther along the coast.'

'He has to be heading there. Get DCI Cox to contact Norfolk Police. They must have some uniform out in cars. Instruct them to watch the Cromer road for the van, and get someone on the approach to Overstrand. Tell them he is violent and dangerous, but there's no intel to suggest he has a firearm. They'll need to make the call about whether to intercept. We presume David Whitlam is heading for the same car park as before, this time with the sister, Claudia, as a hostage, whom we believe is injured. I repeat, there's fresh blood on her father's grave.'

'Is the ARV there still?' asked Malik. 'Cox said to send it with you.'

'Yes, we'll all attend. Cureton and Smith will go ahead in the faster vehicle. We think they'll have the necessary force to take out Whitlam. However, even with lights, we're over sixty minutes away. She'll need to mobilise the local ARV, and it's time to bring in a tactical support unit in case Whitlam gets holed up somewhere and we want snipers.'

'Hang on, sir. Another camera's been lit up at Holt. He's cracking on for a big vehicle, but definitely heading towards Cromer.'

Barton urged himself to think if he'd missed anything. He clicked his fingers. 'Last thing, we reckon he's been operating out of Trimble's house in Wisbech. Get anyone free, a special or a support officer, to secure the scene. They don't need to go in yet, we think we know exactly where the danger is, but it's possible the owner of the house is involved.'

'Will do.'

'And get uniform out to secure Woodston Cemetery. It might be a murder scene.'

82

THE SOUL KILLER

It seems Claudia isn't interested in absconding with me. That's the second time I've been spat at. I'm not Taser trained and wasn't entirely confident with what I was doing or where I was aiming. I'd had it a while, and it didn't hold its charge for long. Tasers shoot prongs into the body and override the nervous system. I did some research and decided if my life was in danger, I wouldn't want to rely on it. Sure enough, one of the prongs hit her thick coat and nothing happened.

Luckily I had brought a stun gun with me as backup. You simply press them against the body, ideally against skin, but they can arc through clothing. The YouTube video I watched recommended I hold it against her neck for five seconds. It was an uncomfortably long time as her teeth clamped in agony. She collapsed afterwards as though I'd removed her heart. The loudest sound of the whole experience was her head hitting the corner of the grave. She remained unconscious and still bled as I taped her up and laid her in the rear of the van.

I had to return to Wisbech to pick up the items I need for my final act. I suspect it will be Barton I have to watch out for because Clavell won't solve another crime.

Unless I escape, nothing remains for me except prison. The only choice I have left is how to end it all. In my job I know how this works. Someone will have noticed Claudia's gone by now. They'll have found Charlie and realised the lecturer wasn't a simple brutal robbery. Armed officers will be fired up over the disappearance of Clavell. They'll have connected some of the dots, perhaps not all of them, but there'll be no doubt that I am to be brought in. I don't want to give one of those cocky firearms types the chance to take me down.

The road to the coast is a single carriageway most of the way. There are few options for rat-running so I can only hope that I'm far enough in front for them to have insufficient time to respond. I'm through Holt. They'll think I'm heading to Overstrand. I bet they now wonder if Annabelle drove herself there and swam out to sea, or if I locked her in the boot and threw her in.

I find myself in good spirits though. There's a lightness in my voice as I sing along to the radio. It can only mean my confession has been accepted. I imagine the crucified Jesus giving me a nod to carry on. I work for him now.

Instead of ploughing on to Overstrand, I turn off to West Runton. Barton won't know Barney and I stayed there in the past. I rang Martha from the caravan park yesterday afternoon:

'Hi, Martha. It's David here. I thought I'd let you know that Barney has passed.'

'I'm sorry to hear that. He was a nice man.'

'Yes. I really miss him. Anyway, it's been a troubling time of late. There's been a lot going on, as you can imagine. My girlfriend and I are having a save-the-relationship break in our campervan. Can we come and stay on your field?'

'I'm sorry, we're closed in the winter. The shop's shut and the facilities are all closed.'

I knew that, of course. 'That's okay. We'll just park there. We don't need anything.'

'I'm sorry, David. Our insurance doesn't permit anyone to stay on the site when it's closed.'

I knew that too. I also know Martha and her husband live in a house at the bottom of the road that leads up to the site. It's there that I've stopped. I push over the body that's been held by the belt in the seat next to me, and prop it against the window. It feels very stiff. Maybe that's for the best.

Martha's a big one for decorations. Through the lounge window, I can see a tinsel laden tree and there's one of those moving reindeer in her front garden. She answers the door with suspicion, but brightens when she recognises me.

'Hi, Martha.'

'David, what are you doing here?'

'We decided to come for the night to get away. We'll park on the edge of the cliff car park, unless you've changed your mind about the site?'

'I'm sorry. We just can't.'

'No problem. You'll probably be able to see us from down here.'

She looks over my shoulder at the campervan. The body has slipped forward at an unnatural angle. Greasy hair smears the window and you can make out a thin protruding chin.

'I better wake her up, or she'll be stiff.'

Martha is still in the doorway as I get back in the van, but it's dark enough to prevent her getting a good look. She definitely wouldn't want to get in the van. I remember the Coughlin character in that film, *Cocktail*, constantly giving Tom Cruise advice. One of his titbits was to 'bury the dead, they stink up the joint,' and he was right – Clavell really hums. He must have had better gut bacteria than Barney. It's the kind of smell that, however much you scrubbed, you'd never be rid of.

There are no other vehicles in the car park. I stop on the left hand side so Martha can see our lights if she looks out of the window. From under the table, I drag out the canisters of petrol I got a few days ago and pour all but one onto the floor. The stinging stench is almost overpowering but still an improvement on rotting flesh. I leave the biggest container attached by a steel wire to the door handle. If anyone races to be a hero, they will open the door and flood more fuel around. Failing that, it's made of metal. It'll make quite a bomb. They'll spot the flames from the house down below, but there'll be no chance of saving anyone.

Out here, the fire brigades are on-call, and the fastest they could arrive is about fifteen minutes. Petrol burns at around 1000 degrees Celsius. That's teeth-melting, bone-disintegrating heat. Hopefully, all they'll find to poke through will be ashes.

83

DI BARTON

Barton, Zander and Strange discussed the facts in the car. They were chilling. Zander came to the same conclusion as Barton.

'You're right. When all this comes out, he's going to go down in history. Peterborough will have a new serial killer.'

'I expect he'll have a name catchier than the Compost Heap Killer. I dread to think how many people he's killed,' replied Barton.

'The twins said it was out of character for their father to have taken the choice to hang himself. Could Whitlam have carried him up the stairs, noosed him, and thrown the body over the balcony?'

Strange nodded. 'From talking to Claudia, that seems more likely than his suicide. What's tough to get your head around is that he did all this while he continued to work. I suppose it's possible that Robin Rowe was involved, but if he wasn't, then his death is down to Whitlam too. What kind of person can chat freely at the water cooler after burying a body in an allotment the previous day?'

None of them commented. Barton's phone broke the silence. A low-key-sounding Malik spoke fast.

'We've used a variety of media to warn the public and ask for sightings. A 999 call has been received from West Runton. A driver spotted a campervan matching the description speeding towards the seafront.'

'What details did the operator get?'

'Black and white campervan, two people in the front seat, driving dangerously fast.'

'Okay, we're twenty minutes away from West Runton. We'll head straight there. Redirect the ARV, which must be in Cromer by now.'

Barton hung up and stared ahead. The finale loomed. They were dealing with a clever detective; one who would know it was over. But would Whitlam surrender to a life in jail? Minutes passed swiftly as Barton contemplated their next move. He might only have seconds to make life-or-death decisions.

Barton ran through Whitlam's options. What did he want? What did he gain by driving to the seaside? He couldn't hide there now; it was too late for that. He had no hope of escaping in that slow van, either. Barton had been to West Runton a couple of times in the past. He recalled an overpriced souvenir shop next to a slip ramp, which allowed the fishing boats to enter the sea. All of a sudden, he feared a *Thelma and Louise*-style ending.

Strange cleared her throat. 'Okay, Boss?'

Barton tutted. 'I've got a nasty feeling this isn't going to end well.'

'His end or ours?'

Barton's phone startled them.

'John, it's Tapper here. The word has got out down here and it's been bedlam. You'd think people would have had something better to do today than stare at a crime scene. It seems Charlie wasn't popular. No surprise there. One of her friends did turn up though. She was another one who never left after her degree. After what you told me about Whitlam studying here, I asked her if she remembered him. She didn't recall the surname, but she said Charlie dated a boy called David in her first year.'

'Do you think it was him?'

'Yep. She described him as tall, thin, and serious to the point where it made you a bit wary around him. She thinks he was the last student Charlie dated before she got tangled up with the lecturer she ended up marrying.'

'Well. I think that solves your crimes for you. I suspect Whitlam's always been a troubled individual. It's hard to maintain a façade for years. Maybe it was a culmination of pressure and he finally lost control.'

'You need to stop him, John. He'll kill again.'

'We're pursuing him now. I can't imagine he's going to let us take him alive, so you probably won't get to question him.'

Barton's phone beeped to let him know someone else was trying to call him. He said goodbye to Tapper and connected Malik.

'Has Whitlam reached Cromer?' asked Barton.

'The fire service received a 999 call. This time for a van on fire at West Runton beach car park. The vehicle stopped at the caller's house before driving on. She knows who it is. The male's name is David. She's known him for years. The other is his girlfriend, who was asleep when they arrived. She looked gaunt with long black hair.'

'Were they inside the campervan when it went up?'

'That's all we have at the moment. The caller's husband has gone to help. They could see the fire raging from their window. We had managed to set up a roadblock at Pinewood Caravan Park outside Cromer but the campervan didn't turn up. Police from there are on their way to West Runton now, too. There's also a team in Overstrand, who'll stay put for the time being, but it doesn't look good.'

'How long for the fire brigade?'

'DCI Cox arrived here a while ago. She expected Whitlam to crash on the country roads, so she'd warned Sheringham Fire Station they might be called out and they were ready to go. The fire engine's arrival is imminent as the station is only two miles away. The ARV might beat you there as well. Cox said not to approach the vehicle until the armed officers have called it safe. They'll liaise with Fire and Rescue on the scene.'

The satnav told them they were only ten minutes away. Barton struggled to believe it was Christmas Day. Only a few hours ago, he'd been opening presents and pulling crackers with his family. The car had steamed up with all the talking, and Barton opened his window fully once they hit West Runton village. His nose wrinkled at the smell of something man made burning in the air.

Strange drove down Water Lane to the caravan park. Two policemen stood in the way, their patrol car blocking the road. Strange eased to a halt and they introduced themselves. Barton showed his warrant card through the window.

'Any survivors?' Barton asked.

'In that?' the taller one said. 'No chance. It's been blazing since we got here ten minutes ago. The flames were fifty feet high. Something just exploded, too. I've never seen something burn like that.'

'Okay. Could you move your car so we can approach?'

'No entry, sir. The watch manager is up there with the ARV making an assessment. It looks as though there were two bodies in the front seats. Turn your engine off, and I'll check whether the situation has changed.'

It was another five minutes before Barton, Zander and Strange were allowed to drive to the burning wreckage. The fire brigade had a large cordon set up around the smouldering campervan. The crew trained their hoses on the vehicle and had commenced dousing. Barton asked who was in charge. He could feel the heat as he approached.

'Keep back, please. I'm guessing you're police?'

'Yes, DI Barton, Peterborough. How long to put it out?'

A flicker of irritation passed over the watch manager's face. He suspected he'd have the same look if a fireman pressed him on his murder investigation. The man remained professional.

'We'll take our time, maybe all night. Caravans don't burn in this manner without accelerants. That individual—' he pointed to a man in his sixties being comforted by a younger firefighter at the edge of the car park, 'came over to assist after spotting the fire. He saw two people burning in the front seats. Both struggled and then stopped.'

'I take it they were beyond help?'

'The cab was filled with flames, so he tried to enter the living unit at the back, but the heat beat him away. That makes him very lucky because, just after we arrived, something blew up and blasted off that door.'

Barton stared into the bushes fifty metres to the left where the blackened door rested on top of a dune.

'There's no rush to put it out as there's nothing for it to spread to. Anyone inside that van will be long dead. We won't risk more lives for little benefit.'

'When will I be able to get closer to have a look?'

'Not for quite a while. Our fire investigator is on the way. He'll make that call due to the loss of life. Besides, we don't know what kind of batteries are in there, or gas canisters, even tyres can blow and kill. There may be booby traps. I've seen an exploding vehicle strut knock a man's leg clean off.'

Barton and the watch manager stepped back a pace as the nearest wall of the campervan slowly collapsed in on itself.

'A well-involved fire like this means there won't be much left for us, or you, to investigate. You might get something from dental, but I doubt it.'

84

THE SOUL KILLER

After the campervan catches fire, I hide and wait to make sure it goes up. It appears I've used more than enough petrol. I put the rucksack containing money, my stun gun, the baseball bat and some clothes on my back. Keeping out of the light, I sprint from the car park into Lavender Caravan Park. I jog hard for a mile along the cliff tops towards the small hill at Beeston Regis, seeing nobody. It looks foreboding in the dark. I could go around it, but I'm less likely to meet anyone over the top.

When I reach the taxi company's office in Sheringham town centre, the building is shuttered. Cursing, I check my watch. I'm half an hour late. My hands pat my jacket pockets and I suddenly remember placing my mobile on the dashboard of the van. My heart races as I check for a phone booth. A pair of headlights flash in the gloom ahead of me. Should I run? A voice carries over.

'Mr Clavell?'

'That's me.' I'd decided if I got this far that I would have a little fun at Barton's expense. It was better than using my own name.

'Taxi to Wisbech?'

'Correct. I thought you'd shut up and gone home.'

'They closed yesterday. It's only me working today. They told me to meet you here. I almost cleared off when you didn't show but, since you paid half up front, I reckoned I'd give it thirty minutes.'

I never know whether to sit in the front or rear of these

normal saloon car taxis, but the back will do this time. I'm not in the talking mood. There's a whiff of petrol on my clothes as I get in. The guy is a grungy-looking, bearded fellow in his fifties. He probably can't smell anything apart from himself.

After thirty seconds, my breathing settles. My eyelids droop with the warmth. I need to be alert. There'll be plenty of sleeping time when this is all over. I listen to the tune on the radio. It sounds like gospel rock. I smile at the positivity and find it soothing.

'Are you religious?' I ask.

'I'm a Christian.'

'Strange day for a Christian to be working.'

'I follow my own path. Anyway, there's nothing in the Bible about Jesus's birthdate. From what I've read concerning shepherds watching their flocks, it's more likely he was born in the summer. The sheep wouldn't have been left out on those hills in the winter.'

'Wasn't he born in Bethlehem? I don't think they have a cold winter there.'

'Oh, yeah.' Something drops out of his beard as he scratches it.

'But I get it. This day is commercial rubbish.'

'Not at all. Anything that celebrates the Lord above can't be bad. And I don't mind working when the pay's so good.'

I wonder whether this man has been sent to test me. Although, it has to be unlikely that a messenger from above would smell so terrible.

'What are your views on heaven?' I ask.

'Personally, I think everybody goes, whatever we've done. God knows we're flawed creatures. He expects us to stray, but he loves us all.'

'That's a reassuring thought.'

'Amen.'

'However, I do have a question.'

'Fire away.'

'If you have a girlfriend, whom you love very much, but you split up, will you see her again in heaven?'

'Of course.'

'What if, after you separate, she gets married to someone else and has twelve children? She's hardly going to want me grinning at her through the pearly gates fifty years later when the big day arrives.'

'You obviously haven't studied the Bible.'

'I know a few stories.'

'To be a Christian on this earth, you need love, faith and hope. When you get to heaven, you don't require faith or hope because you've made it. Only love is left and there's enough for everyone. Marriage is to make babies, educate them in the ways of the Lord, and attain holiness together. That's useful on earth to help us reach paradise. Once we're there, it's no longer necessary.'

'Then it wouldn't matter if we didn't find *the one* on this earth?'

He turns back to me, and nods seriously. 'In heaven, we'll share a love more perfect than anything you can experience down here.'

A glimpse of mother's earnest beliefs flickers on his face before he returns his gaze to the road. In a way, she died a martyr so I could fulfil my promise. I suffered as a child, so I could understand His word.

'How about those we've wronged? What about when we meet them in heaven?'

'All mortal sins are forgiven and forgotten.'

'That's a relief, or I could have quite the welcoming committee.'

I watch him lick his lips. 'Amen,' he whispers.

His is an innocent view, but I prefer my version. I don't relish eternity with Claudia's family, however lenient they may have become. I prefer to think I took the gift of heaven when I answered to their interfering.

'You believe our feelings will transcend human emotions and we'll all be happy together like angels.'

'That's right.'

I catch him looking at me in the mirror.

'What if I only want one person?' I ask.

'Why not find someone new to spend your life with here? All will meet again in the merest scrap of time. After that, it's eternity together.'

'I only want her. Nobody else adds up.'

'There isn't much you can do if she's moved on.'

'Well, what if I killed her, and she went to heaven? Then she'd be there when I arrived.'

He stills and his grip tightens on the wheel. His right hand slips down, and I catch a slight glow.

His next sentence starts with a croak. 'You're him, aren't you? The killer the police are looking for.'

'I am him.'

I watch him moisten his lips. After a lengthy pause, he asks, 'Am I going to die?'

'You might if you don't hand me your phone.'

We travel in a nervous vacuum for a few miles. Finally, he clears his throat.

'Why did you do what you've done?'

It's time to be honest from now on; I have nothing left to lose. Nor does the driver if he believes everything he's said.

'I've never fitted in. I somehow convinced myself that I would find my soul mate and that would be it. I see life's not like that now. Do you know what the vicar called me? A soul killer. Does that sound like someone who's going to end up in heaven?'

'I guess not.'

He mumbles something else but stops himself.

'What? Say it.'

'You might well be a soul killer, but the only one that you've really destroyed is your own.'

85

DI BARTON

The drama of the chase and fire finally drained their last reserves. One of the nearby homeowners brought welcome cups of coffee out. Statements were taken from the site owners but there seemed little doubt when two bodies were seen in the front of the van. But it was hard to think analytically after what the team had seen. The smells that filled the air made it hard for Barton to empty his mind of anything else.

It had taken an hour for the fire to be put out and then the fire investigator had allowed them close. There wasn't much to look at, especially in the dark. The ARV was called back to Cambridge for a possible hostage situation. There seemed little point in staying longer.

At 19:00, Zander rolled his head around his shoulders. 'I think I'd like to go home and at least catch a few hours with the family.'

Barton and Strange nodded at that. Barton spoke with the local DI who'd since arrived, explained they were leaving and exchanged contact details. But as they got in the car, Barton's natural suspicions stirred.

'Let's run through things on the way back.'

Zander drove to give Strange a break. She leaned between the seats as they pulled out of West Runton.

'What are you thinking, Boss?'

'This looks like a murder suicide by Whitlam with his girlfriend. Yet, I'm struggling to fit it to Whitlam's personality. Those types of crimes tend to be really emotional. Like when a woman tries to escape a domestic abuser and he kills them both. The problem is I still can't get a fix on exactly the type of guy Whitlam was.'

'I don't think I spoke to him about anything other than work,' said Strange.

'Are you thinking that it wasn't him in that van?' asked Zander.

'Maybe. I was about to stand it all down, but what if he burned someone else's body with Claudia?'

'That's possible. We still don't know where Clavell is. Maybe he's been cremated with his girlfriend. I'm more inclined to believe that, actually. Think. If he killed the lecturer and his girlfriend for getting together behind his back, maybe he did the same with Clavell and Claudia. But where did he go?'

'I don't know the area. Could he have just run along the cliffs?' said Strange.

The word 'run' caused them all to pause. Running was one of the few things they knew Whitlam liked. They travelled in silence for a minute.

'The fire investigator said the remains won't be much help. We might never know who was in that van,' said Barton. 'I'll ring Cox. We'll need to keep looking for him. If he ran to Cromer or Sheringham, try and think about what he'd do on Christmas Day while I ring my boss.'

Barton updated DCI Cox, while Zander and Strange discussed what Whitlam might do. It was a long call for Barton as he explained his hunches. It sounded to the others that Cox had information to pass on too because Barton did a lot of listening.

'What have you come up with?' asked Barton as he finished the call.

'It's possible he had a car stowed in either place or a hotel booked. I suspect he's lying low, maybe running further up the coast. He might even have a tent in a field. We don't know his state of mind, but look at the kills. They are cold-blooded and planned. If it wasn't him inside the van, then he'll have got away. He'll have had a way out,' said Strange.

'Cox more or less came to that same conclusion. If there's any chance of this lunatic still being out there, we're going to have to keep looking. She's speaking to the super to see if there's any chance of a helicopter. It'll be a struggle getting organised today. It's the worst time of the year to conduct a manhunt.'

'There goes my whisky by the fire,' said Zander.

'She also told me that they entered the property on Norwich Road to find information about Whitlam or the owner. I should have considered that. We didn't know if Trimble was working with Whitlam. They could have discovered a gun case or cartridge boxes. Then we'd have really been in trouble.'

'Did they find evidence of a weapon?' asked Zander.

'No, but they found a long-dead body.'

'Murdered?'

'They have no idea at this point. I assume it was Trimble. The man was dying when we saw him a while back.'

'Cox has got some tough decisions to make. Is there any point in us driving back? Or might we be better going home and having some rest so we can start again in the morning?'

'Yes, I thought the same. I was going to pull over and wait for instructions. The DCI said she'd ring when they decide where to set up a command centre. Most of the Norfolk stations aren't twenty-four hours. She may keep it in Peterborough for the moment. We might as well carry on to Wisbech. There's a twenty-four-hour petrol station there and I'm starving.'

Barton rang the DI at the fire scene while they drove and spent twenty minutes updating him on their suspicions. Barton suspected that the Norfolk police wouldn't be over-keen on hunting hard for Whitlam in the dark without any armed police.

They'd reached the Elme Hall roundabout at Wisbech by then and Barton had an idea.

'We're only five minutes from Trimble's house. Let's go and have a look and see if we can see if Whitlam's left anything behind.'

'I've seen enough stiffs just lately,' said Zander.

'Haven't we all? You stay in the car if you like. If Trimble's been dead a while, then Whitlam had a base to operate from with no interruptions. I just want to see where Whitlam's been sleeping, what he's been eating or drinking, that sort of thing. Try to get in his mind a little. Whitlam's an escalating serial killer. Who knows who else has upset him? If he's not dead, it's possible he's on his way to his next kill.'

86

THE SOUL KILLER

I tell the taxi driver about my childhood. It's another confession of sorts. I start with being dragged through every religion in the country, then my Easter basket and the cellar, and finally I confess to the wicked things I've done. I promise to be different in the future. He hopes there's still a place for me in heaven if I truly repent.

'Do you think when your time comes, you will regret your actions?' he asks.

'What do I have to regret? I've won.'

After that, we travel in silence as my story is finished although I want to believe the taxi driver is right. My mother had two men in her life. It wouldn't be right for her to be in heaven with her first partner and Barney have nobody waiting for him. It makes sense that everyone lives in harmony, with no lust or jealousy. It's a purity that's hard for me to comprehend because I don't want to share Claudia with anyone. The Lord made us in his own image though. It makes sense that he would forgive our mistakes and save us all. Although it does give you a 'get out of hell free' card when you're on earth.

I'm tempted to take over the driving and keep going. Throw this strange man out and search for a place where your past doesn't matter. I'm not entirely sure what I planned to do after all this. Then I remember, not only is Claudia at Barney's place, but so are the objects I kept over the years: Donald's ring and Charlie's necklace, among others. I need those little things; they're mine. I also know I want to talk to Claudia for one final time. Will this be our last goodbye? I had hoped she'd be willing to give us another go, but that sounds far-fetched now. The thought of her being with someone else makes me feel sick. The idea of her waiting for me in heaven sounds more appealing. It's time I called the shots and others waited at my beck and call.

I appreciate there's risk in returning. There'll be at least one officer protecting the scene, but they won't be expecting me. They might have already gone inside and found Barney. If they've discovered Claudia, the place will be heaving with police. They'll know I staged the fire. If that's the case, I'll just drive past.

I get the driver to stop up the road from the Elme Hall roundabout. A path between two fields heads towards a thick wood. I heard that youngsters brought their girlfriends here when they had nowhere else.

'Get out,' I say.

'Please, don't kill me,' says the taxi driver.

I study his petrified face. 'Not keen on experiencing everlasting paradise just yet?'

'No, let me go. I won't tell anyone. Please, have mercy.'

A voice in the depths of me urges me to nod at him. I point to the path. 'Run. Sprint down there as fast as you can, before I change my mind. If I see you stop, heaven will cease to be just a concept shortly afterwards.'

He's quick for an old guy. Yet, before I drive away, I think of what I've learned. Kindness doesn't pay. He will go for help at the first opportunity. Mercy is weakness. I should have killed him, because I can't be any deeper in trouble. There's no difference between six life sentences and seven.

His car drives well and it's full of fuel. Large sporadic drops of rain splatter the windscreen, and I turn on the wipers. The darkening clouds bunch together. I wonder how long the driver will remain silent. Do I still have a chance to escape? Because I realise now that I do want to live, even if Claudia doesn't. As long as I know she's waiting for me in heaven, I'll continue here on Earth. After all, I'll be a long time dead and the way I feel now is incredible. No one can beat me. I've finally got what I never had, and that's power. Power to give and power to take away.

This world is full of those who need to be stopped. I can

even visit those bullies from school and wipe Clavell's old gang from the face of the earth.

If I have the opportunity, I'll swap the number plates with another car. Cornwall might be a great place to hide for a while. Realistically, the cameras will tag this vehicle as soon as it's reported stolen, so I'll need to lie low and use public transport. Barney has more money hidden in his wardrobe. It isn't much, but every little bit should help. I also withdrew the daily limit from his bank card this week and buried it nearby. I should have started doing that earlier. Always thinking ahead is the way to stay ahead.

Then I'll lead a life without sin doing God's work. I'll save my soul by sending others to the abyss. Then, when I'm ready, I'll take my place at her side.

I stop outside the house. There's a young policeman virtually standing to attention. He's only a special constable. That's perfect. I step from the car and look around the street. It's quiet as only Christmas Day evening can be. I sling my bag from the passenger seat onto my shoulder with the baseball bat inside as I close the car door. I approach, showing him my fake warrant card.

'I'm a detective. Who are you?'

'Here protecting the scene, sir. What's your name?'

I hammer a blow into his face, but not too hard. The stun gun handle in my grip will make my fist less elastic and more effective. Too much, though, and I'd damage my hand. The impact is only heavy enough to break his nose.

'Where's your partner? Around the back?'

He sobs confirmation through streaming blood. I grab his collar and drag him to his feet.

'You know who I am?'

He's only just out of his teens. I spin him so we're facing each other. Do I really instil such fear? The police must know nearly everything. I'll need to be quick.

'Keep quiet. You lead,' I say, and shove him towards the rear garden.

The other policeman is middle-aged and smoking near the back door. The cigarette slips from his fingers at the sight of his bleeding friend. I throw his colleague to the floor and punch the older guy in the stomach. It's all too quick and too surreal for him to respond. My power overwhelms him as I grab his throat and place the stun gun to his neck. Part-time police don't want to die, even if they must. That's good, because it makes them weak and compliant.

'Cuff yourselves together.'

Their nervous fumbling hands make the process last longer than I'd hoped but finally they do as they're told. I lift the lid of the coal bunker and stare into the darkness. I know what's in there and it will break any resistance. Grabbing the torch from the older officer's belt, I direct the beam into the black hole. Charlie's severed head stares back at us. While the younger guy chokes and points with shock, the other shakes his head in disbelief.

'No, don't.'

I smash the handle of the stun gun into his forehead and repeat the blow on his partner. I'd rather not use it for its actual purpose as it will lose power. It may come in handy later. I shove them in with a howl.

'If this lid moves, I'll open it, and batter you both to death.' There's still some defiance in the older one's eyes. I simply do not have time for this. They must remain out of my way. Placing the bag on the floor, I show them the glinting baseball bat in the moonlight. For good measure, I give the bolder one a firm tap on the top of his head with it. This does the trick and I drop the lid down.

It's clear where the police entered as Barney's back door has a foot sized print at waist height. There's no time to lose. I place the two weapons on the kitchen work surface and pull open the drawer. The blade on the sharpest kitchen knife would struggle to go through butter. Using it would be too savage and unbefitting. I don't want to remember her like that. The next drawer along has a Stanley knife in it. Perfect.

I stride to the dining room, and listen. Nothing. I run upstairs and grab the box of my special things. Back downstairs, I open the front door and place it in the back of the car.

I return to the house and pull the table away. After sliding the rug off, I lift the trapdoor and shine the torch that I keep on the side into the hole. Claudia's still in the same position in which I left her. Bound that tight, I suppose she'd struggle to move. Barney's sleeping tablets could knock out a rhino, but she is stirring now.

Her left eye is inflamed from the impact of the fall in the cemetery. But the other eye is clear. It's like staring at good and evil. To finish our relationship in this way is a shame because we could have made an excellent team. She coolly regards me. I jump in and remove the gag.

'Claudia, I'm leaving now. I'm sorry about how things turned out. All the best for the future, but we'll meet again. Of that, I'm sure.'

'Where's my sister, you sick fucker? Where's my boyfriend?'

'They're safe from harm.'

'You'll rot in hell.' She kicks out at my shin, but I simply block it. The loathing expression she delivers in return is impressive. She'll understand soon. I stroke her cheek and pull the gag back into place. What a great woman. There's no way I could let her go when the prize is eternity together.

I check the blade and it's sharp. A deep cut of a few centimetres will do. Her good eye rolls with terror. I pause with the blade against her throat. Is this the only way? It's what my mother believed. This life hasn't taught me any different from her lessons. I sense that a shady part of me is going to enjoy it. How dare she screw Clavell? She deserves to find out what happened to him first. I smile, but it drops as I hear a vehicle stop outside.

Shit. A quick decision made, I replace the furniture and step towards the lounge window, my ears twitching for sounds. There's nothing, but I must check. I slowly lift the blind a touch and peer through the gloom. It's a police pool car parked just down the road. The windscreen is steamed up and rain hammers the glass, but I can make out two large shapes. I can see that one is black and one is white. I know them both.

87

DI BARTON

When the team were about thirty metres from the property, the heavens opened and raindrops hammered on the bonnet. Zander turned the headlights off and quickly killed the engine. They all felt a chill of foreboding. The next-door neighbour's curtains billowed from an upstairs window, but the lights in that room were out. Trimble's house, on the other hand, was lit downstairs. As they viewed the front of the building, they all saw the shadow of someone tall walking behind a closed blind in the lounge window.

'CSI?' asked Zander.

'Coming tomorrow,' said Barton.

'I know it's raining, but the guards are supposed to be protecting the scene, not clumping around inside with their size twelves on,' said Strange.

Barton rang Wisbech Control. Two minutes later he hung up. 'Both scene guards should still be here. Neither are answering their radios or their mobiles. They're recent recruits and only specials. They won't be ready for this kind of trouble.'

Strange leaned forward between Zander and Barton. 'Whitlam's been too smart for us all the way.'

The shadow passed across the window again. 'Do I need to ask who's in there if it isn't police?' asked Zander.

'It's got to be Whitlam,' said Strange.

Barton asked the obvious. 'What's happened to the scene guards?'

'Wait,' said Zander. 'Why the hell would Whitlam come

back here? That's madness. How would he get here on Christmas Day night?'

Barton rang Control again. A minute's conversation finished with, 'Get all available to this location, immediately.'

Strange waited for him to hang up so she could talk. 'You know, I think I've got it. Remember we discussed how much Whitlam loved this Claudia? Most of his crimes stem from people getting in his way and trying to split them up. He's taken everyone out, so why kill her at the end? I'd put money on the first person in the campervan being Clavell, and the DNA of the second body might tell us it's Claudia, but only because she'll have the same DNA as her twin sister, Annabelle.'

'Bloody hell!' said Zander. 'Wait, the witness reported they were seen burning alive and surely Annabelle's long dead?'

Barton shook his head. 'The fire investigator said they move into a boxer's posture as they burn even if they're dead. The muscles and tissues shrink due to dehydration by heating. They also may have appeared to struggle due to the moving flames.'

'Who's to say Whitlam didn't keep Annabelle or Claudia alive somewhere?' said Strange.

'Makes sense to me,' said Zander. 'He brings his victims here. Then goes to the coast, sets fire to the van, and drives back in a car stashed away earlier. He might not be aware that we know about this place. This is where he keeps the bodies, dead or alive. He's escaped after frying Claudia's sister and Clavell. He couldn't take Claudia with him as she'd have stopped him making a quick exit. Now, he's back for her.'

'Let's make this a group decision. We can wait ten minutes for the cavalry to arrive, or we go in now,' said Barton.

'The risks of delaying are too big,' said Strange. 'What if he's here to kill her? He murdered Charlie and everyone else who crossed him.'

'I agree. He might be killing the scene guards and Claudia as we speak. Right now, he could be planning on setting light to the place before scarpering out the back way. He may even have planned another murder-suicide,' said Barton.

Zander popped the car door open. 'John and I have twenty stone on this bloke, whatever weapon he's holding. I say we surprise him. Kelly, you go around the rear. Don't engage him, shout if he makes a run for it. Have you got your baton?'

Strange shook her head.

'Take mine. I heard you know how to use it.'

They exited the car as quietly as they could. Strange sidled down the path to the rear while Barton and Zander tensed at the front door. Barton tried the handle. The door creaked open, revealing David Whitlam standing next to the window with narrowed eyes.

88

THE SOUL KILLER

They are a threatening sight together and all I can think is to back away. The Stanley knife isn't much use against meat like these two, but it'll be a nasty surprise that will give me the edge. I slip it in my pocket before they see it. Edging out of the lounge, I pause at the foot of the stairs where my mother died. The pair of them are too wide to come through at the same time. It'll be the only chance I get. I stand up tall and relaxed, empty hands on display, but I'm poised inside. I speak calmly.

'Careful of the stairs, they're a bit of a death trap.'

Zander can't help glancing up them.

I know that if you're going to fight, hit first, so that's what I do. One of the weaker points of a head is the jawbone, especially if the receiver doesn't know it's coming, so that's where my shot lands, with everything I have behind it. Zander's head whips around, and I imagine his brain bouncing off one side of the skull and slamming into the other. I read that such an impact causes a temporary state of paralysis.

It's lights out for Zander and he crashes to the floor. I'm tempted to drive the short blade into his exposed neck, but Barton moves forward. He moves well for someone of his age.

Zander will be out for minutes with anything from a headache to cerebral bleeding and death. I just need to drop Barton and finish them off.

Barton steps over Zander and follows me into the dining room with a look of intent that I've heard others joke about from his younger days. He's as tall as Zander but bulkier. It's like circling a bear. He even growls, 'David Whitlam, you're under arrest.'

'You can't beat me. I have faith in my abilities. There's still time for you to leave.'

'What the hell happened to you? You were a great asset to the team.'

I feel a twinge of guilt for letting everyone down. It was great to be part of a team, but time moves on. I have a new calling.

A dull thud sounds from under the floorboards. Barton ignores the distraction, preventing me from taking a cheap shot. His stance is wide and strong as he edges towards me. I snap out a straight right, and he barely moves. My hand vibrates on his left eyebrow. It probably hurt me more than him, yet his skin splits and bleeds. Barton collapses forwards onto his knees. It's clear he's old now and not on my level.

'You're a big man, Barton. A giant, in fact. But who beat Goliath?'

It's my favourite story and I know who wins. Barton rises to his feet. I send a thunderous hook into his ribs. He flinches in agony as the air whooshes from his lungs. Zander groans from the stairwell beyond Barton and I cast an eye over as he rises to his feet. Using my momentum, I crash another blow into Barton's other side. The audible crack shocks me and stuns him. I stare at him as he falls back. What should I do? Barton is why they're here. I know he'll never forgive or forget. Mercy gains me nothing.

I take the knife from my pocket and push out the blade. Zander first because a kitten could claw Barton. The splintering sound of old wood crashes through the kitchen. I turn to see Sergeant Strange stride through the door. She doesn't seem scared, only determined. It'll be a shame and a pleasure to alter that.

The woman looks tiny compared to the others but the stun gun and bat on the kitchen work surface are a similar distance between us. They are both great equalisers in the right hands. I lunge towards them.

89

DI BARTON

Barton attempted to drag some air into his lungs, but the pain was like nothing he'd experienced before. He struggled upright but his legs gave way under him, and he fell back onto his rear, banging his head on the wall behind him. A mighty stab of pain seared through his side. Taking short gasps, he moved his right hand to the left of his ribcage and could barely touch it without crying out. Whitlam stared down at him without emotion.

Barton couldn't move. He was going to die. A strange smile passed over Whitlam's face, and he reached into his trouser pocket. Barton stared with absolute terror at the small blade, realising there was nothing he could do if Whitlam slit him clean open. He thought to kick Whitlam's legs from under him, but just the act of tensing his stomach sent a bolt of agony up and down his torso. His breath wheezed from his body with the effort.

A crash from the kitchen distracted Whitlam, who turned to the person who entered. It was Strange. Whitlam gave Barton one last glance, showing the glint of madness that must have been present for some time. He wanted to shout out, 'Run,' to Strange but even that was beyond him.

Whitlam moved towards her. His hand snapped out towards the worktop. His arm whipped back as though it had been stung. Then Whitlam's head reared away and twisted to the side, spitting liquid in Barton's direction. Barton saw the baton whistle through the air on the third swing, hitting Whitlam on his right ear, and then on his wrist, knocking the Stanley knife from his grasp.

'Argh,' Whitlam screamed, and cowered back. Blood poured from his head and mouth.

Zander staggered past Barton as the sound of sirens approached. His massive hands grabbed Whitlam's wrists, held them behind his back, and slammed the man against the wall. Strange withdrew her cuffs and slipped them onto Whitlam. He winced, suggesting she had them too tight. Then Whitlam howled as Zander seized the link between the cuffs and rammed downwards, forcing him to his knees.

If Barton moved, it would only have been a millimetre. Whitlam had cracked many of his ribs. If they were displaced, Barton knew he risked puncturing a lung. Zander shoved Whitlam over. Falling with his hands behind his back, Whitlam was forced to put his head to one side, so he didn't hit the ground face first. Zander slumped next to him and rubbed his jaw.

'Whitlam, I still don't think we're even,' he said.

Another, louder thud echoed from under the kitchen table. Strange pulled the table away and yanked a rug back. She fiddled with a catch and lifted up a trapdoor. Barton couldn't see what caused Strange's mouth to widen, but Whitlam's presence hadn't scared her. It must be bad. She reached into a pocket in her jacket, removed a Swiss Army knife, and jumped into the hole. She bent over and out of sight. A few seconds later, a long, high pitched shriek deafened him, and then a roar echoed around the room.

Claudia's wild eyed head rose up. Vicious, inflamed eyes bored into Barton. Dried blood covered her forehead, and red stained her white blouse. She hauled herself out of the hole and staggered towards the prone figure of Whitlam, who had an exhausted Zander leaning back on him. Whitlam turned to face her and grinned. She lurched closer, blinking wildly.

Staggering past them, she grabbed at the kitchen work surface. Claudia spun on her heel. She brandished the baseball bat with a satanic snarl. Barton tried a final shout but keeled over in agony instead. He glanced up as Claudia brought the weapon down in a speeding arc. Strange cried, 'No!' from the edge of the hole.

Claudia's second blow shattered Whitlam's skull. The third sprayed Barton's face with blood. He tried to move as he felt it pour down his face, but a heavy tightness enveloped his chest. The room spun as a panicking Barton realised he couldn't breathe at all.

90

DI BARTON

Steady beeps penetrated Barton's unconsciousness. He attempted to clear his throat and whistled through his teeth with the pain. His mind caught up and he realised that it was the second time he'd woken in the high dependency unit. The first time had been after surgery for his punctured lung. He'd been groggy then but had still managed to get that he was going to be okay out of the nurse. She'd said he'd have been in the ICU otherwise. Regardless, they'd keep him in for a few days for observation and rest.

His condition meant he had to remain sitting up. He stared at the ceiling and tried to drown out the sounds of the machines. The faces of those who'd lost their lives began to materialise in his mind instead. Clavell's mischievous grin had appeared when he heard the door open.

DCI Cox peered down on him and smiled.

'Skiving?'

He laughed and let a small yelp out.

'Sorry, a bit too soon, maybe.' She pulled up a chair next to Barton's hospital bed.

'How are you feeling?'

Barton considered her question while watching her lips purse as she stared at the drains coming from his chest. He tensed various parts of the rest of his bruised body. 'Like the entire world's problems are pushing down on me.' Barton winced. It still hurt to talk.

She shook her head. 'I'd never have believed Whitlam had that in him.'

He took a few quick breaths. It wasn't so painful if he did that. He glanced again at Cox. She had a twinkle in her eyes that he didn't recognise.

'The quiet ones, eh? Is he dead?' he asked.

'No, surprisingly not, from what Sergeant Strange said. He's in a serious but stable condition in Intensive Care, although the doctor suspects he'll spend the rest of his life in a vegetative state. Saves the cost of a trial, I suppose.'

'How are the team?'

'They're fine. Strange did well. She never told me she'd worked the riots in London. I guess Whitlam didn't know either. I've just been to see Zander. His face is a funny colour, but he reckons the impact sent his IQ up twenty points.'

'Wow. Imagine having your IQ doubled with a single blow.'

She chuckled.

'And Claudia?'

'Surprisingly stoic. She refused medication and checked herself out. Said she couldn't bear to be in the same hospital as him. She said there were no regrets about what she did in the heat of the moment.'

'Nothing gets the message across like a baseball bat.'

'Quite.'

'Thanks for coming to let me know.'

'No problem. Strange is taking Zander home tonight. They'll pop in before they leave to keep you company.'

'Excellent. I've only just woken up, and already I'm bored.'

'I also came to give you some other news. Great for me, good for you. I'm nearly four months pregnant.' She gazed out of the window for a few moments.

'That's fantastic. Congratulations.'

Her eyes refocussed on his. 'It's been a very, very long and expensive road. I'm not taking any chances.'

Barton thought about her home life for the first time and blushed. You really never knew what folk were going through. He hadn't even considered it. People show such strength to perform at work, when behind the scenes they're under incredible stress.

'Anyway, I'll take maternity leave at the earliest opportunity and I plan to enjoy having the full time possible. Between you and me, who knows if I'll be back? I recommended that you cover for me and the top brass have agreed. When all this Soul Killer business has been put to bed, we'll work together until I'm gone.'

'The Soul Killer?'

'Yes, that's what the papers have named him. There's been pages and pages written about him and his motivation. The taxi driver made a lot of money if the first six pages of *The Mail on Sunday* are anything to go by. It's certainly captured the nation's attention. Apparently Whitlam believed this life was a rehearsal and he would end up in heaven at the expense of those who got in his way. It's chilling stuff.'

'Did he really think killing people was the way to salvation?'

'Apparently so. That's what's fired up the media. If good people do bad things, are they damned for eternity? Or can bad people atone before they die, and are then rewarded with paradise?'

Barton shook his head. 'It's a complicated world.'

Cox smiled. 'Seems simple to me. Looks like another perfect example of the jobs our parents do on us.'

Barton blinked repeatedly. He managed a weak smile.

Cox stood. 'I'd better go.' She strode to the door, stopped and glanced back.

'Congratulations to you, too, John. You did a brilliant job, don't forget that. You shouldn't rush back to work, either.'

'Thanks.'

'Maybe even take tomorrow off as well.'

He grinned as she left, then placed his head in his hands. He'd just been thinking that perhaps it was time to retire.

ACKNOWLEDGEMENT

Many have given freely of their time, and their assistance and support remain greatly appreciated. However, again, the stand-out supporting act for this novel is Julian. He retired recently after twenty-five years in the police and kindly offered to answer any questions I might have, not realising that it was going to be a trilogy.

Thank you for your time and enthusiasm.

MORE FROM ROSS GREENWOOD

We hope you enjoyed reading *The Soul Killer*. If you did, please leave a review.

If you'd like to gift a copy, this book is also available as an ebook, digital audio download and audiobook CD.

Sign up to Ross Greenwood's mailing list for news, competitions and updates on future books.

http://bit.ly/RossGreenwoodNewsletter

DI Barton's next case, *The Ice Killer*, is available to order now.

ABOUT THE AUTHOR

Ross Greenwood is the author of six crime thrillers. Before becoming a full-time writer he was most recently a prison officer and so worked everyday with murderers, rapists and thieves for four years. He lives in Peterborough.

Follow Ross on social media:

twitter.com/greenwoodross

facebook.com/RossGreenwoodAuthor

bookbub.com/authors/ross-greenwood

instagram.com/rossg555

ABOUT BOLDWOOD BOOKS

Boldwood Books is a fiction publishing company seeking out the best stories from around the world.

Find out more at www.boldwoodbooks.com

Sign up to the Book and Tonic newsletter for news, offers and competitions from Boldwood Books!

http://www.bit.ly/bookandtonic

We'd love to hear from you, follow us on social media:

facebook.com/BookandTonic

twitter.com/BoldwoodBooks

instagram.com/BookandTonic